罗尔德·达尔短篇故事
品读及汉译探索
第7卷

An Interpretation of Short Stories by Roald Dahl and an Exploration of Their Chinese Translations
Volume 7

王　昕　王永胜　著
WANG Xin, WANG Yong-sheng

哈爾濱工業大學出版社

内容提要

本书系对英国作家罗尔德·达尔"非儿童类"(个别篇章具有"儿童类"文学特点,但由于是罗尔德·达尔早期作品,也被收录进来,作为研究的对象)短篇故事(小说)进行研究所著系列图书中的第7卷,包括5部短篇小说。这些小说长短不一、难易各异,按照不同的主题分成三章加以编排,分别为"亦真亦幻""异想天开"和"功成名就"。除第三章外,每章收录两篇作品,先做引导性的介绍,名为"原作导读",再给出小说的原文供读者阅读或作为翻译的参考,同时给出语言点及文化层面上的注释,以辅助理解,名为"原作释读",最后给出探索性的汉语译文,名为"翻译探索"。

本书适合英语专业大学本科生及研究生阅读、研究、翻译之用(不少小说也可供高中生阅读、学习),也适合广大的文学爱好者阅读,更适合从事英汉翻译或外国文学研究的学者、教师、学生等阅读、参考。

图书在版编目(CIP)数据

罗尔德·达尔短篇故事品读及汉译探索.第7卷/王昕,王永胜著. — 哈尔滨 :哈尔滨工业大学出版社,2016.2

ISBN 978-7-5603-5805-5

Ⅰ.①罗… Ⅱ.①王… ②王… Ⅲ.①短篇小说-小说研究-英国-现代②短篇小说-文学翻译-英国-现代 Ⅳ.①I561.074

中国版本图书馆CIP数据核字(2015)第308616号

策划编辑 田新华
责任编辑 李广鑫
封面设计 思 华 高永利
出版发行 哈尔滨工业大学出版社
社 址 哈尔滨市南岗区复华四道街10号 邮编150006
传 真 0451-86414749
网 址 http://hitpress.hit.edu.cn
印 刷 哈尔滨市工大节能印刷厂
开 本 880mm×1230mm 1/32 印张10.625 字数398千字
版 次 2016年2月第1版 2016年2月第1次印刷
书 号 ISBN 978-7-5603-5805-5
定 价 38.00元

前言

对于罗尔德·达尔(Roald Dahl, 1916—1990),中国读者耳熟能详的恐怕是他的一些儿童文学作品,而且国内外对他称呼最多的莫过于"儿童文学作家"。他的儿童文学作品的确十分畅销,已被翻译成多国文字出版发行,知名度颇高。可以说,在儿童文学作家中,罗尔德·达尔是最为成功、最为知名的作家之一。达尔的儿童文学作品得到很多国家小朋友的喜爱,这样的作品包括《詹姆斯与大仙桃》(*James and the Giant Peach*)、《查利与巧克力工厂》(*Charlie and the Chocolate Factory*)、《魔法手指》(*The Magic Finger*)、《查利与大玻璃升降机》(*Charlie and the Great Glass Elevator*)、《了不起的狐狸爸爸》(*Fantastic Mr. Fox*)、《特威特夫妇》(*The Twits*)、《女巫》(*The Witches*)、《好心眼儿的巨人》(*The BFG*,这部小说1983年获"惠特布雷德奖",英文表述为"*Whitbread Award*")以及《玛蒂尔达》(*Matilda*)等。

然而,作为英国儿童文学作家的罗尔德·达尔,还写过其他类型的文学作品,特别是那些"非儿童类"短篇小说(个别篇章具有"儿童类"文学作品特点,但由于是罗尔德·达尔早期作品,也被收录进来,作为研究的对象,也可以说"成人类"短篇小说,也就是说,为成年人写的文学作品。当然,这些作品中有些具有"成人"色彩——含有色情内容,但达尔"成人"作品中的"成人"内容大多是比较"隐晦"的。这样的"成人"作品,基本收录在他的《迷情乱性》(*Switch Bitch*)一书中)也同样精彩。称之为"非儿童类",主要针对达尔"儿童类"作品耀眼的光环而言。其实,这些"非儿童类"短篇故事(小说)绝大多数是达尔转笔写儿童文学作品之前完成的。"儿童类"作品的耀眼光环或多或少掩盖了一些"非儿童类"作品的光芒,而在中国,这些"非儿童类”作品的“光芒”几乎没有散发出来,很少为中国广大读者所熟知。这些作品受到西方19世纪现实主义文学的影响,多数采用现实主义的创作手法。同时,达尔也从美国短篇小说家欧·亨利(O. Henry)那里汲取了一定的营养。就达尔作品本身对人物和景物的描写来看,可以说,他是“20世纪英国变形精神世界的一位工笔画家”①。同他的儿童文学作品一样,他早期的这些“非儿童类”作品同样具有结尾出奇、结局令人意想不到等特点,更进一步说,达尔的此类短篇小说这方面的特点尤为突出。这类作品充满奇思妙想,人物刻画细腻入微,其中不乏道貌岸然者、悲观主义者、心理变态者。此类作品也不乏荒谬、贪婪、邪恶、虚伪的成分,其中的人物大都在“机关用尽”之时,一不小心就“栽了跟头”,或者在“聪明绝顶”之际,反而被自己的“聪明”所误。

罗尔德·达尔的父母是挪威人,但达尔本人1916年出生在英国格拉摩根郡的兰达夫(Llandaff, Glamorgan)②,并在雷普顿公学(Repton School)接受教育。第二次世界大战爆发,他应征入伍,加入英国皇家空军,驻扎在内罗毕。后来,他加入了驻利比亚的一个战斗机中队,受了重伤。之后,又作为一名战斗机飞行员到希腊和叙利亚参加战斗。1942年,达尔作为英国大使馆的空军助理专员去了华盛顿。华盛顿成为他人生的转折点,因为在那里他开始了自己的创作生涯。随后,他被调到情报部。战争结束的时候,他成为英国皇家空军中校。他的第一批短篇小说共有12篇,都是根据自己在战争期间的经历所写。这12篇作品首先发表在美国的一些主流杂志上,后来编撰成书出版,书名为《向你飞跃》(*Over to You*)。

罗尔德·达尔所有受到高度赞誉的作品都被译成多种文字,成为全世界的畅销书。安格利亚电视台(Anglia Television)将他的一些

① 参见“陈钰. 畸形精神世界的工笔画家——谈罗尔德·达尔的小说创作特色. 武汉:外国文学研究,1985(4):66”. 这里只不过将其中的“二十世纪”,规范性修改成“20世纪”。

② 格拉摩根原来是英国南威尔士的一个郡。

短篇小说改编成电视系列剧，冠以标题《出乎意料的故事集》(*Tales of the Unexpected*)。他的作品还包括两本自传——《男孩时代》(*Boy*)和《独闯天下》(*Going Solo*)，还有赢得很多赞誉的小说《我的叔叔奥斯瓦尔德》(*My Uncle Oswald*)以及《罗尔德·达尔倾心的鬼怪故事集》(*Roald Dahl's Book of Ghost Stories*)。最后一本是他自己编辑出版的。在生命的最后一年，他收集了一些奇闻轶事，并跟妻子弗利西蒂(Felicity)一起，整理了一些烹饪食谱，汇编成一本书。这本书1996年由企鹅出版集团出版，书名为《罗尔德·达尔的烹饪书》(*Roald Dahl's Cookbook*)①。

罗尔德·达尔于1990年11月23日去世。英国《泰晤士报》(The Times)称其为"我们这一代人中最有影响力的作家之一，也是拥有极其广泛读者群的作家之一"(One of the most widely read and influential writers of our generation)，并在写给他的讣告中写道："孩子喜欢他写的故事，把他当成自己心目中最喜爱的人……他的作品将成为未来的经典之作。"(Children loved his stories and made him their favourite... They will be classics of the future)据报道，在2000年英国的"世界图书日"(World Book Day)投票中，罗尔德·达尔当选为"读者最喜爱的作家"(Favourite Author)②。

对于20世纪的英国作家罗尔德·达尔及其作品，《爱尔兰时报》(Irish Times)的一篇评论，可谓一语中的："Roald Dahl is one of the few writers I know whose work can accurately be described as addictive. Through his tales runs a vein of macabre malevolence, the more effective because it springs from the slightest, almost inconsequential everyday things. The result is a black humour of the most sophisticated kind."(罗尔德·达尔是我所认识的为数不多的作家之一，可以准确无误地说，

① 参见"DAHL R. *The Best of Roald Dahl*. London: Penguin Books Ltd., 2006"。

② 参见"DAHL R. *The Collected Short Stories of Roald Dahl*. London: Penguin Books Ltd., 1992"。

其作品令人沉醉、上瘾。他的作品始终贯穿着一条主线,这条主线令人毛骨悚然,充满恶意和凶险,但却更加行之有效,因为其来源是一些不起眼的、几乎微不足道的日常事物。结果,最为错综复杂的黑色幽默便应运而生了)①。

抛开后来"儿童类"作品的耀眼光环不说,罗尔德·达尔在20世纪中叶之所以蜚声世界,就是因为他所创作的这些"非儿童类"的短篇小说(当然,个别篇章具有"儿童类"文学特点,预示性地展露出达尔后来作为儿童文学作家的一丝"光芒")。但是,当时中国翻译出版业不是很发达,对他的作品的译介也不是很多。就算是有所译介,也处于零星的"散兵作战"状态,不成体系。在全球化浪潮滚滚而来的今天,研究罗尔德·达尔的这部分作品,并系统地进行翻译研究,如同打开尘封已久的大门,门内的景色依然会令当代中国读者惊喜不已。对于广大的英语学习者和文学爱好者来说,阅读达尔的这部分作品将会带来迥然不同的人生体验。

其实,罗尔德·达尔这部分短篇小说的实质和绝妙,可以从英美主流媒体的评价窥见一斑:

"Roald Dahl is the prince of storytellers." —*Daily Mail*

"罗尔德·达尔是位讲故事的王子。" ——(英国)《每日邮报》

"The absolute master of the twist-in-the-tale." —*The Observer*

"绝对的大师,其故事的结局出人意料。"

——(英国)《观察家报》

"These stories pack their punch." —*The Observer*

"这些故事蓄满了惊人之力。" ——(英国)《观察家报》

---

① 著者译自 Roald Dahl 的"*The Best of Roald Dahl*"(《罗尔德·达尔小说精品集》)一书的封底(back cover)。此书由英国"Penguin Books Ltd."出版公司于2006年出版发行。

"An unforgettable read, don't miss it." —*Sunday Times*

"一次难忘的阅读体验,不可错过。"

——(英国)《星期日泰晤士报》

"Dahl is too good a storyteller to become predictable, so you never know whether the tyrant or the tyrannized will win in the end."

—*Daily Telegraph*

"达尔的故事讲得太精彩了,结局简直令人无法预测。因此,你永远都无法得知,最后的赢家是残暴的人,还是受到残暴对待的人。"

——(英国)《每日电讯报》

"Dahl has the mastery of plot and characters possessed by great writers of the past, along with a wildness and wryness of his own. One of his trademarks is writing beautifully about the ugly, even the horrible."

—*The Los Angeles Times*

"达尔拥有以往伟大作家的资质——善于营造情节、精于刻画人物,但达尔也拥有自己荒诞不经的一面,以及自己的一套挖苦讥讽的手段。其中的一个标志就是他对丑陋之人的精妙刻画,更有甚者是对恐怖之人的精妙刻画。" ——(美国)《洛杉矶时报》

"An ingenious imagination, a fascination with odd and ordinary detail, and a lust for its thorough exploitation are the... strengths of Dahl's storytelling." —*The New York Times Book Review*

"达尔写作的影响力在于其独特的想象力,在于其对稀奇古怪和平淡无奇的细节的着迷程度,在于其对细节完完全全加以利用的欲望。" ——(美国)《纽约时报·书评》

"The mind of Roald Dahl is quintessentially nasty and wicked."

—*The Washington Post*

"罗尔德·达尔的思维具有典型的特点,那就是肮脏和邪恶。"

——(美国)《华盛顿邮报》

在此前提下,研究并翻译罗尔德·达尔的"非儿童类"短篇小说,将具有一定的学术价值和社会价值,会为中国文学的百花园增添一个品种,会为文学爱好者和翻译者提供一个可供参考的文本。

在历时三年多对罗尔德·达尔"非儿童类"短篇小说进行研究和翻译的过程中,共收集到长短不一的此类作品60篇,并站在一定的角度,根据著者个人的理解,细加编排,精心安排,详加注释,分册编辑,最终通过翻译,引介给中国读者。

本书在对罗尔德·达尔短篇小说的翻译探索中,采取了严谨的翻译态度,形成了以下基本的翻译思路:

(1) 人名、地名按照一定的标准进行"异化"式处理(极个别人名做了"归化"式处理),主要依据《世界人名翻译大辞典》(新华社译名室编,中国对外翻译出版公司1993年第一版或2007年第二版)以及《世界地名翻译大辞典》(周定国主编,中国出版集团、中国对外翻译出版公司2008年第一版)等,个别的人名、地名的翻译兼顾了流行的译法。

(2) 绝大多数非国际化的度量衡单位,特别是英制的度量衡单位,采用"同化"或"归化"的处理方法,以便汉语思维者能形象化地加以理解。

(3) 每一篇的题目都采用汉语四字格来处理,以求汉语的工整,发挥汉语四字格表达的优势,但同时最大限度地兼顾原文题目的字面含义。

(4) 就汉语译文整体而言,尽量杜绝"翻译腔",以保持汉语语言的纯洁性和规范性,但前提是确保对达尔小说原文的"忠实"。

(5) 尽量完美地再现原文的风格,虽然做到这一点并不是轻而易举的事情。原文有些风格,在翻译中只能退其次而求之——基本上采用"归化"处理手法,照顾了汉语的通畅性。比如,原文中很多非标准的英语表达,汉译时就没有在"风格"上充分加以体现,这也是以后有待继续探索的一个翻译问题。

当然,“金无足赤,人无完人”,匆忙且蹒跚的步履必将会迈出“不和谐”的步伐。在对罗尔德·达尔的“非儿童类”短篇小说进行研究、翻译并成书的过程中,不当甚至错误之处在所难免,还望读者不吝赐教,多多批评,特别是多做文学翻译方面的批评。

需要特别声明的是,本系列书中所引用的罗尔德·达尔原著内容以及所做的翻译探索,旨在学术研究,不做商业用途。涉及相关版权的地方,已经做了引用和标注。

王昕　王永胜

2015 年 9 月

目　录

第一章　亦真亦幻

在这个世界上，有些事情忽而让你觉得是真的，忽而又让你觉得是虚幻的，真真假假、假假真真，让人难以捉摸，可谓亦真亦幻。

粤西孙子楚，名士也。生有枝指；性迂讷，人诳之辄信为真。或值座有歌妓，则必遥望却走。或知其然，诱之来，使妓狎逼之，则赪颜彻颈，汗珠珠下滴，因共为笑。遂貌其呆状相邮传，作丑语而名之"孙痴"。

这是蒲松龄《聊斋志异·阿宝》这篇故事的开篇，阅读至此，恐怕没人会怀疑蒲老前辈要讲述的故事的真实性——有名有姓有地点，真人真事真性情。然而，随着故事的展开，当你读到"家旧养一鹦鹉，忽毙，小儿持弄于床。生自念：倘得身为鹦鹉，振翼可达女室。心方注想，身已翩然鹦鹉，遽飞而去，直达宝所"时，你恐怕要心生疑问：真的会发生这样的事情吗？可谓亦真亦幻。但是，回顾《聊斋志异》的书名，蒲松龄的书房名为"聊斋"，"志"则有对发生的事件如实记录的意思，只不过实际记录的是"异"罢了，也就是"奇异的事件"。这就奠定了故事真实性的基础，但是，人变鹦鹉，飞向阿宝的住所，又让人心生"幻"觉——觉得这不是真实发生的事情。可是，书名却暗示：这是实际发生的事情，我蒲松龄只是加以记录罢了。亦真亦幻，这恐怕就是文学的魅力所在。

英国作家罗尔德·达尔在其为数不少的作品中都宣称：这是真

实发生的故事,我一点也没加更改。读完他这样的作品,人们对其真实性也没有半点怀疑。但是,这样的作品,有很多完完全全是他虚构出来的,由此可见罗尔德·达尔创作功底之一——想象力的丰富程度。难怪英国《每日邮报》(*Daily Mail*)对他有这样的评价:"罗尔德·达尔是位讲故事的王子。"(Roald Dahl is the prince of storytellers.)像《宝藏风波》这样真实发生的事情,达尔讲述起来也是绘声绘色、生动形象的,毫无纪实性文学作品如报告文学或新闻报道"骨子"里所特有的枯燥感;对于《非洲往事》的记录,更具传奇色彩和离奇特性,可谓亦真亦幻,真假难辨,令人难以捉摸。

走进罗尔德·达尔的"真实"世界,去体会"亦真亦幻"的魅力吧。

第一节 《宝藏风波》*The Mildenhall Treasure*

罗尔德·达尔的《宝藏风波》(*The Mildenhall Treasure*)首次发表在《女士家庭杂志》(*Ladies' Home Journal*)上,后又收录在《〈非凡亨利〉及另外六篇故事集》(*The Wonderful Story of Henry Sugar and Six More*)等书中。这个真实的故事开篇前,作者写了一段序言,交代了事情的来龙去脉:一个专门替人犁田谋生的、老实巴交的农夫名叫戈登·布彻,一次犁田时偶然发现了一批罗马时代的银器。达尔前去采访,之后写下了这篇真实的故事,名为《宝藏风波》。

一、原作导读

一月份一个寒冷的早晨,戈登·布彻早早就起床,吻别妻子和孩子,骑上自行车,冒着凛冽的寒风,赶往福特家去开自己存放在那里的拖拉机。戈登和福特都靠替人犁田挣钱来谋生,只不过戈登是"小打小闹"型的,而福特摊子铺得大一些,活儿多的自然就忙不过来了,有些活儿就再雇像戈登这样的小户来干。

前天，他将拖拉机留在福特家，因为下一个活要为福特干，要犁的田在西斯利格林，有二十七亩多地。但是，要记住的重点就是，那块田地不是福特的，只不过是福特求他去犁那块田。

事实上，那块面积为二十七亩的田地的主人是一个名叫罗尔夫的农夫。

He had left his tractor at Ford's the day before because his next job was to plough up four and a half acres on Thistley Green for Ford. It was not Ford's land. It is important to remember this, but Ford was the one who had asked him to do the work.

Actually, a farmer called Rolfe owned the four and a half acres.

戈登替罗尔夫犁的那块田预计要种的是甜菜，这种作物不同于其他的作物，地要犁得深一些。

"往深处犁，"前天福特这样对布彻说道。"那地要改种糖用甜菜。罗尔夫要在那块地里种甜菜了。"

要是种大麦，只需往下犁十多厘米就足够了，但是要种甜菜，就得往深处犁，要二十五厘米或三十厘米深才行……

"Deep-plough it," Ford had said to Butcher the day before. "It's for sugar-beet. Rolfe's putting sugar-beet in there."

They only plough about four inches down for barley, but for sugar-beet they plough deep, to ten or twelve inches...

正因为如此，戈登拖拉机后面挂的犁铧尖就触碰了一批沉睡已久的罗马时代的银器，但戈登不知道它们究竟为何物。于是，他匆忙赶回去叫福特来查看。福特到来一看，就知道那些是什么东西了。但是，他不动声色，跟戈登一起将这些古董挖了出来，却据为己有。英国有一项很有意思的法律规定：从地里挖出一件金银器物要立刻报告,归国家所有,发现者则有权得到政府奖励的一笔奖金——“这项有意思的法律条文另一个有意思的方面就是,直接从政府那儿得到奖金的是宝藏的发现者本人,而不是宝藏发现地的拥有者。当然,擅自闯入他人领地进行发掘,是得不到奖金的。可是,如果宝藏的发现者被土地的拥有者雇来干活,那么,发现者也会得到所有的奖金。”(The other curious part of this curious law is this: it is the person who discovers the treasure in the first place who gets the reward from the government. The owner of the land gets nothing—unless of course the finder is trespassing on the land when he makes the discovery. But if the finder of the treasure has been hired by the owner to do a job on his land, then he, the finder, gets all the reward.)

回到家中,福特偷偷将这些宝物擦得铮亮,花费了相当长的时间。擦亮后的宝物令福特暗自惊喜,将它们藏起来,偷偷欣赏达四年之久。

1946年复活节刚刚过去的那一天,休·奥尔德森·福西特博士到福特家拜访,他是一位考古学家。这次拜访,他偶然发现了福特的这一秘密,要求福特报告给警察。事已至此,福特只得照做。经过裁决,发现者不是布彻自己,而是福特和布彻两个人。最后,这批宝藏被大英博物馆收购。

博物馆为了表示鼓励,奖励给两个发现者每人一千英镑。布彻这位真正的发现者是乐坏了,怎么也没有想到会得到这么多的钱。他没有意识到的是,要是起先发现的时候容许他将财宝带回家的话,几乎可以肯定的是,他会报告的。那样的话,他就有资格得到与全部财宝的价值相同数额的奖金,数额在五十万到一百万之间。

As a gesture, the Museum rewarded the co-finders with one thousand pounds each. Butcher, the true finder, was happy and surprised to receive so much money. He did not realize that had he been allowed to take the treasure home originally, he would almost certainly have revealed its existence and would thus have become eligible to receive one hundred per cent of its value, which could have been anything between half a million and a million pounds.

二、原作释读

罗尔德·达尔的这篇小说纪实性很强，但不乏生动形象、引人入胜的描写，阅读起来并无枯燥之感。阅读中，涉及农耕、历史、收藏以及希腊语方面的知识或多或少构成了理解上的障碍，应注意体会。

A Note about the Next Story①

In 1946, more than thirty years ago, I was still unmarried and living with my mother. I was making a fair income by writing two short stories a year. Each of them took four months to complete, and fortunately there were people both at home and abroad who were willing to buy them.

One morning in April of that year, I read in the newspaper about a remarkable find of Roman silver. It had been discovered four years before by a ploughman near Mildenhall, in the county of Suffolk②, but the discovery had for some reason been kept secret until then. The newspaper article said it was the greatest treasure ever found in the British Isles, and it had now been acquired by the British Museum. The name of the ploughman was given as Gordon Butcher.

True stories about the finding of really big treasure send shivers of e-

① 本部小说原文出自"DAHL R. *The Wonderful Story of Henry Sugar and Six More*. London: Penguin Books Ltd., 2002"。注：这里的"Next Story"指的就是本节所研究的"*The Mildenhall Treasure*"（《宝藏风波》）。

② Suffolk: *Noun* a county of eastern England, on the coast of East Anglia; county town, Ipswich 萨福克郡（英格兰东部一郡，位于东英吉利海岸，郡首府为伊普斯威奇）

lectricity all the way down my legs to the soles of my feet. The moment I read the story, I leapt up from my chair without finishing my breakfast and shouted good-bye to my mother and rushed out to my car. The car was a nine-year-old Wolseley①, and I called it "The Hard Black Slinker". It went well but not very fast.

Mildenhall was about a hundred and twenty miles from my home, a tricky cross-country trip along twisty toads and country lanes. I got there at lunchtime, and by asking at the local police station, I found the small house where Gordon Butcher lived with his family. He was at home having his lunch when I knocked on his door.

I asked him if he would mind talking to me about how he found the treasure.

"No, thank you," he said. "I've had enough of reporters. I don't want to see another reporter for the rest of my life."

"I'm not a reporter," I told him. "I'm a short-story writer and I sell my work to magazines. They pay good money." I went on to say that if he would tell me exactly how he found the treasure then I would write a truthful story about it. And if I was lucky enough to sell it, I would split the money equally with him.

In the end, he agreed to talk to me. We sat for several hours in his kitchen, and he told me an enthralling story. When he had finished, I paid a visit to the other man in the affair, an older fellow called Ford. Ford wouldn't talk to me and closed the door in my face. But by then I had my story and I set out for home.

The next morning, I went up to the British Museum in London to see the treasure that Gordon Butcher had found. It was fabulous. I got the shivers all over again just from looking at it.

---

① Wolseley：一个汽车的品牌，这里根据读音译作"沃尔斯利"。

I wrote the story as truthfully as I possibly could and sent it off to America. It was bought by a magazine called the Saturday Evening Post, and I was well paid. When the money arrived, I sent exactly half of it to Gordon Butcher in Mildenhall.

One week later, I received a letter from Mr. Butcher written upon what must have been a page torn from a child's school exercise-book. It said, "... you could have knocked me over with a feather when I saw your cheque. It was lovely. I want to thank you..."

Here is the story almost exactly as it was written thirty years ago. I've changed it very little. I've simply toned down① some of the more flowery passages and taken out a number of superfluous② adjectives and unnecessary sentences.

The Mildenhall Treasure

Around seven o'clock in the morning, Gordon Butcher got out of bed and switched on the light. He walked barefoot to the window and drew back the curtains and looked out.

This was January and it was still dark, but he could tell③ there hadn't been any snow in the night.

"That wind," he said aloud to his wife. "Just listen to that wind."

---

① tone sth. down: to make sth. such as a speech, an opinion, etc. less offensive, critical or harsh than it was originally 使(讲话、意见等)缓和;使温和(e. g. He had to tone down his article before it was published. 他得在文章发表之前把措辞缓和一下。)

② superfluous: *Adjective* unnecessary, especially through being more than enough 过多的;过量的;过剩的(e. g. The purchaser should avoid asking for superfluous information. 买方应当避免询问过多的信息。)

③ tell: *Verb* [with clause] decide or determine correctly or with certainty 断定;判断(e. g. You can tell they're in love. 你可以断定他们在恋爱。)

His wife was out of bed now, standing beside him near the window, and the two of them were silent, listening to the swish of the icy wind as it came sweeping in over the fens①.

"It's a nor'-easter②," he said.

"There'll be snow for certain before nightfall," she told him. "And plenty of it."

She was dressed before him, and she went into the next room and leaned over the cot③ of her six-year-old daughter and gave her a kiss. She called out a good morning to the two other older children in the third room, then she went downstairs to make breakfast.

At a quarter to eight, Gordon Butcher put on his coat, his cap and his leather gloves, and walked out of the back door into the bitter early-morning winter weather. As he moved through the half-daylight over the yard to the shed where his bicycle stood, the wind was like a knife on his cheek. He wheeled out the bike and mounted and began to ride down the middle of the narrow road, right into the face of the gale.

Gordon Butcher was thirty-eight. He was not an ordinary farm labourer. He took orders from no man unless he wished. He owned his own tractor, and with this he ploughed other men's fields and gathered other men's harvests under contract. His thoughts were only for his wife, his son, his two daughters. His wealth was in his small brick house, his two cows, his tractor, his skill as a ploughman.

Gordon Butcher's head was very curiously shaped, the back of it protruding like the sharp end of an enormous egg, and his ears stuck out,

---

① fen: *Noun* a low and marshy or frequently flooded area of land 低位沼泽;沼泽

② nor'-easter = north-easter:这里指的应该是东北风。

③ cot: *Noun* (Brit.) a small bed with high barred sides for a baby or very young child(英国英语)(两边有高围栏的)婴儿床;幼儿床

and a front tooth was missing on the left side. But none of this seemed to matter very much when you met him face to face in the open air. He looked at you with steady blue eyes that were without any malice① or cunning② or greed. And the mouth didn't have those thin lines of bitterness around the edges which one so often sees on men who work the land and spend their days fighting the weather.

His only eccentricity③, to which he would cheerfully admit if you asked him, was in talking aloud to himself when he was alone. This habit, he said, grew from the fact that the kind of work he did left him entirely by himself for ten hours a day, six days a week. "It keeps me company," he said, "hearing me own voice now and again."

He biked on down the road, pedalling hard against the brutal wind.

"All right," he said, "all right, why don't you blow a bit? Is that the best you can do? My goodness me. I hardly know you're there this morning!" The wind howled around him and snapped at his coat and squeezed its way through the pores of the heavy wool, through his jacket underneath, through his shirt and vest, and it touched his bare skin with an icy finger-tip.

"Why," he said, "it's lukewarm you are today. You'll have to do

---

① malice: *Noun* [mass noun] the intention or desire to do evil; ill will 恶意;怨恨(e. g. I bear no malice towards anybody. 我对任何人都没有恶意。)

② cunning: *Noun* [mass noun] skill in achieving one's ends by deceit 狡猾;诡诈;狡诈(e. g. A statesman to whom cunning had come as second nature. 一个以狡诈为第二本性的政客。)

③ eccentricity: *Noun* [count noun] (usu. as "eccentricities") an eccentric act, habit, or thing 古怪的举止(或习惯、事物)(e. g. Her eccentricities were amusing rather than irritating. 她古怪的举止与其说是令人反感倒不如说是有趣的。)

a sight[①] better than that if you're going to make me shiver."

And now the darkness was diluting[②] into a pale grey morning light, and Gordon Butcher could see the cloudy roof of the sky very low above his head and flying with the wind. Grey-blue the clouds were, flecked[③] here and there with black, a solid mass from horizon to horizon, the whole thing moving with the wind, sliding past above his head like a great grey sheet of metal unrolling. All around him lay the bleak and lonely fen-country of Suffolk, mile upon mile of it that went on for ever.

He pedalled on. He rode through the outskirts of the little town of Mildenhall and headed for the village of West Row where the man called Ford had his place.

He had left his tractor at Ford's the day before because his next job was to plough up four and a half acres on Thistley Green for Ford. It was not Ford's land. It is important to remember this, but Ford was the one who had asked him to do the work.

Actually, a farmer called Rolfe owned the four and a half acres.

Rolfe had asked Ford to get it ploughed because Ford, like Gordon Butcher, did ploughing jobs for other men. The difference between Ford and Gordon Butcher was that Ford was somewhat grander. He was a fairly prosperous small-time agricultural engineer who had a nice house and a

---

① a sight ... : (informal) used to indicate that something is so described to a considerable extent(非正式)相当;非常(e. g. The old lady is a sight cleverer than Sarah. 这位老太太要比萨拉机灵得多。)

② dilute: *Verb* make (something) weaker in force, content, or value by modifying it or adding other elements to it (用掺杂的方法)削弱(力量);减少(内容);降低(价值)(e. g. The reforms have been diluted. 改革的力度已经削弱了。)

③ fleck: *Verb* [with obj.] (often as "be flecked") mark or don't with small patches of colour or particles of something 给……洒上小色点;用碎花点缀……(e. g. The minarets are flecked with gold leaf. 点缀着金叶的尖塔。)

large yard full of sheds filled with farm implements① and machinery. Gordon Butcher had only his one tractor.

On this occasion, however, when Rolfe had asked Ford to plough up his four and a half acres on Thistley Green, Ford was too busy to do the work so he hired Gordon Butcher to do it for him.

There was no one about in Ford's yard when Butcher rode in. He parked his bike, filled up his tractor with paraffin and petrol, warmed the engine, hitched② the plough behind, mounted the high seat and drove out to Thistley Green.

The field was not half a mile away, and around eight-thirty Butcher drove the tractor in through the gate on to the field itself. Thistley Green was maybe a hundred acres all told, with a low hedge running round it. And although it was actually one large field, different parts of it were owned by different men. These separate parts were easy to define because each was cultivated in its own way. Rolfe's plot of four and a half acres was over to one side near the southern boundary fence. Butcher knew where it was and he drove his tractor round the edge of the field, then inward until he was on the plot.

The plot was barley③ stubble④ now, covered with the short and rotting yellow stalks of barley harvested last autumn, and only recently it had been broad-sheared so that now it was ready for the plough.

---

① implement: *Noun* a tool, utensil, or other piece of equipment, especially as used for a particular purpose 工具；器具

② hitch: *Verb* [with obj.] fasten or tether with a rope(用绳索)拴；系(e. g. He returned to where he had hitched his horse. 他回到他拴马的地方。)

③ barley: *Noun* [mass noun] a hardy cereal which has coarse bristles extending from the ears. It is widely cultivated, chiefly for use in brewing and stockfeed 大麦

④ stubble: *Noun* [mass noun] the cut stalks of cereal plants left sticking out of the ground after the grain is harvested(谷类植物收割后残留的)残梗；茬

"Deep-plough it," Ford had said to Butcher the day before. "It's for sugar-beet[①]. Rolfe's putting sugar-beet in there."

They only plough about four inches down for barley, but for sugar-beet they plough deep, to ten or twelve inches. A horse-drawn plough can't plough as deep as that. It was only since motor-tractors came along that the farmers had been able to deep-plough properly. Rolfe's land had been deep-ploughed for sugar-beet some years before this, but it wasn't Butcher who had done the ploughing and no doubt the job had been skimped[②] a bit and the ploughman had not gone quite as deep as he should. Had he done so, what was about to happen today would have happened then, and that would have been a different story.

Gordon Butcher began to plough. Up and down the field he went, lowering the plough deeper and deeper each trip until at last it was cutting twelve inches into the ground and turning up a smooth even wave of black earth as it went.

The wind was coming faster now, rushing in from the killer sea, sweeping over the flat Norfolk[③] fields, past Saxthorpe[④] and Reepham and Honingham and Swaffham and Larling and over the border to Suffolk, to Mildenhall and to Thistley Green where Gordon Butcher sat upright

---

① sugar-beet or sugar beet: *Noun* [mass noun] beet of a variety from which sugar is extracted. It provides an important alternative sugar source to cane, and the pulp which remains after processing is used as stockfeed 甜菜;糖用甜菜

② skimp: *Verb* [no obj.] expend or use less time, money, or material on something than is necessary in an attempt to economize 节省;舍不得用(e. g. Don't skimp on insurance when you book your holidays. 当你为假期而订票时,别在保险方面节省。)

③ Norfolk: *Noun* a county on the east coast of England, east of the Wash; county town, Norwich 诺福克郡(英格兰东海岸的一个郡,位于沃什湾以东,首府诺里奇)

④ 这里的"Saxthorpe"以及随后出现的"Reepham""Honingham""Swaffham""Larling"都是英国诺福克郡境内的一些村镇。

high on the seat of his tractor, driving back and forth over the plot of yellow barley stubble that belonged to Rolfe. Gordon Butcher could smell the sharp crisp smell of snow not far away, he could see the low roof of the sky—no longer flecked with black, but pale and whitish grey—sliding by overhead like a solid sheet of metal unrolling.

"Well," he said, raising his voice above the clatter of the tractor, "you are surely fashed① at somebody today. What an almighty fuss it is now of blowin'② and whistlin'③ and freezin'④. Like a woman," he added. "Just like a woman does sometimes in the evening," and he kept his eye upon the line of the furrow⑤, and he smiled.

At noon he stopped the tractor, dismounted and fished in his pocket for his lunch. He found it and sat on the ground in the lee⑥ of one of the huge tractor-wheels. He ate large pieces of bread and very small pieces of cheese. He had nothing to drink, for his only Thermos⑦ had got smashed by the jolting of the tractor two weeks before, and in wartime, for this was in January 1942, you could not buy another anywhere. For about fifteen minutes he sat on the ground in the shelter of the wheel and

---

① fash: *Verb* (fash oneself) (Scottish) feel upset or worried(苏格兰用法)忧虑;焦虑;心烦(e.g. She'll be coming soon, don't fash yourself. 她很快就会来了,你不要自寻烦恼。)

② blowin' = blowing

③ whistlin' = whistling

④ freezin' = freezing

⑤ furrow: *Noun* a long narrow trench made in the ground by a plough, especially for planting seeds or irrigation 犁沟

⑥ lee: *Noun* [mass noun] shelter from wind or weather given by a neighbouring object 背风处;庇荫(e.g. He went round the front of the cab to be out of the wind and lit a cigarette in its lee. 他绕过车前部避风并在背风处点了香烟。)

⑦ Thermos: *Noun* trademark of a vacuum flask(商标)膳魔师牌(真空保冷用具,如杯子等)

ate his lunch. Then he got up and examined his peg①.

Unlike many ploughmen, Butcher always hitched his plough to the tractor with a wooden peg so that if the plough fouled② a root or a large stone, the peg would simply break at once, leaving the plough behind and saving the shares③ from serious damage. All over the black fen country, just below the surface, lie enormous trunks of ancient oak trees, and a wooden peg will save a ploughshare many times a week out there. Although Thistley Green was well-cultivated land, field-land, not fen-land, Butcher was taking no chances with his plough.

He examined the wooden peg, found it sound, mounted the tractor again, and went on with his ploughing.

The tractor nosed back and forth over the ground, leaving a smooth black wave of soil behind it. And still the wind blew colder but it did not snow.

Around three o'clock the thing happened.

There was a slight jolt, the wooden peg broke, and the tractor left the plough behind. Butcher stopped, dismounted and walked back to the plough to see what it had struck. It was surprising for this to have happened here, on field-land. There should be no oak trees underneath the soil in this place.

He knelt down beside the plough and began to scoop the soil away

---

① peg: *Noun* a short cylindrical piece of wood, metal, or plastic, typically tapered at one end, that is used for holding things together, hanging things on, or marking a position 螺钉;栓;挂物钉;标度钉

② foul: *Verb* cause (a cable, anchor, or other object) to become entangled or jammed 使(缆、锚等)缠结(或堵塞)(e. g. Watch out for driftwood which might foul up the engine. 当心可能堵塞发动机的漂流的木头。)

③ share: *Noun* short for "ploughshare" "ploughshare"的简称. ploughshare or plowshare: *Noun* the main cutting blade of a plough, behind the coulter(犁)铧;铧头

around the point of the ploughshare. The lower tip of the share was twelve inches down. There was a lot of soil to be scooped up. He dug his gloved fingers into the earth and scooped it out with both hands. Six inches down... eight inches... ten inches... twelve. He slid his fingers along the blade of the ploughshare until they reached the forward point of it. The soil was loose and crumbly①, and it kept falling back into the hole he was digging. He could not therefore see the twelve-inch-deep point of the share. He could only feel it. And now he could feel that the point was indeed lodged against something solid. He scooped away more earth. He enlarged the hole. It was necessary to see clearly what sort of an obstacle he had struck. If it was fairly small, then perhaps he could dig it out with his hands and get on with the job. If it was a tree-trunk he would have to go back to Ford's and fetch a spade.

"Come on," he said aloud. "I'll have you out of there, you hidden demon, you rotten old thing." And suddenly, as the gloved fingers scraped away a final handful of black earth, he caught sight of the curved rim of something flat, like the rim of a huge thick plate sticking up out of the soil. He rubbed the rim with his fingers and he rubbed again. Then all at once, the rim gave off a greenish glint, and Gordon Butcher bent his head closer and closer still, peering down into the little hole he had dug with his hands. For one last time, he rubbed the rim clean with his fingers, and in a flash of light, he saw clearly the unmistakable blue-green crust of ancient buried metal, and his heart stood still.

It should be explained here that farmers in this part of Suffolk, and particularly in the Mildenhall area, have for years been turning up ancient objects from the soil. Flint arrowheads from very long ago have

---

① crumbly: *Adjective* consisting of or easily breaking into small fragments 碎裂的;易碎的(e.g. The cheese has a sharp flavour and is crumbly and moist. 这种奶酪口味很重,含水分,很松脆。)

been found in considerable numbers, but more interesting than that, Roman pottery and Roman implements have also been found. It is known that the Romans favoured this part of the country during their occupation of Britain, and all local farmers are therefore well aware of the possibility of finding something interesting during a day's work. And so there was a kind of permanent awareness among Mildenhall people of the presence of treasure underneath the earth of their land.

Gordon Butcher's reaction, as soon as he saw the rim of that enormous plate, was a curious one. He immediately drew away. Then he got to his feet and turned his back on what he had just seen. He paused only long enough to switch off the engine of his tractor before he walked off fast in the direction of the road.

He did not know precisely what impulse caused him to stop digging and walk away. He will tell you that the only thing he can remember about those first few seconds was the whiff of danger that came to him from that little patch of greenish blue. The moment he touched it with his fingers, something electric went through his body, and there came to him a powerful premonition① that this was a thing that could destroy the peace and happiness of many people.

In the beginning, all he had wished was to be away from it, and to leave it behind him and be done with it for ever. But after he had gone a few hundred yards or so, he began to slow his pace. At the gate leading out from Thistley Green, he stopped.

"What in the world is the matter with you, Mr. Gordon Butcher?" he said aloud to the howling wind. "Are you frightened or something? No, I'm not frightened. But I'll tell you straight. I'm not keen to han-

---

① premonition: *Noun* a strong feeling that something is about to happen, especially something unpleasant(尤指不祥的)预感(e.g. He had a premonition of imminent disaster. 他有一种灾难临头的预感。)

dle this alone."

That was when he thought of Ford.

He thought of Ford at first because it was for him that he was working. He thought of him second because he knew that Ford was a kind of collector of old stuff, of all the old stones and arrowheads which people kept digging up from time to time in the district, which they brought to Ford and which Ford placed upon the mantel① in his parlour②. It was believed that Ford sold these things, but no one knew or cared how he did it.

Gordon Butcher turned towards Ford's place and walked fast out of the gate on to the narrow road, down the road around the sharp left-hand corner and so to the house. He found Ford in his large shed, bending over a damaged harrow③, mending it. Butcher stood by the door and said, "Mr. Ford!"

Ford looked around without straightening his body.

"Well, Gordon," he said, "what is it?"

Ford was middle-aged or a little older, bald-headed, long-nosed, with a clever foxy look about his face. His mouth was thin and sour, and when he looked at you, and when you saw the tightness of his mouth and the thin, sour line of his lips, you knew that this was a mouth that never smiled. His chin receded, his nose was long and sharp and he had the air about him of a sour old crafty fox from the woods.

"What is it?" he said looking up from the harrow.

---

① mantel or mantle: *Noun* a mantelpiece or mantelshelf 壁炉架;壁炉台

② parlour or parlor: *Noun* (dated) a sitting room in a private house(过时用法)客厅;起居室

③ harrow: *Noun* an implement consisting of a heavy frame set with teeth or tines which is dragged over ploughed land to break up clods, remove weeds, and cover seed 耙

Gordon Butcher stood by the door, blue-cheeked with cold, a little out of breath, rubbing his hands slowly one against the other.

"The tractor left the plough behind," he said quietly. "There's metal down there. I saw it."

Ford's head gave a jerk. "What kind of metal?" he said sharply.

"Flat. Quite flat like a sort of huge plate."

"You didn't dig it out?" Ford had straightened up now and there was a glint of eagles in his eyes.

Butcher said. "No, I left it alone and came straight on here."

Ford walked quickly over to the corner and took his coat off the nail. He found a cap and gloves, then he found a spade and went towards the door. There was something odd, he noticed, in Butcher's manner.

"You're sure it was metal?"

"Crusted up," Butcher said. "But it was metal all right."

"How deep?"

"Twelve inches down. At least the top of it was twelve inches down. The rest is deeper."

"How d'you know it was a plate?"

"I don't." Butcher said. "I only saw a little bit of the rim. But it looked like a plate to me. An enormous plate."

Ford's foxy face went quite white with excitement. "Come on," he said. "We'll go back and see."

The two men walked out of the shed into the fierce, ever-mounting fury of the wind. Ford shivered.

"Curse this filthy weather," he said. "Curse and blast① this filthy freezing weather," and he sank his pointed foxy face deep into the collar

① blast: exclamation (Brit. informal) expressing annoyance(英国英语非正式用法)该死;讨厌(e. g. "Blast! The car won't start!" "该死! 车子起动不了!")

of his coat and began to ponder upon the possibilities① of Butcher's find.

One thing Ford knew which Butcher did not know. He knew that back in 1932 a man called Lethbridge, a lecturer in Anglo-Saxon② Antiquities at Cambridge University, had been excavating in the district and that he had actually unearthed the foundations of a Roman villa on Thistley Green itself. Ford was not forgetting that, and he quickened his pace. Butcher walked beside him without speaking and soon they were there. They went through the gate and over the field to the plough which lay about ten yards behind the tractor.

Ford knelt down beside the front of the plough and peered into the small hole Gordon Butcher had dug with his hands. He touched the rim of green- blue metal with a gloved finger. He scraped away a bit more earth. He leaned further forward so that his pointed nose was right down the hole. He ran fingers over the rough green surface. Then he stood up and said, "Let's get the plough out of the way and do some digging." Although there were fireworks exploding in his head and shivers running all over his body, Ford kept his voice very soft and casual.

Between them they pulled the plough back a couple of yards.

"Give me the spade," Ford said, and he began cautiously to dig the soil away in a circle about three feet in diameter around the exposed patch of metal. When the hole was two feet deep, he threw away the spade and used his hands. He knelt down and scraped the soil away, and gradually the little patch of metal grew and grew until at last there lay ex-

---

① possibility: *Noun* (possibilities) unspecified qualities of a promising nature; potential 发展前景;潜能(e.g. The house was old but it had possibilities. 这座房屋很古老,但却有升值空间。)

② Anglo-Saxon: *Adjective* relating to or denoting the Germanic inhabitants of England from their arrival in the 5th century up to the Norman Conquest(与)盎格鲁撒克逊人(有关)的(指从公元5世纪到达英格兰至诺曼征服时居住在英格兰的日耳曼部族居民)

posed before them the great round disc of an enormous plate. It was fully twenty-four inches in diameter. The lower point of the plough had just caught the raised centre rim of the plate, for one could see the dent①.

Carefully Ford lifted it out of the hole. He got to his feet, and stood wiping the soil away from it, turning it over and over in his hands. There was nothing much to see, for the whole surface was crusted over with a thick layer of a hard greenish-blue substance. But he knew that it was an enormous plate or dish of great weight and thickness. It weighed about eighteen pounds!

Ford stood in the field of yellow barley stubble and gazed at the huge plate. His hands began to shake. A tremendous and almost unbearable excitement started boiling up inside him and it was not easy for him to hide it. But he did his best.

"Some sort of a dish," he said.

Butcher was kneeling on the ground beside the hole. "Must be pretty old," he said.

"Could be old," Ford said. "But it's all rusted up and eaten away."

"That don't look like rust to me," Butcher said. "That greenish stuff isn't rust. It's something else..."

"It's green rust," Ford said rather superbly, and that ended the discussion.

Butcher, still on his knees, was poking about casually in the now three-feet-wide hole with his gloved hands. "There's another one down here," he said.

Instantly, Ford laid the great dish on the ground. He knelt beside Butcher, and within minutes they had unearthed a second large green-

① dent: *Noun* a slight hollow in a hard even surface made by a blow or the exertion of pressure 凹陷

encrusted plate. This one was a shade smaller than the first, and deeper. More of a bowl than a dish.

Ford stood up and held the new find in his hands.

Another heavy one. And now he knew for certain they were on to something absolutely tremendous. They were on to Roman Treasure, and almost without question it was pure silver. Two things pointed to its being pure silver. First the weight, and second, the particular type of green crust caused by oxidation①.

How often is a piece of Roman silver discovered in the world?

Almost never any more. And had pieces as large as this ever been unearthed before?

Ford wasn't sure, but he very much doubted it.

Worth millions it must be.

Worth literally millions of pounds.

His breath, coming fast, was making little white clouds in the freezing atmosphere.

"There's still more down here, Mr. Ford," Butcher was saying. "I can feel bits of it all over the place. You'll need the spade again."

The third piece they got out was another large plate, somewhat similar to the first. Ford placed it in the barley stubble with the other two.

When Butcher felt the first flake of snow upon his cheek he looked up and saw over to the north-east a great white curtain drawn across the sky, a solid wall of snow flying forward on the wings of the wind.

"Here she comes!" he said, and Ford looked round and saw the snow moving upon them and he said, "It's a blizzard. It's a filthy

---

① oxidation: *Noun* [mass noun] (Chemistry) the process or result of oxidizing or being oxidized(化学)氧化(作用)

stinking① blizzard!"

The two men stared at the blizzard as it raced across the fens towards them. Then it was on them, and all around was snow and snowflakes in the eyes and ears and mouth and down the neck and all around. And when Butcher glanced down at the ground a few seconds later it was already white.

"That's all we want," Ford said. "A filthy rotten stinking blizzard," and he shivered and sunk his sharp and foxy face deeper into the collar of his coat. "Come on," he said. "See if there's any more."

Butcher knelt down again and poked around in the soil, then in the slow and casual manner of a man having a lucky dip② in a barrel of sawdust, he pulled out another plate and held it out to Ford. Ford took it and placed it with the other three. Now Ford knelt down beside Butcher and began to dip into the soil with him.

For a whole hour the two men stayed out there digging and scratching in that little three-foot patch of soil. And during that hour they found and laid upon the ground beside them no less than thirty-four separate pieces! There were dishes, bowls, goblets③, spoons, ladles④ and several other things, all of them crusted over but each one recognizable for what it was. And all the while the blizzard swirled around them and

① stinking: *Adjective* (informal) very bad or unpleasant(非正式)很糟的;极坏的;令人讨厌的

② lucky dip: (Brit.) a game in which small prizes are concealed in a container and chosen at random by participants, usually in return for a small payment(英国英语)摸彩

③ goblet: *Noun* (archaic) a metal or glass bowl-shaped drinking cup, sometimes with a foot and a cover(古旧用法)(金属或玻璃的)碗状酒杯

④ ladle: *Noun* a large long-handled spoon with a cup-shaped bowl, used for serving soup, stew, or sauce 长柄勺

the snow gathered in little mounds[1] upon their caps and on their shoulders and the flakes melted on their faces so that rivers of icy water trickled down their necks. A large globule[2] of half-frozen liquid dangled continually, like a snow drop[3], from the end of Ford's pointed nose.

They worked in silence. It was too cold to speak. And as one precious article after the other was unearthed, Ford laid them carefully on the ground in rows, pausing every now and then to wipe the snow away from a dish or a spoon which was in danger of being completely covered.

At last Ford said, "That's the lot, I think."

"Yes."

Ford stood up and stamped his feet on the ground. "Got a sack in the tractor?" he said, and while Butcher walked over to fetch the sack, he turned and gazed upon the four-and-thirty pieces lying in the snow at his feet. He counted them again. If they were silver, which they surely must be, and if they were Roman, which they undoubtedly were, then this was a discovery that would rock the world.

Butcher called to him from the tractor, "It's only a dirty old sack."

"It'll do."

Butcher brought the sack over and held it open while Ford carefully put the articles into it. They all went in except one. The massive two-foot plate was too large for the neck of the sack.

The two men were really cold now. For over an hour they had knelt and scratched about out there in the open field with the blizzard swirling around them. Already, nearly six inches of snow had fallen. Butcher was

---

① mound: *Noun* a rounded mass projecting above a surface 堆;垛

② globule: *Noun* a small round particle of a substance; a drop 小球;滴

③ snow drop or snowdrop: a bulbous European plant which bears drooping white flowers during the late winter (欧洲产)雪花莲

half-frozen. His cheeks were dead-white, blotched[1] with blue, his feet were numb like wood, and when he moved his legs he could not feel the ground beneath his feet. He was much colder than Ford. His coat and clothes were not so thick, and ever since early morning he had been sitting high up on the seat of the tractor, exposed to the bitter wind. His blue-white face was tight and unmoving. All he wanted was to get home to his family and to the fire that he knew would be burning in the grate.

Ford, on the other hand, was not thinking about the cold. His mind was concentrated solely upon one thing—how to get possession for himself of this fabulous treasure. His position, as he knew very well, was not a strong one.

In England there is a very curious law about finding any kind of gold or silver treasure. This law goes back hundreds of years, and is still strictly enforced today. The law states that if a person digs up out of the ground, even out of his own garden, a piece of metal that is either gold or silver, it automatically becomes what is known as Treasure Trove[2] and is the property of the Crown[3]. The Crown doesn't in these days mean the actual King or Queen. It means the country or the government. The law also states that it is a criminal offence to conceal such a find. You are simply not allowed to hide the stuff and keep it for yourself. You must report it at once, preferably to the police. And if you do report it at once, you as the finder will be entitled to receive from the government in money the full amount of the market value of the article. You are not re-

---

① blotch: *Verb* (usu. as "be blotched") cover with blotches 给……弄上斑块;弄脏

② trove: *Noun* a store of valuable or delightful things 有价值(或令人喜爱)的藏品(e.g. the museum's trove of antique treasure 博物馆的古董收藏)

③ crown: *Noun* (usu. as "the Crown") the power or authority residing in the monarchy 王权;王位(e.g. They claimed immunity on behalf of the Crown. 他们以王室名义宣布豁免。)

quired to report the digging up of other metals. You are allowed to find as much valuable pewter①, bronze, copper or even platinum② as you wish, and you can keep it all, but not gold or silver.

The other curious part of this curious law is this: it is the person who discovers the treasure in the first place who gets the reward from the government. The owner of the land gets nothing—unless of course the finder is trespassing③ on the land when he makes the discovery. But if the finder of the treasure has been hired by the owner to do a job on his land, then he, the finder, gets all the reward.

In this case, the finder was Gordon Butcher. Furthermore, he was not trespassing. He was performing a job which he had been hired to do. This treasure therefore belonged to Butcher and to no one else. All he had to do was to take it and show it to an expert who would immediately identify it as silver, then turn it in to the police. In time, he would receive from the government one hundred per cent of its value—perhaps a million pounds.

All this left Ford out in the cold and Ford knew it. He had no rights whatsoever to the treasure by law. Thus, as he must have told himself at the time, his only chance of getting hold of the stuff for himself lay in the fact that Butcher was an ignorant man who didn't know the law and who did not anyway have the faintest idea of the value of the find. The proba-

---

① pewter: *Noun* [mass noun] a grey alloy of tin with copper and antimony (formerly, tin and lead) [as modifier] 锡

② platinum: *Noun* [mass noun] a precious silvery-white metal, the chemical element of atomic number 78. It was first encountered by the Spanish in South America in the 16th century, and is used in jewellery, electrical contacts, laboratory equipment, and industrial catalysts (Symbol: Pt) (化学元素)铂;白金(符号:Pt)

③ trespass: *Verb* [no obj.] enter someone's land or property without their permission 擅闯某人领地;侵犯某人财产(e. g. There is no excuse for trespassing on railway property. 铁路财产不容侵犯。)

bility was that in a few days Butcher would forget all about it. He was too simple-minded a fellow, too artless, too trusting, too unselfish to give the matter much thought.

Now, out there in the desolate snowswept field, Ford bent down and took hold of the huge dish with one hand. He raised it but he did not lift it. The lower rim remained resting on the snow. With his other hand, he grasped the top of the sack. He didn't lift that either. He just held it. And there he stooped amid the swirling snowflakes, both hands embracing, as it were, the treasure, but not actually taking it. It was a subtle and a canny① gesture. It managed somehow to signify② ownership before ownership had been discussed. A child plays the same game when he reaches out and closes his fingers over the biggest chocolate éclair③ on the plate and then says, "Can I have this one, Mummy?" He's already got it.

"Well, Gordon," Ford said, stooping over, holding the sack and the great dish in his gloved fingers. "I don't suppose you want any of this old stuff."

It was not a question. It was a statement of fact framed as a question.

The blizzard was still raging. The snow was falling so densely the two men could hardly see one another.

"You ought to get along home and warm yourself up," Ford went on. "You look frozen to death."

"I feel frozen to death," Butcher said.

---

① canny: *Adjective* having or showing shrewdness and good judgement, especially in money or business matters (尤指在钱财或生意上)精明的

② signify: *Verb* (of a person) indicate or declare (a feeling or intention)(人)表明(情感或意图)(e.g. Signify your agreement by signing the letter below. 在下面这封信中署名,表明你同意。)

③ éclair or eclair: *Noun* a small, soft, log-shaped cake of choux pastry filled with cream and typically topped with chocolate icing 奶油松饼;狭长形松饼(一种顶部常裹有巧克力糖衣的奶油馅饼)

"Then you get on that tractor quick and hurry home," said the thoughtful, kind-hearted Ford. "Leave the plough here and leave your bike at my place. The important thing is to get back and warm yourself up before you catch pneumonia."

"I think that's just what I will do, Mr. Ford," Butcher said. "Can you manage all right with that sack? It's mighty heavy."

"I might not even bother about it today," Ford said casually. "I just might leave it here and come back for it another time. Rusty old stuff."

"So long then, Mr. Ford."

"Bye, Gordon."

Gordon Butcher mounted the tractor and drove away into the blizzard.

Ford hoisted the sack on to his shoulder, and then, not without difficulty, he lifted the massive dish with his other hand and tucked it under his arm.

"I am carrying," he told himself, as he trudged① through the snow, "I am now carrying what is probably the biggest treasure ever dug up in the whole history of England."

When Gordon Butcher came stamping and blowing through the back door of his small brick house late that afternoon, his wife was ironing by the fire. She looked up and saw his blue-white face and snow-encrusted clothes.

"My goodness, Gordon, you look froze to death!" She cried.

"I am," he said. "Help me off with these clothes, love. My fingers aren't hardly working at all."

She took off his gloves, his coat, his jacket, his wet shirt. She

---

① trudge: *Verb* [no obj., with adverbial of direction] walk slowly and with heavy steps, typically because of exhaustion or harsh conditions(尤指在疲劳状态或恶劣环境中)步履艰难地走(e.g. She trudged through blinding snow. 她在令人目眩的雪地中跋涉。)

pulled off his boots and socks. She fetched a towel and rubbed his chest and shoulders vigorously all over to restore the circulation. She rubbed his feet.

"Sit down there by the fire," she said, "and I'll get you a hot cup of tea."

Later, when he was settled comfortably in the warmth with dry clothes on his back and the mug of tea in his hand, he told her what had happened that afternoon.

"He's a foxy one, that Mr. Ford," she said, not looking up from her ironing. "I never did like him."

"He got pretty excited about it all, I can tell you that," Gordon Butcher said. "Jumpy as a jack-rabbit① he was."

"That may be," she said. "But you ought to have had more sense than to go crawling about on your hands and knees in a freezing blizzard just because Mr. Ford said to do it."

"I'm all right," Gordon Butcher said, "I'm warming up nicely now."

And that, believe it or not, was about the last time the subject of the treasure was discussed in the Butcher household for some years.

The reader should be reminded that this was wartime, 1942. Britain was totally absorbed in the desperate war against Hitler and Mussolini②.

---

① jack-rabbit or jackrabbit: *Noun* a hare found on the prairies and steppes of North America(北美草原上的)长耳大野兔

② Benito Mussolini (1883—1945), Italian Fascist statesman, Prime Minister 1922—1943; known as Il Duce ("the leader"). He founded the Italian Fascist Party in 1919. He annexed Abyssinia in 1936 and entered the Second World War on Germany's side in 1940. Forced to resign after the Allied invasion of Sicily, he was rescued from imprisonment by German paratroopers, but was captured and executed by Italian communist partisans 贝尼托·墨索里尼(1883—1945):意大利法西斯政客,1922~1943年间任首相,通称"领袖",1919年建立意大利法西斯党,1936年吞并阿比西尼亚,1940年与德国联盟加入二战,在盟军进入西西里后被迫辞职,遭监禁后被德国伞兵救出,但最后被意大利共产党游击队俘获并处决。

Germany was bombing England, and England was bombing Germany, and nearly every night Gordon Butcher heard the roar of motors from the big aerodrome at nearby Mildenhall as the bombers took off for Hamburg①, Berlin②, Kiel③, Wilhelmshaven④ or Frankfurt⑤. Sometimes he would wake in the early hours and hear them coming home, and sometimes the Germans flew over to bomb the aerodrome, and the Butcher house would shake with the crumph⑥ and crash of bombs not far away.

Butcher himself was exempt from military service. He was a farmer, a skilled ploughman, and they had told him when he volunteered for the army in 1939 that he was not wanted. The island's food supplies must be kept going, they told him, and it was vital that men like him stay on their

---

① Hamburg: *Naun* a port in northern Germany, on the River Elbe; pop. 1,668,760 (1991). Founded by Charlemagne in the 9th century, it is now the largest port in Germany, with extensive shipyards. 汉堡:德国北部港市,在易北河畔,1991年人口1,668,760,公元9世纪时由查理曼大帝建造,现为德国最大港口,拥有大规模的造船厂。

② Berlin: *Noun* the capital of Germany; pop. 3,102,500 (est. 1990) 柏林:德国首都,1990年估计人口3,102,500。

③ Kiel: *Noun* a naval port in northern Germany, capital of Schleswig-Holstein, on the Baltic Sea coast at the eastern end of the Kiel Canal; pop. 247,100 (1991) 基尔:德国北部军港,石勒苏益格-赫尔斯泰因州首府,位于波罗的海沿岸,基尔运河东端;1991年人口247,100。

④ Wilhelmshaven: *Noun* a port and resort in NW Germany, on the North Sea; pop. 91,150 (1991). It was a major naval base until 1945. 威廉港:德国西北部港口和度假胜地,濒临北海;1991年人口91,150;1945年以前是一重要的海军基地。

⑤ Frankfurt: *Noun* a commercial city in western Germany, in Hesse; pop. 645,500 (est. 2002). The headquarters of the Bundesbank are located there. 法兰克福:德国西部黑森州商业城市;2002年估计人口645,500;德意志银行总部设在该市。

⑥ 此处的"crumph"疑为"crump"之误,抑或"crump"的异体形式。

crump: *Noun* a loud thudding sound, especially one made by an exploding bomb or shell(炸弹或炮弹的)爆炸声

jobs and cultivate the land.

Ford, being in the same business, was also exempt. He was a bachelor, living alone, and he was thus able to live a secret life and to do secret things within the walls of his home.

And so, on that terrible snowy afternoon when they dug up the treasure, Ford carried it home and laid everything out on a table in the back room.

Thirty-four separate pieces! They covered the entire table. And by the look of it, they were in marvellous condition. Silver does not rust. The green crust of oxidation can even be protection for the surface of the metal underneath. And with care, it could all be removed.

Ford decided to use an ordinary domestic silver polish known as Silvo, and he bought a large stock of it from the ironmonger's[①] shop in Mildenhall. Then he took first the great two-foot plate which weighed more than eighteen pounds. He worked on it in the evenings. He soaked it all over with Silvo. He rubbed and rubbed. He worked patiently on this single dish every night for more than sixteen weeks.

At last, one memorable evening, there showed beneath his rubbing a small area of shining silver, and on the silver, raised up and beautifully worked, there was a part of a man's head.

He kept at it, and gradually the little patch of shining metal spread and spread, the blue-green crust crept outward to the edges of the plate until finally the top surface of the great dish lay before him in its full glory, covered all over with a wondrous pattern of animals and men and many odd legendary things.

Ford was astounded by the beauty of the great plate. It was filled with life and movement. There was a fierce face with tangled hair, a

---

① ironmonger: *Noun* (Brit.) a person or shop selling hardware such as tools and household implements(英国英语)金属器具商;小五金商

dancing goat with a human head, there were men and women and animals of many kinds cavorting[1] around the rim, and no doubt all of them told a story.

Next, he set about cleaning the reverse side of the plate. Weeks and weeks it took. And when the work was completed and the whole plate on both sides was shining like a star, he placed it safely in the lower cupboard of his big oak sideboard and locked the cupboard door.

One by one, he tackled the remaining thirty-three pieces. A mania had taken hold of him now, a fierce compulsion to make every item shine in all its silver brilliance. He wanted to see all thirty-four pieces laid out on the big table in a dazzling array of silver. He wanted that more than anything else, and he worked desperately hard to achieve his wish.

He cleaned the two smaller dishes next, then the large fluted[2] bowl, then the five long-handled ladles, the goblets, the wine-cups, the spoons. Every single piece was cleaned with equal care and made to shine with equal brilliance, and when they were all done, two years had passed and it was 1944.

But no strangers were allowed to look. Ford discussed the matter with no man or woman, and Rolfe, the owner of the plot on Thistley Green where the treasure had been found, knew nothing except that Ford, or someone Ford had hired, had ploughed his land extremely well and very deep.

One can guess why Ford hid the treasure instead of reporting it to the police as Treasure Trove. Had he reported it, it would have been taken away and Gordon Butcher would have been rewarded as the finder.

---

① cavort: *Verb* [no obj.] jump or dance around excitedly 跳跃;欢腾;欢跃 (e. g. The players cavorted about the pitch. 运动员们为这一投球而欢跃。)

② fluted: *Adjective* having grooves 有凹槽的(e. g. fluted columns 刻有凹槽的柱子)

Rewarded with a fortune. So the only thing Ford could do was to hang on to it and hide it in the hope, presumably, of selling it quietly to some dealer or collector at a later date.

It is possible, of course, to take a more charitable① view and assume that Ford kept the treasure solely because he loved beautiful things and wanted to have them around him. No one will ever know the true answer.

Another year went by.

The war against Hitler was won.

And then, in 1946, just after Easter, there was a knock on the door of Ford's house. Ford opened it.

"Why hello, Mr. Ford. How are you after all these years?"

"Hello, Dr Fawcett," Ford said. "You been keeping all right?"

"I'm fine, thank you," Dr Fawcett said. "It's been a long time, hasn't it?"

"Yes," Ford said. "That old war kept us all pretty busy."

"May I come in?" Dr Fawcett asked.

"Of course," Ford said, "Come on in."

Dr Hugh Alderson Fawcett was a keen and learned archaeologist who before the war had made a point of visiting Ford once a year in search of old stones or arrowheads. Ford had usually collected a batch of such itemsduring the twelve months and he was always willing to sell them to Fawcett. They were seldom of great value, but now and again something quite good had turned up.

"Well," said Fawcett, taking off his coat in the little hall. "Well, well, well. It's been nearly seven years since I was here last."

---

① charitable: *Adjective* apt to judge others leniently or favourably 宽容的;仁慈的;称赞的(e.g. Those who were less charitable called for his resignation. 那些不太宽容的人要求他辞职。)

"Yes, it's been a long time," Ford said.

Ford led him into the front room and showed him a box of flint arrowheads which had been picked up in the district. Some were good, others not so good. Fawcett picked through them, sorted them, and a deal was done.

"Nothing else?"

"No, I don't think so."

Ford wished fervently that Dr Fawcett had never come. He wished even more fervently that he would go away.

It was at this point that Ford noticed something that made him sweat. He saw suddenly that he had left lying on the mantel over the fireplace the two most beautiful of the Roman spoons from the treasure hoard①. These spoons had fascinated him because each was inscribed with the name of a Roman girl child to whom it had been given, presumably as a christening present, by Roman parents who had been converted to Christianity. One name was Pascentia, the other was Papittedo. Rather lovely names.

Ford, sweating with fear, tried to place himself between Dr Fawcett and the mantelpiece. He might even, he thought, be able to slip the spoons into his pocket if he got the chance.

He didn't get the chance.

Perhaps Ford had polished them so well that a little flash of reflected light from the silver caught the doctor's eye. Who knows? The fact remains that Fawcett saw them. The moment he saw them, he pounced like a tiger.

"Great heavens alive!" he cried. "What are these?"

---

① hoard: *Noun* a stock or store of money or valued objects, typically one that is secret or carefully guarded 储藏(或秘藏)的钱财(或贵重物品)(e.g. He came back to rescue his little hoard of gold. 他回来抢救他储藏的一小批金子。)

"Pewter," Ford said, sweating more than ever. "Just a couple of old pewter spoons."

"Pewter?" cried Fawcett, turning one of the spoons over in his fingers. "Pewter! You call this pewter ?"

"That's right," Ford said. "It's pewter."

"You know what this is?" Fawcett said, his voice going high with excitement. "Shall I tell you what this really is?"

"You don't have to tell me," Ford said, truculent①. "I know what it is. It's old pewter. And quite nice, too."

Fawcett was reading the inscription in Roman letters on the scoop of the spoon. "Papittedo!" he cried.

"What's that mean?" Ford asked him.

Fawcett picked up the other spoon. "Pascentia," he said. "Beautiful! These are the names of Roman children! And these spoons, my friend, are made of solid silver! Solid Roman silver!"

"Not possible." Ford said.

"They're magnificent!" Fawcett cried out, going into raptures. "They're perfect! They're unbelievable! Where on earth did you find them? It's most important to know where you found them! Was there anything else?" Fawcett was hopping about all over the room.

"Well..." Ford said, licking dry lips.

"You must report them at once!" Fawcett cried. "They're Treasure Trove! The British Museum is going to want these and that's for certain! How long have you had them?"

"Just a little while," Ford told him.

"And who found them?" Fawcett asked, looking straight at him.

---

① truculent: *Adjective* eager or quick to argue or fight; aggressively defiant 好争论的;好勇斗狠的;咄咄逼人的(e.g. the truculent attitude of farmers to cheaper imports 农场主对价格较低的进口货所持的敌视态度)

"Did you find them yourself or did you get them from somebody else? This is vital! The finder will be able to tell us all about it!"

Ford felt the walls of the room closing in on him and he didn't quite know what to do.

"Come on, man! Surely you know where you got them! Every detail will have to come out when you hand them in. Promise me you'll go to the police with them at once?"

"Well ..." Ford said.

"If you don't, then I'm afraid I shall be forced to report it myself," Fawcett told him. "It's my duty."

The game was up① now and Ford knew it. A thousand questions would be asked. How did you find it? When did you find it? What were you doing? Where was the exact spot? Whose land were you ploughing? And sooner or later, inevitably, the name of Gordon Butcher would have to come into it. It was unavoidable. And then, when Butcher was questioned, he would remember the size of the hoard and tell them all about it.

So the game was up. And the only thing to do at this point was to unlock the doors of the big sideboard and show the entire hoard to Dr Fawcett.

Ford's excuse for keeping it all and not turning it in would have to be that he thought it was pewter. So long as he stuck to that, he told himself, they couldn't do anything to him.

Dr Fawcett would probably have a heart-attack when he saw what there was in that cupboard.

"There is actually quite a bit more of it," Ford said.

"Where?" cried Fawcett, spinning round. "Where, man, where? Lead me to it!"

---

① The game is up: The deception or crime is revealed or foiled(诡计或罪行)被戳穿(或被挫败)

"I really thought it was pewter," Ford said, moving slowly and very reluctantly forward to the oak sideboard. "Otherwise I would naturally have reported it at once."

He bent down and unlocked the lower doors of the sideboard. He opened the doors.

And then Dr Hugh Alderson Fawcett very nearly did have a heart-attack. He flung himself on his knees. He gasped. He choked. He began spluttering① like an old kettle. He reached out for the great silver dish. He took it. He held it in shaking hands and his face went as white as snow. He didn't speak. He couldn't. He was literally and physically and mentally struck absolutely dumb by the sight of the treasure.

The interesting part of the story ends here. The rest is routine. Ford went to Mildenhall Police Station and made a report. The police came at once and collected all thirty-four pieces, and they were sent under guard to the British Museum for examination.

Then an urgent message from the Museum to the Mildenhall Police. It was far and away② the finest Roman silver ever found in the British Isles. It was of enormous value. The Museum (which is really a public governmental institution) wished to acquire it. In fact, they insisted upon acquiring it.

The wheels of the law began to turn. An official inquest③ and hear-

---

① splutter: *Verb* [reporting verb] say something rapidly, indistinctly, and with a spitting sound, as a result of anger, embarrassment, or another strong emotion (因愤怒、窘迫、激动而)气急败坏(或结结巴巴、含糊不清)地说;(因激动而)急促地说

② far and away: by a very large amount 极大地;极其悬殊地(e.g. He is far and away the most accomplished player. 他是最有成就的运动员,别的运动员无法望其项背。)

③ inquest: *Noun* (Law) a judicial inquiry to ascertain the facts relating to an incident(法律)审讯;审问

ing was arranged at the nearest large town, Bury St Edmunds. The silver was moved there under special police guard. Ford was summoned to appear before the Coroner and a jury of fourteen, while Gordon Butcher, that good and quiet man, was ordered also to present himself to give evidence.

On Monday, July the first, 1946, the hearing took place, and the Coroner① cross-questioned Ford closely.

"You thought it was pewter?"

"Yes."

"Even after you had cleaned it?"

"Yes."

"You took no steps to inform any experts of the find?"

"No."

"What did you intend to do with the articles?"

"Nothing. Just keep them."

And when he had concluded his evidence, Ford asked permission to go outside into the fresh air because he said he felt faint. Nobody was surprised.

Then Butcher was called, and in a few simple words he told of his part in the affair.

Dr Fawcett gave his evidence, so did several other learned archaeologists, all of whom testified to the extreme rarity of the treasure. They said that it was of the fourth century after Christ; that it was the table silver of a wealthy Roman family; that it had probably been buried by the

---

① coroner: *Noun* an official who holds inquests into violent, sudden, or suspicious deaths, and (in Britain) inquiries into cases of treasure trove 验尸官；(英国)无主珍宝调查官

owner's bailiff① to save it from the Picts② and Scots③ who swept down from the north in about A.D. 365-7 and laid waste many Roman settlements. The man who buried it had probably been liquidated④ either by a Pict or a Scot, and the treasure had remained concealed a foot below the soil ever since. The workmanship, said the experts, was magnificent. Some of it may have been executed⑤ in England, but more probably the articles were made in Italy or in Egypt. The great plate was of course the finest piece. The head in the centre was that of Neptune⑥, the sea-god, with dolphins in his hair and seaweed in his beard. All around him, sea-nymphs⑦ and sea-monsters gambolled⑧. On the broad rim of the plate

---

① bailiff: *Noun* (chiefly Brit.) a sheriff's officer who executes writs and processes and carries out distraints and arrests(主要为英国英语用法)(负责执行令状传唤、扣押财产及逮捕)郡副司法长官

② Pict: *Noun* a member of an ancient people inhabiting northern Scotland in Roman times(古罗马时代居住在苏格兰北部的)皮可特人

③ Scot: *Noun* A native or inhabitant of Scotland 苏格兰人

④ liquidate: *Verb* eliminate, typically by violent means; kill 除掉;杀戮

⑤ execute: *Verb* produce (a work of art) 创作(艺术作品)(e.g. Not only does she execute embroideries, she designs them too. 她不仅进行刺绣而且还进行绣花设计。)

⑥ Neptune: *Noun* (Roman Mythology) the god of water and of the sea. Greek equivalent Poseidon(罗马神话)尼普顿(海神,相当于希腊神话中的"Poseidon"。)

⑦ nymph: *Noun* a mythological spirit of nature imagined as a beautiful maiden inhabiting rivers, woods, or other locations 神话中居于山林水泽的美丽仙女

⑧ gambol: *Verb* [no obj., usu. with adverbial] run or jump about playfully 欢跳;雀跃(e.g. The mare gambolled towards Constance. 马儿撒开蹄子向康斯坦茨奔去。)

stood Bacchus① and his attendants. There was wine and revelry②. Hercules③ was there, quite drunk, supported by two satyrs④, his lion's skin fallen from his shoulders. Pan⑤ was there, too, dancing upon his goat-legs with his pipes in his hand. And everywhere there were maenads⑥, female devotees of Bacchus, rather tipsy⑦ women.

The court was told also that several of the spoons bore the mono-

---

① Bacchus: *Noun* (Greek Mythology) another name for Dionysus(希腊神话)酒神巴克斯(另一个称呼"Dionysus",即狄俄尼索斯)

② revelry: *Noun* [mass noun] lively and noisy festivities, especially when these involve drinking a large amount of alcohol 狂欢作乐;纵酒狂欢(e. g. Sounds of revelry issued into the night. 纵酒狂欢的喧闹声响彻夜空。)

③ Hercules: *Noun* (Greek & Roman Mythology) a hero of superhuman strength and courage who performed twelve immense tasks or "labours" imposed on him and who after death was ranked among the gods. (希腊罗马神话)大力神赫拉克勒斯(一位有超人力量和勇气的英雄,他完成了强加于他的12项艰巨任务,死后被立为神。)

④ satyr: *Noun* (Greek Mythology) one of a class of lustful, drunken woodland gods. In Greek art they were represented as a man with a horse's ears and tail, but in Roman representations as a man with a goat's ears, tail, legs, and horns. (希腊神话)撒梯(森林之神,好酒色,在希腊神话中被描绘为人身马耳马尾,而在罗马神话中则为生有羊耳羊尾羊腿羊角的人形。)

⑤ Pan: *Noun* (Greek Mythology) a god of flocks and herds, typically represented with the horns, ears, and legs of a goat on a man's body. His sudden appearance was supposed to cause terror similar to that of a frightened and stampeding herd, and the word panic is derived from his name. (希腊神话)潘(人身羊角、羊耳、羊脚的畜牧神;据说他的突然出现会造成受惊畜群那样的恐慌,"panic"[恐慌]一词因其得名。)

⑥ maenad: *Noun* (in ancient Greece) a female follower of Bacchus, traditionally associated with divine possession and frenzied rites(古希腊)酒神的女随从;酒神的女祭司

⑦ tipsy: *Adjective* slightly drunk 喝醉的;微醉的

gram① of Christ (Chi-Rho②), and that the two which were inscribed with the names Pascentia and Papittedo were undoubtedly christening presents.

The experts concluded their evidence and the court adjourned. Soon the jury returned, and their verdict was astonishing. No blame was attached to anyone for anything, although the finder of the treasure was no longer entitled to receive full compensation from the Crown because the find had not been declared at once. Nevertheless, there would probably be a measure of compensation paid, and with this in view, the finders were declared to be jointly Ford and Butcher.

Not Butcher. Ford and Butcher.

There is no more to tell other than that the treasure was acquired by the British Museum, where it now stands proudly displayed in a large glass case for all to see. And already people have travelled great distances to go and look upon those lovely things which Gordon Butcher found beneath his plough on that cold and windy winter afternoon. One day, a book or two will be compiled about them, full of suppositions and abstruse③ conclusions, and men who move in archaeological circles will talk for ever about the Treasure of Mildenhall.

As a gesture, the Museum rewarded the co-finders with one thousand pounds each. Butcher, the true finder, was happy and surprised to receive so much money. He did not realize that had he been allowed to

---

① monogram: *Noun* a motif of two or more interwoven letters, typically a person's initials, used to identify a personal possession or as a logo 交织字母;花押字(由两个或多个字母,尤指姓名首字母交织组成的图案,用以标明物属或用作标识。)

② chi-rho: *Noun* a monogram of chi (X) and rho (P) as the first two letters of Greek Khristos Christ 耶稣基督:希腊语"Khristos"(基督)头两个字母"chi"(X)和"rho"(P)的组合。

③ abstruse: *Adjective* difficult to understand; obscure 深奥难懂的;晦涩的(e.g. an abstruse philosophical inquiry 玄奥的哲学探讨)

take the treasure home originally, he would almost certainly have revealed its existence and would thus have become eligible to receive one hundred per cent of its value, which could have been anything between half a million and a million pounds.

Nobody knows what Ford thought about it all. He must have been relieved and perhaps somewhat surprised when he heard that the court had believed his story about pewter. But above all he must have been shattered by the loss of his great treasure. For the rest of his life he would be kicking himself for leaving those two spoons on the mantel above the fireplace for Dr Fawcett to see.

三、翻译探索

本篇小说的翻译中,要处理好两个问题:一个是所涉及的英国历史方面的知识,如人名、地名等;还有一个棘手的地方就是有关希腊、罗马一些神的名称的翻译,值得探索:音译?意译?还是二者的结合?

序　言

三十多年前,也就是1946年,我仍然单身未婚,跟我兄弟住在一起。当时,我一年写两部短篇小说,每部小说四个月完成。幸运的是,国内外都有人愿意买我的作品阅读,我的收入还算可以。

那年四月的一个早晨,我从报纸上看到一则消息,说的是发现了罗马时代的银器,是一个非同凡响的发现,是四年前一个犁田的农夫在萨福克郡的米尔登霍尔附近发现的。但是,出于某种原因,那个发现直到那年才公布于世。报纸的那篇文章说,那是在不列颠群岛上所发现的最大的宝藏,已经被大英博物馆收购。报道中说,犁田农夫的名字叫戈登·布彻。

关于发现这笔巨大宝藏的真实故事如阵阵电流,电得我从头部到腿部,甚至脚底都颤抖不已。看到这则故事的那一刻,我早饭还没有吃完,就从椅子上跳了起来,大声对母亲说完再见,就冲出门,跳上了小汽车,是一辆用了九年的沃尔斯利牌汽车,我称之为“黑硬懒虫”,性能良好,但跑不快。

米尔登霍尔离我家大约有一百八十公里。这一段基本都是土路,弯弯曲曲、拐弯抹角,还要穿过乡村小径,走起来需要细心和技巧。我到达那儿的时候正是吃午饭的时间,通过当地的警察局,我找到了戈登·布彻家住的小房子。敲门的时候,他正在家吃午饭。

我问他,是否介意跟我谈谈是如何找到珍宝的。

“不,谢谢,”他说。“一个一个记者让我受够了,我这辈子再也不想看到记者。”

“我不是记者呀,”我对他说。“我是写短篇小说的,我向杂志社出售自己的作品,杂志社会付给我一笔丰厚的稿酬。”我继续对他说,要是他一五一十地跟我讲讲发现珍宝的过程,我就能写出一篇真实的故事来。如果很幸运能卖出这篇故事,我就将稿酬一劈两半,跟他均分。

最后,他同意跟我谈谈。我们在他家厨房一坐就是好几个小时,其间,他讲述了一个引人入胜的故事。讲完后,我拜访了与这件事儿有关的另一个人,是一位名叫福特的、上了年纪的男子。问题是,福特不愿意跟我谈,将我拒之门外,让我吃了闭门羹。可是,我要的故事已经成形,就出发回家了。

第二天早晨,我去了一趟位于伦敦的大英博物馆,看了看戈登·布彻发现的宝藏。宝藏无与伦比,单单看上那么一眼,又使我浑身颤抖不已。我将这个故事原封不动、一五一十地写了出来,然后寄到了美国。美国的一家名为《星期六晚邮报》的杂志买下了这篇故事,也付给我一笔丰厚的稿酬。钱到手后,我就不多不少,将正好一半的钱寄给了米尔登霍尔的戈登·布彻。

一周后,我收到了布彻先生的一封信,那页信纸一定是从孩子的学校练习本上撕下来的。信中说:“……看到支票的那一刻,我目瞪口呆,一根羽毛就能将我击倒。太美妙了,我想感谢你……”

下面就是这篇故事,与三十年前我写的几乎是一模一样,只是稍作改动。我只是把某些辞藻华丽段落的措辞缓和了一下,去除了很多累赘的形容词和一些没有必要的句子。

宝藏风波

早晨大约七点钟的时候，戈登·布彻从床上爬起来，开了灯，赤脚走到窗前，拉开窗帘向外观看。

时值一月，外面仍然一片漆黑，但他可以断定，夜里一点雪都没有下。

“听听啊，”他对妻子说。“听听那风声吧。”

他妻子现在也起床了，靠近了窗户，站到他的身旁。他俩站在那儿，静静地听着寒风发出“飕飕”的声响，那风从平坦的沼泽低地一路狂扫而来。

“是东北风。”他说。

“夜幕降临前，一定会下雪，”她对他说。“而且，会下得很大。”

她先穿好了衣服，去隔壁房间，俯身婴儿车的上方，吻了一下里面躺着的六岁的小女儿。接着，她又去了另外一个房间跟另外两个年纪大一些的孩子说了声“早晨好”，就下楼做早饭了。

离八点还有十五分钟的时候，戈登·布彻穿好外衣，戴上帽子和皮手套，从后门走了出去，外面的寒冬天气冰冷刺骨。时候还早，借着半明半暗的光线，他穿过院落，走进棚屋取自行车。此时，寒风如刀一般刮过他的脸颊，但他依然将自行车推了出来，跨上车座，迎着狂风，沿着窄窄的小道骑着车走了。

戈登·布彻的年纪有三十八岁了。他可不是一般的农场劳作人员，若不如愿，谁的活他都不会接的。他自己有一辆拖拉机，他就用这辆拖拉机按照合同帮别人犁田、收获庄稼。他的心思仅仅放在妻子、儿子以及两个女儿身上，他所有的财富就是那座砖砌的小房子、两头奶牛、一台拖拉机以及他自己犁田的手艺。

戈登·布彻脑袋的形状很是奇特，脑袋后面凸出，就像一只大大鸡蛋尖的那一端，两只耳朵向外侧凸出，左侧门牙掉了。可是，在外边跟他碰面的时候，这一切看起来似乎都无关紧要。他那双蓝色的眼睛稳稳地看着你，没有任何的恶意、狡诈或者贪婪，在他的嘴边也看不出任何细细的、饱含苦涩滋味的线条,而在那些整日在田里劳作、每日与天气抗争、靠天吃饭的人的嘴边,经常会看到这样的线条。

如果你问起他,他会笑呵呵地承认,他唯一怪癖的行为习惯就是,一个人独处的时候,他会大声地自言自语。他说,这一习惯源自他工作的性质:一周有六天的时间,一天有多达十个小时完全没人陪伴。“不时地听到自己的声音,”他说,“我感觉有人陪伴左右。”

他骑车沿着窄路走着,使劲儿蹬着车子,以化解肆虐的风带来的阻力。

“好啦,”他说,“好啦,你为什么不再吹得狂一点?这就是你最大的能耐吗?我的老天啊,今天早晨,我几乎没有察觉到还有风在吹呢!”风在他周围号叫着,猛烈撕扯着他的外衣,拼了命从厚重羊毛外衣的缝隙挤进去,穿透里层的夹克衫,再穿透衬衫和背心,最后用冰冷的指尖触摸着他赤裸的皮肤。

“嗨,”他说,“你今天怎么不冷不热的啊。要想让我浑身发抖的话,你需要更加卖力气才行。”

现在,黑暗逐渐融化,融化成早晨浅灰色的光线。戈登·布彻能够看清,头顶上方的天空很低,阴云密布,且随风飞舞。云彩呈暗蓝色,黑乎乎地往这儿堆几块、往那儿砌几片,那些阴云与四周的地平线连到了一起,整体随风移动,从头顶上方掠过,就像一大块灰色的金属板铺展开来。他周围是萨福克郡的一片荒凉而孤独的平坦沼泽区域,那片区域一公里、一公里地向远处延伸,一望无际。

他继续往前骑行,穿过米尔登霍尔小镇的郊区,奔向西罗村,名叫福特的男子就住在那个村子里。

前天,他将拖拉机留在福特家,因为下一个活要为福特干,要犁的田在西斯利格林,有二十七亩多地。但是,要记住的重点就是,那块田地不是福特的,只不过是福特求他去犁那块田。

事实上,那块面积为二十七亩的田地的主人是一个名叫罗尔夫的农夫。

罗尔夫最先求的是福特,因为福特跟戈登·布彻一样,也为别人干犁田的活儿。但是,福特跟戈登·布彻的不同之处在于,福特的级别多多少少要高一点:他算作一位名不见经传的农业工程师,家境殷实,房子漂亮,大大的院子里盖满了各式棚子,里面装满了各式农场用具和机械设备,而戈登·布彻只有一台拖拉机。

但是,即使在这种情况之下,当初罗尔夫求福特犁那块地时,那块地位于西斯利格林,有二十七亩,福特也是忙得团团转,干不过来。于是,福特就雇戈登·布彻替他干这个活儿。

布彻骑车进入福特家院子的时候,院子四周空无一人。他将自行车停放好,把拖拉机灌满煤油和汽油,发动引擎,在拖拉机后面挂上犁,登上那高高的驾驶座位,驶离院子,开往西斯利格林。

那块地离这儿还不到一公里远,约八点半的时候,布彻就穿过田地的栅栏门,驶入那块地。西斯利格林的那块地面积估计总共才六百多亩,这些地周边用低矮的树篱围了起来。尽管这六百多亩实际上是连在一起的一大块土地,不同的地段却分属不同的拥有者。每一地段的边界很容易划分,因为每人的耕作方式各不相同。罗尔夫拥有的那块二十七亩的土地是在另一边,就是在靠近南部边界栅栏的地方。布彻清楚地知道它的位置,于是,他开着拖拉机绕着田地的边缘走,然后再向里面拐,一直开到那块地所在的位置。

这块地里现在只剩下大麦的根茬,上面覆盖着去年秋天收割后留下的短短的、黄黄的、快要腐烂的大麦的茎秆。不久前,才有人将那些茎秆粗略地割了一遍,所以现在犁田正是时候。

“往深处犁,”前天福特这样对布彻说道。“那地要改种糖用甜菜。罗尔夫要在那块地里种甜菜了。”

要是种大麦,只需往下犁十多厘米就足够了,但是要种甜菜,就得往深处犁,要二十五厘米或三十厘米深才行,而马拉的犁却犁不到那个深度。只有到了机动拖拉机面世以后,农夫方能彻底地深犁。罗尔夫的这块地多年前因为种植糖用甜菜曾经深犁过,但那次的活不是布彻干的。毫无疑问,那次的活干得有点图省事了,那个犁田的农夫并没有将地犁到应该达到的深度。要是当时那个农夫深犁的话,今天要发生的当时就会发生了,今天的故事就得改写,完全不同啦。

戈登·布彻开始犁地。他沿着田地来来往往地忙活着,每一趟他都将犁深深地、深深地往下放。最后,把这块地往下深深地犁了三十厘米,每经过一处,黑土都被翻了出来,形成了平滑、匀称的泥土波浪。

现在,风刮得越来越紧,从凶猛无比的大海上一路狂吹而来。它肆虐着吹过位于东海岸的诺福克郡平坦而广袤的田野,一路掠过萨克斯索普、里弗姆、哈宁厄姆、斯沃弗姆、拉灵,接着越过萨福克郡边界,吹向米尔登霍尔,最终到达西斯利格林,也就是那个笔直地坐在高高的拖拉机驾驶座位上的戈登·布彻犁田的地方。在这块黄色的、满是大麦根茬的、属于罗尔夫的田地上,他来来回回地忙碌着。戈登·布彻能够闻到不远处白雪散发出的那股浓烈而清爽的味道,也能够看到低低的天空轮廓,不再那么黑乎乎的,而是灰暗中带有少许的白色。低低的天空在头顶上方滑过,就像一张结实的金属板铺展开来。

"好啊,"他说着,提高了嗓门,声音盖过了拖拉机发出的"咔嗒咔嗒"的声响。"今天,你确实让某个人心烦了。你现在吹着口哨呼啸而过,冰冷刺骨,貌似强大无比,实则小题大做,简直像娘们一样,"他补充道。"简直就像娘们有时候在晚上所干的事儿一样。"说完,他看了一眼犁出来的波浪形线条,微笑起来。

中午时分,他停下拖拉机,下了驾驶座位,伸手到兜子里摸午餐,摸到后就席地而坐,坐在拖拉机其中一只大轮子的背风处吃了起来。他吃的是大片的面包,还有小片的乳酪,但没有带什么喝的,因为他唯一的一个膳魔师牌暖水瓶两周前由于拖拉机的颠簸震动,打碎了。况且,当时还是战争年代——1942年1月,没地方再去买一个回来。他在轮子避风处的地面上坐了大约十五分钟,吃着午饭,然后站起身,检查了一下连接栓。

跟其他犁田农夫不一样的是,布彻总是用一个木制的连接栓将犁挂到拖拉机后面,好处就是,犁一旦钩住植物的根,或者碰到大块的石头,就会当场断开,掉在后头,避免犁铧头受到严重的损坏。整个土质黝黑的沼泽旷野上,就在表面之下,横七竖八地躺着远古时代的橡树树干,这样的话,木制的连接栓一周就会从那片区域里不知挽救多少次犁铧头。尽管西斯利格林是一块开垦得不错的土地,是农耕地而不是沼泽野地，但是，布彻也绝不会拿他的犁冒险的。

他仔细检查了一下木制连接栓，发现它安然无恙，就又装了上去，继续犁地。

拖拉机在土地上来来回回、小心翼翼地行驶着，后面留下了翻好的、平滑的、黝黑的波浪形土壤。风依然不停地刮着，天越来越冷，但是并没有下雪。

三点左右，大事发生了。

一阵轻微的震动过后，木制连接栓断开了，拖拉机将犁落到了后头。布彻停了下来，从驾驶座位上下来，往回向犁走去，想看看碰到了什么东西。在农耕地的这块地方发生这样的事情，着实让人吃惊，难以想象。这个地方的土壤下面，不应该有什么橡树存在啊。

他在犁旁边跪下，开始将犁铧头周围的泥土捧走。犁铧尖插进三十厘米深，所以有很多泥土需要捧走。他戴着手套，将手指往泥土里挖，再用双手将挖出来的泥土捧走，挖的深度达到十五厘米……二十厘米……二十五厘米……三十厘米。他沿着犁铧刃滑动着手指，最终摸到了犁铧前面的尖儿。泥土疏松易碎，不断地向他挖出的坑里掉落，因此他始终看不到插入泥土三十厘米深的犁铧头的尖部，只能摸到。现在，摸起来感觉到犁铧尖儿的的确确卡在某个硬物上。于是，他捧走了更多的泥土，扩大了土坑的体积，有必要清清楚楚地看看到底碰到了什么样的障碍物。要是障碍物很小的话，或许用两只手就可以将其挖出来，然后继续工作。障碍物要是树干的话，他就得去福特家，取来一把铁锹帮忙。

"加油，"他大声说。"我要把你连根挖出，你这个隐藏的恶魔，你这个腐烂的老东西。"他用戴上手套的手指将最后一捧黑色的泥土捧走的时候，突然间，他看到某种扁平东西弧形的边缘，就像是一个大大的、厚厚的盘子的边，那东西从土里凸出来。他用手指摩擦了一下那个边缘，接着又摩擦了一下，那个边缘露出淡绿的光亮，戈登·布彻低下头靠近，再靠近，眼睛向小小的土坑里观看，那是他用双手挖出来的。然后，他用手指最后一次将那个边缘擦干净。亮光一闪，他清清楚楚地看到古时候埋下的金属器物那蓝绿色的外壳。

一点没错,是金属器物,他的心跳戛然而止。

到此为止,应该解释一下的是,这一带萨福克郡的农夫,特别是米尔登霍尔地区的农夫,多年以来,一直能从土壤里挖出古代的器物。已经发现了相当数量的、很久以前的燧石箭头。但是,比箭头更令人感兴趣的是,还发现了罗马时期的陶器和用具。众所周知,罗马人占领不列颠期间,他们钟情于这个国家的这一区域,因此,当地的所有农夫都充分意识到,一天的劳作中,有可能发现有意思的东西。正因为如此,米尔登霍尔地区的人的头脑中始终有一根弦,认为他们的土地下面会有宝藏出现。

一看到那个巨大盘子的边缘,戈登·布彻的反应是很奇特的,他立即收回身体,站了起来,背对着刚才所见。在短暂停顿的时间里,他将拖拉机的引擎熄了火,然后快速向马路方向走去。

到底是哪根神经促使他停下,不接着挖下去,而是转身走开,他说不清楚。他能说清楚的是,在当初的几秒钟之内,他唯一能够记得的就是,一看到那小块蓝色中稍微带点绿色的东西,就感觉一股危险的气息向他袭来。手指碰到那东西的一瞬间,某种带电的物质贯穿他的整个身体,一种强烈的、不祥的预感随之而来:这个东西有可能毁灭祥和的局面,破坏很多人的幸福。

刚开始的时候,他所有的希望就是:立即走开,弃之不理,万事大吉。可是,走出去还不到几百米的距离,他就放慢了脚步。眼看就要跨出西斯利格林的栅栏门了,这时候,他停了下来。

"戈登·布彻先生,你到底是怎么回事啊?"他冲着呼啸的风大声说道。"你是害怕了,还是怎么了?不,我没有害怕,但我直率地告诉你,这件事情要我单独处理的话,我没有那个积极性。"

就在那时,他想到了福特。

他首先想到了福特,其主要原因就是,这活是为福特干的。其次,他知道,福特喜欢收藏老物件。这一地区的人们时不时地就从地下挖出古老的石头和箭头。每每此时,他们都将这些老物件拿给福特,福特就将它们放到他家客厅的壁炉台上陈列起来。人们也知道,福特卖这些东西挣钱,但是,没有谁知道,也没有谁关心他是如何卖掉的。

戈登·布彻转身朝着福特的住处快速走去。他走出栅栏门，迈上窄窄的马路，再沿着马路绕过一个向左的急转弯，就来到了福特家。他看见福特在一个大棚屋里，正俯身修理一个损坏的耙子。布彻站在门边说道："福特先生！"

福特向两旁看了看，但并没有挺直身体。

"哦，戈登啊，"他说，"什么事儿？"

福特已经人到中年，或者中年偏老一点儿，秃头，长鼻子，嘴唇很薄，有一种尖酸的感觉，脸上一副聪明而又带有狐狸般狡猾的表情。他看着你的时候，你就看到他那张紧闭的嘴、薄薄的嘴唇、尖酸的唇线，你也就看得出，他那张嘴从来都没笑过。他的下巴向后缩去，鼻子又长又尖，那副神情既尖酸，又狡猾，跟树林里的老狐狸没有什么两样。

"什么事儿？"他从耙子那儿抬起头问道。

戈登·布彻站在门边，由于寒冷，下巴铁青，整个人有点上气不接下气，还将两只手叠起来，不断地揉搓着。

"拖拉机将犁甩到后头啦，"他轻声说道。"犁卡住那地方的下面有金属物，我也看见了。"

福特的脑袋猛地一动。"什么样的金属物？"他尖声问道。

"扁平的，又扁又平，就像是某种类型的大盘子。"

"你怎么不把它挖出来呢？"现在，福特已经挺直了身体，眼里闪烁出尖锐的目光，这种目光只有老鹰的眼里才有。

布彻说："没挖出来，还是原封不动的状态，我直接奔你这里来了。"

福特快步走向屋子一角，从挂钉上取下外衣，又找出一顶帽子、一副手套，然后拿起一把铲子，向门口走去。他注意到，布彻的行事方式中带有某种古怪、反常的因素。

"你肯定它是金属质地的吗？"

"那东西表面起了一层硬皮，"布彻说。"但，是金属，不会错。"

"有多深？"

“有三十厘米深,盘子的顶部至少有三十厘米深,其余部分更深。”

“你怎么知道,它就是一只盘子呢?”

“我不知道,”布彻回答。“我只看到一点儿边缘部分,但在我看来,它就像是一只盘子,一只大大的盘子。”

由于兴奋,福特那张狐狸脸变得惨白。“走吧,”他说。“我俩回去看看吧。”

这两名男子走出棚屋,迎面袭来的是凶猛呼啸的狂风,愈刮愈烈。福特浑身颤抖起来。

“这鬼天气,真是该死,”他说。“这鬼天气冰冻刺骨,真是该死,令人讨厌。”说完,他将自己那张尖尖的狐狸脸深深地埋进外衣的领子里,暗自思忖:布彻的发现最后可能是什么。

有一件事情福特是知道的,但布彻并不知道。那就是,往回追溯到1932年,有一名叫莱斯布里奇的人一直在这一地区发掘,这个人是剑桥大学盎格鲁—撒克逊时期古器物专业的讲师。实际上,就在西斯利格林这块地方曾挖掘出古罗马时期的一个庄园的地基。这一点,福特一直记着呢,于是,他加快了脚步。布彻与他并肩而行,默不作声,他们很快就到达现场。他俩穿过栅栏大门,走过田地,来到犁旁,那只犁距离前面的拖拉机有九米多远。

福特在犁前旁边的位置跪了下来,向戈登·布彻用双手挖出的土坑里面看去,然后用自己的一只戴上手套的手指触摸蓝绿色金属物的边缘部分。他稍微刮去更多的泥土,身体更向前倾斜一下,这样他那尖尖的鼻子就正好能伸进坑里,然后用手指在粗糙的绿色表面摸了一遍。他站起来说道:“我们把犁弄出来,再挖一挖。”尽管福特内心如朵朵烟花怒放,浑身阵阵颤抖,但他说话的声音还是很轻柔,一副随意的样子。

他俩合力将犁向后拉出两三米远。

“把铲子给我,”福特说。然后,以露出的那块金属物为中心,以约九十厘米为直径,他小心谨慎地将这一圆圈范围内的泥土铲除。这个圆坑挖到约六十厘米深的时候,他扔掉了铲子,开始用手挖。他跪在那儿，将泥土清除。随着泥土被清除，那小块金属物渐渐地越来越大、越来越大。最后，他俩眼前出现了一只大盘子的圆碟形表面，是一只直径足足有六十厘米的盘子。犁的最低处正好卡在盘子凸出边缘的中间部位，这从盘子上的凹痕看得出来。

福特小心谨慎地将盘子从坑里提了出来。他站稳脚跟，擦去上面的泥土，双手将其翻来翻去，看个不停。根本看不出来什么，因为盘子整个表面由一层厚厚的、硬硬的、蓝色中稍微带点儿绿色的物质包裹着，但是他知道，它不是一只大大的盘子，就是一只厚重的碟子，大约有七公斤重！

福特站在满是黄色大麦残茎的田地里，盯着大盘子看，双手开始发抖，一股强大的、几乎令他无法忍受的兴奋开始在他整个身体内翻腾。这一点掩藏起来并不容易，但是，他却竭力控制着。

"某种类型的碟子吧，"他说。

布彻跪在圆坑旁边的地面上。"一定是相当的古老，"他说。

"可能吧，"福特回应。"但是，上面起了层硬皮，腐蚀得差不多啦。"

"那硬皮看起来不像是铁锈，"布彻说。"那稍微绿一点儿的东西不是锈，是某种其他的……"

"是绿锈，"福特十分庄重地说，这场争论也随之结束。

布彻仍然跪在那儿，用戴着手套的手指在直径已经达到九十厘米的圆坑里拨弄着。"下面还有一个，"他说。

福特立即将手里的大盘子放到地上，在布彻旁边跪了下来。没用几分钟的功夫，他们挖出了第二只大盘子，上面覆盖了一层绿色的硬皮。这一只比第一只小一点，却更深一些，更像是一只碗。

福特站立起来，将新挖出的举在手里打量着，感觉很有分量。现在，他确定，他们将会有绝对重大的发现，离罗马宝藏近在咫尺。几乎毫无疑问的是，这会是一笔纯银宝藏。有两点可以表明宝藏是纯银的：第一，是重量；第二，是氧化作用引起的那层特定类型的绿色物质。

世界上发现一件罗马银器的频率是多少呢？

几乎没有发现过。那么，像这样大块的物件以前出土过吗？

福特不敢肯定,但不相信出土过这样的物件。

一定会值数百万的价钱。

事实上,会值数百万英镑。

他呼吸急促,热气在冰冷的环境中凝结成团团白色的气雾。

“福特先生,下面还有不少呢,”布彻说。“我摸得出,这地方周边还有不少呢,你还得用铲子。”

他们挖出的第三件是一只盘子,跟第一只很相似。福特将这只放到大麦的残茎上,跟另外两只放到了一起。

布彻感觉到第一片雪花落到脸颊上时,抬头看向东北部的天空,那儿有一面白色的大幕横过天空拉了下来——大雪伴着大风滚滚而来。

“终于下雪了!”他说。福特向四周看了看,看到大雪直奔他们而来。他说:“是暴风雪,是讨厌的暴风雪,真该死啊!”

两名男子盯着来袭的暴风雪,只见它穿越沼泽,一路向他们奔来。紧接着,他们头顶上方,还有身体周围都下起雪来,雪花飘进眼睛、耳朵、嘴,沿着脖子往衣服里落,周围雪落纷纷。几秒钟过后,布彻低头看了一眼,发现地面已是白茫茫的一片。

“就这些了吧,”福特说。“真是一场讨厌的暴风雪,糟透了,真该死。”他颤抖起来,随即将棱角分明的狐狸脸埋进外衣的领子里。“快啊,”他说。“看看还有没有。”

布彻又跪了下来,在泥土里拨弄起来。然后,他慢慢地、随意地从里面拎出另一只盘子,递给了福特,那架势就好像一个男子从锯末桶里摸出头彩一样。福特接过盘子,跟其他三件放到了一起。现在,福特也在布彻旁边跪了下来,跟他一起在泥土里摸了起来。

在整整一个小时的时间里,这两名男子就待在那儿,在那块直径为九十厘米的土坑里挖呀、刮呀……最后,在他们旁边的地面上堆起的物品已多达三十四件!它们之中有碟、碗、碗状酒杯、勺子、长柄勺等,所有的物件都包裹了一层硬皮,却都能辨别出东西的质地。在这一小时的时间里,暴风雪在他们周围旋转、飞扬,雪片在他们帽子上、肩膀上形成小小的山丘,雪花在他们脸上融化,以至于冰冷的雪水形成了小小的溪流往他们的脖子里流淌。一只大大的、半冷冻半融化状态的冰球从福特尖尖的鼻子那儿开始一直悬垂下来，如同一棵雪花莲。

他俩默不作声地忙活着，太冷了无法说话。随着一件接着一件的宝物被挖出来，福特仔仔细细地将它们在地面上排列着放好，还不时地停下来，将碟子或者勺子上的积雪清理干净，以免被大雪盖住找不到。

最后，福特说："就这么多了，我想。"

"是的。"

福特站了起来，双脚在地面上跺了一下。"拖拉机上有麻袋吗？"他问。布彻走开，去取麻袋，他则转身盯着脚边雪地里躺着的那三十四件物品，而且又数了一遍。这些物件要是银质的话——肯定是银质的，要是罗马时期的话——无疑是罗马时期的，那么，这一发现将会震惊全世界。

布彻从拖拉机那儿向他喊道："只有一条脏兮兮的旧麻袋。"

"可以的。"

布彻拿来麻袋、张开，福特则仔仔细细将这些物件放了进去，除了其中一件，其余的都能放进去。放不进去的那件是一只大大的、直径为六十厘米的盘子，太大了，从麻袋口放不进去。

现在，这两个人真的是冻坏了，因为这一个多小时，他们一直跪在那儿，不停地在开阔的土地上抓啊、刮啊，周围暴风雪肆虐，而且雪的厚度已达十五厘米。布彻处于半冻僵状态，两颊惨白，还起了青紫色的斑块，双脚如木头般麻木，双腿移动时，他甚至无法感觉到脚下地面的存在。比起福特，他被冻得更惨。他的外衣以及其他衣服不是很厚实，况且从一大早开始，他就一直高高地坐在拖拉机的驾驶座位上，任凭寒风刺骨。他那张惨白的、带有青紫色斑块的脸绷得紧紧的，好像僵住了。此时，他一心只想回家跟家人待在一起，待在火炉旁。他知道，家中的炉火在壁炉的炉膛烧得正旺呢。

福特则不一样了。他没有想冷不冷的问题，他的心思完全集中在一件事情上面——如何独自拥有这笔巨额财富，因为他十分清楚，自己独吞的理由不是很充足。

在英国,关于发现金银宝藏,也不管是什么种类的金银宝藏,制定了一项很有意思的法律条文。这项条文可以追溯到数百年前,至今依然得到严格的执行。此项法律规定,如果一个人从地里——哪怕是自己家花园里——挖出一块金属物,不管这块金属物是金质的,还是银质的,都自动归入国家宝藏库,成为王权的财产。当时那些年代里,王权并不是指哪一个具体的国王或王后,而是指整个国家或者政府。此项法律也明确说明,藏匿这样一笔宝藏属于犯罪行为。简单来说,就是不允许你将发现之物藏匿起来,或者据为己有,必须立刻报告,最好向警察报告。要是当场就报告的话,作为发现人,你将有权得到政府奖励的钱,钱的数量相当于所发现物品的市场最高价。要是发掘出其他种类的金属物,你就用不着报告了。换句话说,其他很多贵重值钱的金属物品——锡质的、青铜质的、红铜质的,甚至是白金质的,谁发现即归谁所有,但金银质的物品却不行。

这项有意思的法律条文另一个有意思的方面就是,直接从政府那儿得到奖金的是宝藏的发现者本人,而不是宝藏发现地的拥有者。当然,擅自闯入他人领地进行发掘,是得不到奖金的。可是,如果宝藏的发现者被土地的拥有者雇来干活,那么,发现者也会得到所有的奖金。

目前情况下,发现者是戈登·布彻,而且,他不是擅自闯入者,他是被雇来干活的。因此,这笔宝藏属于布彻,而不是其他什么人。他所要做的就是,把东西拿到专家那儿,给专家看看。如果专家立刻能辨认出宝藏是银质的,就交给警察。这样的话,他就会得到政府的奖金,数额相当于宝藏自身全部的价值,或许有一百万英镑之多。

所有这一切让福特置寒冷于度外,福特也清楚这一点。根据法律,他没有一丁点儿的权利拥有这笔宝藏。因此,他当时一定会自言自语地说,将这些物件据为己有的唯一的机会就在于这样一个事实:布彻孤陋寡闻,根本不知道这项法律的事儿,也根本没有丝毫的想法,认为这些东西价值不菲。很有可能的是,几天过后,布彻就把这件事儿忘得一干二净。布彻这个家伙就是头脑简单、不谙世故、轻信别人、大公无私，根本不会对这件事儿过多考虑的。

现在，在野外雪片横飞的、荒凉的田地里，福特弯下了腰，一只手抓住了那只大个儿的碟子，将它抬起一些，但并没有提起来。这样，碟子较低的边缘仍然留在雪中。接着，他用另一只手抓住麻袋口，但也没有提起来，只是抓住。就这样，在盘旋飞舞的雪片之中，他弯腰曲背，两只手围拢着可以说是宝藏的东西，但没有将其抱在怀里。这一姿势惟妙惟肖、无比精妙：在探讨拥有权之前，想方设法表明所有权的倾向。小孩子也同样的游戏：伸出手，将手指扣在盘子里最大的一块巧克力棒上，说道："妈咪，我能吃这块吗？"事实上，他早已将这一块据为己有啦。

"噢，戈登，"福特说着，弯腰曲背的同时抬起头，带手套的手指分别捏住了麻袋和那只大大的碟子。"我想呢，这种老玩意，你一件也不会看上眼的。"

这句话并不是问句，却用问句的架势陈述了一个事实。

暴风雪仍在肆虐，鹅毛般的浓密的雪花纷纷落下，他俩几乎看不见彼此。

"你应该赶回家，暖和一下，"福特继续说。"你看起来冻得要死。"

"我的确感觉快要冻死了，"布彻说。

"那么，赶快跨上拖拉机往家开吧，"考虑周全、心肠仁慈的福特说道。"犁就放到这儿，自行车就放到我家吧。重要的是赶快回家暖和一下，省得患上肺炎。"

"福特先生，我想，你说的正是我要做的，"布彻说。"那条麻袋你自己能搞定吗？它可不是一般的沉啊。"

"今天，我是不用对麻袋费神费力的啦，"福特漫不经心地说。"我大可将它丢到这儿，找个时间再拿回去，里面尽是些生锈的老玩意。"

"那我走了，福特先生。"

"走好，戈登。"

戈登跨上拖拉机，驶入暴风雪中。

福特将麻袋举上肩膀,另一只手毫不费力地将那只大大的碟子提起来,夹到胳膊底下。

"我正在搬运,"他一边步履艰难地在雪地跋涉,一边自言自语地说道,"我现在正在搬运一笔财宝,或许是整个英国历史上所发掘出的最大一笔财宝。"

那天下午晚些时候,戈登·布彻跺着脚,通过后门,呼地一下冲进他家那栋小小的砖房子,当时他的妻子正在火炉旁熨衣服。她抬头看了他一眼,发现他脸色惨白,还带有青紫色的斑块,衣服上覆盖了一层雪。

"我的老天啊,戈登,看样你都要冻死了!"她叫道。

"是的,"他说。"亲爱的,帮我把这些衣服脱下,我的手指几乎不听使唤。"

她帮丈夫摘下手套,脱下外衣、夹克衫,还有湿漉漉的衬衫,又帮他脱去靴子和袜子。她取来一条毛巾,使劲把他的胸部和双肩擦了个遍,以恢复血液循环,再为他擦干脚。

"到那儿坐下,坐到火炉旁,"她说,"我再给你倒杯热茶。"

他穿上干衣服,手里捧着一杯茶,暖和而舒服地坐着。缓和一段时间之后,他给妻子讲述了当天下午发生的事情。

"那个福特先生,他就是一只狡猾的狐狸,"她说,头也不抬地熨着衣服。"我从来就不喜欢像他那样的人。"

"我可以对你讲,他始终兴奋不已,"戈登·布彻说。"他就像一只长耳大野兔跳上跳下的。"

"或许吧,"她说。"可是,在冰冻刺骨的暴风雪天气里,你不应该任凭他说什么,你就做什么呀。俯首帖耳、爬来爬去、跪这儿跪那儿,你也不至于那么傻呀。"

"我没事儿啊,"戈登·布彻说,"我现在暖和过来了,很舒服。"

不管你相信与否,那一次是多年以来布彻家最后一次讨论宝藏这一话题。

应该提醒读者的是,当时是战争年代,时间是1942年。英国完全彻底地陷入战争之中,全力以赴对抗希特勒和墨索里尼。德国轰炸英国,英国也在轰炸德国。几乎每一天夜里,戈登·布彻都能听到马达的轰鸣声,是从米尔登霍尔附近的一个大型机场传过来的,是轰炸机起飞发出的声音,它们飞往汉堡、柏林、基尔港、威廉港以及法兰克福等地执行轰炸任务。有时候,在凌晨时分,那些飞机返回的声音就会把他吵醒;有时候还听到德国飞机飞过上空去轰炸那个飞机场。每每此时,随着不远处炸弹爆炸发出的巨响,布彻家的房子也不停地抖动。

布彻本人得到豁免,不用服兵役。他是一位农夫——技艺高超的犁田农夫。1939 年他报名自愿参军的时候,军方对他说,不会吸纳他入伍的,不列颠岛国的粮食供给不能中断,而像他这样的人应该继续干老本行,继续耕地种田。

福特跟他是同行,也得到豁免,但他是个单身汉,一个人居住。因此呢,他就能够过着一种隐秘的生活,在自己家院墙之内做些隐秘的事情。

正因为如此,在那个大雪纷飞的糟糕的下午,他们将宝藏挖出来之后,福特就将其带回家,然后将东西一件一件倒出来,摆放到自家后屋的一张桌子上。

想想啊,总共三十四件宝物!整张桌子都摆满了。从外表这么一看,就知道它们保存的状况完好。银是不生锈的,外表那层绿色的氧化硬皮恰恰对里面的金属起到了很好的保护作用。处理好的话,硬皮都能够去除干净。

福特决定使用一种普通的家用银器抛光剂,名叫“西尔沃”。于是,他从米尔登霍尔的五金商店里买回了大量的西尔沃。然后,他利用晚上的时间,从那只直径六十厘米、重量超过七公斤的大盘子开始干起。他将它全部浸泡到西尔沃里,然后不断地擦呀、擦呀。每天晚上,他都耐心地清理这只盘子,一清理就是十六周的时间。

最终,在一个值得纪念的晚上,在他的擦拭之下,一小块银光闪闪的区域露了出来,在银器的这块区域上,一部分人的头像露了出来,那头像凸起,加工得十分漂亮。

他没有停歇,继续干着。那小块闪耀金属光芒的区域逐渐地、逐渐地变得越来越大、越来越大,蓝绿色的硬皮脱落到盘子的边缘部分。最后,这只大大盘子正面部分的全部风采在他面前亮丽地呈现出来。上面布满了令人叹为观止的动物图案、人物图案,还有许多奇异的传说中的物品的图案。

这只大盘子的美艳让福特惊得目瞪口呆。盘子上面充满了活力和动感:凶狠的面孔上散落着乱糟糟的头发,长着人头的山羊跳跃着,盘子的边缘有男人、女人,还有各种动物在欢呼跳跃。毫无疑问,所有这一切都在讲述一个故事。

接下来,他开始着手清理盘子的背面,清理了一周又一周的时间。清理完毕之时,整只盘子的两个面都如星星般亮闪闪的。为安全起见,他将这只大盘子放进他家大橡木餐具柜低层的一个柜橱里,并锁上了这个柜橱的门。

随着时间一天一天地流逝,他开始清理剩下的三十三件器物。现在,他简直是着了迷,一门心思要将每一件银器都清理得闪闪发光,以恢复其美丽迷人的本来面目。他想看着所有三十四件器物在他家的大桌子上摆放开来,发射出夺目的光彩。除此之外,他别无所求,只想拼了命地去清理,以实现他的愿望。

下一步,他清理的是两个小一些的碟子,接着是带有凹槽的大碗,再接着是五只长柄勺,还有碗状酒杯、葡萄酒杯、勺子。每一件器物都得到同样精心的清理,清理完毕都闪耀着同样夺目的光彩。清理完毕的时候,已经是1944年,两年已经过去了。

可问题是,这些宝物他不允许陌生人观看。不管是男人还是女人,福特都不与之讨论这件事,就连西斯利格林那块地的主人罗尔夫,也对此事一无所知。正是在那块地上,他得到了这批宝藏。罗尔夫知道的是,有人给他犁田,犁得到位、够深,犁田的人不是福特,就是福特雇的人。

福特将宝藏隐藏起来,却没有报告警察,然后纳入国家宝藏库,其原因是猜得出来的。要是他报告警察的话,宝物就会被拿走,他就一无所有,奖金也会发给发现者戈登·布彻,那奖金可是一笔巨大的财富啊。所以嘛,福特唯一能做的就是,把宝藏藏好,坚持住,希望有朝一日将其秘密出手卖掉,卖给某个经销商或者收藏者什么的。这可以说是他的一厢情愿。

当然,也可以更宽容地替福特想想,可能的情况就是,他保存这批宝藏纯粹是因为他酷爱漂亮的东西,想让它们陪伴他左右。真正原因是什么,没人知道答案。

又一年过去了。

对抗希特勒的战争打赢了。

接着有一天,也就是1946年复活节刚过的一天,有人敲响了福特家的房门,他随即开门。

“嗨,你好啊,福特先生。这么多年了,你过得怎么样?”

“你好,福西特博士,”福特招呼道。“别来无恙啊?”

“我很好,谢谢,”福西特博士说。“真是好久、好久不见了,是不是呢?”

“是的,”福特说。“那场旷日持久的战争把我们大家都忙活得够戗。”

“我可以进来吗?”福西特博士问道。

“当然,”福特回答,“请进。”

休·奥尔德森·福西特博士是一位考古学家,既机敏又博学。战争爆发前,他每年都会特地拜访福特一次,为的是搜寻古老的石头或者箭头什么的,而这样的东西福特一年之中通常会收集一批,也愿意卖给福西特。这样的东西很少能值什么大价钱,但是,偶尔也会发现某件奇珍异宝。

“哎呀,”福西特边说边在大厅里脱下了外衣。“哎呀,哎呀,哎呀,我有将近七年没到你这儿来啦。”

“是啊,一晃很长时间了。”福特说。

福特将他领进前屋,拿出一盒燧石箭头给他看。那些箭头是他在本地区捡到的,有些很不错,有些不怎么样。福西特挑挑拣拣、筛来选去,最后成交了。

“还有别的吗?”

“没了,我想没了。”

福特多么希望福西特博士永远也不要来,甚至更希望他立即走开。

就在这个节骨眼儿上,福特注意到某个东西,这东西令他冒汗。他突然间看到,壁炉那边的壁炉台上躺着两只最为漂亮的罗马时期的勺子,那两只勺子是他从藏宝柜橱里拿出来的,但忘了收起来。这两只勺子令他如痴如醉,因为每只勺子上都刻着一个罗马女孩的名字,或许是罗马时代的父母在洗礼命名仪式上,把勺子作为礼物送给孩子的,那时候,孩子的父母已经皈依基督教。其中一个名字是帕谢缇娅,另一个是帕皮苔朵,都是相当可爱的名字。

福特由于恐惧而冒汗,设法站到福西特博士和壁炉台之间。他寻思着,只要逮着机会,他甚至能够将其滑入衣兜。

但是,他并没有逮着什么机会。

或许是由于福特将勺子擦得太亮了,一丝光线从银器上反射出来,射入博士的眼中。是不是这个原因,谁知道呢?实际情况就是,福西特看到了勺子。一看到那两只勺子,他一跃而起,就像一只老虎。

"老天在上!"他叫道。"什么东西?"

"锡制品,"福特回答,汗出得更多了。"就那么两三只锡勺子。"

"锡的?"福西特叫道,用手将其中一只勺子翻了过来。"锡制的!你说这是锡制的?"

"没错,"福特回答。"是锡制的。"

"你知道这是什么吗?"福西特问道,由于兴奋,声音高出许多。"我可以告诉你这东西原本是什么吗?"

"你不必告诉我这个,"福特说,有些挑衅的意味。"我知道这是什么,不就是旧锡器嘛,而且质量也相当不错。"

福西特正在读勺柄上刻的罗马文字。"帕皮苔朵!"他叫道。

"什么意思?"福特问。

福西特拿起另一只。"帕谢缇娅,"他说。"真漂亮啊!这是两个罗马儿童的名字。我的朋友,这两只勺子是用纯银做的!纯正的罗马银啊!"

“不可能，”福特说。

“太棒了！”福西特叫道，开始欣喜若狂。“太完美了！太不可思议了！你到底在什么地方发现的？知道发现地点是极其重要的啊！还有别的吗？”福西特在屋子里跳来跳去。

“哦……”福特舔了舔干巴巴的嘴唇说。

“你必须立刻报告！”福西特叫道。“它们应该归入国家宝藏库啊！毫无疑问的是，大英博物馆需要这些东西！你发现多长时间了？”

“就一小会儿，”福特对他说。

“那么，是谁发现的？”福西特径直盯着他问。“是你本人亲自发现的，还是从他人那里弄来的？这一点至关重要！发现者会讲出实情的！”

福特感觉屋子四周的墙壁向他步步逼近，他顿时慌了手脚、不知所措。

“快说啊，伙计！你肯定知道从哪里弄到的！上交的时候，每一个细节都要说出来。你立刻去警察那儿报告，答应我吗？”

“哦……”福特说。

“要是你不去，我想，我不得不亲自去了，”福西特对他说。“我有这个义务。”

现在，纸里包不住火了，福特清楚这一点。一大堆问题等着他回答呢。你是怎么发现的？什么时候发现的？在哪儿发现的？具体的地点在哪里？你犁的是谁家的田地？或早或晚，戈登·布彻的名字就会被说出来，这是不可避免、无法逃避的。接下来，要是问布彻的话，他就会回忆起宝藏的规模，对警察和盘托出。

所以说，纸里包不住火了。此时此刻，唯一能做的就是，打开那个大餐具柜的柜门，将全部宝藏都拿出来给福西特博士看。

福特保留宝物没有上交的借口就是，他认为这批东西是锡制的。他对自己说，只要坚持这一点，他们不会对他怎么样的。

福西特博士要是看到餐具柜里的东西，也许他会当场突发心脏病。

"实际上,此类东西还有不少,"福特说。

"在哪儿?"福西特将身体旋转过来问道。"哪儿呢,伙计,在哪儿?带我看看!"

"我真的认为,都是锡制的,"福特一边说,一边慢慢地、十分不情愿地挪向那个橡木餐具柜。"否则的话,我就一定会立刻去报告了。"

他弯下腰,打开了餐具柜低层的柜门。

就在那时,休·奥尔德森·福西特博士的确就要突发心脏病了,只见他"扑通"一下跪在地上,嘴里喘着粗气,窒息得说不出话来,嘴里"啪嗒啪嗒"作响,就像一只旧水壶烧开水时发出的声响。他将手伸向那只大大的银碟子,拿了起来,双手一边举着,一边颤抖不止。他的脸变得如雪一般白,没有说话,也说不出话来。看到这批宝藏,他整个人实际上是完完全全瘫痪、麻木了,不管从身体上来说,还是从精神上来说,他都瘫痪、麻木了。

这个故事有意思的部分到此结束,其余部分就没有那么跌宕起伏、激动人心了。福特去了警察局,做了报告。警察随即到达,收走了所有三十四件宝物,然后宝物被护送到大英博物馆接受检查。

接下来,博物馆给米尔登霍尔警署发来一个紧急消息:这批宝藏是不列颠群岛上所发现的最好的,价值连城,远远超过其他宝藏。这个博物馆是真正的政府性的公共机构,希望收购这批宝藏。事实上,博物馆硬是坚持要收购的。

法律的车轮开始转动起来。在距离最近的一个大城镇——贝里圣埃德蒙兹,举行了一次正式授权的审问听证会,银器也在特种警察护卫下搬到了那里。福特被传唤出庭,面对一位无主珍宝调查官以及十四人的陪审团,而那位沉默寡言、好心肠的戈登·布彻也被要求出庭作证。

1946年7月1日,星期一,听证会开始,这位无主珍宝调查官严密盘问福特。

"你认为那东西是锡的?"

"是的。"

"即使在你清理完毕之后,也那么认为?"

“是的。”

“你没有采取任何行动把你的发现告诉专家吗?”

“没有。”

“这些物品你打算怎么办?”

“没什么打算,只是想保存它们。”

作证结束后,福特请求允许他到外面透口新鲜空气,他说的理由是,他感到眩晕,对此没有人感到有什么可惊奇的。

接着,传唤布彻,他只是简单的几句话就说明了他在整个事件中的角色。

福西特博士出示了证据,其他几位博学的考古学家也做了证明,所有人都证明,这批宝藏十分罕见、珍贵。他们说,宝藏是耶稣基督诞生后第四世纪的东西,是一户富有的罗马家庭餐桌上使用的银器,或许是主人的管家埋下的,以防皮可特人和苏格兰人抢走。当时大约处于公元 365 至 367 年之间,这些人从北方一路横扫而下,致使很多罗马人定居点变成了废墟。埋下宝藏的那个人不是被皮可特人,就是被苏格兰人杀害,自那之后,宝藏就一直沉睡在土壤下方三十厘米深的地方。专家异口同声地说,银器的工艺无与伦比,其中有些是在英国创作完成,但更多的物件是在意大利或者埃及制作的。当然,那只大大的盘子是最为精美的一只,盘子的中央是海神尼普顿的头像。海神的头发里尽是海豚,胡须里满是海草,在海神周围欢呼雀跃的是众多的海仙女和海怪。盘子开阔的边缘处站立着酒神巴克斯及其随从,上面有酒,也有纵酒狂欢的场面。大力神赫拉克勒斯在那儿,喝得醉醺醺的,由两名森林之神搀扶着,他身上的狮子皮从肩膀处脱落下来。牧神潘也在那儿,手里拿着排笛,抬起他的羊腿跳着舞。盘子上到处都有酒神巴克斯的女随从,她们个个都摇摇晃晃、醉意十足。

专家也告知法庭,其中的好几只勺子上带有耶稣基督希腊语姓名的首字母“Chi”(X)和“Rho”(P)的交织图案。毫无疑问,刻有帕谢缇娅和帕皮苔朵两个名字的勺子,是命名洗礼仪式上的礼物。

专家出示完证据,法庭就暂时休庭。没过多久,陪审团回到法庭,做出裁定,结果令人惊讶不已。不管是谁做了什么事情,都不予以追究,只是宝藏的发现者不再有权得到政府发放的全额奖金,因为当时没有立刻上报。不管怎么说,或许还会付给一定数额的奖金。考虑到这一点的话,发现者就是福特和布彻两个人了。

发现者不是布彻自己,而是福特和布彻两个人。

这批宝藏被大英博物馆收购,高傲地陈列在一只大大的玻璃箱子中,供来人参观,除此之外,没有什么过多的事情可说。人们不远万里赶来,观看那些可爱的物件,那些东西是戈登·布彻在那个寒冷刺骨、狂风呼啸的午后发现的,是在他的犁铧下面发现的。关于这一切,将来有一天或许有人会编撰一两本书出版发行,书中尽是臆想推测,还有深奥玄妙的结论。以后从事考古行当的人会永远地谈论起米尔登霍尔的宝藏风波。

博物馆为了表示一下,奖励给两个发现者每人一千英镑。布彻这位真正的发现者是乐坏了,怎么也没有想到会得到这么多的钱。他没有意识到的是,要是起先发现的时候容许他将财宝带回家的话,几乎可以肯定的是,他会报告的。那样的话,他就有资格得到与全部财宝的价值相同数额的奖金,数额在五十万到一百万之间。

谁也不知道福特是怎么想的。法庭相信他所说的锡制品故事的时候,他一定会如释重负,或许也会有那么一点点的吃惊。但是,最为重要的是,失去一大批宝藏,他一定是心力交瘁、心烦意乱。在他余生的时间里,一想起让福西特博士看到了那两只落在壁炉台上的勺子,他就会对自己连踢带打、懊悔不已。

第二节 《非洲往事》*An African Story*

罗尔德·达尔的《非洲往事》(*An African Story*)首次发表在《向你飞跃:十篇飞行员与飞行故事集》(*Over to You: Ten Stories of Flyers and Flying*)上,但是,这篇故事与“飞行”这一主题只是沾上一点点边儿——叙述者“我”(其实就是达尔本人)从一名在训练中丧生的皇家空军飞行员的手提箱里发现了一份手稿,手稿记录的是这名飞行员生前从迫降地的一名非洲老人那里听来的故事。接着,达尔就展开了这个非洲故事。可以说,《非洲往事》是一个故事引出的另一个故事,属于故事的“嵌套”。后来,这个故事又收录在《罗尔德·达尔短篇故事集锦》(*The Collected Short Stories of Roald Dahl*)、《五部畅销书集》(*5 Bestsellers*)以及《〈人皮刺青〉及其他故事集》(*Skin and Other Stories*)等书中。

一、原作导读

一名年轻的英国皇家空军飞行员得到允许,首次独立越野飞行——从内罗毕飞往埃尔多雷特,那是一座高原小镇,海拔两千四百米。飞行途中,油箱进水导致引擎失灵,紧急迫降在一座简陋的小屋附近。

那座小屋孤零零地立在高原平坦的地面上,看不到周围还有其他什么住户。那里可真是一片高高的、孤独的乡野。

... a little shack which stood alone on the highland plain with no other habitation in sight. That is lonely country up there.

小屋的主人是一位非洲老人,老人收留了他,给他讲了一段奇异的非洲往事。飞行员拿出纸笔将这个故事记录了下来。

两周后,他在训练中丧生。我们检查了他的遗留物品,在他的手提箱里发现了那篇故事。他似乎没有什么亲人,再加上他是我的朋友,于是,我就拿走了这份手稿,替他保管、处理。

We found it in his suitcase two weeks later when we were going through his belongings after he had been killed in training, and because he seemed to have no relatives, and because he was my friend, I took the manuscript and looked after it for him.

下面就是“我”转述的这位英国皇家空军飞行员所记录的故事。

这位非洲老人住在一个简陋的小屋里,陪伴他的是一条狗、几只鸡、一头奶牛,还有一个名叫贾德森的帮手。贾德森是一个暴躁的家伙,受不了狗舔爪子发出的声音,那声音令他几乎疯掉。于是,他用竹竿打了狗,将狗的后背打断了。老人用铁棒砸向小狗的头部,提前帮助小狗解除了痛苦。

后来,老人养的那头奶牛发生了一件奇怪的事情:牛奶在夜间不翼而飞,第二天早晨所剩无几。一天晚上,老人蹲在奶牛附近守候,看到了令人吃惊的一幕:一条致命的非洲曼巴毒蛇竟然前来吸吮牛奶!经过几个夜晚的观察,老人发现这条蛇每天晚上都是很有规律地前来吸吮牛奶。但是,老人却告诉贾德森说,偷牛奶的是一个小子,一定要逮住这小子。

“今天,”老人继续说,“你得在奶牛的旁边挖出一条浅沟,能容你躺进去,我再用干草和绿草将你盖起来。这样,贼要是走不到你身边,就发现不了你。”

“Today,” continued the old man, “you will dig a shallow trench right beside the cow. If you lie in it and if I cover you over with hay and grass, the thief won't notice you until he's right alongside.”

贾德森虽然同样受不了奶牛反刍发出的声音,但也只得照做。结果,贾德森被毒蛇咬中,痛苦地死去。但是,老人却端坐窗前,没有采取任何行动,继续观察着毒蛇移动身体,吸吮牛奶。

“你可以将他的那一份喝掉,”老人安静地说。“你喝掉他的那一份,我们不介意的。”……

“没错,”他又说道,“你喝掉他的那一份,我们不介意的。”

“You can have his share,” he said quietly. “We don't mind you having his share," . . .

"Yes," he said again, "we don't mind your having his share."

二、原作释读

这篇小说篇幅短小，但内容不乏精彩之处，结局令人深思。阅读中，要体会好主人公——老人心理状态的变化，还要理解好作家罗尔德·达尔对老人的帮工——贾德森一些行为的细节描写。

An African Story①

For England, the war began in September, 1939. The people on the island knew about it at once and began to prepare themselves. In farther places the people heard about it a few minutes afterwards, and they too began to prepare themselves.

And in East Africa, in Kenya Colony, there was a young man who was a white hunter, who loved the plains and the valleys and the cool nights on the slopes of Kilimanjaro. He too heard about the war and began to prepare himself. He made his way over the country to Nairobi, and he reported to the RAF and asked that they make him a pilot. They took him in and he began his training at Nairobi airport, flying in little Tiger Moths and doing well with his flying.

After five weeks he nearly got court-martialled② because he took his

① 本部小说原文出自"DAHL R. *The Collected Short Stories of Roald Dahl*. London: Penguin Books Ltd., 1992"。

② court-martial: *Verb* to try by military tribunal 军事法庭审判(或判决)

plane up and instead of practising spins and stall-turns① as he had been ordered to do, he flew off in the direction of Nakuru② to look at the wild animals on the plain. On the way, he thought he saw a Sable antelope③, and because these are rare animals, he became excited and flew down low to get a better view. He was looking down at the antelope out of the left side of the cockpit, and because of this he did not see the giraffe on the other side. The leading edge④ of the starboard⑤ wing struck the neck of the giraffe just below the head and cut clean through it. He was flying as low as that. There was damage to the wing, but he managed to get back to Nairobi, and as I said, he was nearly court-martialled, because you cannot explain away a thing like that by saying you hit a large bird, not when there are pieces of giraffe skin and giraffe hair sticking to the wing and the stays⑥.

After six weeks he was allowed to make his first solo cross-country flight, and he flew off from Nairobi to a place called Eldoret, which is a little town eight thousand feet up in the Highlands. But again he was un-

---

① stall-turn or stall turn: an aerobatic manoeuvre in which the aircraft climbs vertically before being stalled, when it turns on one wing into a dive(特技飞行中的)失速转弯;跃升失速倒转

② Nakuru: *Noun* an industrial city in western Kenya; pop. 162,800 (1989). Nearby is Lake Nakuru, famous for its spectacular flocks of flamingos 纳库鲁(肯尼亚西部工业城市,1989 年人口 162,800,附近有闻名的火烈鸟栖息地纳库鲁湖。)

③ Sable antelope or sable antelope: a large African antelope with long curved horns, the male of which has a black coat and the female a russet coat, both having a white belly 貂羚

④ leading edge: (Aeronautics) the foremost edge of an aerofoil, especially a wing or propeller blade(航天)(机翼或叶片的)前缘

⑤ starboard: *Noun* the side of a ship or aircraft that is on the right when one is facing forward. The opposite of port(船舶、飞机的)右舷;右边(port 的反义词)

⑥ stay: *Noun* a supporting wire or cable on an aircraft(飞机的)拉杆;拉索

lucky. This time he had engine failure on the way, due to water in the fuel tanks. He kept his head and made a beautiful forced landing① without damaging the aircraft, not far from a little shack② which stood alone on the highland plain with no other habitation in sight. That is lonely country up there.

He walked over to the shack, and there he found an old man, living alone, with nothing but a small patch of sweet potatoes, some brown chickens and a black cow.

The old man was kind to him. He gave him food and milk and a place to sleep, and the pilot stayed with him for two days and two nights, until a rescue plane from Nairobi spotted his aircraft on the ground, landed beside it, found out what was wrong, went away and came back with clean petrol which enabled him to take off and return.

But during his stay, the old man, who was lonely and had seen no one for many months, was glad of his company and of the opportunity to talk. He talked much and the pilot listened. He talked of the lonely life, of the lions that came in the night, of the rogue③ elephant that lived over the hill in the west, of the hotness of the days and of the silence that came with the cold at midnight.

On the second night he talked about himself. He told a long, strange story, and as he told it, it seemed to the pilot that the old man was lifting a great weight off his shoulders in the telling. When he had finished, he said that he had never told that to anyone before, and that

---

① forced landing: an act of abruptly bringing an aircraft to the ground or the surface of water in an emergency 迫降

② shack: *Noun* a roughly built hut or cabin 简陋木屋;棚屋

③ rogue: *Noun* [usu. as modifier] an elephant or other large wild animal driven away or living apart from the herd and having savage or destructive tendencies 野生的离群兽;野生的离群象(e. g. a rogue elephant 一只野生的离群象)

he would never tell it to anyone again, but the story was so strange that the pilot wrote it down on paper as soon as he got back to Nairobi. He wrote it not in the old man's words, but in his own words, painting it as a picture with the old man as a character in the picture, because that was the best way to do it. He had never written a story before, and so naturally there were mistakes. He did not know any of the tricks with words which writers use, which they have to use just as painters have to use tricks with paint, but when he had finished writing, when he put down his pencil and went over to the airmen's canteen for a pint of beer, he left behind him a rare and powerful tale.

We found it in his suitcase two weeks later when we were going through his belongings after he had been killed in training, and because he seemed to have no relatives, and because he was my friend, I took the manuscript and looked after it for him.

This is what he wrote.

The old man came out of the door into the bright sunshine, and for a moment he stood leaning on his stick, looking around him, blinking at the strong light. He stood with his head on one side, looking up, listening for the noise which he thought he had heard.

He was small and thick and well over seventy years old, although he looked nearer eighty-five, because rheumatism[①] had tied his body into knots. His face was covered with grey hair, and when he moved his mouth, he moved it only on one side of his face. On his head, whether indoors or out, he wore a dirty white topee.

---

① rheumatism: *Noun* [mass noun] any disease marked by inflammation and pain in the joints, muscles, or fibrous tissue, especially rheumatoid arthritis 风湿病(尤指类风湿性关节炎)

He stood quite still in the bright sunshine, screwing up① his eyes, listening for the noise.

Yes, there it was again. The head of the old man flicked around and he looked towards the small wooden hut standing a hundred yards away on the pasture. This time there was no doubt about it: the yelp② of a dog, the high-pitched, sharp-piercing yelp of pain which a dog gives when he is in great danger. Twice more it came and this time the noise was more like a scream than a yelp. The note was higher and more sharp, as though it were wrenched③ quickly from some small place inside the body.

The old man turned and limped fast across the grass towards the wooden shed where Judson lived, pushed open the door and went in.

The small white dog was lying on the floor and Judson was standing over it, his legs apart, his black hair falling all over his long, red face; standing there tall and skinny, muttering to himself and sweating through his greasy white shirt. His mouth hung open in an odd way, lifeless way, as though his jaw was too heavy for him, and he was dribbling④ gently down the middle of his chin. He stood there looking at the small white dog which was lying on the floor, and with one hand he was slowly twis-

---

① screw up: (of the muscles of one's face or around one's eyes) contract, typically so as to express emotion or because of bright light(面部或眼睛周围的肌肉,尤指为表达情感或因强光刺激)收缩;皱紧

② yelp: *Noun* a short sharp cry, especially of pain or alarm(尤指因痛楚或惊慌而)尖声急叫;叫喊(e. g. She uttered a yelp as she bumped into a table. 当她撞上桌子时,她尖叫了一声。)

③ wrench: *Verb* [with obj.] pull or twist (someone or something) suddenly and violently 猛扭;猛拧(e. g. Casey grabbed the gun and wrenched it from my hand. 凯西一把抓住了枪,猛地一扭,从我手中抢了过去。)

④ dribble: *Verb* [no obj.] allow saliva to run from the mouth 流口水(e. g. His mouth was open and he was dribbling. 他的嘴张着,并且在流口水。)

ting his left ear; in the other he held a heavy bamboo.

The old man ignored Judson and went down on his knees beside his dog, gently running his thin hands over its body. The dog lay still, looking up at him with watery eyes. Judson did not move. He was watching the dog and the man.

Slowly the old man got up, rising with difficulty, holding the top of his stick with both hands and pulling himself to his feet. He looked around the room. There was a dirty rumpled① mattress lying on the floor in the far corner; there was a wooden table made of packing cases and on it a Primus② stove and a chipped blue-enamelled③ saucepan. There were chicken feathers and mud on the floor.

The old man saw what he wanted. It was a heavy iron bar standing against the wall near the mattress, and he hobbled over towards it, thumping④ the hollow wooden floorboards with his stick as he went. The eyes of the dog followed his movements as he limped across the room. The old man changed his stick to his left hand, took the iron bar in his right, hobbled back to the dog and without pausing, he lifted the bar and brought it down hard upon the animal's head. He threw the bar to the ground and looked up at Judson, who was standing there with his legs apart, dribbling down his chin and twitching around the corners of his

---

① rumple: *Verb* [with obj.] [usu. as adj. "rumpled"] give a creased, ruffled, or dishevelled appearance to 弄皱;压皱;弄乱

② primus: *Noun* (also called "Primus stove") (Cookery) a portable paraffin cooking stove, used esp. by campers(烹饪)普里默斯炉(一种便携式煤油炉)

③ enamel: *Noun* [mass noun] an opaque or semi-transparent glassy substance applied to metallic or other hard surfaces for ornament or as a protective coating 搪瓷;珐琅

④ thump: *Verb* [with obj.] hit (someone or something) heavily, especially with the fist or a blunt implement 重击;捶击;撞击(e.g. She thumped on the cottage door. 她"嘭嘭嘭"地敲打村舍的门。)

eyes. He went right up to him and began to speak. He spoke very quietly and slowly, with a terrible anger, and as he spoke he moved only one side of his mouth.

"You killed him," he said. "You broke his back."

Then, as the tide of anger rose and gave him strength, he found more words. He looked up and spat them into the face of the tall Judson, who twitched around the corners of his eyes and backed away towards the wall.

"You lousy, mean, dog-beating bastard. That was my dog. What the hell right have you got beating my dog, tell me that. Answer me, you slobbering① madman. Answer me."

Judson was slowly rubbing the palm of his left hand up and down on the front of his shirt, and now the whole of his face began to twitch. Without looking up, he said, "He wouldn't stop licking that old place on his paw. I couldn't stand the noise it made. You know I can't stand noises like that, licking, licking, licking. I told him to stop. He looked up and wagged his tail; but then he went on licking. I couldn't stand it any longer, so I beat him."

The old man did not say anything. For a moment it looked as though he were going to hit this creature. He half raised his arm, dropped it again, spat on the floor, turned around and hobbled out of the door into the sunshine. He went across the grass to where a black cow was standing in the shade of a small acacia tree, chewing its cud②, and the cow watched him as he came limping across the grass from the shed. But it

---

① slobber: *Verb* [no obj.] have saliva dripping copiously from the mouth 流口水(e.g. big slobbering kisses 满嘴口水的吻)

② chew the cud: (of a ruminant animal) further chew partly digested food (动物)反刍

went on chewing, munching[1] its cud, moving its jaws regularly, mechanically, like a metronome[2] in slow time. The old man came limping up and stood beside it, stroking its neck. Then he leant against its shoulder and scratched its back with the butt end of his stick. He stood there for a long time, leaning against the cow, scratching it with his stick; and now and again he would speak to it, speaking quiet little words, whispering them almost, like a person telling a secret to another.

It was shady under the acacia tree, and the country around him looked lush and pleasant after the long rains, for the grass grows green up in the Highlands of Kenya; and at this time of the year, after the rains, it is as green and rich as any grass in the world. Away in the north stood Mount Kenya itself, with snow upon its head, with a thin white plume[3] trailing[4] from its summit where the city winds made a storm and blew the white powder from the top of the mountain. Down below, upon the slopes of that same mountain there were lion and elephant, and sometimes during the night one could hear the roar of the lions as they looked at the moon.

The days passed and Judson went about his work on the farm in a silent, mechanical kind of way, taking in the corn, digging the sweet potatoes and milking the black cow, while the old man stayed indoors away

---

① munch: *Verb* [with obj.] eat (something) with a continuous and often audible action of the jaws 用力咀嚼;出声地咀嚼

② metronome: *Noun* a device used by musicians that marks time at a selected rate by giving a regular tick 节拍器

③ plume: *Noun* a long cloud of smoke or vapour resembling a feather as it spreads from its point of origin 羽状烟柱(或气流)(e.g. As he spoke, the word was accompanied by a white plume of breath. 他说话时,话语伴随着白色的哈气。)

④ trail: *Verb* [with adverbial] draw or be drawn along the ground or other surface behind someone or something 拖;拉(e.g. Alex trailed a hand through the clear water. 亚历克斯伸出一只手在清澈的水中划过。)

from the fierce African sun. Only in the late afternoon when the air began to get cool and sharp, did he hobble outside, and always he went over to his black cow and spent an hour with it under the acacia tree. One day when he came out he found Judson standing beside the cow, regarding it strangely, standing in a peculiar attitude with one foot in front of the other and gently twisting his ear with his right hand.

"What is it now?" said the old man as he came limping up.

"Cow won't stop chewing," said Judson.

"Chewing her cud," said the old man. "Leave her alone."

Judson said, "It's the noise, can't you hear it? Crunchy① noise like she was chewing pebbles, only she isn't; she's chewing grass and spit. Look at her, she goes on and on crunching, crunching, crunching, and it's just grass and spit. Noise goes right into my head."

"Get out," said the old man. "Get out of my sight."

At dawn the old man sat, as he always did, looking out of his window, watching Judson coming across from his hut to milk the cow. He saw him coming sleepily across the field, talking to himself as he walked, dragging his feet, making a dark green trail in the wet grass, carrying in his hand the old four-gallon kerosene② tin which he used as a milk pail. The sun was coming up over the escarpment③ and making long shadows behind the man, the cow and the little acacia tree. The old man

---

① crunchy: *Adjective* making a sharp noise when bitten or crushed and (of food) pleasantly crisp 发出"嘎吱嘎吱"声的;(食物)松脆的;易碎的

② kerosene or kerosine: *Noun* [mass noun] a light fuel oil obtained by distilling petroleum, used especially in jet engines and domestic heating boilers; paraffin oil 煤油;火油

③ escarpment: *Noun* a long, steep slope, especially one at the edge of a plateau or separating areas of land at different heights(尤指高原边缘处或不同高度地块之间的)急斜坡;陡坡

saw Judson put down the tin and he saw him fetch the box from beside the acacia tree and settle himself upon it, ready for the milking. He saw him suddenly kneeling down, feeling the udder① of the cow with his hands and at the same time the old man noticed from where he sat that the animal had no milk. He saw Judson get up and come walking fast towards the shack. He came and stood under the window where the old man was sitting and looked up.

"Cow's got no milk," he said.

The old man leaned through the open window, placing both his hands on the sill.

"You lousy bastard, you've stole it."

"I didn't take it," said Judson. "I bin② asleep."

"You stole it." The old man was leaning farther out of the window, speaking quietly with one side of his mouth. "I'll beat the hell out of③ you for this," he said.

Judson said, "Someone stole it in the night, a native, one of the Kikuyu④. Or maybe she's sick."

It seemed to the old man that he was telling the truth. "We'll see," he said, "if she milks this evening; and now for Christ's sake, get out of my sight."

By evening the cow had a full udder and the old man watched Judson draw two quarts of good thick milk from under her.

---

① udder: *Noun* the mammary gland of female cattle, sheep, goats, horses, and related ungulates, hanging near the hind legs as a bag-like organ with two or more teats(牛、羊、马等有蹄类动物)乳房;乳腺

② 这里的"bin"是"been"的非标准发音的拼写形式。

③ beat the hell out of: (informal) beat (someone) very severely(非正式)痛打;狠揍(某人)

④ Kikuyu: *Noun* a member of a people forming the largest ethnic group in Kenya(肯尼亚的最大种族)基库尤人

The next morning she was empty. In the evening she was full. On the third morning she was empty once more.

On the third night the old man went on watch. As soon as it began to get dark, he stationed himself at the open window with an old twelve-bore shot gun① lying on his lap, waiting for the thief who came and milked his cow in the night. At first it was pitch dark and he could not see the cow even, but soon a three-quarter moon came over the hills and it became light, almost as though it was day time. But it was bitter cold because the Highlands are seven thousand feet up, and the old man shivered at his post and pulled his brown blanket closer around his shoulders. He could see the cow well now, just as well as in daylight, and the little acacia tree threw a deep shadow across the grass, for the moon was behind it.

All through the night the old man sat there watching the cow, and save when he got up once and hobbled back into the room to fetch another blanket, his eyes never left her. The cow stood placidly under the small tree, chewing her cud and gazing at the moon.

An hour before dawn her udder was full. The old man could see it; he had been watching it the whole time, and although he had not seen the movement of its swelling any more than one can see the movement of the hour hand of a watch, yet all the time he had been conscious of the filling as the milk came down. It was an hour before dawn. The moon was low, but the light had not gone. He could see the cow and the little tree and the greenness of the grass around the cow. Suddenly he jerked his head. He heard something. Surely that was a noise he heard. Yes, there it was again, a rustling in the grass right underneath the window

---

①　shot gun or shotgun: *Noun* a smooth-bore gun for firing small shot at short range 滑膛枪；散弹枪（e.g. The robbers used a sawn-off shotgun in the raid. 劫匪在袭击中用锯断的散弹猎枪。）

where he was sitting. Quickly he pulled himself up and looked over the sill on to the ground.

Then he saw it. A large black snake, a Mamba, eight feet long and as thick as a man's arm, was gliding through the wet grass, heading straight for the cow and going fast. Its small pear-shaped head was raised slightly off the ground and the movement of its body against the wetness made a clear hissing sound like gas escaping from a jet. He raised his gun to shoot. Almost at once he lowered it again, why he did not know, and he sat there not moving, watching the Mamba as it approached the cow, listening to the noise it made as it went, watching it come up close to the cow and waiting for it to strike.

But it did not strike. It lifted its head and for a moment let it sway gently back and forth; then it raised the front part of its black body into the air under the udder of the cow, gently took one of the thick teats into its mouth and began to drink.

The cow did not move. There was no noise anywhere, and the body of the Mamba curved gracefully up from the ground and hung under the udder of the cow. Black snake and black cow were clearly visible out there in the moonlight.

For half an hour the old man watched the Mamba taking the milk of the cow. He saw the gentle pulsing① of its black body as it drew the liquid out of the udder and he saw it, after a time, change from one teat② to another, until at last there was no longer any milk left. Then the Mamba gently lowered itself to the ground and slid back through the grass in the direction whence it came. Once more it made a clear hissing noise as

---

① pulse: *Verb* [no obj.] throb rhythmically; pulsate 有节奏地悸动;搏动;跳动

② teat: *Noun* a nipple of the mammary gland of a female mammal, from which the milk is sucked by the young(雌性哺乳动物的)乳头

it went, and once more it passed underneath the window where the old man sat, leaving a thin dark trail in the wet grass where it had gone. Then it disappeared behind the shack.

Slowly the moon went down behind the ridge of Mount Kenya. Almost at the same time the sun rose up out of the escarpment in the east and Judson came out of his hut with the four-gallon kerosene tin in his hand, walking sleepily towards the cow, dragging his feet in the heavy dew as he went. The old man watched him coming and waited. Judson bent down and felt the udder with his hand and as he did so, the old man shouted at him. Judson jumped at the sound of the old man's voice.

"It's gone again," said the old man.

Judson said, "Yes, cow's empty."

"I think," said the old man slowly, "I think that it was a Kikuyu boy. I was dozing a bit and only woke up as he was making off①. I couldn't shoot because the cow was in the way. He made off behind the cow. I'll wait for him tonight. I'll get him tonight," he added.

Judson did not answer. He picked up his four-gallon tin and walked back to his hut.

That night the old man sat up again by the window watching the cow. For him there was this time a certain pleasure in the anticipation of what he was going to see. He knew that he would see the Mamba again, but he wanted to make quite certain. And so, when the great black snake slid across the grass towards the cow an hour before sunrise, the old man leaned over the window sill and followed the movements of the Mamba as it approached the cow. He saw it wait for a moment under the belly of the animal, letting its head sway slowly backwards and forwards half a dozen times before finally raising its body from the ground to take the teat of the

---

① make off: leave hurriedly, especially in order to avoid duty or punishment (尤指为了避开责任或惩罚)匆忙离开;逃脱

cow into its mouth. He saw it drink the milk for half an hour, until there was none left, and he saw it lower its body and slide smoothly back behind the shack whence it came. And while he watched these things, the old man began laughing quietly with one side of his mouth.

Then the sun rose up from behind the hills, and Judson came out of his hut with the four-gallon tin in his hand, but this time he went straight to the window of the shack where the old man was sitting wrapped up in his blankets.

"What happened?" said Judson.

The old man looked down at him from his window. "Nothing," he said. "Nothing happened. I dozed off again and the bastard came and took it while I was asleep. Listen, Judson," he added, "we got to catch this boy, otherwise you'll be going short of milk, not that that would do you any harm. But we got to catch him. I can't shoot because he's too clever; the cow's always in the way. You'll have to get him."

"Me get him? How?"

The old man spoke very slowly. "I think," he said, "I think you must hide beside the cow, right beside the cow. That is the only way you can catch him."

Judson was rumpling his hair with his left hand.

"Today," continued the old man, "you will dig a shallow trench right beside the cow. If you lie in it and if I cover you over with hay and grass, the thief won't notice you until he's right alongside."

"He may have a knife," Judson said.

"No, he won't have a knife. You take your stick. That's all you'll need."

Judson said, "Yes, I'll take my stick. When he comes, I'll jump up and beat him with my stick." Then suddenly he seemed to remember something. "What about her chewing?" he said. "Couldn't stand her chewing all night, crunching and crunching, crunching spit and grass like it was pebbles. Couldn't stand that all night," and he began twisting again at his left ear with his hand.

"You'll do as you're bloody well told," said the old man.

That day Judson dug his trench beside the cow which was to be tethered to the small acacia tree so that she could not wander about the field. Then, as evening came and as he was preparing to lie down in the trench for the night, the old man came to the door of his shack and said, "No point in doing anything until early morning. They won't come till the cow's full. Come in here and wait; it's warmer than your filthy little hut."

Judson had never been invited into the old man's shack before. He followed him in, happy that he would not have to lie all night in the trench. There was a candle burning in the room. It was stuck into the neck of a beer bottle and the bottle was on the table.

"Make some tea," said the old man, pointing to the Primus stove standing on the floor. Judson lit the stove and made tea. The two of them sat down on a couple of wooden boxes and began to drink. The old man drank his hot and made loud sucking noises as he drank. Judson kept blowing on his, sipping it cautiously and watching the old man over the top of his cup. The old man went on sucking away at his tea until suddenly Judson said, "Stop." He said it quietly, plaintively① almost, and as he said it he began to twitch around the corners of his eyes and around his mouth.

"What?" said the old man.

Judson said, "That noise, that sucking noise you're making."

The old man put down his cup and regarded the other quietly for a few moments, then he said, "How many dogs you killed in your time,

---

① plaintive: *Adjective* sounding sad and mournful 伤心的;哀伤的

Judson?"

There was no answer.

"I said how many? How many dogs?"

Judson began picking the tea leaves out of his cup and sticking them on to the back of his left hand. The old man was leaning forward on his box.

"How many dogs, Judson?"

Judson began to hurry with his tea leaves. He jabbed his fingers into his empty cup, picked out a tea leaf, pressed it quickly on to the back of his hand and quickly went back for another. When there were not many left and he did not find one immediately, he bent over and peered closely into the cup, trying to find the ones that remained. The back of the hand which held the cup was covered with wet black tea leaves.

"Judson!" The old man shouted, and one side of his mouth opened and shut like a pair of tongs①. The candle flame flickered② and became still again.

Then quietly and very slowly, coaxingly, as someone to a child. "In all your life, how many dogs has it been?"

Judson said, "Why should I tell you?" He did not look up. He was picking the tea leaves off the back of his hand one by one and returning them to the cup.

"I want to know, Judson." The old man was speaking very gently. "I'm getting keen about this too. Let's talk about it and make some plans for more fun."

---

① tongs: *Noun* [plural noun] an instrument with two movable arms that are joined at one end, used for picking up and holding things 钳;夹剪

② flicker: *Verb* [no obj.] (of light or a source of light) shine unsteadily; vary rapidly in brightness(光或光源)闪烁

Judson looked up. A ball of saliva① rolled down his chin, hung for a moment in the air, snapped and fell to the floor.

"I only kill'em② because of a noise."

"How often've you done it? I'd love to know how often."

"Lots of times long ago."

"How? Tell me how you used to do it. What did you like best?"

No answer.

"Tell me, Judson. I'd love to know."

"I don't see why I should. It's a secret."

"I won't tell. I swear I won't tell."

"Well, if you'll promise." Judson shifted his seat closer and spoke in a whisper. "Once I waited till one was sleeping, then I got a big stone and dropped it on his head."

The old man got up and poured himself a cup of tea. "You didn't kill mine like that."

"I didn't have time. The noise was so bad, the licking, and I just had to do it quick."

"You didn't even kill him."

"I stopped the noise."

The old man went over to the door and looked out. It was dark. The moon had not yet risen, but the night was clear and cold with many stars. In the east there was a little paleness in the sky, and as he watched, the paleness grew and it changed from a paleness into a brightness, spreading over the sky so that the light was reflected and held by the small drops of dew upon the grass along the highlands; and slowly,

① saliva: *Noun* [mass noun] watery liquid secreted into the mouth by glands, providing lubrication for chewing and swallowing, and aiding digestion 唾液; 涎

② 'em = them

the moon rose up over the hills. The old man turned and said, "Better get ready. Never know; they might come early tonight."

Judson got up and the two of them went outside. Judson lay down in the shallow trench beside the cow and the old man covered him over with grass, so that only his head peeped out above the ground. "I shall be watching, too," he said, "from the window. If I give a shout, jump up and catch him."

He hobbled back to the shack, went upstairs, wrapped himself in blankets and took up his position by the window. It was early still. The moon was nearly full and it was climbing. It shone upon the snow on the summit of Mount Kenya.

After an hour the old man shouted out of the window: "Are you still awake, Judson?"

"Yes," he answered, "I'm awake."

"Don't go to sleep," said the old man. "Whatever you do, don't go to sleep."

"Cow's crunching all the time," said Judson.

"Good, and I'll shoot you if you get up now," said the old man.

"You'll shoot me?"

"I said I'll shoot you if you get up now."

A gentle sobbing noise came up from where Judson lay, a strange gasping sound as though a child was trying not to cry, and in the middle of it, Judson's voice, "I've got to move; please let me move. This crunching."

"If you get up," said the old man, "I'll shoot you in the belly."

For another hour or so the sobbing continued, then quite suddenly it stopped.

Just before four o'clock it began to get very cold and the old man huddled deeper into his blankets and shouted, "Are you cold out there, Judson? Are you cold?"

"Yes," came the answer. "So cold. But I don't mind because cow's not crunching any more. She's asleep."

The old man said, "What are you going to do with the thief when you catch him?"

"I don't know."

"Will you kill him?"

A pause.

"I don't know. I'll just go for him.

"I'll watch," said the old man. "It ought to be fun." He was leaning out of the window with his arms resting on the sill.

Then he heard the hiss under the window sill, and looked over and saw the black Mamba, sliding through the grass towards the cow, going fast and holding its head just a little above the ground as it went.

When the Mamba was five yards away, the old man shouted. He cupped his hands to his mouth and shouted, "Here he comes, Judson; here he comes. Go and get him."

Judson lifted his head quickly and looked up. As he did so he saw the Mamba and the Mamba saw him. There was a second, or perhaps two, when the snake stopped, drew back and raised the front part of its body in the air. Then the stroke. Just a flash of black and a slight thump as it took him in the chest. Judson screamed, a long, high-pitched scream which did not rise nor fall, but held its note until gradually it faded into nothingness and there was silence. Now he was standing up, ripping open his shirt, feeling for the place in his chest, whimpering① quietly, moaning and breathing hard with his mouth wide open. And all the while the old man sat quietly at the open window, leaning forward

① whimper: *Verb* [no obj.] (of a person or animal) make a series of low, feeble sounds expressive of fear, pain, or discontent(人或动物)(因恐惧、痛苦或不满等而)抽泣,抽搭,呜咽

and never taking his eyes away from the one below.

Everything comes very quick when one is bitten by a black Mamba, and almost at once the poison began to work. It threw him to the ground, where he lay humping his back and rolling around on the grass. He no longer made any noise. It was all very quiet, as though a man of great strength was wrestling with a giant whom one could not see, and it was as though the giant was twisting him and not letting him get up, stretching his arms through the fork of his legs and pushing his knees up under his chin.

Then he began pulling up the grass with his hands and soon after that he lay on his back kicking gently with his legs. But he didn't last very long. He gave a quick wriggle, humped his back again, turning over as he did it, then he lay on the ground quite still, lying on his stomach with his right knee drawn up underneath his chest and his hands stretched out above his head.

Still the old man sat by the window, and even after it was all over, he stayed where he was and did not stir. There was a movement in the shadow under the acacia tree and the Mamba came forward slowly towards the cow. It came forward a little, stopped, raised its head, waited, lowered its head, and slid forward again right under the belly of the animal. It raised itself into the air and took one of the brown teats in its mouth and began to drink. The old man sat watching the Mamba taking the milk of the cow, and once again he saw the gentle pulsing of its body as it drew the liquid out of the udder.

While the snake was still drinking, the old man got up and moved away from the window.

"You can have his share," he said quietly. "We don't mind you having his share," and as he spoke he glanced back and saw again the black body of the Mamba curving upward from the ground, joining with the belly of the cow.

"Yes," he said again, "we don't mind your having his share."

三、翻译探索

本篇小说的翻译中,除了几个地名和动物名称外,障碍不是很多,可以在表达的准确性和"雅"(elegance)上多做探索。

非洲往事

对于英国而言,这场战争(这里指的是第二次世界大战——译者注)始于1939年9月。战争一开始,这座岛屿上的人民立刻得知了这一消息,并开始各自准备起来。而在这座岛上稍远的地方,人们也在几分钟之后得知了这一消息,开始各自准备起来。

当时,有一位年轻的白人小伙子在东非的肯尼亚殖民地狩猎。他热爱那里的平原和山谷,喜欢在乞力马扎罗山坡度过一个又一个凉爽的夜晚。他也听到了有关这场战争的消息,开始自我准备起来。他独自穿越广袤的乡野,来到了首都内罗毕,到英国皇家空军报道,要求军方允许他做一名飞行员参战。军方吸纳了他,他也就开始在内罗毕机场接受培训,驾驶的是小型的虎蛾战机,驾驶技术相当不错。

五周过后,他差点受到军法惩处,原因是,他驾机升空后,没有按照预先的命令来驾机旋转以及跃升失速倒转,而是飞向纳库鲁上空,俯瞰那里平原上的野生动物。他想,在飞行途中,自己看到了貂羚,感到很兴奋,因为貂羚是珍稀物种。于是,他飞得很低,以便看得更清楚。当时,他是从驾驶舱的左舷观看貂羚的。正因如此,他没有看到另一侧还有长颈鹿呢。结果,右舷机翼的前缘刮到了长颈鹿的脖子——正好是头部下面的脖子部分,干净利落地切断了脖子。这就是他当时的飞行高度。其结果是,机翼受损,但是,他还是设法飞回了内罗毕。就像我刚才说的,他差点受到军法惩处,因为机翼受损到了那个程度,你要说撞上了一只大鸟,是无法解释清楚的,更何况,机翼及拉索上还粘着几块长颈鹿皮和些许毛发呢。

六周后,他得到允许,首次独立越野飞行——从内罗毕飞往埃尔多雷特,那是一座高原小镇,海拔两千四百米。但这次飞行,他照样运气不佳。飞行途中,油箱进水导致引擎失灵,但是,他拉直机头,紧急迫降,飞机没有受损,干得很漂亮。战机最终降落在一座简陋的小屋附近。那座小屋孤零零地立在高原平坦的地面上,看不到周围还有其他什么住户。那里可真是一片高高的、孤独的乡野。

他向小屋走去,发现只有一位老年男子在那里独自生活。除了一小块地瓜田、几只棕毛鸡和一头黑奶牛外,老人就一无所有了。

老人家对他很好,给他东西吃,送他牛奶喝,还提供地方供他过夜睡觉。这名飞行员跟老人一起待了两天两夜。随后,内罗毕飞来的一架救援机发现他的战机停在地面上,就在一旁降落,查出故障后就飞了回去。然后,又带着干净的汽油返回。这样,他就能够起飞返航了。

但是,在他逗留期间,这位老人因为有他的陪伴十分开心,也很乐意借此机会跟他谈这说那,因为老人孑然一身,颇感孤独,况且,已经好几个月了,老人没有看到任何人前来拜访。其间,老人讲了很多、很多,他就一直听着。老人谈起了孤独寂寞的生活,谈起了夜晚造访的狮子,谈起了西边的小山那边凶猛的离群野象,谈起了白天的炎热,还谈起了伴随午夜的寒冷而来的那种死寂。

第二天夜晚,老人谈起了自己,讲了很长一段奇异的往事。这名飞行员似乎觉得,老人在讲述的过程中,逐渐从肩上卸掉了一件沉重的包袱。讲完后,老人说,这段往事从来没有对任何人讲过;还说,永远不会再讲给任何人听了。但是,这段往事过于奇异,这名飞行员返回内罗毕后,就立刻拿起纸笔,把它写了下来。他是以自己的口吻,而不是以老人的口吻写下来的。他当时犹如画了一幅画,那位老人就是画中的一个人物。他这样做,再好不过了,因为他以前什么东西都没有写过。自然而然地,错误是在所难免的。他根本不了解作家写作的用词技巧,而这些用词技巧就如同画家的绘画技法。不管怎么说,写完放下铅笔、走进空军食堂喝完一大瓶啤酒的时候,他留在身后的却是一篇奇异稀有、极具震撼力的故事。

两周后，他在训练中丧生。我们检查了他的遗留物品，在他的手提箱里发现了那篇故事。他似乎没有什么亲人，再加上他是我的朋友，于是，我就拿走了这份手稿，替他保管、处理。

下面就是他写下的内容。

老人走出屋子，站在明亮的阳光下。他靠着拐棍站了一会儿，向四周观瞧，冲着强烈的光线眨着眼睛。他抬起头，脑袋歪向一侧，耳朵倾听着某种声音。他想，他听见了某种什么声音。

他个头矮小，但身体粗壮，肯定超过了古稀之年，尽管看起来更接近八十五岁的高龄。要知道，他的身体饱受风湿病之苦。他的脸上长出一层灰色的须发，嘴巴动弹时，只有脸部一侧的嘴巴能动弹。不管是在屋内还是在屋外，头上总是戴着一顶脏兮兮的白色遮阳软帽。

他一动不动地站在明亮的阳光下，眯起眼睛，倾听着那种可疑的声音。

没错，有声音，又听见了。老人向四周轻轻地探探头，眼睛看向草场上九十多米开外的一座小木屋。这一次，声音的性质明确无疑了：狗发出的短促尖叫声——高调、尖锐的痛苦叫声，这种叫声是狗处于极度危险之中才发出的。紧接着，又传出两声，这两声与其说是尖叫，不如说是狂叫——声调更高、更尖，就好像某个东西，其身体内部某个狭小的部位，被人快速而猛烈地扭了一下似的。

这位老人转过身，一瘸一拐地快速穿过草地，走向那个小木屋，那是贾德森住的地方。他推开门，走了进去。

那条白色的小狗躺倒在地板上，而贾德森则岔开双腿站在小狗的上方，黑色的头发散落在他那张红色的长脸上。他高高地站在那儿，显得骨瘦如柴，嘴里在自言自语地嘟囔着，汗水湿透了他那件油腻的白色衬衫。他那张嘴悬吊在空中，合拢不上，样子很是古怪，显得毫无生气，就好像下颌过于沉重似的，而口水则沿着下巴中间部位轻轻往下流淌。他站在那儿，看着那条躺在地上的白色的小狗，一只手慢慢地扭着自己的左耳，另一只手则握着一根很沉的竹竿。

老人没有理会贾德森,而是跪到了小狗旁边,消瘦的双手在小狗的身体上轻轻地抚摸。小狗一动不动地躺着,抬起一双水汪汪的眼睛看着老人。贾德森仍然没有动地方,眼睛盯着小狗和老人。

老人双手握紧拐棍的顶部,支撑着身体,慢慢地站了起来,显得十分吃力。他向屋子四周看了看,发现远处角落里的地板上铺了一张皱巴巴的床垫子,屋子里放着一张木桌子,是由几只包装箱拼成的,桌子上放了一只普里默斯炉——便携式煤油炉,还放了一个蓝色的搪瓷平底锅,地面上还有鸡毛和泥巴。

老人看到了自己想要找的东西,也就是一根沉重的铁棒,铁棒靠在床垫附近的墙壁上。于是,老人拄着拐棍蹒跚地走了过去,拐棍撞击在悬空的地板上,发出"嘭、嘭、嘭"的声响。小狗的双眼随着一瘸一拐走过屋子的老人转动着。老人将拐棍换到左手,右手拾起了铁棒,然后蹒跚地返回小狗那儿,紧接着举起铁棒,使劲砸向小狗的头部。老人将铁棒扔到地上,抬头看了眼贾德森,贾德森仍然岔开双腿站在那儿,口水沿着下巴流淌,双眼的眼角抽搐着。老人径直朝他走去,开始跟他说话。老人说得很慢、很轻,但语气充满了愤怒。他说话时,只有脸部一侧的嘴巴在动弹。

"你把它弄成这样的,"他说。"是你弄断了它的后背。"

接着,愤怒的浪潮高涨起来,给他增添了力量,使他有更多的话要讲。于是,他抬起头,将要说的话一股脑儿喷到高个子贾德森的脸上,只见贾德森眼角抽搐着,身体向后面的墙壁退缩着。

"你这个该死的、卑鄙的、打狗的杂种。那可是我养的狗啊,你到底有什么权利来打我的狗,告诉我啊。说啊,你这个淌口水的疯子,说啊。"

贾德森左手手掌放到衬衫前面慢慢地上下揉搓起来。到了现在,他整张脸都开始抽搐起来。他头也不抬地说:"它老是舔爪子的同一个地方,一刻不停,而我忍受不了它舔爪子发出的噪音。你知道,我忍受不了那样舔来舔去发出的噪音,而且不停地舔。我喊它停下,它抬起头,摇了摇尾巴,却接着舔了起来。我再也无法忍受了,就打了它。"

老人没有说什么。有那么一会儿,看起来他要揍这个家伙一顿:胳膊举到一半的位置,却又放了下来。他往地板上吐了口唾沫,转过身,出了门,走到阳光下。他穿过草地,走到黑奶牛那儿。黑奶牛站在一颗金合欢树的阴影里,嚼着反刍的食物。奶牛看着他一瘸一拐地从小屋出来,穿过了草地,但嘴的动作却没有停下来,继续嚼着反刍的食物:上下颚机械地、有规律地运动着,就像节拍器慢慢地拍打着节奏。这位老人一瘸一拐地走上前来,站在奶牛旁边,轻轻抚摸它的脖子,靠在它的肩头,用拐棍的平头端挠着它的背。他靠着奶牛站了很长时间,用拐棍给它挠痒痒,还不时地轻轻对它说上只言片语,几乎是低声耳语,就如同一个人在向另一个人透露着内心的秘密。

金合欢树下很是阴凉,老人周围的乡野看起来郁郁葱葱。长时间降雨过后,景色令人心旷神怡,肯尼亚高原上绿草繁茂。每年的这个时候,雨过天晴,跟世界上其他地方一样,这里的草也生长得翠绿、繁茂。北部以远的地方耸立着肯尼亚山,山顶积雪覆盖,一股细长的羽状气流从其主峰顶端蜿蜒而出。城市吹来的风在峰顶形成暴风雪,并将白色的雪粒从山顶吹走。山顶以下,沿着山坡分布着狮子和大象等动物。夜间有的时候,狮子仰头对月,吼声不断。

日子一天天过去,贾德森还是那样一声不吭地、机械般地干着农场里的活计:收割玉米、挖掘地瓜、挤黑牛的牛奶,而老人则待在屋内,免受非洲炽烈阳光的烘烤。只有到了下午晚些时候,老人才蹒跚地走出屋子,走到金合欢树下他的那头黑奶牛跟前,一待就是一个小时,因为那时候空气凉爽而清新。有一天从屋里出来的时候,他发现贾德森站在奶牛旁边,用奇异的眼神打量着奶牛。他当时的步态很是怪异:一只脚站在另一只脚的前方,右手则轻轻扭着自己的一只耳朵。

"现在什么情况?"老人一瘸一拐地走上前来问道。

"这头奶牛一个劲儿地咀嚼着,"贾德森回答。

"那是在咀嚼反刍的食物,"老人说。"不要理会。"

贾德森说:"发出的是噪音啊,难道你听不见吗?那声音,'嘎吱、嘎吱'的,就好像在嚼小圆石头,但它嚼的却不是石头,而是草和唾液。看看啊,它一个劲儿地‘嘎吱、嘎吱、嘎吱’嚼个不停,嚼的却只是草和唾液。那噪音径直钻入我的脑袋。”

“滚开,”老人说。“从我眼前消失。”

黎明时分,老人就像以往那样,坐在窗前向窗外观瞧,看着贾德森从小木屋一路走过来挤牛奶。只见他睡眼惺忪地穿越田地走过来,边走边自言自语,拖着双脚往前走,双脚在草地上蹚出一道暗绿色的印记,手里拎着一只能装十八升煤油的旧锡桶,这只桶是他用来装牛奶用的。太阳从高原的陡坡处缓缓升起,在贾德森、奶牛以及矮小的金合欢树后面投下了长长的影子。老人看到,贾德森放下锡桶,从金合欢树的旁边取来箱子,坐到上面,准备挤奶。只见他一下子跪到地上,双手触摸着奶牛的奶头,与此同时,老人从坐的位置上看去,奶头根本没有牛奶流出来。这时,他看到贾德森站起身,快速向屋子这边走来,站在老人坐着的位置的窗户下面,抬起了头。

“奶牛没有牛奶可挤了,”他说。

老人探身窗外,双手放在窗台上。

“你这个该死的杂种,是你偷的吧。”

“我没偷,”贾德森回答。“我一直在睡觉呢。”

“是你偷的。”老人将身体向外多探出了一些,脸部一侧的嘴巴动弹着,静静地说道。“这事儿我绝饶不了你。”他说。

贾德森说:“有人夜间偷了牛奶,应该是一个当地人——其中的一名基库尤人吧,或许奶牛生病了。”

在这位老人看来,他说的是实情。“我们看一看,”老人说,“看看它今晚能否产奶。但是现在,看在耶稣基督的分上,从我眼前消失。”

到了晚上,奶牛的乳房胀满了,老人看着贾德森从奶牛的身底下挤走了两升多的香浓牛奶。

第二天早晨,它又没有牛奶了。到了晚上,它的乳房又胀满了。到了第三天早晨,它的乳房又空空如也。

第三天的晚上，老人继续观察。天一擦黑儿，老人就在打开着的窗前坐定，膝盖上放了一支十二口径霰弹枪，等待着夜晚前来偷牛奶的贼。起先，周围漆黑一片，甚至连奶牛也看不清，但是没过多久，大半个月亮就从小山顶部升起，周围一下子亮了起来，如同白昼一般。但问题是，由于高原的这一段海拔二千一百米高，夜晚冷得要命，老人坐在那儿瑟瑟发抖。于是，他拉紧那条棕色的毛毯，缠到双肩上。现在，他可以清楚地看到那头奶牛了，就像白天看到的一样清楚，还看到那棵矮小的金合欢树的影子穿过草地长长地延伸开来，因为月亮就是从树的背后升起来的。

整个夜晚的时间里，老人坐在那儿看着那头奶牛，除了有一次站起身来，蹒跚地走回屋子取来另一条毛毯，他的眼睛从未离开过奶牛。奶牛则温和、平静地站在那棵矮小的树下，一边嚼着反刍的食物，一边盯着月亮看。

天亮前一个小时的时候，它的乳房胀满了，这一点，老人能够看出来。他一直目不转睛地看着它，尽管他没有看到它的乳房一点点胀满的过程，那过程类似于手表时针的走动过程。但是自始至终，牛奶淌下来填满乳房的这一过程，他是意识到了。胀满的时间是黎明前一个小时的时候。月亮已经落得很低了，但是光亮依旧。他能够看得见那头奶牛、那棵矮小的树，还有奶牛周围绿油油的草地。突然间，他的头猛地动了一下，听到了什么声响，肯定是听到了什么响动。没错，又一次听到了这种响动，窸窣作响，就是从他坐的位置的窗户底下的草地里发出的。他快速站起身，通过窗台向地面看去。

接下来，他看到了，原来是条大黑蛇，也就是非洲曼巴毒蛇，约两米半长，粗细的程度跟一名男子的胳膊差不多。这条蛇正滑过湿漉漉的草地，径直爬向那头奶牛，爬的速度很快。它那只鸭梨形的脑袋挺了起来，离开地面稍微有一点距离，身体贴着湿地移动时发出清晰的“嘶嘶”的声音，就像气体从喷嘴喷出时发出的声音。他举起枪就要射击，但是几乎与此同时，他又把枪放下，他也不知道为什么要这样做。他一动不动地坐在那儿，看着曼巴毒蛇爬近奶牛，听着它爬行时发出的声音，继续看着它接近奶牛，等着它发起攻击。

但是,它并没有进攻,只是举起了头,并轻轻地前后摇摆了一会儿,然后将其黑色身体的前端举到空中,举到奶牛乳房的下方,将其中一个浑圆的奶头吸入嘴里,开始吮吸起来。

奶牛没有动弹,四处一点声音都没有。曼巴毒蛇的身体从地面优雅地向上卷曲,悬吊在奶牛乳房的下方。月光下,那里的那条黑色的毒蛇和那头黑色的奶牛清晰可辨。

在长达半个小时的时间里,老人就这样看着曼巴毒蛇吮吸着牛奶,看见它的身体随着牛奶的吸入而轻轻地搏动,过了一段时间又看见它从一个奶头换到另一个奶头,到了最后,一点牛奶都没有剩下。然后,这条曼巴毒蛇轻柔地将身体放低,落到地面上,滑过草地,沿着来时的方向返回。返回途中,它又发出清晰可闻的"嘶嘶"声,并再次经过老人坐的位置的窗户的下方,在它爬过的湿漉漉的草地上留下一道细长的黑色印记。紧接着,消失到小屋的后面,不见了踪迹。

月亮缓缓地沉入肯尼亚山脊的后面。几乎与此同时,太阳从东方高原的陡坡处冉冉升起,贾德森也拎着那只能装十八升煤油的锡桶从他的小木屋走出来,睡眼惺忪地拖着双脚趟过浓稠的露水,朝奶牛走来。老人看着他走过来,等待着。贾德森弯下腰,一只手触摸着牛乳。就在这当儿,老人喊了一声。贾德森闻声跳了起来。

"奶又没了,"老人说。

贾德森接道:"是啊,乳房空了。"

"我想,"老人慢条斯理地说,"我想,是一名基库尤小子干的。当时我打了个盹儿,醒来后竟让他得逞了。我无法开枪,因为奶牛挡在前面碍事。他在奶牛后面得以逃脱。今晚我还会等着他,今晚一定能逮住他。"他补充道。

贾德森没有吱声,拎起容量为十八升的锡桶,走回自己的小木屋。

那天晚上,老人又一夜未睡,坐在窗前,看着奶牛。对他来说,这一次有了乐趣,因为他将看到预期会出现的情景。他清楚,自己将会再次看到曼巴毒蛇,但是,他想进一步肯定一下:结果是否会如他所愿。最终,日出前一个小时,这条大黑蛇滑过草地,爬向奶牛。老人就倚靠在窗台上,眼睛随着曼巴毒蛇移动:毒蛇接近奶牛,在奶牛肚子底下等待了一会儿,头部前后慢慢地摇晃了六七次,最后,身体从地面举到空中,然后将奶牛的奶头吸入嘴中。老人看着它吮吸了半个小时,吸到一点也不剩为止。然后,老人看见它放低身体,沿着来时的方向,流畅地滑回小屋后面,消失不见。看着这一切,老人开始暗自笑了起来——脸部一侧的嘴巴动弹着,笑了起来。

接下来,太阳从小山的后方升起,贾德森也拎着他那只容量为十八升的锡桶走出了自己的小木屋。但是,这一次,他径直走向身上裹着毯子的老人坐着的那间小屋。

"情况咋样?"贾德森问道。

老人从窗户那儿往下看了一眼。"什么事儿都没有,"他回答。"一点儿动静都没有。我又打了个盹儿。这个杂种趁我睡着,来了,偷走了。听着,贾德森,"接着,他补充道,"我们逮住这小子,否则,你喝的牛奶可就短缺了。并不是说,这样对你有多大的害处,但是,我们要逮住他。他太聪明了,我无法开枪,再说,那头奶牛总是碍事。你必须得抓住他。"

"我,抓他?怎么抓?"

老人说起话来语速很慢。"我想,"他说,"我想,你必须藏到奶牛的旁边,紧挨着奶牛。只有这样,你才能抓住他。"

贾德森伸出左手抓挠起头发,将头发都抓乱了。

"今天,"老人继续说,"你得在奶牛的旁边挖出一条浅沟,能容你躺进去,我再用干草和绿草将你盖起来。这样,贼要是走不到你身边,就发现不了你。"

"贼或许会带着刀啊,"贾德森说。

"不会的,他不会带刀来。你带上棍子,别的什么都不用带。"

贾德森说:"嗯,我得带上棍子。他一上来,我就跳起来,用棍子打他。"接着,他突然间好像想起了什么事儿。"那么,它总嚼来嚼去,怎么办呢?"他问。"它整晚都在那儿咀嚼着,我忍受不了。'嘎吱、嘎吱、嘎吱'嚼着唾液和草,就像嚼小圆石头一样。整晚那样,我忍受不了。"说完,他就又开始用一只手扭着自己的左耳朵。

“怎么告诉你的,你就怎么做,甭废话。”老人说道。

那天白天,贾德森在奶牛旁边挖好了沟,奶牛则被栓到了金合欢树上,以防在地里到处溜达。接下来,随着夜幕的降临,贾德森准备着,要在沟里面躺下,度过这个夜晚。此时,老人走到屋子的门口说道:“不到大清早,什么事儿都做不了。奶牛乳房不胀满的话,贼是不会来的。进屋来等着吧,这里比你那间脏兮兮的小破屋要暖和多了。”

贾德森以前从没得到过邀请,进入老人的屋子坐坐。由于不用整晚躺在沟里,他感到很高兴。于是,他跟着老人进去。屋子里点燃了一根蜡烛,蜡烛插在一只啤酒瓶口上,瓶子则放在桌子上。

“你自己沏茶吧,”老人边说,边用手指着放在地板上的那只普里默斯炉。贾德森点燃煤油炉,烧水沏茶。他们两个人坐在几只木箱上,喝起茶来。老人趁着茶的热乎劲儿喝了起来,一边将茶水舔吸进嘴里,一边发出很大的声响。贾德森一个劲儿吹着自己杯子里的茶,谨慎地小口品着茶,透过茶杯的顶部向老人观瞧,老人则一直不停地大声舔吸着茶水。突然之间,贾德森说:“停。”他说话的声音很轻,似乎带着一丝的哀怨。说话的同时,眼角和嘴角也随着开始抽搐。

“什么?”老人问。

贾德森说:“那种声音,就是你舔吸茶水时发出的声音。”

老人放下茶杯,静静地打量着对方,看了好一会儿,说道:“贾德森,你一生中杀死过多少条狗了?”

没有回答。

“我说,多少条了? 多少条狗?”

贾德森开始从杯子里往外拣茶叶,然后将拣出来的茶叶粘到左手的手背上。老人坐在箱子上,身体向前倾斜着。

“贾德森,多少条狗呢?”

贾德森开始忙活着拣自己杯子里的茶叶。只见他将手指戳入喝空的杯子里,拣出一片茶叶,很快地压到左手的手背上粘住,然后很快地再次将手指戳入杯子,拣出另一片茶叶。茶叶没剩下几片,几乎拣不出来的时候,他就弯下腰,贴近杯子,往里面观瞧,试图要找到剩下那几片茶叶。托着茶杯的那只手的背面沾满了潮湿的黑色茶叶。

“贾德森!”老人喊了起来。从脸部的侧面看过去,老人的嘴巴张开,又合上,活像一把钳子。烛火闪烁、摇曳几下,又稳住了。

接下来,老人的语调和缓下来,就像对待小孩子一般,轻轻地、连哄带骗地说:“你一生中,一共要了多少条狗的命?”

贾德森问道:“我为什么要告诉你?”说完,仍然低着头,将手背上的茶叶一片、一片拣回到杯子里。

“我想知道,贾德森。”老人很是轻柔地说道。“对这件事,我也变得很感兴趣。我们谈谈,看看是否有一些更有趣的想法。”

贾德森抬起了头。一股口水沿着他的下巴淌下,淌着淌着就结成球状,在空中悬吊了一小会儿,然后“啪”地一声落到地板上。

“我杀死它们,就因为那种声响。”

“干一次,会有多久?我很想知道时间间隔。”

“很久前,干了好多次。”

“怎么干的?告诉我,你以前是怎么干的。你最喜欢怎么干?”

没有回答。

“贾德森,告诉我。我很想知道。”

“我看不出,为什么要告诉你。这是一个秘密。”

“我不会讲出去的。我发誓,我不会告诉别人的。”

“噢,要是你发誓的话。”贾德森在座位上挪动一下,靠得更近一些,小声说:“有一次,等大家都睡着了,我就弄到一块石头,让其落下,砸到狗的头上。”

老人站了起来,给自己倒了一杯茶。“我的那条狗,你不是那样砸死的吧。”

“当时没有那个时间。那种声音实在是糟糕,就是舔舌头发出的声音,于是,我只得干快些。”

“你甚至没有将他杀死。”

“我让那种声音停止了。”

老人走到门口,向外看去。外面很黑,月亮还没有升起,但繁星点点,夜色清澈,天气寒冷。东方天空露出了点儿灰白的色调。他观看的时候,那点儿灰白的色调逐渐扩大,由灰白色调变成了明亮色调,明亮的色调继而弥漫了整个天空。最终,高原田野里绿草上的滴滴露珠将明亮的色调反射开来,周围变亮,月亮随之从小山上方缓缓地升起来了。老人转过身,说道:"该做好准备了,贼今晚或许会来得早些,谁也说不准。"

贾德森起身,他们两个来到屋外。随即,贾德森到奶牛旁边的浅沟里躺了下来,老人用草将其覆盖起来,只把头部留出来,以便探出地面向外观瞧。"从窗户那儿,"老人说,"我也会观望着。听到我的喊声,你就跳起来抓住他。"

他蹒跚地走回屋子,上了楼,用毯子将自己裹住,坐到靠近窗户的那个位置上。时候还早,但是,月亮几乎圆了,还在不断爬升。月光照在肯尼亚山顶部的积雪上。

一个小时过后,老人从窗户那儿喊道:

"贾德森,你没有睡着吧?"

"没有,"他回答,"我醒着呢。"

"不要睡着了,"老人继续说。"做什么都可以,就是别睡着了。"

"奶牛总是咀嚼着,"贾德森说。

"稳住,要是你现在起身,我就向你射击,"老人说。

"你要向我射击?"

"我说过,要是你现在起身,我就向你射击。"

从贾德森躺着的地方传来一声轻轻的啜泣,是一种很奇怪的喘息声,就像是一个孩子强忍着不哭出声来。其间,贾德森的声音传来:"我得动动地方,请让我动一动,受不了这种'嘎吱'的声音。"

"要是你起身,"老人说,"我就朝你的肚子开枪。"

这种啜泣的声音持续着,大约持续了一个小时。接着,突然之间,声音停止了。

快要到四点的时候,天气变得很是寒冷,老人缩成一团,将毯子裹得更紧了,接着喊道:"你在那儿冷吗,贾德森?你冷吗?"

"是的,"他回答。"太冷了,但是,我不介意的,奶牛睡着了,不再'嘎吱'咀嚼了。"

老人说："抓到贼，你要拿他怎么办？"

"我不知道。"

"你会要他的命吗？"

暂停了一会儿。

"我不知道。我只是要逮住他。"

"我会继续看着，"老人说。"应该很有意思的。"他将胳膊搭到窗台上，身体探到了窗外。

接下来，他听到窗台下发出"嘶嘶"的声音，就一眼看了过去，看到了那条黑色的曼巴毒蛇，毒蛇正穿过草地，滑向奶牛，滑行速度很快。一边滑行，一边将头部举起，稍稍离开了地面。

还差四米半远的时候，老人喊了起来。只见他将两手窝成杯状，拢在嘴边，喊道："他来了，贾德森；他来了。快去抓住他。"

贾德森快速举起头，向上看去。就在这一瞬间，他看到了曼巴毒蛇，曼巴毒蛇也看到了他。有一秒钟的时间——或许有两秒钟的时间，毒蛇戛然而止，后退了一下，将身体前部举到了半空中。紧接着，进攻开始了。只见黑影一闪，随即"啪"的一声，毒蛇咬到了他的胸部。贾德森大叫一声，一声长长的、尖尖的大叫，叫的音调始终如一：既没有升高，也没有降低。接下来，大叫声慢慢地消失，四周静悄悄的。此刻，他站了起来，扯开衬衫，摸着胸部被咬的部位，微弱地啜泣着、呻吟着，同时，嘴巴张得大大的，使劲儿喘息着。自始至终，老人安静地坐在敞开的窗户前，身体向前倾斜着，眼睛一刻也没有从下方移开。

人一旦被黑曼巴毒蛇咬中，随后的一切都会以迅雷不及掩耳之势到来。几乎在被咬的同时，蛇毒就开始起作用了。只见他跌倒在地，背部隆起，躺在那儿，同时在草地上打着滚，什么声音都发不出来了。一切都静悄悄的，好似一名大力士与一位隐形的巨人在摔跤，巨人扭住了大力士，不让他站立起来，将他的两只胳膊紧紧地拉向两腿的分叉处，同时将他的双膝也推到了下巴底下。

接着，他的双手将绿草从土里拔出，之后，他仰卧在地，双腿轻轻地踢着，但没有踢多长时间。紧接着，他快速扭动一下，又一次隆起了背部,同时翻了一个身,脸朝下趴在地上,一动不动了。他就这样趴着,右膝抬起放在胸部下方,双手伸展开来,围在脑袋上方。

老人仍然端坐窗前,即便是一切都结束了,他还坐在原地,没有动弹。金合欢树的阴影下有东西在移动,那是曼巴毒蛇在缓慢滑行,爬向奶牛。只见它向前移动一点距离,停了下来,举起了头,等待着。然后,放低头部,又向前滑行,径直爬到奶牛肚子底下。接着,它将身体举到半空中,将奶牛的一个棕色奶头吸入嘴中,开始吮吸起来。老人坐在那儿,看着曼巴毒蛇吸着牛奶。随着毒蛇从奶头里将牛奶吸入嘴中,他又一次看到毒蛇的身体在轻轻地搏动。

趁着毒蛇吮吸的当儿,老人站起身来,离开了窗户。

“你可以将他的那一份喝掉,”老人安静地说。“你喝掉他的那一份,我们不介意的。”他边说,边回头看了一眼,又一次看到曼巴毒蛇黑色的身体从地面向上卷曲,跟奶牛的肚子连到了一起。

“没错,”他又说道,“你喝掉他的那一份,我们不介意的。”

第二章　异想天开

异想天开的想法往往是一些不可思议的想法，异想天开的事情往往是一些荒唐离奇的事情，但异想天开，同时又预示着超强的想象力。晚清四大谴责小说之一——吴趼人的《二十年目睹之怪现状》第八十六回有这样的描述：

迭三这宝货，他揣摩到了这一层，却异想天开，夸说他的药膏，可以在枪上戒烟：譬如吃一钱烟的，只要秤出九分烟，加一分药膏在烟里，如此逐渐减烟加膏，至将烟减尽为止，自然断瘾。

迭三的行径固然异想天开，但看起来似乎不是不"靠谱"，这一点跟英国作家罗尔德·达尔笔下的小男孩有些相似：一个小男孩看着地毯上的图案，浮想联翩，甚至"意愿突发"，决定一试身手、加大难度来挑战自我要穿越地毯。不管结局是否离奇或恐怖，这个小男孩算是异想天开了。

离奇的不"靠谱"的恐怕要属阿道夫·奈普了。样子邋里邋遢的阿道夫·奈普是自动计算机器方面的天才。在休假期间，他竟突发奇想，异想天开地要制造出一台自动写作小说的机器。令人意想不到的是，他还真的做成了。他发明的这种自动化的"伟大写手"甚至危及当时一些知名作家的生存。

走进罗尔德·达尔《意愿突发》的世界，去体会《伟大写手》的魅力吧。

第一节 《意愿突发》*The Wish*

罗尔德·达尔的《意愿突发》(*The Wish*)被收录在《罗尔德·达尔短篇故事集锦》(*The Collected Short Stories of Roald Dahl*)、《如你之人》(*Someone like You*)、《〈人皮刺青〉及其他故事集》(*Skin and Other Stories*)、《五部畅销书集》(*5 Bestsellers*)、《罗尔德·达尔选集》(*The Roald Dahl Omnibus*)以及《罗尔德·达尔二十九篇成人故事集》(*Twenty Nine Kisses from Roald Dahl*)等书中。

这篇小说篇幅虽然短小,但却生动形象,充满了悬疑,正如克里斯廷·霍华德(Kristine Howard)所发出的疑问:"那些毒蛇只是小男孩想象出来的吗? 题目里'意愿'指的是什么? 小男孩真的掉进满是毒蛇的坑中了吗?"(Are the snakes only in the boy's imagination? What is "the wish" that the title refers to? Has he really disappeared into the snake pit?)①。

一、原作导读

一个小男孩腿上早先留下的伤口结了痂,于是,小男孩就要把这个痂剥掉,哪怕剥掉会留下新的伤口,因为剥痂这件事情充满了挑战和诱惑力。小男孩将剥下来的痂弹飞,落到了地毯的边缘,这时候小男孩才意识到这块地毯的存在:

那是很大、很大的一块地毯,上面有红、黑、黄相间的图案,从他

① 这段叙述由本书著者译自"罗尔德·达尔粉丝网"(Roald Dahl Fans),具体可参见克里斯廷·霍华德(Kristine Howard)创建并维护的网站"*Roald Dahl Fans.com*",网址为:http://www.roalddahlfans.com/。

坐的台阶处铺过整个门厅,一直延伸到远处的正门。真是一块巨毯啊,比网球场还大一些,甚至大多了。

... the enormous red and black and yellow carpet that stretched the whole length of the hall from the stairs on which he sat to the front door in the distance. A tremendous carpet. Bigger than the tennis lawn. Much bigger than that.

小男孩盯着地毯看了许久,奇想突发,决定挑战一下:穿越那块地毯,但不是一般的穿越,而是一段加大了难度的穿越之旅:

地毯的红色部分是炽热燃烧的煤块。我一定得这样去做:必须沿着地毯走到正门,但却不能碰上红色的煤块。要是碰上,我就会被烧掉。事实上,我会被烧成灰烬。那么,地毯的黑色部分……好的,黑色部分就是一条条蛇——有毒的蛇,多数是蝰蛇,还有眼镜蛇,蛇身中间粗如树干。要是我碰上哪怕是一条这样的蛇,我就会被咬到,不用等到下午茶点的时间,我就会死去。

The red parts of the carpet are red-hot lumps of coal. What I must do is this: I must walk all the way along it to the front door without touching them. If I touch the red I will be burnt. As a matter of fact, I will be burnt up completely. And the black parts of the carpet... yes, the black parts are snakes, poisonous snakes, adders mostly, and cobras, thick like tree-trunks round the middle, and if I touch one of them, I'll be bitten and I'll die before tea time.

小男孩的穿越之旅充满了惊险和刺激,那些毒蛇张开了大口等待着……他的身体开始摇晃,坠向黑色区域……

外面阳光明媚,房后很远的地方,母亲正在寻找自己的儿子。

Outside in the sunshine, far away behind the house, the mother was looking for her son.

二、原作释读

读罢这部篇幅短小的故事,作家罗尔德·达尔非凡的叙述功力就可见一斑了。普通得不能再普通的人生场景,在达尔笔下则具有了神奇的地方。阅读理解之余,达尔这种化"腐朽"为"神奇"的笔力,值得我们认真体会。

The Wish①

Under the palm of one hand the child became aware of the scab② of an old cut on his kneecap③. He bent forward to examine it closely. A scab was always a fascinating thing; it presented a special challenge he was never able to resist.

Yes, he thought, I will pick it off, even if it isn't ready, even if the middle of it sticks, even if it hurts like anything.

With a fingernail he began to explore cautiously around the edges of the scab. He got a nail underneath it, and when he raised it, but ever so slightly, it suddenly came off, the whole hard brown scab came off beautifully, leaving an interesting little circle of smooth red skin.

Nice. Very nice indeed. He rubbed the circle and it didn't hurt.

---

① 本部小说原文出自"DAHL R. *The Collected Short Stories of Roald Dahl*. England: Penguin Books Ltd., 1992"。

② scab: *Noun* a dry, rough protective crust that forms over a cut or wound during healing(伤口或疮口上所结的)痂(e.g. When you cut yourself, blood clots and forms a scab. 割破了皮肤,血就会凝固、结痂。)

③ kneecap: *Noun* the convex bone in front of the knee joint; the patella 膝盖骨;髌

He picked up the scab, put it on his thigh and flipped[①] it with a finger so that it flew away and landed on the edge of the carpet, the enormous red and black and yellow carpet that stretched the whole length of the hall from the stairs on which he sat to the front door in the distance. A tremendous carpet. Bigger than the tennis lawn. Much bigger than that. He regarded it gravely, setting his eyes upon it with mild pleasure. He had never really noticed it before, but now, all of a sudden the colours seemed to brighten mysteriously and spring out at him in a most dazzling[②] way.

You see, he told himself, I know how it is. The red parts of the carpet are red-hot lumps of coal. What I must do is this: I must walk all the way along it to the front door without touching them. If I touch the red I will be burnt. As a matter of fact, I will be burnt up completely. And the black parts of the carpet... yes, the black parts are snakes, poisonous snakes, adders[③] mostly, and cobras, thick like tree-trunks round the middle, and if I touch one of them, I'll be bitten and I'll die before tea time[④]. And if I get across safely, without being burnt and without being bitten, I will be given a puppy[⑤] for my birthday tomorrow.

---

① flip: *Verb* [with obj. and adverbial] move, push, or throw (something) with a sudden sharp movement(猛地)移动;弹;推;扔(e.g. She flipped a few coins on to the bar. 她把几枚硬币扔在吧台上。)

② dazzling: *Adjective* extremely bright, especially so as to blind the eyes temporarily 耀眼的;眼花缭乱的(e.g. The sunlight was dazzling. 阳光耀眼。)

③ adder: *Noun* a small venomous Eurasian snake which has a dark zigzag pattern on its back and bears live young. It is the only poisonous snake in Britain. 极北蝰;蝰蛇

④ teatime or tea time: *Noun* (chiefly Brit.) the usual or traditional time for serving tea, as late afternoon(主要为英国英语的用法)下午吃茶点的时间(通常在下午四五点钟)

⑤ puppy: *Noun* a young dog 小狗;幼犬

He got to his feet and climbed higher up the stairs to obtain a better view of this vast tapestry① of colour and death. Was it possible? Was there enough yellow? Yellow was the only colour he was allowed to walk on. Could it be done? This was not a journey to be undertaken lightly; the risks were far too great for that. The child's face—a fringe② of white-gold hair, two large blue eyes, a small pointed chin peered down anxiously over the banisters. The yellow was a bit thin in places and there were one or two widish gaps, but it did seem to go all the way along to the other end. For someone who had only yesterday triumphantly travelled the whole length of the brick path from the stables③ to the summer-house without touching the cracks, this carpet thing should not be too difficult. Except for the snakes. The mere thought of snakes sent a fine electricity of fear running like pins down the backs of his legs and under the soles of his feet.

He came slowly down the stairs and advanced to the edge of the carpet. He extended one small sandalled foot and placed it cautiously upon a patch of yellow. Then he brought the other foot up, and there was just enough room for him to stand with the two feet together. There④! He had

---

① tapestry: *Noun* (figurative) used in reference to an intricate or complex sequence of events(比喻)复杂的一连串的事件(e. g. The loopiness of the Commons adds to life's rich tapestry. 下院议员们的愚笨使已经错综复杂的生活更加扑朔迷离。)

② fringe: *Noun* (chiefly Brit.) the front part of someone's hair, cut so as to hang over the forehead(主要为英国英语的用法)刘海

③ stable: *Noun* a building set apart and adapted for keeping horses 马厩

④ there: Exclamation used to focus attention on something and express satisfaction or annoyance at it(用于引起注意,表示满意或生气)你瞧(e. g. There, I told you she wouldn't mind!. 你看! 我告诉过你她不会在意的。)

started! His bright oval face was curiously intent, a shade① whiter perhaps than before, and he was holding his arms out sideways to assist his balance. He took another step, lifting his foot high over a patch of black, aiming carefully with his toe for a narrow channel of yellow on the other side. When he had completed the second step he paused to rest, standing very stiff and still. The narrow channel of yellow ran forward unbroken for at least five yards and he advanced gingerly② along it, bit by bit, as though walking a tightrope③. Where it finally curled off sideways, he had to take another long stride, this time over a vicious-looking mixture of black and red. Halfway across he began to wobble④. He waved his arms around wildly, windmill fashion, to keep his balance, and he got across safely and rested again on the other side. He was quite breathless now, and so tense he stood high on his toes all the time, arms out sideways, fists clenched⑤. He was on a big safe island of yellow. There was lots of room on it, he couldn't possibly fall off, and he stood there resting, hesitating, waiting, wishing he could stay for ever on this big safe yellow island. But the fear of not getting the puppy compelled him to go on. Step by step, he edged further ahead, and between each one he paused to decide exactly where he should put his foot. Once, he had a

---

① a shade...: a little... 有点;略微(e.g. He was a shade hung-over. 他有点醉后头晕。)

② gingerly: *Adverb* in a careful or cautious manner 小心地;谨慎地;战战兢兢地(e.g. She gingerly picked the flower. 她小心翼翼地摘下那朵花。)

③ tightrope: *Noun* a rope or wire stretched tightly high above the ground, on which acrobats perform feats of balancing(供杂技演员表演用的)绷紧的钢丝(或绳索)

④ wobble: *Verb* [no obj.] move unsteadily from side to side 摇晃;摇摆(e.g. The table wobbles where the leg is too short. 桌子短腿的那一边摇摇晃晃。)

⑤ clench: *Verb* (with reference to the fingers or hand) close into a tight ball, especially when feeling extreme anger(手,手指)紧握成拳(尤以表示愤怒)

choice of ways, either to left or right, and he chose the left because although it seemed the more difficult, there was not so much black in that direction. The black was what had made him nervous. He glanced quickly over his shoulder to see how far he had come. Nearly halfway. There could be no turning back now. He was in the middle and he couldn't turn back and he couldn't jump off sideways either because it was too far, and when he looked at all the red and all the black that lay ahead of him, he felt that old sudden sickening surge of panic in his chest—like last Easter① time, that afternoon when he got lost all alone in the darkest part of Piper's Wood.

He took another step, placing his foot carefully upon the only little piece of yellow within reach, and this time the point of the foot came within a centimetre of some black. It wasn't touching the black, he could see it wasn't touching, he could see the small line of yellow separating the toe of his sandal from the black; but the snake stirred as though sensing his nearness, and raised its head and gazed at the foot with bright beady eyes②, watching to see if it was going to touch.

"I'm not touching you! You mustn't bite me! You know I'm not touching you!"

Another snake slid up noiselessly beside the first, raised its head, two heads now, two pairs of eyes staring at the foot, gazing at a little naked place just below the sandal strap where the skin showed through. The child went high up on his toes and stayed there, frozen stiff with terror. It

---

① Easter: *Noun* the most important and oldest festival of the Christian Church, celebrating the resurrection of Christ and held (in the Western Church) between 21 March and 25 April, on the first Sunday after the first full moon following the northern spring equinox. 复活节(基督教最重要、最古老的节日,庆祝"耶稣复活",西方教会在每年3月21日至4月25日之间北半球春分后月圆后的第一个星期日庆祝。)

② beady eyes: *Noun* small, glinting eyes 晶亮如小珠的眼睛

was minutes before he dared to move again.

The next step would have to be a really long one. There was this deep curling river of black that ran clear across the width of the carpet, and he was forced by his position to cross it at its widest part. He thought first of trying to jump it, but decided he couldn't be sure of landing accurately on the narrow band of yellow on the other side. He took a deep breath, lifted one foot, and inch by inch he pushed it out in front of him, far far out, then down and down until at last the tip of his sandal was across and resting safely on the edge of the yellow. He leaned forward, transferring his weight to his front foot. Then he tried to bring the back foot up as well. He strained and pulled and jerked his body, but the legs were too wide apart and he couldn't make it. He tried to get back again. He couldn't do that either. He was doing the splits① and he was properly② stuck. He glanced down and saw this deep curling river of black underneath him. Parts of it were stirring now, and uncoiling③ and beginning to shine with a dreadfully oily glister④. He wobbled, waved his arms frantically to keep his balance, but that seemed to make it worse. He was starting to go over. He was going over to the right, quite slowly he was going over, then faster and faster, and at the last moment, in-

---

① split: *Noun* (the splits) (Brit.) (in gymnastics and dance) an act of leaping in the air or sitting down with the legs straight and at right angles to the body, one in front and the other behind, or one at each side(英国英语)(体操、舞蹈中的)劈叉动作(e. g. I could never do the splits before. 我以前根本就不能做劈叉动作。)

② properly: *Adjective* [usu. as submodifier] (informal, chiefly Brit.) thoroughly; completely(主要为英国英语中的非正式用法)彻底地;完全地(e. g. On the first day she felt properly well, Millie sat out on the front steps. 密丽在感觉自己彻底好了的第一天就到屋外门前的台阶上坐了坐。)

③ uncoil: *Verb* straighten or cause to straighten from a coiled or curled position 伸开;展开(e. g. The snake slowly uncoiled. 蛇身慢慢伸开。)

④ glister: *Noun* a sparkle 闪光;发光

stinctively he put out a hand to break[1] the fall and the next thing he saw was this bare hand of his going right into the middle of a great glistening mass of black and he gave one piercing cry as it touched.

Outside in the sunshine, far away behind the house, the mother was looking for her son.

三、翻译探索

本篇小说的翻译难度不是很大,关键是要再现原文那"扣人心弦"的文风,特别是那几个大段描写风格的再现。这恐怕要在"雅"这方面多做探索了。

奇想突发

手掌捂到膝盖骨上面的时候,这个孩子才意识到,那里早先的一处切口已经结痂。孩子弯腰向前,仔细查看结下的痂。伤口结了痂,总是一件令人着迷的事情。对他而言,那儿结下一个痂,就代表一种特殊的挑战,而这种挑战他永远都无法抗拒。

他想,没错,我要把这个痂剥掉,就算还没有结好,就算中间还粘连着,就算切口疼得要命,我也要把这个痂剥掉。

他用一个指甲尖儿开始小心翼翼地在这个痂的边缘探查。指甲探到了痂下,他就开始向外撬,但是,用力轻轻。突然,痂脱落下来——整块棕色的硬痂利索地脱落下来,露出一小块圆圆的、光滑的红色皮肤,看上去很有意思。

漂亮,的确很漂亮。他揉了揉那圈皮肤——不疼。他将痂捡起,放在大腿部位,然后猛地一弹。这个痂随即飞走,落到地毯的边缘。那是很大、很大的一块地毯,上面有红、黑、黄相间的图案,从他坐的台阶处铺过整个门厅,一直延伸到远处的正门。真是一块巨毯啊,比

① break: *Verb* lessen the impact of (a fall) 减轻(落体的)冲击力度

网球场还大一些,甚至大多了。他庄严地注视着这块地毯,眼光落在上面,轻微露出喜悦之色。以前,他从未真正注意到它的存在,可是现在,突然之间,它上面的颜色似乎闪耀着神秘的光芒,光芒直奔他而来,令他眼花缭乱。

他对自己说,知道嘛,我知道怎么回事儿啦。地毯的红色部分是炽热燃烧的煤块。我一定得这样去做:必须沿着地毯走到正门,但却不能碰上红色的煤块。要是碰上,我就会被烧掉。事实上,我会被烧成灰烬。那么,地毯的黑色部分……好的,黑色部分就是一条条蛇——有毒的蛇,多数是蝰蛇,还有眼镜蛇,蛇身中间粗如树干。要是我碰上哪怕是一条这样的蛇,我就会被咬到,不用等到下午茶点的时间,我就会死去。要是我成功穿越——没有被烧掉、没有被咬到,明天我就会得到一只小狗作为自己的生日礼物。

他站了起来,爬上几级台阶,要好好看看这一连串的色彩图案和生死未卜的穿越。有可能吗?黄色够多吗?黄色是允许踩着行走的唯一颜色。能穿越成功吗?这可不是一段轻松可以走完的旅程。成功跨越,风险极大。这个孩子留着金白色的刘海儿,两只蓝色的眼睛大大的,尖尖的下巴小小的。他的脸伏在阶梯扶手上,眼睛焦虑地向下凝视着。地毯上有些地方,黄色部分有点稀薄,还有一两处稍宽一点的间隙,但是,黄色部分看上去,似乎确实一直通到了地毯的另一端。就在昨天,从马厩到凉亭的整条用砖铺成的小路,都能胜利走过,而没有碰到砖的缝隙。对这样的胜利者而言,这件穿越地毯的事情不应该太困难——那些蛇另当别论。只要一想到那些蛇,一股细细的恐惧电流,就如同大头针一般,从他的腿后和脚掌底下穿过。

他慢慢地走下台阶,走到地毯的边缘,然后,伸出一只小脚,谨慎地踏在一块黄色区域上面,那只脚上穿的是凉鞋。接着,他又抬起另一只脚,黄色区域上的空间刚好够两只脚一起站到上面。瞧啊!他已经开始啦!他那张椭圆形的脸蛋闪闪发亮,或许比先前白了一点。他表情专注,样子很有趣儿。他的胳膊在身体的两侧举起,辅助身体的平衡。他又迈出一步,只见他抬起脚,高高地举到一块黑色区域上方,脚趾头仔细地对准另一头的一块狭窄的长条形黄色区域。第二步完成后,他暂停下来,笔直站立,一动不动,歇息了一会儿。这块狭窄的长条形黄色区域向前延伸,没有间断,距离至少有四米半。他战战兢兢地沿着这块区域前行,一点儿、一点儿地挪移,如同走钢丝一般。在这块长条地带最终向一侧弯曲的地方,他不得不向前再大跨一步,这次跨步跃过的是一块面目狰狞的黑红混合的区域。跨越到一半的时候,他开始摇晃起来,只见他胳膊狂舞,如风车一般,意欲保持平衡。安全跨越后,他在另一头又休息了一会儿。现在,他已经上气不接下气了,绷紧身体,始终踮起脚尖高高地站立,两只胳膊向两侧伸展,双手握成拳头紧紧地攥住。他身处一大片黄色的安全岛上,岛上空间很大,不可能跌落的。他站在岛上休息,显得犹豫不决、有所等待,希望永远待在这大片黄色的安全岛上。可问题是,由于担心得不到小狗这件礼物,他被迫继续穿越。

他进一步向前移动,慢慢地、一步一步地挪动,每挪一步,他就暂停一下,以确定脚究竟该放到什么位置。有一次,他面临着两种选择:向左走,还是向右走。他选择了向左走,理由是,尽管左边看起来似乎困难重重,但那个方向上没有如此多的黑色区域。黑色是令他紧张不安的颜色。他扭头快速向后看了看,看看一路走来,走出了多远的距离:几乎走到一半了,现在已经没有回头路可走。他已经跨越一半的距离,骑虎难下了:不可能返回,也不可能跳到一边,落荒而逃,原因就是,他已经走得太远。看到前方一块块红色和一块块黑色的时候,他突然间感到胸前涌起曾经有过的一种恐惧感,这种恐惧感令他难受得想吐。比如,去年复活节午后的感觉——当时,在派珀氏树林最幽暗的地方,他独自一人走迷了路。

他又跨出一步,小心翼翼地将一只脚踏进了一小块黄色区域,能够得着的范围内就这么一小块黄色区域。这一次,脚尖踩到一块黑色区域上方有一厘米的地方,但是没有触碰到黑色。他看得出来,脚尖没有触碰到黑色。他看得出来,黄色区域细细的边线将凉鞋的脚尖部位跟黑色分割开来。尽管如此,蛇还是动弹了几下,好像感觉到他在靠近,只见它抬起头,用明亮的、小粒珍珠般的眼睛警惕地盯着那只脚,想看看那只脚会不会碰到自己。

“我没有碰到你呀！你绝对不可以咬我！你知道，我没有碰到你呀！”

第一条蛇的旁边，又有一条蛇悄无声息地爬上前来，抬起了头。现在，已经有两个蛇头从脚下抬了起来，有两双蛇眼盯着他的脚，直勾勾地就盯着凉鞋带下面一小块裸露的地方，因为那地方有皮肤裸露出来。这个孩子高高地踮起脚尖，待在那儿，恐惧得僵直起来。过了好几分钟，他才壮着胆，再次移动起来。

下一步要迈的距离真的很长。一条深深的黑色河流在眼前弯弯曲曲地横过地毯流淌。从他所在的位置上看，他必须得在河段的最宽部位跃过河流。起先，他想试着跳过去，但是，他不敢肯定是否能准确无误地落到对岸那块狭窄的黄色地带。他深深吸了一口气，抬起一只脚，在身体前方一点儿、一点儿向外伸出，一次伸出两三厘米的距离，伸出的距离越来越远、越来越远，脚也放得越来越低、越来越低。最终，他那只凉鞋的鞋尖横跨过去，安全地落到黄色的边沿。于是，他向前倚身，将体重转移到前面那只脚上。接着，尽力将后面的脚也抬了起来，全力向前拉，猛地抽动身体，但是，双腿分得距离太宽，办不到。于是，他尽量要退回去，但是，也办不到。他做着劈叉动作，完全卡在那儿了。他低头看去，看到了下方这条深深而弯曲的黑色河流。现在，河流的一些地方开始翻腾，卷起了浪花，开始闪耀着可怕的油亮的光芒。他摇晃起来，双臂狂舞着要保持平衡，但是，这一切似乎使事情变得更糟。他开始翻转过去，向右翻转，十分缓慢地翻转。接着，越来越快、越来越快地翻转。就在最后的时刻，他本能地伸出一只手要减缓下落的冲击力。紧接着，他看到他那只裸露的手径直落入一大片闪着光芒的黑色区域中间。手触碰到黑色区域表面的时候，他尖锐地大叫一声。

外面阳光明媚，房后很远的地方，母亲正在寻找自己的儿子。

第二节 《伟大写手》*The Great Automatic Grammatizator*

罗尔德·达尔的《伟大写手》(*The Great Automatic Grammatizator*)被收录在《罗尔德·达尔短篇故事集锦》(*The Collected Short Stories of Roald Dahl*)、《如你之人》(*Someone like You*)、《五部畅销书集》(*5 Bestsellers*)、《〈伟大写手〉及其他故事集》(*The Great Automatic Grammatizator and Other Stories*)、《〈卖伞男子〉及其他故事集》(*The Umbrella Man and Other Stories*)、《罗尔德·达尔选集》(*The Roald Dahl Omnibus*)以及《罗尔德·达尔二十九篇成人故事集》(*Twenty Nine Kisses from Roald Dahl*)等书中。

从达尔最初发表《伟大写手》的时间来看,这部小说颇具科幻色彩,但讽刺的意味很浓,具有"含沙射影"之嫌,读罢令人感觉达尔在美国投稿吃了太多的"闭门羹",对美国的一些杂志"恨之入骨"。所以,个人看来,达尔写这部小说过于"感情用事",但也不失为一篇精彩之作。就这个故事本身的情节而言,在20世纪五六十年代造这样一部自动写作的机器,就算在今天看来,也有点"天方夜谭",未免有些"异想天开"了。

一、原作导读

计算机的兴起是20世纪八九十年代的事情,而在达尔发表这篇小说的20世纪五六十年代,计算机远没有达到今天的水平。因此,达尔具有很强的超前性和惊人的想象力,但当时真要制造出达到小说中所描述的写作能力的"伟大写手"不亚于"痴人说梦",那只能算是"异想天开"的事了。从达尔写作动机(也许出于个人恩怨)来看,这篇小说显得"平淡",甚至流于"平庸",但总体上也淋漓尽致地体现出达尔的写作风格,不乏悬念和精彩的文笔,仅以克里斯廷·霍华

德(Kristine Howard)的一个看法为例:

这个故事也不乏悬念,因为我们知道,其真正的主题在于达尔当时作为一个作家所处的地位方面。这种主题中固有的"隐含意识"会在很多地方显露原形,其中我最喜欢的就是主人公奈普解释每一位作家都具有的写作嗜好那一段:每一位作家都习惯在自己的每一部作品中插入一个古旧的长词,这样好使自己显得胜人一筹。于是,博伦先生就问,这样的"词"存在什么地方。奈普解释说"在'单词记忆'部件里",感觉对方有点"画蛇添足"。我至少读了三遍才注意到达尔用"画蛇添足"这个词实则是开了一个晦涩的玩笑。这一点,每次阅读时都被我一带而过了。

There's also a constant strain of tension present in the story, simply because we know the real subject is Dahl's status as a writer himself. This "hidden consciousness" peeks out in many places; my favorite is the paragraph where Knipe explains that nearly every writer makes a practice of inserting one long archaic word into each story to make himself sound smarter. When Mr. Bohlen asks where these words are stored, Knipe "epexegetically" answers "in the 'word-memory' section." It took me at least three readings to notice that Dahl was making a subtle joke simply with that one word, which I repeatedly skimmed over. ①

在这部小说中,主人公阿道夫·奈普是一个计算机方面的天才,却总是怀揣一个要当作家的梦想。一次休假过程中,他突发奇想,要制造一台能够自动写小说的计算机。于是,他设法说服上司博伦先生投资制造这样一台机器。最终,这样的一部机器——"伟大写手"——研制成功,随后又加以改进,可以写出长篇小说来。他又跟

① 这段叙述由本书著者译自"罗尔德·达尔粉丝网"(Roald Dahl Fans),具体可参见克里斯廷·霍华德(Kristine Howard)创建并维护的网站"*Roald Dahl Fans. com*",网址为:http://www.roalddahlfans.com/。

博伦先生创建了一家公司,大规模"生产"小说卖给出版社,大赚了一笔。紧接着,他们更进一步,要垄断整个出版业,"买断"了大部分作家,让他们白拿钱而不写作。这危及某些拒绝"就范"的作家,使他们生存出现了危机,他们的孩子开始挨饿,吃不饱饭。

小说的最后,达尔将视角转向其中一位"苦苦挣扎"的作家,叙事角度转到了第一人称:

就在这一刻,我坐在这儿,听着另一个房间里,我那九个挨饿的孩子正在那儿号叫,我感觉自己的手越来越靠近、越来越靠近那份黄金一般的合同了——那份合同就放在书桌的另一头。

赐予我们力量吧,噢,上帝,哪怕是让我们的孩子挨饿。

This very moment, as I sit here listening to the howling of my nine starving children in the other room, I can feel my own hand creeping closer and closer to that golden contract that lies over on the other side of the desk.

Give us strength, Oh Lord, to let our children starve.

二、原作释读

阅读本篇小说要体会好主人公阿道夫·奈普前后心境的变化,要领会好英国英语中特有的一些词的用法,还要体会好结尾处角度的切换。同时,也要注意体会作家罗尔德·达尔那种讽刺的笔调。

The Great Automatic Grammatizator①

Well, Knipe, my boy. Now that it's finished. I just called you in to tell you I think you've done a fine job."

---

① 本部小说原文出自"DAHL R. *The Collected Short Stories of Roald Dahl*. England: Penguin Books Ltd., 1992"。

Adolph Knipe stood still in front of Mr. Bohlen's desk. There seemed to be no enthusiasm in him at all.

"Aren't you pleased?"

"Oh yes, Mr. Bohlen."

"Did you see what the papers said this morning?"

"No sir, I didn't."

The man behind the desk pulled a folded newspaper towards him, and began to read: "The building of the great automatic computing engine①, ordered by the government some time ago, is now complete. It is probably the fastest electronic calculating machine in the world today. Its function is to satisfy the ever-increasing need of science, industry, and administration for rapid mathematical calculation which, in the past, by traditional methods, would have been physically② impossible, or would have required more time than the problems justified. The speed with which the new engine works, said Mr. John Bohlen, head of the firm of electrical engineers mainly responsible for its construction, may be grasped by the fact that it can provide the correct answer in five seconds to a problem that would occupy a mathematician for a month. In three minutes, it can produce a calculation that by hand (if it were possible) would fill half a million sheets of foolscap③ paper. The automatic computing engine uses pulses of electricity, generated at the rate of a million a

---

① engine: *Noun* a thing that is the agent or instrument of a particular process 工具;手段(e. g. Exports used to be the engine of growth. 出口曾经是促进经济增长的手段。)

② physically: Adverb (informal) actually or completely(非正式)实际上;完全地(e. g. He no longer found her physically attractive. 他认为她的外表已经失去吸引力。Every time I think about it I feel physically sick. 一想起那件事我就感到极恶心。)

③ foolscap: *Noun* [mass noun] (Brit.) a size of paper, about 330 × 200 (or 400) mm(英国英语)大裁(纸张尺寸规格:约 330×200(或 400)毫米)

second, to solve all calculations that resolve① themselves into addition, subtraction, multiplication, and division. For practical purposes there is no limit to what it can do..."

Mr. Bohlen glanced up at the long, melancholy② face of the younger man. "Aren't you proud, Knipe? Aren't you pleased."

"Of course, Mr. Bohlen."

"I don't think I have to remind you that your own contribution, especially to the original plans, was an important one. In fact, I might go so far as to say that without you and some of your ideas, this project might still be on the drawing-boards③ today."

Adolph Knipe moved his feet on the carpet, and he watched the two small white hands of his chief, the nervous fingers playing with a paperclip④, unbending⑤ it, straightening out the hairpin⑥ curves. He didn't like the man's hands. He didn't like his face either, with the tiny mouth and the narrow purple-coloured lips. It was unpleasant the way

---

① resolve: *Verb* [with obj.] (resolve something into) reduce a subject, statement, etc. by mental analysis into (separate elements or a more elementary form) 将(问题、陈述等)分解为(各个不同因素或更基础的形式)来分析(e.g. the ability to resolve facts into their legal categories 把不同事实分解纳入各自法律范畴的能力)

② melancholy: *Adjective* sad, gloomy, or depressed 忧愁的,忧郁的,沮丧的(e.g. The dog has a melancholy expression. 这只狗表情忧郁。)

③ on the drawing board: (of an idea, scheme, or proposal) under consideration and not yet ready to put into practice(观点、计划、建议)在计划阶段;处于初级阶段(e.g. There are plans to enlarge the runway, but at present all this remains on the drawing board. 有计划要扩建机场跑道,但目前一切仍处于计划阶段。)

④ paperclip or paper clip: *Noun* a piece of bent wire or plastic used for holding several sheets of paper together 回形针

⑤ unbend: *Verb* make or become straight from a bent or twisted form or position 把……弄直;变直(e.g. I had trouble unbending my cramped knees. 我麻木的膝盖很难伸直。)

⑥ hairpin: *Noun* a U-shaped pin for fastening the hair "U"形发夹

only the lower lip moved when he talked.

"Is anything bothering you, Knipe? Anything on your mind?"

"Oh no, Mr. Bohlen. No."

"How would you like to take a week's holiday? Do you good. You've earned it."

"Oh, I don't know, sir."

The older man waited, watching this tall, thin person who stood so sloppily① before him. He was a difficult② boy. Why couldn't he stand up straight? Always drooping③ and untidy, with spots on his jacket, and hair falling all over his face.

"I'd like you to take a holiday, Knipe. You need it."

"All right, sir. If you wish."

"Take a week. Two weeks if you like. Go somewhere warm. Get some sunshine. Swim. Relax. Sleep. Then come back, and we'll have another talk about the future."

Adolph Knipe went home by bus to his two-room apartment. He threw his coat on the sofa, poured himself a drink of whisky, and sat down in front of the typewriter that was on the table. Mr. Bohlen was right. Of course he was right. Except that he didn't know the half of it. He probably thought it was a woman. Whenever a young man gets depressed, everybody thinks it's a woman.

---

① sloppy: *Adjective* (of a garment) casual and loose-fitting; marked by a lack of neatness or order; untidy(衣服)不合身的;肥大的;衣着不整的;邋遢的(e.g. Mother constantly picked at him for being sloppy. 母亲不断地批评他衣着不整。)

② difficult: *Adjective* (of a person) not easy to please or satisfy; awkward(人)难以取悦的;挑剔的;难对付的

③ droop: *Verb* [no obj.] bend or hang downwards limply(松沓沓地)垂下(e.g. A long black cloak drooped from his shoulders. 一件黑色的长斗篷从他肩膀上垂下。)

He leaned forward and began to read through the half-finished sheet of typing still in the machine. It was headed "A Narrow Escape", and it began "The night was dark and stormy, the wind whistled in the trees, the rain poured down like cats and dogs..."

Adolph Knipe took a sip of whisky, tasting the malty① - bitter flavour, feeling the trickle of cold liquid as it travelled down his throat and settled in the top of his stomach, cool at first, then spreading and becoming warm, making a little area of warmness in the gut. To hell with Mr. John Bohlen anyway. And to hell with the great electrical computing machine. To hell with...

At exactly that moment, his eyes and mouth began slowly to open, in a sort of wonder, and slowly he raised his head and became still, absolutely motionless, gazing at the wall opposite with this look that was more perhaps of astonishment than of wonder, but quite fixed now, unmoving, and remaining thus for forty, fifty, sixty seconds. Then gradually (the head still motionless), a subtle change spreading over the face, astonishment becoming pleasure, very slight at first, only around the corners of the mouth, increasing gradually, spreading out until at last the whole face was open wide and shining with extreme delight. It was the first time Adolph Knipe had smiled in many, many months.

"Of course," he said, speaking aloud, "it's completely ridiculous." Again he smiled, raising his upper lip and baring his teeth in a queerly sensual② manner.

---

① malty: *Adjective* containing, or like, malt 麦芽的;有麦芽的 malt: *Noun* [mass noun] barley or other grain that has been steeped, germinated, and dried, used especially for brewing or distilling and vinegar-making 麦芽

② sensual: *Adjective* of or arousing gratification of the senses and physical, especially sexual, pleasure 撩人的;情欲的(e.g. The production of the ballet is sensual and passionate. 那部芭蕾作品又刺激又充满激情。)

"It's a delicious idea, but so impracticable it doesn't really bear thinking about at all."

From then on, Adolph Knipe began to think about nothing else. The idea fascinated him enormously, at first because it gave him a promise—however remote—of revenging himself in a most devilish① manner upon his greatest enemies. From this angle alone, he toyed idly with it for perhaps ten or fifteen minutes; then all at once he found himself examining it quite seriously as a practical possibility. He took paper and made some preliminary notes. But he didn't get far. He found himself, almost immediately, up against the old truth that a machine, however ingenious②, is incapable of original thought. It can handle no problems except those that resolve themselves into③ mathematical terms—problems that contain one, and only one, correct answer.

This was a stumper④. There didn't seem any way around it. A machine cannot have a brain. On the other hand, it can have a memory, can it not? Their own electronic calculator had a marvellous memory. Simply by converting electric pulses, through a column of mercury, into supersonic waves, it could store away at least a thousand numbers at a

① devilish: *Adjective* mischievous and rakish 好恶作剧的;爱惹麻烦的;放荡的(e.g. a wide, devilish grin 龇牙咧嘴地奸笑。)

② ingenious: *Adjective* (of a person) clever, original, and inventive(人)机灵的;有独创性的;具创造力的(e.g. He was ingenious enough to overcome the limited budget. 他足智多谋,足以克服预算有限的困难。)

③ resolve itself/themselves into sth.: If sth. you see or hear at a distance resolves into sth. or resolves itself into sth., you gradually see it or hear it clearly as a particular thing (远处景物、响声等)逐渐呈现为……(e.g. The grey shape resolved into a group of walkers. 灰色的影子慢慢呈现为一群走路的人。)

④ stumper: *Noun* (informal) a puzzling question(非正式)疑难问题

time, extracting[①] any one of them at the precise moment it was needed. Would it not be possible, therefore, on this principle, to build a memory section of almost unlimited size?

Now what about that?

Then suddenly, he was struck by a powerful but simple little truth, and it was this: that English grammar is governed by rules that are almost mathematical in their strictness! Given the words, and given the sense of what is to be said, then there is only one correct order in which those words can be arranged.

No, he thought, that isn't quite accurate. In many sentences there are several alternative positions for words and phrases, all of which may be grammatically correct. But what the hell[②]. The theory itself is basically true. Therefore, it stands to reason[③] that an engine built along the lines of the electric computer could be adjusted to arrange words (instead of numbers) in their right order according to the rules of grammar. Give it the verbs, the nouns, the adjectives, the pronouns, store them in the memory section as a vocabulary, and arrange for them to be extracted as required. Then feed it with plots and leave it to write the sentences.

There was no stopping Knipe now. He went to work immediately, and there followed during the next few days a period of intense labour.

---

① extract: *Verb* obtain (a substance or resource) from something by a special method 提取;提炼(e. g. Lead was extracted from the copper. 铅是从这些铜料中提炼出来的。)

② what the hell: (spoken) It doesn't matter; I don't care(口语)没关系;我不在乎(e. g. "Do you want a cigarette?" "No, thanks, I've given up. Oh, what the hell! Yes, I will have one, after all." "抽烟吗?""不,谢谢,我已经戒了。哦,管它那么多呢,我还是来一支吧。")

③ It stands to reason: It is obvious or logical 合情理;是当然的;自不待言(e. g. It stands to reason that if you can eradicate the fear the nervousness will subside. 如果你根除恐惧心理,紧张感会随之减轻,这是显而易见的事情。)

The living-room became littered with sheets of paper: formulae and calculations; lists of words, thousands and thousands of words; the plots of stories, curiously broken up and subdivided; huge extracts from Roget's[①] Thesaurus; pages filled with the first names of men and women; hundreds of surnames taken from the telephone directory; intricate drawings of wires and circuits and switches and thermionic valves[②]; drawings of machines that could punch holes of different shapes in little cards, and of a strange electric typewriter that could type ten thousand words a minute. Also a kind of control panel with a series of small push-buttons, each one labelled with the name of a famous American magazine.

He was working in a mood of exultation[③], prowling[④] around the room amidst this littering of paper, rubbing his hands together, talking out loud to himself; and sometimes, with a sly curl of the nose he would

---

① Peter Mark Roget (1779—1869), English scholar. He worked as a physician but is remembered as the compiler of Roget's Thesaurus of English Words and Phrases, first published in 1852 彼得·马克·罗热(1779—1869):英国学者,以医生为职业,但是以编《罗热英语单词和短语汇编》(1852 年首次出版)而为世人记住。

② thermionic valve or thermionic tube: *Noun* (Electronics) a device giving a flow of thermionic electrons in one direction, used especially in the rectification of a current and in radio reception(电子)热离子管;热阴极电子管

③ exultation: *Noun* the act or condition of rejoicing greatly 狂喜;非常得意

④ prowl: *Verb* (of a person or animal) move stealthily or restlessly as or like a hunter(人或动物)(偷偷而又不安地)徘徊(e.g. David had been prowling about in the garden, waiting for her car. 戴维一直在花园里徘徊,等着她的车出现。)

mutter a series of murderous[1] imprecations[2] in which the word "editor" seemed always to be present. On the fifteenth day of continuous work, he collected the papers into two large folders which he carried—almost at a run—to the offices of John Bohlen Inc., electrical engineers.

Mr. Bohlen was pleased to see him back.

"Well Knipe, good gracious me, you look a hundred per cent better. You have a good holiday? Where'd you go?"

He's just as ugly and untidy as ever, Mr. Bohlen thought. Why doesn't he stand up straight? He looks like a bent stick. "You look a hundred per cent better, my boy." I wonder what he's grinning about. Every time I see him, his ears seem to have got larger.

Adolph Knipe placed the folders on the desk. "Look, Mr. Bohlen!" he cried. "Look at these!"

Then he poured out his story. He opened the folders and pushed the plans in front of the astonished little man. He talked for over an hour, explaining everything, and when he had finished, he stepped back, breathless, flushed, waiting for the verdict.

"You know what I think, Knipe? I think you're nuts[3]." Careful now, Mr. Bohlen told himself. Treat him carefully. He's valuable, this one is. If only he didn't look so awful, with that long horse face and the

---

① murderous: *Adjective* (informal) (of a person or their expression) extremely angry(非正式)(人或表情)大怒的;怒极的(e. g. Mary emerged from the changing room, looking murderous. 玛丽满面怒容地从更衣室里出来。)

② imprecation: *Noun* (formal) a spoken curse(正式)咒骂(e. g. She hurled her imprecations at anyone who might be listening. 她对每个可能在听的人都骂骂咧咧。)

③ nuts: *Adjective* (informal) mad(非正式)疯狂的(e. g. The way he turns on the television as soon as he walks in drives me nuts. 他那种一走进房间就打开电视机的习惯让我发疯。)

big teeth. The fellow had ears as big as rhubarb① leaves.

"But Mr. Bohlen! It'll work! I've proved to you it'll work! You can't deny that!"

"Take it easy now, Knipe. Take it easy, and listen to me."

Adolph Knipe watched his man, disliking him more every second.

"This idea," Mr. Bohlen's lower lip was saying, "is very ingenious—I might almost say brilliant—and it only goes to confirm my opinion of your abilities, Knipe. But don't take it too seriously. After all, my boy, what possible use can it be to us? Who on earth wants a machine for writing stories? And where's the money in it, anyway? Just tell me that."

"May I sit down, sir?"

"Sure, take a seat."

Adolph Knipe seated himself on the edge of a chair. The older man watched him with alert brown eyes, wondering what was coming now.

"I would like to explain something Mr. Bohlen, if I may, about how I came to do all this."

"Go right ahead, Knipe." He would have to be humoured② a little now, Mr. Bohlen told himself. The boy was really valuable—a sort of genius, almost—worth his weight in gold③ to the firm. Just look at these

---

① rhubarb: *Noun* [mass noun] the thick leaf stalks of a cultivated plant of the dock family, which are reddish or green and eaten as a fruit after cooking 大黄叶柄

② humour or humor: *Verb* [with obj.] comply with the wishes of (someone) in order to keep them content, however unreasonable such wishes might be 纵容;迁就,迎合(e. g. She was always humouring him to prevent trouble. 她总是迁就他以防止麻烦。)

③ be worth one's weight in gold: (of a person) exceedingly useful or helpful (人)极其有用(或有帮助)的

papers here. Darndest① thing you ever saw. Astonishing piece of work. Quite useless, of course. No commercial value. But it proved again the boy's ability.

"It's a sort of confession, I suppose, Mr. Bohlen. I think it explains why I've always been so... so kind of worried."

"You tell me anything you want, Knipe. I'm here to help you—you know that."

The young man clasped his hands together tight on his lap, hugging himself with his elbows. It seemed as though suddenly he was feeling very cold.

"You see, Mr. Bohlen, to tell the honest truth, I don't really care much for my work here. I know I'm good at it and all that sort of thing, but my heart's not in it. It's not what I want to do most."

Up went Mr. Bohlen's eyebrows, quick like a spring. His whole body became very still.

"You see, sir, all my life I've wanted to be a writer."

"A writer!"

"Yes, Mr. Bohlen. You may not believe it, but every bit of spare time I've had, I've spent writing stories. In the last ten years I've written hundreds, literally hundreds of short stories. Five hundred and sixty-six, to be precise. Approximately one a week."

"Good heavens, man! What on earth did you do that for?"

"All I know, sir, is I have the urge."

"What sort of urge?"

"The creative urge, Mr. Bohlen." Every time he looked up he saw Mr. Bohlen's lips. They were growing thinner and thinner, more and more purple.

---

① darnedest or darndest: *Noun & Adjective* the most possible; (a euphemistic word for damnedest) most amazing or extraordinary 最后可能的事;极其令人吃惊的;非同一般的

"And may I ask you what you do with these stories, Knipe?"

"Well sir, that's the trouble. No one will buy them. Each time I finish one, I send it out on the rounds. It goes to one magazine after another. That's all that happens, Mr. Bohlen, and they simply send them back. It's very depressing."

Mr. Bohlen relaxed. "I can see quite well how you feel, my boy." His voice was dripping with sympathy. "We all go through it one time or another in our lives. But now—now that you've had proof—positive proof—from the experts themselves, from the editors, that your stories are—what shall I say—rather unsuccessful, it's time to leave off[①]. Forget it, my boy. Just forget all about it."

"No, Mr. Bohlen! No! That's not true! I know my stories are good. My heavens, when you compare them with the stuff some of those magazines print—oh my word, Mr. Bohlen! —the sloppy[②], boring stuff that you see in the magazines week after week—why, it drives me mad!"

"Now wait a minute, my boy..."

"Do you ever read the magazines, Mr. Bohlen?"

"You'll pardon me, Knipe, but what's all this got to do with your machine?"

"Everything, Mr. Bohlen, absolutely everything! What I want to tell you is, I've made a study of magazines, and it seems that each one tends to have its own particular type of story. The writers—the successful ones—know this, and they write accordingly."

"Just a minute, my boy. Calm yourself down, will you. I don't

---

① leave off: stop doing or using sth. 停止做某事;不再使用(e. g. The rain left off at daybreak. 破晓时雨停了。)

② sloppy: *Adjective* (of literature or behaviour) weakly or foolishly sentimental(文学或行为)感情脆弱的;无聊伤感的(e. g. lovers of sloppy romance 喜欢伤感浪漫故事的人)

think all this is getting us anywhere."

"Please, Mr. Bohlen, hear me through. It's all terribly important." He paused, to catch his breath. He was properly worked up now, throwing his hands around as he talked. The long, toothy face, with the big ears on either side, simply shone with enthusiasm, and there was an excess of saliva① in his mouth which caused him to speak his words wet. "So you see, on my machine, by having an adjustable co-ordinator between the 'plot-memory' section and the 'word-memory' section I am able to produce any type of story I desire simply by pressing the required button."

"Yes, I know, Knipe, I know. This is all very interesting, but what's the point of it?"

"Just this, Mr. Bohlen. The market is limited. We've got to be able to produce the right stuff, at the right time, whenever we want it. It's a matter of business, that's all. I'm looking at it from your point of view now—as a commercial proposition."

"My dear boy, it can't possibly be a commercial proposition ever. You know as well as I do what it costs to build one of these machines."

"Yes sir, I do. But with due respect②, I don't believe you know what the magazines pay writers for stories."

"What do they pay?"

"Anything up to twenty-five hundred dollars. It probably averages arounda thousand."

Mr. Bohlen jumped.

---

① saliva: *Noun* [mass noun] watery liquid secreted into the mouth by glands, providing lubrication for chewing and swallowing, and aiding digestion 唾液;涎

② with due respect or with all due respect: used as a polite formula preceding, and intended to mitigate the effect of, an expression of disagreement or criticism 尽管(对您)尊敬之至(用于表示异议或批评的话之前)(e. g. With all due respect, Father, I think you've got to be more broad-minded these days. 恕我直言,父亲,我认为这些日子您必须心胸更开阔些。)

"Yes sir, it's true."

"Absolutely impossible, Knipe! Ridiculous!"

"No sir, it's true."

"You mean to sit there and tell me that these magazines pay out money like that to a man for... just for scribbling off a story! Good heavens, Knipe! Whatever next①! Writers must all be millionaires!"

"That's exactly it, Mr. Bohlen! That's where the machine comes in. Listen a minute, sir, while I tell you some more. I've got it all worked out. The big magazines are carrying approximately three fiction stories in each issue. Now, take the fifteen most important magazines—the ones paying the most money. A few of them are monthlies, but most of them come out every week. All right. That makes, let us say, around forty big stories being bought each week. That's forty thousand dollars. So with our machine—when we get it working properly—we can collar② nearly the whole of this market!"

"My dear boy, you're mad!"

"No sir, honestly, it's true what I say. Don't you see that with volume alone we'll completely overwhelm them! This machine can produce a five-thousand word story, all typed and ready for despatch③, in thirty seconds. How can the writers compete with that? I ask you, Mr. Bohlen, how?"

At that point, Adolph Knipe noticed a slight change in the man's

① what next or whatever next: an expression of surprise or amazement(用以表示惊讶或惊奇)下一步怎么样;还会有何等的荒唐事

② collar: *Verb* [with obj.] (informal) seize, grasp, or apprehend (someone)(非正式)抓住;逮捕(e.g. Police collared the culprit. 警察逮捕了犯人。)

③ despatch: *Verb & Noun* variant spelling of dispatch "dispatch"的变体拼写形式 dispatch: *Noun* [mass noun] the sending of someone or something to a destination or for a purpose 派遣;发送(e.g. A resolution authorizing the dispatch of a peacekeeping force. 批准派遣维和部队的一项决议。)

expression, an extra brightness in the eyes, the nostrils distending①, the whole face becoming still, almost rigid. Quickly, he continued. "Nowadays, Mr. Bohlen, the handmade article hasn't a hope. It can't possibly compete with mass-production, especially in this country you know that. Carpets... chairs... shoes... bricks... crockery②... anything you like to mention they're all made by machinery now. The quality may be inferior, but that doesn't matter. It's the cost of production that counts. And stories—well—they're just another product, like carpets and chairs, and no one cares how you produce them so long as you deliver the goods. We'll sell them wholesale, Mr. Bohlen! We'll undercut③ every writer in the country! We'll corner④ the market!"

Mr. Bohlen edged up straighter in his chair. He was leaning forward now, both elbows on the desk, the face alert, the small brown eyes resting on the speaker.

"I still think it's impracticable, Knipe."

"Forty thousand a week!" cried Adolph Knipe. "And if we halve the price, making it twenty thousand a week, that's still a million a year!" And softly he added, "You didn't get any million a year for building the old electronic calculator, did you, Mr. Bohlen?"

---

① distend: *Verb* [no obj.] swell out because of pressure from inside 膨胀(e.g. The abdomen distended rapidly. 腹部迅速鼓起。)

② crockery: *Noun* [mass noun] plates, dishes, cups, and other similar items, especially ones made of earthenware or china 陶器;瓦器;瓷器

③ undercut: *Verb* [with obj.] offer goods or services at a lower price than (a competitor) 低于(对手)价格出售(商品或服务)(e.g. These industries have been undercut by more efficient foreign producers. 这些工业遇上更有效率的外国厂商的低价销售。)

④ corner: *Verb* control (a market) by dominating the supply of a particular commodity 垄断;囤积(e.g. Whether they will corner the market in graphics software remains to be seen. 还不清楚他们是否要垄断制图软件市场。)

"But seriously now, Knipe. D'you really think they'd buy them?"

"Listen, Mr. Bohlen. Who on earth is going to want custom-made stories when they can get the other kind at half the price? It stands to reason, doesn't it?"

"And how will you sell them? Who will you say has written them?"

"We'll set up our own literary agency, and we'll distribute them through that. And we'll invent all the names we want for the writers."

"I don't like it, Knipe. To me, that smacks of trickery①, does it not?"

"And another thing, Mr. Bohlen. There's all manner of valuable by-products once you've got started. Take advertising, for example. Beer manufacturers and people like that are willing to pay good money these days if famous writers will lend their names to their products②. Why, my heavens, Mr. Bohlen! This isn't any children's plaything we're talking about. It's big business."

"Don't get too ambitious, my boy."

"And another thing. There isn't any reason why we shouldn't put your name, Mr. Bohlen, on some of the better stories, if you wished it."

"My goodness, Knipe. What should I want that for?"

"I don't know, sir, except that some writers get to be very much

---

① smack of sth.: to seem to contain an unpleasant attitude or quality 有(否定的)态度;带有(消极的)意味(e.g. His comments smack of racism. 他的评论带有种族主义的味道。)

② lend your name to sth: (formal) let it be known in public that you support or agree with sth. (正式)以你的名义表示支持;公开支持(e.g. Famous actors sometimes lend their names to political causes. 有些著名演员有时会公开支持一些政治活动。)

respected—like Mr. Erle Gardner① or Kathleen Morris, for example. We've got to have names, and I was certainly thinking of using my own on one or two stories, just to help out."

"A writer, eh②?" Mr. Bohlen said, musing. "Well, it would surely surprise them over at the club when they saw my name in the magazines—the good magazines."

"That's right, Mr. Bohlen!"

For a moment, a dreamy, faraway look came into Mr. Bohlen's eyes, and he smiled. Then he stirred himself and began leafing through the plans that lay before him.

"One thing I don't quite understand, Knipe. Where do the plots come from? The machine can't possibly invent plots."

"We feed those in, sir. That's no problem at all. Everyone has plots. There's three or four hundred of them written down in that folder there on your left. Feed them straight into the 'plot-memory' section of the machine."

"Go on."

"There are many other little refinements③ too, Mr. Bohlen. You'll see them all when you study the plans carefully. For example, there's a

---

① Erle Stanley Gardner (1899—1970), American novelist and short-story writer. He practised as a defence lawyer before writing his novels featuring the lawyer-detective Perry Mason 埃勒·斯坦利·加德纳(1899—1970):美国小说家和短篇小说作家,曾任辩护律师,后写出以律师兼侦探佩里·梅森为中心人物的一些小说。

② eh: Exclamation used to represent a sound made in speech in a variety of situations, in particular to ask for something to be repeated or explained or to elicit agreement(尤用于要求重复、解释某事或征求同意等情境)啊;嗯;什么;是吗;好吗(e.g. "Eh? What's this?""嗯? 这是什么?")

③ refinement: *Noun* a detail or device added to improve something 细微的改良(e.g. All programs have bugs and need endless refinement. 所有的程序都有漏洞,都需要不断改进。)

trick that nearly every writer uses, of inserting at least one long, obscure word into each story. This makes the reader think that the man is very wise and clever. So I have the machine do the same thing. There'll be a whole stack of long words stored away just for this purpose."

"Where?"

"In the 'word-memory' section," he said, epexegetically①.

Through most of that day the two men discussed the possibilities of the new engine. In the end, Mr. Bohlen said he would have to think about it some more. The next morning, he was quietly enthusiastic. Within a week, he was completely sold on② the idea.

"What we'll have to do, Knipe, is to say that we're merely building another mathematical calculator, but of a new type. That'll keep the secret."

"Exactly, Mr. Bohlen."

And in six months the machine was completed. It was housed in a separate brick building at the back of the premises, and now that it was ready for action, no one was allowed near it excepting Mr. Bohlen and Adolph Knipe.

It was an exciting moment when the two men—the one, short, plump, breviped③—the other tall, thin and toothy—stood in the corridor before the control panel and got ready to run off the first story. All around them were walls dividing up into many small corridors, and the walls were covered with wiring and plugs and switches and huge glass valves. They were both nervous, Mr. Bohlen hopping from one foot to the other,

---

① epexegetical: *Adjective* of, serving as, or like an epexegesis 解释性;补充性 epexegesis: *Noun* [mass noun] the addition of words to clarify meaning 增词

② be sold on sth.: (informal) to be convinced that sth. is very good(非正式)相信……很好(e.g. I could see she was sold on the idea. 我看得出她非常赞同这个主意。)

③ breviped: *Adjective* having short legs 有矮脚的

quite unable to keep still. "Which button?" Adolph Knipe asked, eyeing a row of small white discs that resembled the keys of a typewriter. "You choose, Mr. Bohlen. Lots of magazines to pick from—Saturday Evening Post, Collier's, Ladies' Home Journal—any one you like."

"Goodness me, boy! How do I know?" He was jumping up and down like a man with hives①.

"Mr. Bohlen," Adolph Knipe said gravely, "do you realize that at this moment, with your little finger alone, you have it in your power to become the most versatile writer on this continent?"

"Listen Knipe, just get on with it, will you please—and cut out the preliminaries②."

"Okay, Mr. Bohlen. Then we'll make it... let me see—this one. How's that?" He extended one finger and pressed down a button with the name TODAY'S WOMAN printed across it in diminutive③ black type. There was a sharp click, and when he took his finger away, the button remained down, below the level of the others.

"So much for the selection," he said. "Now—here we go!" He reached up and pulled a switch on the panel. Immediately, the room was filled with a loud humming noise, and a crackling of electric sparks, and the jingle of many, tiny, quickly-moving levers; and almost in the same

① hives: *Plural Noun* (treated as sing. or pl.) another term for urticaria(单复数相同)荨麻疹

② preliminary: *Noun* (preliminaries) business or talk, especially of a formulaic or polite nature, taking place before an action or event(尤指程序性或礼节性的)预备性事务(或对话)(e.g. She began speaking, without preliminaries. 她开始说了,没有任何客套话。)

③ diminutive: *Adjective* extremely or unusually small 极小的;非常小的(e.g. A diminutive figure dressed in black. 身着黑衣的微小身影。)

instant, sheets of quarto[①] paper began sliding out from a slot to the right of the control panel and dropping into a basket below. They came out quick, one sheet a second, and in less than half a minute it was all over. The sheets stopped coming.

"That's it!" Adolph Knipe cried. "There's your story!"

They grabbed the sheets and began to read. The first one they picked up started as follows: "Aifkjmbsaoegweztpplnvoqudskigt&, - fuhpekanvbertyuiolkjhgfdsazxcvbnm, peruitrehdjkg mvnb, wmsuy..." They looked at the others. The style was roughly similar in all of them. Mr. Bohlen began to shout. The younger man tried to calm him down.

"It's all right, sir. Really it is. It only needs a little adjustment. We've got a connection wrong somewhere, that's all. You must remember, Mr. Bohlen, there's over a million feet of wiring in this room. You can't expect everything to be right first time."

"It'll never work," Mr. Bohlen said.

"Be patient, sir. Be patient."

Adolph Knipe set out to discover the fault, and in four days' time he announced that all was ready for the next try.

"It'll never work," Mr. Bohlen said. "I know it'll never work."

Knipe smiled and pressed the selector button marked Reader's Digest. Then he pulled the switch, and again the strange, exciting, humming sound filled the room. One page of typescript[②] flew out of the slot into the basket.

"Where's the rest?" Mr. Bohlen cried. "It's Stopped! It's gone wrong!"

"No sir, it hasn't. It's exactly right. It's for the Digest, don't

---

① quarto: *Noun* [mass noun] (Printing) a size of book page resulting from folding each printed sheet into four leaves (eight pages)(印刷)四开

② typescript: *Noun* a typed copy of a text 打字稿

you see?" This time it began. "Fewpeople yet know that are volution ary new cure hasbeen discovered which may well bring per manent relieftosuf ferersof them ostdreaded diseaseo fourtime. . ." And so on.

"It's gibberish①!" Mr. Bohlen shouted.

"No sir, it's fine. Can't you see? It's simply that she's not breaking up the words. That's an easy adjustment. But the story's there. Look, Mr. Bohlen, look! It's all there except that the words are joined together."

And indeed it was.

On the next try a few days later, everything was perfect, even the punctuation. The first story they ran off, for a famous women's magazine, was a solid, plotty② story of a boy who wanted to better himself with his rich employer. This boy arranged, so that story went, for a friend to hold up the rich man's daughter on a dark night when she was driving home. Then the boy himself, happening by, knocked the gun out of his friend's hand and rescued the girl. The girl was grateful. But the father was suspicious. He questioned the boy sharply. The boy broke down and confessed. Then the father, instead of kicking him out of the house, said that he admired the boy's resourcefulness③. The girl admired his honesty—and his looks. The father promised him to be head of the Accounts Department. The girl married him.

"It's tremendous, Mr. Bohlen! It's exactly right!"

"Seems a bit sloppy to me, my boy!"

---

① gibberish: *Noun* [mass noun] unintelligible or meaningless speech or writing; nonsense 令人费解(或毫无意义)的话(或文字);胡言乱语(e. g. He talks gibberish. 他满口莫名其妙的话。)

② plotty: *Adjective* (informal) (of a novel, play, or film) having an excessively elaborate or complicated plot(非正式)(小说、戏剧、电影)情节复杂的

③ resourceful: *Adjective* having the ability to find quick and clever ways to overcome difficulties 善于随机应变的;足智多谋的

"No sir, it's a seller, a real seller!"

In his excitement, Adolph Knipe promptly ran off① six more stories in as many minutes. All of them—except one, which for some reason came out a trifle lewd②—seemed entirely satisfactory.

Mr. Bohlen was now mollified. He agreed to set up a literary agency in an office downtown, and to put Knipe in charge. In a couple of weeks, this was accomplished. Then Knipe mailed out the first dozen stories. He put his own name to four of them, Mr. Bohlen's to one, and for the others he simply invented names.

Five of these stories were promptly accepted. The one with Mr. Bohlen's name on it was turned down with a letter from the fiction editor saying, "This is a skilful job, but in our opinion it doesn't quite come off. We would like to see more of this writer's work..." Adolph Knipe took a cab out to the factory and ran off another story for the same magazine. He again put Mr. Bohlen's name to it, and mailed it immediately. That one they bought.

The money started pouring in. Knipe slowly and carefully stepped up the output, and in six months' time he was delivering thirty stories a week, and selling about half.

He began to make a name for himself in literary circles as a prolific and successful writer. So did Mr. Bohlen; but not quite such a good name, although he didn't know it. At the same time, Knipe was building up a dozen or more fictitious persons as promising young authors. Everything was going fine.

---

① run something off: reproduce copies of a piece of writing on a machine 印出;复印出

② lewd: *Adjective* crude and offensive in a sexual way 淫荡的;猥亵的(e. g. She began to gyrate to the music and sing a lewd song. 她开始随着音乐旋转,并唱起下流的歌。)

At this point it was decided to adapt the machine for writing novels as well as stories. Mr. Bohlen, thirsting now for greater honours in the literary world, insisted that Knipe go to work at once on this prodigious① task.

"I want to do a novel," he kept saying. "I want to do a novel."

"And so you will, sir. And so you will. But please be patient. This is a very complicated adjustment I have to make."

"Everyone tells me I ought to do a novel," Mr. Bohlen cried. "All sorts of publishers are chasing after me day and night begging me to stop fooling around with stories and do something really important instead. A novel's the only thing that counts—that's what they say."

"We're going to do novels," Knipe told him. "Just as many as we want. But please be patient."

"Now listen to me, Knipe. What I'm going to do is a serious novel, something that'll make 'em② sit up and take notice. I've been getting rather tired of the sort of stories you've been putting my name to lately. As a matter of fact, I'm none too③ sure you haven't been trying to make a monkey out of me."

"A monkey, Mr. Bohlen?"

"Keeping all the best ones for yourself, that's what you've been doing."

"Oh no, Mr. Bohlen! No!"

"So this time I'm going to make damn sure I write a high class intelligent book. You understand that."

---

① prodigious: *Adjective* remarkably or impressively great in extent, size, or degree(范围、规模、程度)巨大的;庞大的(e. g. The stove consumed a prodigious amount of fuel. 这种炉子消耗大量燃料。)

② 'em = them

③ none too...: far from; not very 完全不;一点也不(e. g. Her sight's none too good. 她的视力一点也不好。)

"Look, Mr. Bohlen. With the sort of switchboard I'm rigging up①, you'll be able to write any sort of book you want." And this was true, for within another couple of months, the genius of Adolph Knipe had not only adapted the machine for novel writing, but had constructed a marvellous new control system which enabled the author to pre-select literally any type of plot and any style of writing he desired. There were so many dials and levers on the thing, it looked like the instrument panel of some enormous aeroplane.

First, by depressing one of a series of master buttons, the writer made his primary decision; historical, satirical, philosophical, political, romantic, erotic, humorous, or straight②. Then, from the second row (the basic buttons), he chose his theme: army life, pioneer days, civil war, world war, racial problem, wild west, country life, childhood memories, seafaring, the sea bottom and many, many more. The third row of

---

① rig up: *Verb* set up (equipment or a device or structure), typically hastily or as a makeshift(尤指匆匆或临时)搭起(设备、装置或结构)(e.g. He had rigged up a sort of tent. 他简单搭了个帐篷。)

② straight: *Adjective* (especially of drama) serious as opposed to comic or musical; employing the conventional techniques of its art form(尤指戏剧，与喜剧和音乐剧相对)严肃的;(艺术形式)用传统方法的(e.g. a straight play 一部严肃的戏剧)。

buttons gave a choice of literary style: classical, whimsical①, racy②, Hemingway③, Faulkner④, Joyce⑤, feminine, etc. The fourth row was for characters, the fifth for wordage—and so on and so on—ten long rows

① whimsical: *Adjective* playfully quaint or fanciful, especially in an appealing and amusing way 异想天开的;想入非非的;离奇的;古怪的(e.g. a whimsical sense of humour 离奇的幽默感)

② racy: *Adjective* (of speech, writing, or behaviour) lively, entertaining, and typically mildly sexually titillating(言谈、著述、举止)生动的;栩栩如生的;有趣的;泼辣的(尤指略带猥亵的)(e.g. The novel was considered rather racy at the time. 当时认为这部小说相当刺激。)

③ Ernest Hemingway (1899—1961), American novelist, short-story writer, and journalist. He achieved success with The Sun also Rises (1926), which reflected the disillusionment of the post-war 'lost generation'. Other notable works: A Farewell to Arms (1929), For Whom the Bell Tolls (1940), and The Old Man and the Sea (1952, Pulitzer Prize 1953). Nobel Prize for Literature (1954) 欧内斯特·海明威(1899—1961):美国长短篇小说家、记者,他因《太阳照样升起》(1926)而获成功,这本书反映了战后"迷惘的一代"的幻想破灭。其他著名作品包括:《永别了,武器》(1929)、《丧钟为谁而鸣》(1940)以及获1953年普利策奖的《老人与海》(1952)。1954年,海明威获诺贝尔文学奖。

④ William Faulkner (1897—1962), American novelist. His works deal with the history and legends of the American South and have a strong sense of a society in decline. Notable works: The Sound and the Fury (1929), As I Lay Dying (1930), and Absalom! Absalom! (1936). Nobel Prize for Literature (1949) 威廉·福克纳(1897—1962):美国小说家,其作品讲述美国南方的历史和传奇,表现出强烈的世风日下之感;代表作品:《喧嚣与骚动》(1929)、《在我弥留之际》(1930)和《押沙龙,押沙龙!》(1936);1949年,福克纳获诺贝尔文学奖。

⑤ James Joyce (1882—1941), Irish writer. One of the most important writers of the modernist movement, he made his name with Dubliners (short stories, 1914). His novel Ulysses (1922) revolutionized the structure of the modern novel and developed the stream-of-consciousness technique. Other notable novels: A Portrait of the Artist as a Young Man (1914—1915) and Finnegans Wake (1939) 詹姆斯·乔伊斯(1882—1941):爱尔兰作家。现代主义运动最重要的作家之一,1914年的短篇小说集《都柏林人》使他一举成名,小说《尤利西斯》(1922)使现代小说结构产生了巨大的变革并发展了意识流创作技巧;其他代表作品:《青年艺术家肖像》(1914—1915)和《芬尼根的苏醒》(1939)。

of pre-selector buttons.

But that wasn't all. Control had also to be exercised during the actual writing process (which took about fifteen minutes per novel), and to do this the author had to sit, as it were, in the driver's seat, and pull (or push) a battery of labelled stops, as on an organ. By so doing, he was able continually to modulate or merge fifty different and variable qualities such as tension, surprise, humour, pathos①, and mystery. Numerous dials and gauges on the dashboard itself told him throughout exactly how far along he was with his work.

Finally, there was the question of "passion". From a careful study of the books at the top of the best-seller lists for the past year, Adolph Knipe had decided that this was the most important ingredient of all—a magical catalyst that somehow or other could transform the dullest novel into a howling② success at any rate financially. But Knipe also knew that passion was powerful, heady stuff, and must be prudently dispensed③—the right proportions at the right moments; and to ensure this, he had devised an independent control consisting of two sensitive sliding adjustors operated by foot-pedals, similar to the throttle and brake in a car. One pedal governed the percentage of passion to be injected, the other regulated its intensity. There was no doubt, of course and this was the only drawback—that the writing of a novel by the Knipe methods was going to be rather like flying a plane and driving a car and playing an organ all at

---

① pathos: *Noun* [mass noun] a quality that evokes pity or sadness 激起怜悯(或同情的)因素;伤感力(e. g. The actor injects his customary humour and pathos into the role. 这个演员把他惯常的幽默和哀婉感染力融入这个角色之中。)

② howling: *Adjective* (informal) extreme; great(非正式)极大的;极度的(e. g. The meal was a howling success. 这顿饭非常成功。)

③ dispense: *Verb* [with obj.] distribute or provide (a service or information) to a number of people 分发;提供(服务、信息)(e. g. Orderlies went round dispensing drinks. 勤务兵四处分发饮料。)

the same time, but this did not trouble the inventor. When all was ready, he proudly escorted Mr. Bohlen into the machine house and began to explain the operating procedure for the new wonder.

"Good God, Knipe! I'll never be able to do all that! Dammit① man, it'd be easier to write the thing by hand!"

"You'll soon get used to it, Mr. Bohlen, I promise you. In a week or two, you'll be doing it without hardly thinking. It's just like learning to drive."

Well, it wasn't quite as easy as that, but after many hours of practice, Mr. Bohlen began to get the hang of it, and finally, late one evening, he told Knipe to make ready for running off the first novel. It was a tense moment, with the fat little man crouching nervously in the driver's seat, and the tall toothy Knipe fussing excitedly around him.

"I intend to write an important novel, Knipe."

"I'm sure you will, sir. I'm sure you will."

With one finger, Mr. Bohlen carefully pressed the necessary pre-selector buttons:

Master button—satirical

Subject—racial problem

Style—classical

Characters—six men, four women, one infant

Length—fifteen chapters.

At the same time he had his eye particularly upon three organ stops marked power, mystery, profundity.

"Are you ready, sir?"

"Yes, yes, I'm ready."

Knipe pulled the switch. The great engine hummed. There was a

---

① dammit: Interjection used to express anger and frustration 该死的

deep whirring① sound from the oiled movement of fifty thousand cogs② and rods and levers; then came the drumming of the rapid electrical typewriter, setting up a shrill, almost intolerable clatter. Out into the basket flew the typewritten pages—one every two seconds. But what with the noise and the excitement and having to play upon the stops, and watch the chapter-counter and the pace-indicator and the passion-gauge, Mr. Bohlen began to panic. He reacted in precisely the way a learner driver does in a car—by pressing both feet hard down on the pedals and keeping them there until the thing stopped.

"Congratulations on your first novel," Knipe said, picking up the great bundle of typed pages from the basket.

Little pearls of sweat were oozing out all over Mr. Bohlen's face. "It sure was hard work, my boy."

"But you got it done, sir. You got it done."

"Let me see it, Knipe. How does it read?"

He started to go through the first chapter, passing each finished page to the younger man.

"Good heavens, Knipe! What's this!" Mr. Bohlen's thin purple fish-lip was moving slightly as it mouthed the words, his cheeks were beginning slowly to inflate③.

---

① whirr or whir: *Verb* [no obj.] (especially of a machine or a bird's wings) make a low, continuous, regular sound(尤指机器或鸟翅)发出呼呼(或嗡嗡)声;呼呼(或嗡嗡)地响(e.g. The ceiling fans whirred in the smoky air. 吊扇在烟雾弥漫的空气中呼呼地转。)

② cog: *Noun* a wheel or bar with a series of projections on its edge, which transfers motion by engaging with projections on another wheel or bar 齿轮;嵌齿轮

③ inflate: *Verb* [usu. with obj.] fill (a balloon, tyre, or other expandable structure) with air or gas so that it becomes distended; [no obj.] become distended in this way 给(气球、轮胎等可扩张物)充气;膨胀;胀大

"But look here, Knipe! This is outrageous[①]!"

"I must say it's a bit fruity[②], sir."

"Fruity! It's perfectly revolting! I can't possibly put my name to this!"

"Quite right, sir. Quite right!"

"Knipe! Is this some nasty trick you've been playing on me?"

"Oh no, sir! No!"

"It certainly looks like it."

"You don't think, Mr. Bohlen, that you mightn't have been pressing a little hard on the passion-control pedals, do you?"

"My dear boy, how should I know."

"Why don't you try another?"

So Mr. Bohlen ran off a second novel, and this time it went according to plan.

Within a week, the manuscript had been read and accepted by an enthusiastic publisher. Knipe followed with one in his own name, then made a dozen more for good measure[③]. In no time at all, Adolph Knipe's Literary Agency had become famous for its large stable[④] of promising young novelists. And once again the money started rolling in.

---

① outrageous: *Adjective* shockingly bad or excessive 丑恶的;肆无忌惮的;毫无节制的;难以容忍的(e.g. an outrageous act of bribery 肆无忌惮的贿赂行为)

② fruity: *Adjective* (Brit. informal) sexually suggestive in content or style(非正式英国英语表达)(内容或风格上)挑逗性的;挑动春情的

③ for good measure: in addition to what has already been done, said, or given 另外;额外(e.g. He added a couple of chillies for good measure. 他额外加了几个辣椒。)

④ stable: *Noun* an organization or establishment providing the same background or training for its members(为其成员提供相同背景或训练的)组织;机构(e.g. The player comes from the same stable as Agassi. 这个运动员与阿加西来自同一个训练机构。)

It was at this stage that young Knipe began to display a real talent for big business.

"See here, Mr. Bohlen," he said. "We still got too much competition. Why don't we just absorb all the other writers in the country?"

Mr. Bohlen, who now sported a bottle-green velvet jacket and allowed his hair to cover two-thirds of his ears, was quite content with things the way they were. "Don't know what you mean, my boy. You can't just absorb writers."

"Of course you can, sir. Exactly like Rockefeller① did with his oil companies. Simply buy 'em out, and if they won't sell, squeeze 'em out. It's easy!"

"Careful now, Knipe. Be careful."

"I've got a list here sir, of fifty of the most successful writers in the country, and what I intend to do is offer each one of them a lifetime contract with pay. All they have to do is undertake never to write another word; and, of course, to let us use their names on our own stuff. How about that."

"They'll never agree."

"You don't know writers, Mr. Bohlen. You watch and see."

"What about the creative urge, Knipe?"

① John D. Rockefeller (1839—1937), American industrialist and philanthropist; full name John Davison Rockefeller. By 1880 he exercised a virtual monopoly over oil refining in the US. Both he and his son, John D. Rockefeller Jr. (1874—1960), established many philanthropic institutions. 约翰·D·洛克菲勒(1839—1937):美国实业家和慈善家,全名约翰·戴维森·洛克菲勒,到1880年时他几乎垄断美国整个炼油业;他和他的儿子小约翰·D·洛克菲勒(1874—1960)建立了许多慈善机构。

"It's bunk[1]! All they're really interested in is the money—just like everybody else."

In the end, Mr. Bohlen reluctantly agreed to give it a try, and Knipe, with his list of writers in his pocket, went off in a large chauffeur-driven Cadillac[2] to make his calls.

He journeyed first to the man at the top of the list, a very great and wonderful writer, and he had no trouble getting into the house. He told his story and produced a suitcase full of sample novels, and a contract for the man to sign which guaranteed him so much a year for life. The man listened politely, decided he was dealing with a lunatic, gave him a drink, then firmly showed him to the door.

The second writer on the list, when he saw Knipe was serious, actually attacked him with a large metal paper-weight[3], and the inventor had to flee down the garden followed by such a torrent of abuse and obscenity[4] as he had never heard before.

But it took more than this to discourage Adolph Knipe. He was disappointed but not dismayed, and off he went in his big car to seek his next client. This one was a female, famous and popular, whose fat romantic books sold by the million across the country. She received Knipe graciously, gave him tea, and listened attentively to his story.

---

① bunk: *Noun* [mass noun] (informal) nonsense(非正式)废话;胡说(e.g. Anyone with a brain cell would never believe such bunk. 有点头脑的人都不会相信这些胡说八道。)

② Cadillac:一个著名汽车的品牌,通常译作"凯迪拉克",也有人译作"卡迪拉克"。本书采用的是前一个翻译。

③ paper-weight or paperweight: *Noun* a small, heavy object for keeping loose papers in place 镇纸;压纸器

④ obscenity: *Noun* [count noun] an extremely offensive word or expression 污言秽语(e.g. The men scowled and muttered obscenities. 那些人满面怒容,嘴里咕哝着污言秽语。)

"It all sounds very fascinating," she said. "But of course I find it a little hard to believe."

"Madam," Knipe answered. "Come with me and see it with your own eyes. My car awaits you."

So off they went, and in due course, the astonished lady was ushered into the machine house where the wonder was kept. Eagerly, Knipe explained its workings, and after a while he even permitted her to sit in the driver's seat and practise with the buttons.

"All right," he said suddenly, "you want to do a book now?"

"Oh yes!" she cried. "Please!"

She was very competent and seemed to know exactly what she wanted. She made her own pre-selections, then ran off a long, romantic, passion-filled novel. She read through the first chapter and became so enthusiastic that she signed up on the spot.

"That's one of them out of the way," Knipe said to Mr. Bohlen afterwards. "A pretty big one too."

"Nice work, my boy."

"And you know why she signed?"

"Why?"

"It wasn't the money. She's got plenty of that."

"Then why?"

Knipe grinned, lifting his lip and baring a long pale upper gum. "Simply because she saw the machine-made stuff was better than her own."

Thereafter①, Knipe wisely decided to concentrate only upon mediocrity②. Anything better than that—and there were so few it didn't mat-

① thereafter: *Adverb* (formal) after that time (正式)之后;以后(e. g. Thereafter their fortunes suffered a steep decline. 之后他们的财富大幅度减少。)

② mediocrity: *Noun* [count noun] a person of mediocre ability 庸人;庸才

ter much—was apparently not quite so easy to seduce.

In the end, after several months of work, he had persuaded something like seventy per cent of the writers on his list to sign the contract. He found that the older ones, those who were running out of ideas and had taken to drink, were the easiest to handle. The younger people were more troublesome. They were apt to become abusive, sometimes violent when he approached them; and more than once Knipe was slightly injured on his rounds.

But on the whole, it was a satisfactory beginning. This last year—the first full year of the machine's operation—it was estimated that at least one half of all the novels and stories published in the English language were produced by Adolph Knipe upon the Great Automatic Grammatizator.

Does this surprise you?

I doubt it.

And worse is yet to come. Today, as the secret spreads, many more are hurrying to tie up with Mr. Knipe. And all the time the screw turns tighter① for those who hesitate to sign their names.

This very moment, as I sit here listening to the howling② of my nine starving children in the other room, I can feel my own hand creeping closer and closer to that golden contract that lies over on the other side of the desk.

Give us strength, Oh Lord, to let our children starve.

---

① turn (tighten) the screw (screws): (informal) exert strong pressure on someone(非正式)施加压力

② howl: *Verb* weep and cry out loudly 号啕大哭(e. g. A baby started to howl. 婴儿开始号啕大哭。)

三、翻译探索

本篇小说的翻译难度适中，但为使译文流畅，有些地方需要做调整，如增词表达等。另外，个别异体词翻译起来有一定的难度，需要多方查找，确定好词义。

伟大写手

“哦，奈普，好小子。现在完工啦。我把你叫进来，只想对你说，我认为你的这份工作做得很出色。”

阿道夫·奈普一声不响地站在博伦先生的书桌前，看起来完全是一副无精打采的样子。

“你不开心吗？”

“噢，不，博伦先生。”

“今天早上，你看到报纸上都说了些什么吗？”

“没，先生，我没看到。”

坐在书桌后面的男子将一份折叠起来的报纸翻开，往自己跟前拉了拉，然后读了起来：“政府前一段时间下令建造的这台伟大的自动计算工具，现在已经完工。这或许是当今世界上计算速度最快的机器，其功能就是满足日益增加的在科学、工业和管理方面进行快速数学计算的需要，而这种计算，要是用过去传统的方法来处理，实际上是不可能的，即使可能，也需要更多的时间，得不偿失。约翰·博伦是电器工程师公司的负责人，主要负责这台机器的制造工作。他说，通过如下事实，你就会明白，这种新型工具的计算速度有多快了：它能够在五秒之内给出一个问题的答案，而这个问题，一名数学家需要一个月的时间才能解出；三分钟之内，它做出的计算，要是用人工（如果可能的话）进行处理的话，会写满五十万张大裁的纸（规格为330毫米×200毫米——译者注）。这台自动计算机器采用电流脉冲来工作，速率为一秒钟一百万次，能将所有的计算化解为加、减、乘、除来处理。从实用的目的而言，它能做到的，没有极限……”

博伦先生抬起头来,看了看眼前这位年轻人那张忧郁的长脸。“奈普,你不引以为荣吗?你不开心吗?”

“当然不是的,博伦先生。”

“我想,我没有必要提醒你说,你自己在其中所做的贡献——特别是对原始规划所做的贡献,是至关重要的。事实上,目前我或许可以这样说:没有你以及你的一些想法,这个项目今天或许仍然处在规划设计的初级阶段呢。”

阿道夫·奈普的双脚在地毯上动了动,双眼看着上司那两只白色的小手。他很紧张,手指摆弄着一枚回形针,将其弄直,就连那上面的发卡状的“U”形弯也给弄直了。他不喜欢上司的那两只手,也不喜欢他那张脸——嘴很小,双唇很窄,呈紫色。上司说话时,只有下嘴唇在动,这个样子令人感到不愉快。

“奈普,有什么事儿令你烦恼吗?有什么想法吗?”

“哦,没,博伦先生,没有。”

“给你放一周的假,觉得怎么样?对你有好处的,也是你应得的。”

“哦,我不知道,先生。”

这位年长一些的男子等待着,观察着这个站在自己眼前这位衣衫不整、高个子的、单薄的年轻男子。他是一位难以取悦的男孩子。他为什么不能站得直溜一点儿呢?总是耷拉个脑袋,一副邋遢的样子,夹克衫上残留着块块斑点,头发从前额垂下,把整张脸都挡住了。

“我想让你休假一周,奈普。你需要假期。”

“好吧,先生,如果你希望的话。”

“休一周吧。要是你喜欢,就休两周。去某个温暖的地方走走,晒晒太阳。在那儿游泳、放松、睡觉,干什么都可以。然后,返回,我们好再谈谈未来的计划。”

阿道夫·奈普乘公共汽车回到了家——一套两居室的公寓。他脱掉外衣扔到沙发上,倒了一杯威士忌,在一台打字机前坐了下来。那台打字机放在一张桌子上面。博伦先生说得对。当然,博伦说得没错,但有一点除外:他只知其一。他当时或许想,那个样子与女人有关——无论何时，年轻人穿戴讲究些，人人都会认为那与女人有关。

奈普倚身向前，开始浏览仍然夹在打字机上的那张打完一半的稿子，稿子的标题是《侥幸脱险》，是这样开篇的："夜很黑，暴风雨肆虐。风从林间呼啸而过，雨如瓢泼般倾泻而下……"

阿道夫·奈普喝了一小口威士忌，品尝到了麦芽的苦味。他感觉有一股清凉顺着嗓子流淌，沉淀到胃的顶部，起先感觉凉爽，接着就扩展开来，变得暖和起来，在肚子里形成一小块温暖的区域。不管怎么说，见鬼去吧，约翰·博伦。见鬼去吧，伟大的计算机器。见鬼去吧……

就在那一刻，他的眼睛开始慢慢地睁开，他的嘴开始慢慢地张开，显露出某种惊奇的样子。他的头慢慢地抬起，一动不动地待着，而且纹丝不动。眼睛则盯着对面的墙壁，还是那副表情——与其说是惊奇的表情，倒不如说是诧异的表情，可是，整个头部还是僵挺地待着，丝毫未动。他就这样保持了四十秒，五十秒，直至六十秒的时间。然后，头部仍然保持不动，脸部却慢慢地出现一种微妙的变化——诧异变成了喜悦。起先，这种变化很细微，只是在嘴角周围出现，接着，逐渐扩大，扩散开来。最后，整个脸部都舒张开，闪耀着极度欣喜之情。很多、很多个月以来，阿道夫·奈普的脸上都没有这样的笑容了。

"当然啦，"他大声说，"这想法完全荒谬可笑。"他抬起上嘴唇，露出一排牙齿，又笑了起来，那样子很古怪，也很撩人。

"这想法很令人开心，但却是如此不切实际，根本不值得去考虑。"

从那时起，除了这个想法，阿道夫·奈普就什么也不去想了。这个想法令他极其着迷，首先是因为这个想法让他有了一个指望——不管这个指望有多么遥远——指望能以最为恶作剧的方式报复一下他那些最大的敌人。单单从这个角度来说，或许是十分钟，或许是十五分钟的时间里，如同儿戏一般，他懒洋洋地考虑着这一想法。接着，突然之间，他竟然认认真真、仔仔细细地思考起来，认为这是个可行的主意。他拿起纸,做了一些初始性的记录,但没有涉及过多。他发现,自己立马与古老的真理背道而驰了,那个古老的真理说:一部机器,不管设计得多么精巧,是没有能力做出独创性思考的;这样的机器所能处理的问题,只能局限在数学项目上,也就是那些包含一个正确答案的问题,而且是只有一个正确答案的问题。

这下遇到了难关,似乎没有可以绕开的路可走。机器是不能有大脑的,但是,从另一方面来说,它能有记忆力,难道不是吗?机器本身的电子计算器部分记忆力惊人。通过水银柱将电脉冲转换成超声波,它一次能够存储至少一千个数字,而且,什么时候需要,就可以什么时候准确提取其中任何一个数字。因此呢,基于这个原理,建造一个几乎拥有无限制容量的记忆组件,难道是不可能的事情吗?

现在,刚才那个想法怎么样呢?

接着,突然之间,他一下子想到了一个简单而又不起眼的事实,这个事实却是效力强大,那就是:英语语法是由规则限制的,而这些规则简直就像数学一般严谨!给出单词,再给出要表达的意思,那么,将这些单词排列起来,只能有一个正确的顺序。

不对,他想,那不是十分精确。很多句子中,有好几个可供选择的位置可以用来放置单词和短语,放到这些位置上,语法都没有问题。但是,管那么多干吗,这理论本身基本上是正确的。所以,有理由推测,沿着一排排计算机器建造一个装置,就可以调整这个装置,让其根据语法规则,将一个个单词排列起来(而不是数字)。给这个装置配备动词、名词、形容词、代词,并将这些词作为词汇库储存到记忆组件里。然后,根据需要,将它们抽取出来进行排列。再给这个装置输入情节,让其书写出句子来。

现在,没有什么能阻止奈普,他立刻投入到工作中。在接下来的几天时间里,他的工作强度很大,起居室里乱糟糟的一片,到处都是一张张的纸,上面写满了公式和计算式,列出各种单词——成千上万个单词,写上了各式故事情节——划分得很是详细,摘录了《罗热英语单词和短语汇编》中的大量词条。有些纸上写满了男男女女的名字,有些抄满了从电话簿里找来的姓氏,有些画满了复杂的金属线、电路、开关以及热阴极电子管，有些画上了能在不同形状小卡片上打孔的机器，还有一种奇怪的电动打字机，一分钟能打出一万个单词。有的纸上还画上了一种控制面板类的东西，上面排列了一系列的按钮，每个按钮上都标上了美国有名杂志的名字。

他处于一种欢欣鼓舞的工作情绪之中，在屋子里小心翼翼地来回移动，在乱纸堆中忙活着，摩擦着双手，还大声地自言自语。有的时候，鼻子诡异地一卷，嘴里就愤怒地发出一连串骂骂咧咧的词语，而每一次咒骂似乎都带有“编辑”一词。连续工作到第十五天的时候，他将这些纸收拾起来，放进两个大文件夹里。然后，他几乎是一路小跑，将这两个大文件夹带到了约翰·博伦公司的电气工程师办公室。

见到他回来，博伦先生很是高兴。

“哦，奈普，我的天呐，你看起来要强百倍啊。假期过得好吗？去哪里了？”

博伦心里说，他跟以前一样难看和邋遢。他为什么不能站得直溜一点儿呢？他看起来就像是一根弯曲的棍子。“我的伙计，你看起来要强上百倍啊。”我想知道的是，他龇牙咧嘴笑什么呢。每一次我看到他，他的两只耳朵似乎都变大一些。

阿道夫·奈普将两个大文件夹放到书桌上。“看啊，博伦先生！”他大声喊道。“看看这些！”

接着，他道出了自己的所作所为。他打开了文件夹，将所有计划推到了这位面露惊愕的小个子男子面前。他不停地说了一个多小时，将所有的一切都做了解释。解释完之后，他向后一退，等待着裁决。这时，他已经是上气不接下气，脸色也激动得发了红。

“奈普，你知道我是怎么想的吗？我想，你疯了。”博伦对自己说，现在要谨慎了，要小心谨慎地对待他。他价值无限，就是眼前这个家伙。要是他看起来不是那么凌乱，没长那张长长的马脸，没有那些大大的牙齿，那该多好啊。这个伙计的耳朵有大黄那种植物的叶子般大小了。

“可是，博伦先生！这个想法会奏效的啊！我已经向你做了证明！你不能否认！"

"奈普，现在别着急。慢慢来，听我说。"

阿道夫·奈普看着眼前这个男子，时间每过去一秒钟，他对这个男子不喜欢的程度就加深一点儿。

"这个想法，"博伦先生用下嘴唇说道，"很具有独创性——美妙绝伦，我或许可以这样说。这个想法只能证实我对你的能力的首肯。但是，不要太当回事儿。毕竟嘛，我的伙计，它对我们会有什么可能的用处呢？究竟有谁需要一部写故事的机器呢？无论如何，它能从什么地方赚到钱呢？只要对我说说这些就可以。"

"先生，我可以坐下说吗？"

"当然，坐下吧。"

阿道夫·奈普坐到椅子边上，而这位年长一些的男子则用棕色的眼睛警觉地观察着他，想知道现在从他嘴里能说出些什么话语。

"博伦先生，如果可以的话，我想解释点儿事情，一点儿有关我是怎么想到做这一切的事情。"

"照直说吧，奈普。"博伦先生在心里对自己说，现在自己得迎合、迁就对方一点儿。这个男孩子真的是价值无限——近似于某种天才，对公司会有极大的用处。就看看堆在这儿的这些纸吧——是你所看到过的最棒的东西。工作量之大令人吃惊。当然，毫无用处，没有商业价值，但是，它却再一次证明这个男孩子的能力。

"我想，博伦先生，说这事就等于是向你坦白啦。我想，这事儿解释起来，就会说明我为什么总是会如此……如此这般忧心忡忡。"

"对我，你有什么就说什么，奈普。我在这儿就是帮你的——这个你是知道的。"

这个年轻人将双手紧紧叉到一起，放到一条大腿上，用两只胳膊肘将自己抱作一团，就好像突然间感觉发冷似的。

"要知道，博伦先生，实话实说，我真的不是十分在意这里的这份工作。我知道，对于这份工作以及诸如此类的工作，我很精通，但是，我的心思没有放在这上面。这儿的工作不是我最想做的。"

博伦先生的眉毛向上挑起，快得向弹簧一般，整个身体却一动不动地待着。

“要知道,先生,我这一辈子,早就想做一名作家。”

“一名作家!”

“是的,博伦先生。你或许不相信,所有的业余时间,我都用来写故事。在过去的十年里,我写出了好几百——几乎是数以百计的短篇故事。准确地说,有五百六十六篇,大约一周写一篇。”

“天呐,伙计!你写那玩意干什么?”

“先生,我所知道的就是,我有种冲动。”

“什么样的冲动?”

“创作的冲动,博伦先生。”他每一次抬起头,就能看到博伦的双唇,发现他那双嘴唇变得越来越薄、越来越薄,同时也越来越紫、越来越紫。

“奈普,我可以问问,你写这些故事干什么用吗?”

“这个嘛,先生,可就麻烦了。没有谁会买下。每写完一篇,我就往各处投一遍,从一个杂志投到另一个杂志,就是这样的,博伦先生。这些杂志只是将我投的故事退给我,很令人郁闷、沮丧。”

博伦先生松弛下来。“我的伙计,我看得出,你会有什么样的感觉。”他的声音满是同情。“一生之中的某个时刻,我们都会有这样的经历。可问题是,现在,既然你有了证据——确凿的证据,而且是一些专家和编辑亲自给出的证据,证明你写的故事——怎么说呢——相当不成功,那么,你就该停笔啦。忘记这件事情吧,我的伙计。干脆把这一切都忘掉。”

“不,博伦先生!不!不是那样的啊!我就是知道,我写的故事很好。我的天啊,要是你将我写的跟那些杂志上印刷出来的东西一比较——噢,博伦先生,我的文采啊!一周一周过去,你在杂志上看到的全是些无病呻吟的、枯燥乏味的东西——哇,简直令我疯掉!”

“我的伙计,现在,请等一等……”

“博伦先生,你读过那些杂志吗?”

“恕我冒昧,奈普,可是,这一切跟你的机器有什么相关的?”

“紧密相关,博伦先生,绝对是紧密相关!我想告诉你的就是,我已经研究了所有的杂志,每一种杂志刊登的故事似乎都有自己特定的风格类型。这一点,作家了解,特别是功成名就的作家了解。了解后,他们就对号写作。"

"且慢,我的伙计。冷静一下,好吗?我认为,这一切对我们不会有什么改观。"

"拜托了,博伦先生,听我把话说完。这一切至关重要。"他暂停一下,喘了口气。他彻底激动起来,边说边挥舞着两只手。他那张露出很多牙齿的长脸,还有那两只大大的耳朵,都闪现出热切的光芒,而且嘴里充斥了过多的口水,令他说起话来,唾沫星横飞。"因此啊,你知道,在我这台机器上,在'情节记忆'部件和'单词记忆'部件之间,我安装了可以加以调节的协调器。这样,只需按动所需的按钮,我渴望得到什么类型的故事,就能生产出什么类型的故事。"

"是的,我知道,奈普,这个我知道。这一切很有意思,可是,能有什么意义呢?"

"博伦先生,意义是这样的。由于市场的限制,只要我们需要,就能够在适当的时间生产出适当的东西来。这就是生意经,仅此而已。我现在是站在你的立场上说话,向你提出了一个商业性的建议啊。"

"我亲爱的伙计啊,这不可能是一个商业性的建议——永远不可能是。得花多大一笔钱来建造其中的一台机器啊。这一点,你清楚,我也清楚。"

"是的,先生,我清楚。但是,恕我鲁莽,我相信,你不知道杂志付给作者写故事的稿酬是多少。"

"多少?"

"至少这个数——两千五百美元。平均起来,或许有一千左右。"

博伦先生惊跳起来。

"是的,先生,事实如此。"

"绝对不可能,奈普!荒谬!"

"不,先生,事实如此。"

"你的意思是想告诉我,往那儿一坐,就用笔划拉几下子,写出一篇故事……这些杂志就像你说的那样,付钱给一个人啊!天呐,奈普！岂有比这更荒唐的事！作家一定都是百万富翁啦！”

“一点没错，博伦先生！那就是造这台机器的原因所在。且听我说，先生，我跟你多说一些，我已经将这一切都制定好了。大型的杂志每期大约刊登三篇小说。现在，就拿其中十五家最重要的杂志来说吧——那些付钱最丰厚的杂志。它们中有些是月刊，但多数一周出刊一次。好啦，我们算算，每周约有四十篇大作被他们买走，那就是四万美元啊。那么，就我们这台机器而言，要是让其完全运转起来，我们就能抓住几乎整个这方面的市场呢！”

“我亲爱的伙计，你疯啦！”

“没有，先生，说实话，我说的是实情。难道你看不出来啊，光靠量大这一点，我们就能彻底取胜！这台机器可以生产五千字的故事，完整打印好，等待三十秒就可发送出去。作家怎么竞争得过呢？我问你，博伦先生，怎么竞争？”

就在那一刻，阿道夫·奈普注意到眼前这位男子的表情发生了一个轻微的变化，双眼格外亮了一下，鼻孔鼓胀起来，整个脸变得一动不动，几乎僵直了。于是，他不失时机地继续说了下去。“博伦先生，现如今，手写的文章没有一点儿希望，特别是在这个国家，没法跟大规模生产竞争。这一点，你知道的。你想拿什么来说明都可以——地毯……椅子……砖头……陶瓷品……不一而足，现在都是机器生产的。质量也许会低一等，但是，那没有关系，重要的是生产成本。那么，故事——不过是另一种产品，跟地毯和椅子一样，只要你送货，没有人会在意你是如何生产出来的。博伦先生，我们就做故事批发生意！我们卖得比全国任何一个作家的价都要低！我们要垄断这个市场！”

博伦先生挨着椅子边慢慢地坐直了身体。现在，他将身体向前倾斜，两只胳膊肘撑到书桌上，一脸警觉的样子，那双小小的棕色眼睛落在对方身上。

“奈普，我仍然认为，这不切实际。”

“一周四万美元啊！”阿道夫·奈普叫道。“就算减掉一半，一周两万美元，那么，一年还剩一百万啊！”接着，他轻轻地补充了一句：

"造那样老旧的计算机器,一年你也挣不来一百万,博伦先生,对吧?"

"可是,现在说正经的,奈普。你真的认为他们会购买故事吗?"

"听着,博伦先生。在能够半价买到其他类型故事的情况下,这个世界上还有谁会去购买定制的故事呢?我这样说,经得起推敲,难道不是吗?"

"你怎么将故事销售出去呢?你会跟他们说,这些都是谁写的呢?"

"我们将建立起我们自己的文学代办处,通过代办处分销。我们想要什么样的作家名字,就创造出什么样的名字。"

"那我不喜欢,奈普。对我而言,那有行骗的味道,不是吗?"

"还有就是,博伦先生,一旦开了头,还有各式有利可图的副产品呢,比方说,做广告。现今,名作家要是愿意以自己的名誉代言产品的话,啤酒制造商之类的人物十分乐意花大价钱的。哇,我的天,博伦先生!我们所谈的,可不是小孩子玩家家的事情,我们谈的是生意经。"

"我的伙计,野心不可太大。"

"还有一件事情。博伦先生,要是你愿意的话,我们没有任何理由不在某些上等的作品里署上你的名字。"

"我的天啊,奈普。署我的名字干什么用呢?"

"一些作家非常受到敬重,比如说像埃勒·加德纳,或者凯瑟琳·莫里斯。除此之外,我就不知道了,先生。我们得有名字可署才行。我当然想到将其中的一两篇署上我自己的名字,以解燃眉之急。"

"当个作家,嗯?"博伦先生说完话,沉思起来。"嗯,到俱乐部一去,大家看到我的名字出现在杂志上——某些优秀的杂志上,一定会惊奇不已。"

"正是啊,博伦先生!"

顷刻之间,博伦先生的眼睛里浮现出一种出神的、恍惚的神情,随即微笑起来。然后,他站起身,开始梳理摆在他面前的这一项项计划。

"奈普,有一件事儿我不太明白。情节出自哪里?机器是不可能创造出情节的。"

"我们将那些情节输进去,先生,根本没有什么问题的。人人都有情节的。在你左边那个文件夹里,有三四百个情节写了进去,直接将它们输入机器的'情节记忆'部件就可以了。"

"接着讲。"

"博伦先生,还有其他许多细微的操作部件。要是你仔细研究一下这些计划,你都会看到的。比方说,几乎每位作家都会使用的一个技巧,那就是,在每篇故事中至少插入一个很长的、意义模糊的单词。这样,读者就会认为,这位作家很机智、很聪明。因此呢,我设计了一台机器,做同样的事情。就是为了这一目的,那台机器里储存了一大堆长长的单词。"

"在哪儿?"

"在'单词记忆'部件里。"他解释说,感觉对方有点画蛇添足。

那一天的大部分时间里,这两个人都在讨论这种新机器的可行性。最后,博伦先生说,他得多考虑考虑。第二天早晨,他变得极其感兴趣。一周之内,他就完全相信,认为这个主意很好了。

"我们要做的,奈普,就是说我们只是要建造另一台计算器。但型号是新的,那样就能保密了。"

"正是,博伦先生。"

六个月的时间内,这台机器造好了,放置在生产场地后面一间单独的砖砌的建筑物里。既然机器要准备运行,除了博伦先生和阿道夫·奈普之外,自然不允许任何人靠前。

这两个人,一个个头矮小,身体圆胖,长着矮脚,另一个则个头高大,身体消瘦,露出牙齿。当他俩站在过道里的控制面板前,准备运行机器生产第一篇故事时,激动人心的时刻到来了。他俩周围都是一些墙壁,这些墙壁隔出很多小过道,墙上布满了电线、插头、开关,还有大大的玻璃阀。他俩都很紧张,博伦先生蹦跳着换着双脚,无法安静下来。

"哪个按钮?"阿道夫·奈普眼睛看着一排小小的白色圆盘,问道。那些圆盘很像打字机的一个个按键。“你选择,博伦先生。有很多杂志可选,像《星期六晚邮报》《科里尔杂志》《妇女家庭杂志》等,喜欢哪个,就选哪个。”

“我的老天呐,伙计!我怎么知道?”他上下跳跃,如同患上荨麻疹一般。

“博伦先生,”阿道夫·奈普一脸严肃地说,“此时此刻,只需动用你一根小小的手指,你就能够成为这块陆地上最为多才多艺的作家,你意识到没有?”

“听着,奈普,直接往下进行,拜托——去除繁文缛节。”

“好的,博伦先生。我们就要成功了……让我瞧瞧——就这个,怎么样呢?”他伸出一根手指,摁下了一个按钮,按钮上面印上了极小的黑色字体“今日妇女”。接着,听到尖锐的“咔嚓”声。等他松开手指后,那个按钮还保持着按下的状态——保持在比其他按钮低的位置上。

“选择到此结束,”他说。“现在——妥啦!”他向上够去,拉动面板上的一个开关。屋子里就立刻传来很响的嗡嗡声,还有“噼里啪啦”电火花的声音,以及很多、很多微小的操纵杆快速移动发出的“叮叮当当”的声音。几乎与此同时,从控制面板右侧的一个狭槽里,滑出一张张四开本的纸,落入下方的一只篮子里。这些纸滑出的速度很快,一秒钟滑出一张,不到半分钟的工夫,一切都结束了,纸张也不再往外滑了。

“搞定!”阿道夫·奈普说。“那就是你的故事!”

他俩抓起一张张纸,开始阅读起来。第一张纸是这样开始的:“阿佛姆斯格味特爬四其,副何破卡波于噢可个副洒字符吧恩,陪路特若和的可和 母恩波……”他俩又看了看其余的纸,所有的纸上都是类似的风格。博伦先生开始大喊起来,而年轻一点的那位则尽量让他冷静下来。

“没有问题的,先生,真的没问题的,只需小小调整一下。某个地方接错了,仅此而已。你必须记得的是,博伦先生,这个屋子里布线的长度多达三十万米,你无法从一开始就期望一切都会那么稳妥。”

"这玩意永远都不会奏效的。"博伦先生说。

"耐心点儿，先生。要有耐心。"

阿道夫·奈普着手查找出错的地方。只需四天的时间，他就声称，一切就绪，可以进行下一次运行试验了。

"它永远都不会奏效的，"博伦先生说。"我就知道，它永远都不会奏效的。"

奈普微微一笑，按下了标记着《读者文摘》的选择按钮。接着，他拉动了开关，满屋子又响起那种奇怪的、令人兴奋的嗡嗡声。一页打满文字的稿子从狭槽中飞出，落入篮子中。

"其余那些页呢？"博伦叫道。"停下不打啦！出错啦！"

"没有，先生，没出错。一点儿都没出错。这篇是为文摘类杂志写的，难道你没看出来吗？"

这一次，稿子是这样开始的："没有几个人还知道一种革命性的治疗新药已经被发现或许能很好地带来永久性的疼痛缓解给患有最为可怕的疾病的人们在我们这个时代……"等等。

"这是胡言乱语啊！"博伦先生大喊。

"不，先生，这很好呀。难道你没看出来吗？只不过，这个可爱的家伙没有把字句断开。这个容易调整，但是，故事是有了。看啊，博伦先生，看啊！故事摆在那儿，只是字句都连到了一块儿。"

的确，情况如他所言。

几天后的另一次试验，一切都很完美，连标点也无可挑剔。他们的第一篇故事是为一家有名的女性杂志写的。这是一个内容严谨、结构复杂的故事，写的是一个男孩子，他想跟自己有钱的上司搞好关系，就这样展开了故事情节。男孩子安排好一个朋友，在一个漆黑的夜晚，趁有钱上司的女儿开车回家的时候，将她劫持。就在这当儿，男孩碰巧路过，将朋友手中的枪夺走，救出了女孩子。女孩子感激不尽，但是，她的父亲有些怀疑，尖锐地查问男孩子，男孩子垮了下来，坦白承认了一切。接下来，这位父亲非但没有将他踢出门去，还赞赏起他的足智多谋来，而女孩子则钦佩他的诚实——还有他的形象。这位父亲答应让他来做会计部总管，女孩子也嫁给了他。

"这故事真出色,博伦先生!正合适!"

"对我来说,似乎有点粗糙,我的伙计啊!"

"不,先生,能卖出去,真的能卖出去!"

兴奋之下,阿道夫·奈普立刻又印出了另外六篇故事,用去的时间几乎是一样的。除了其中的一篇有点低俗之外,其余的似乎完全令人满意。

博伦先生现在缓和下来,同意在市区的一间办公室设立文学代办处,让奈普去负责。这一切,两三周的时间就完成了。然后,奈普将首批的十二篇故事邮寄出去。其中的四篇,他署了自己的名字,一篇署上了博伦先生的名字,而剩下的,他干脆编造了几个名字署上了。

首批故事中,有五篇立马得到采纳。署上博伦先生名字那篇被退了回来,小说编辑附上一封信,写道:"技巧运用得不错,但以我们的眼光,不很成功。我们想看看这位作家更多的作品……"于是,阿道夫·奈普打出租车去了工厂,为这家杂志又印出了一篇,又一次署上博伦先生的名字,立刻寄了出去。这一篇,他们买走了。

钱源源不断地涌入。奈普十分谨慎,一点点儿慢慢提高产量。半年的时间里,他每周邮出三十篇故事,其中有一半销售出去。

他开始为自己在文学界树立了一个多产而成功的作家形象。博伦先生也一样,但是没有他的形象那么好,尽管博伦本人并不知道这一点。与此同时,奈普编造了十多个虚假的名字,把他们当作年轻有为的作家来培养。一切进展顺利。

到了这一阶段,奈普决定对机器加以改造,让它写故事的同时,也写长篇小说。此时,博伦先生十分渴望在文学界获得更大的声望,就坚持要奈普立即投入工作,来完成这一庞大的工程。

"我要写长篇小说,"他不断地说。"我要写长篇小说。"

"你会如愿以偿的,先生,会的。但是,请耐心一些。我必须得做出很复杂的调整。"

"大家都说我应该创作长篇小说,"博伦大声说道。"各种类型的出版商都昼夜不停地追着我,恳求我不要再捣鼓故事了,要我做些真正重要的事情。写小说是唯一真正重要的——他们就是这样说的。”

“我们就要创作长篇小说了，”奈普对他说。“想创作多少，我们就创作多少，但是，我们得有耐心。”

“奈普，现在听我说。我要创作的是一部严肃认真的长篇大作，这样的作品能够让那些人眼睛一亮，刮目相看。最近，对于你署上我的名字的这类故事，我感到相当厌倦了。事实上，对于你有没有拿我赚上一笔这一点，我一点儿都不敢肯定。”

“赚上一笔，博伦先生？”

“将所有最好的都留给你自己，那就是你一直在做的。”

“噢，没有，博伦先生！没有！”

“所以，这一次，我要把握十足，写出一部高层次大作。你明白我说的是什么。”

“听着，博伦先生。使用我即将调配出来的交换台，你想写什么类型的书，就能够写出什么类型的书。”

这话不假，因为又过了两三个月的时间，阿道夫·奈普这位天才不仅将机器改装完毕，可以创造小说，而且，他还建造了一个绝妙的新控制系统，这个系统能让作者预先选择自己渴望写出的几乎任何类型的情节和风格。这个东西上面有那么多的仪表盘和操纵杆，看起来就像是某种大型飞机的仪器控制面板。

首先，作者按下一系列主按钮中的一个，做个初始的选择：历史型的、讽刺型的、哲理型的、政治型的、浪漫型的、色情型的、幽默型的，或者传统类型的。接着，从第二排按钮（基本按钮）中，按下一个来选择主题：军旅生活、开拓岁月、内部战争、世界战争、种族问题、狂野西部、乡村生活、儿时记忆、远洋航海、海底世界，以及很多、很多其他的主题。第三排按钮用来选择文风：古典风格、奇幻风格、泼辣刺激风格、海明威风格、福克纳风格、乔伊斯风格以及女性风格等。第四排按钮可供选择人物，第五排用来选择篇幅长短，等等，等等。一共有十大长排可供预先做出选择的按钮。

但是，还有更多的呢。实际写作过程中，控制方面还需要练习

(每部小说大约需要练习十五分钟)。练习的时候,作者必须——也许可以这么说——坐在驾驶员的位置上,拉(或推)一些贴上标签的止动器——类似风琴按键一类的东西。照这样做,作者就能够连续地调节或者融合不同的,甚至是多变的特性,如紧张度、惊奇度、幽默度、怜悯度、神秘度等。整个过程中,仪表面板上数量众多的刻度盘、仪表盘可以显示出作者写作的进展情况。

最后,还有一个"热情度"方面的问题。仔细研究了过去一年中的畅销书排行榜之后,阿道夫·奈普认为"热情度"是重中之重的一个元素——相当于魔力催化剂,不知怎么的,就能够将一部最乏味的小说转化为一本成功的力作。无论如何,"热情度"最终会达到这个效果。可是,奈普也清楚,热情度是一种能量强大的、令人陶醉的东西,一定得小心谨慎地加以分配,也就是说,要在适当的时候,分配适当的比例。为了确保这一点,他设计出一套独立的控制系统,由两个敏感度很好的滑动式调节器组成,使用脚踏板来操作。类似于汽车里的油门控制阀和刹车制动器,其中一只脚踏板控制注入的热情度比例,另一只用来调节其浓度。当然,毋庸置疑的是,用奈普的这些方法写小说,更像是在同一时间里,既开飞机,又驾汽车,又拉风琴,这也是唯一的不足之处。但是,对于发明者而言,这种不足不算是什么问题。一切就绪之后,奈普自豪地陪着博伦先生步入机器房,开始解释这件新奇之物的操作程序。

"老天呐,奈普！这一切,我永远都操作不好！要命啊,伙计,手写比这儿要容易多了啊!"

"博伦先生,我向你保证,用不了多久,你就会习惯的。一两周之内,你几乎不用思考就能操作了,这跟学开车很相似。"

可以说,这不像学车一样容易,但是,经过很多小时的练习之后,博伦先生开始掌握操作的窍门了。最终,一天晚上很晚的时候,他告诉奈普做好准备,要印出第一部小说。紧张的时刻到来了。胖胖的小个子博伦紧张兮兮地蹲伏在驾驶座位上,而露出大牙的高个子奈普则在他的周围兴奋地忙活着。

"奈普,我打算写一部力作。"

“我敢肯定，你会写出来的，先生。我敢肯定，你会写出来的。”

博伦先生用一根手指谨慎地按下所需的预选按钮：

主按钮——讽刺性的

主题——种族问题

风格——古典风格

人物——六名男子、四名女子、一名婴儿

长度——十五章

与此同时，他特地将眼睛盯到类似风琴音钮的三个按键上，上面分别标着“强弱度”“神秘度”“深奥度”。

“准备好了吗，先生？”

“是的，是的，准备好了。”

奈普拉动了开关，这部巨型机器随之嗡嗡响起。多达五万个齿轮、金属棒、操纵杆在油的润滑下发出低沉的“呼呼”声，接着传来电子打字机连续而有节奏的“咔嗒、咔嗒”快速敲打声，那种尖尖的声音几乎令人难以忍受。一页页打印好的纸张飞出来——两秒钟飞出一页，落入篮子中。可能由于噪音，可能由于兴奋，可能由于必须得摆弄那几个类似风琴按键的东西，同时还得看着章节计数器、进度指示器、热情度控制器，博伦先生开始惊慌失措起来。他的反应跟初学驾车的人的反应一样——双脚使劲踩到脚踏板上，踩着不松开，直至整部机器停止。

“你的第一部长篇小说，祝贺你，”奈普说着，从篮子里将一大摞打印好的稿子拿了出来。

一小滴、一小滴汗珠从博伦先生的脸部渗出。“我的伙计，这工作，做起来当然辛苦。”

“可是，先生，你完成了。你做完了。”

“让我看看，奈普。读起来怎么样？”

他开始浏览第一章，每看完一页，就将其递给那个比他年纪小一些的男人。

“老天啊，奈普！这是什么呢？”博伦先生的嘴在说出这些话语的同时，那张薄薄的紫色的鱼唇轻微移动着，脸颊开始慢慢肿胀起来。

“可是,奈普,看这儿！简直令人难以容忍!”

“我必须说的是,这里面有点儿挑逗性,先生。”

“挑逗！完全令人反胃啊！我怎么可能往这样的东西上面署我的名字!”

“相当没错,先生,相当没错!”

“奈普！这是不是你一直跟我开的恶意玩笑?”

“噢,不,先生！不是!”

“看起来确实像。”

“博伦先生,踩热情度控制踏板的时候,你或许一直踩得重了点儿,难道你不这样认为吗?”

“我亲爱的伙计,我怎么会知道?”

“为什么不再试试?”

所以,博伦先生又印出一部小说,这一次的内容跟预计的一致。

一周之内,一位热情的出版商读完了这份手稿,同意出版。奈普紧接着又印出一部,署上自己的名字,然后,为了保险起见,又多印出十二部。转瞬之间,阿道夫·奈普的文学代办处因为拥有一大批前途光明的年轻长篇小说家而变得名声大振。金钱再一次奔涌而入。

就在这个阶段,年轻的奈普开始展露出做大买卖的真才实学来。

“听着啊,博伦先生,”他说。“我们仍然有很多竞争对手。为什么不将本国所有的作家都真正地吸收进来呢?”

现在,一身深绿色天鹅绒夹克衫打扮的博伦先生,已经任由头发遮住自己耳朵的三分之二,对目前的状态已是相当满足了。“不知道你说的是什么意思,我的伙计。你不能将作家真正地吸收进来。”

“你当然能的,先生,就跟洛克菲勒当初对那些石油公司的做法一模一样。直接将他们全部买来。要是他们不肯卖,就向他们施加压力逼其全部卖掉。很容易办到!”

“现在阶段,要当心啊,奈普。要当心。”

“先生,我这儿有一份清单,上面列出本国最为成功的五十名作家的名字。我打算要做的就是,给他们每一位提供一份终身的带薪合同,而他们必须做到的就是,承诺永远不再动笔写一个字。当然,他们得允许我们将他们的名字署到我们自己的东西上。这个提议，你觉得呢？"

"他们永远都不会同意的。"

"你不了解作家，博伦先生。你就睁开眼睛看着吧。"

"创作欲望怎么办，奈普？"

"都是扯淡！他们真正感兴趣儿的是钱——这一点，跟其他人没有什么两样。"

最终，博伦先生勉强同意他去试一试。于是，奈普衣兜里揣着他的那份清单，坐上专职司机开的一辆大个头凯迪拉克车就出发了，要一一拜访那些名作家。

他先去拜访的是清单最上面那位作家，是一位很伟大而非凡的作家。进入那位作家的家门，他一点都没费什么周折。然后，他对这位作家说明了自己的来由，随后拿出一只装满小说样本的手提箱，并出示了一份合同要这位男作家签，这份合同为其提供终身保障，一年支付的数额很大。这位男子有礼貌地听着，认为自己在跟一个精神病患者打交道，给他一杯喝的之后，就果断地将他请出了家门。

当名单上的第二位作家看到奈普并没有开玩笑的意思，竟然操起压纸用的大大的金属块朝奈普砸来，逼得奈普这位发明家循着花园一路逃窜。一边逃，一边听到后面传来一阵激烈的谩骂之声，骂声中包含的污言秽语，他以前从未听到过。

但是，让阿道夫·奈普泄气的远不止这件事呢。他失望，但不沮丧，于是，又坐上他那辆大车，去寻访下一位客户，是一位女性作家，很有名气，很受人欢迎。她的书极其富有浪漫色彩，畅销全国，销量上百万。她很谦和地接待了他，为他沏茶，仔细地听他说明了来由。

"这一切听起来很令人着迷，"她回应道。"可是，当然，我想这有点难以相信。"

"夫人，"奈普说。"跟我来亲眼看看吧。我的车等着你呢。"

就这样，他们出发了。没用多长时间，这位面露惊讶的女士就被迎进了产生奇迹的机器间。奈普迫不及待地向她解释机器的工作原理。没过多久，他甚至允许她坐在驾驶位置上，让她操作按钮练习起来。

“好啦,”他突然说道,“你现在想出一本书吗?”

“哦,是的!”她大声说。“请启动吧!”

她很胜任,似乎准确地知道自己要的是什么,只见她分别按下预选按钮,随即印出一部浪漫的、充满激情的长篇小说。通读完第一章后,她热情洋溢,当场就签了合同。

“其中的一个已经解决了,”奈普过后对博伦先生说。“也算是一位大人物啦。”

“干得不错,我的伙计。”

“你知道她为什么签了吗?”

“为什么?”

“不是因为钱,她有的是钱。”

“那为什么?”

奈普咧嘴一笑,将嘴唇抬起,露出一排长长的、灰色的上牙龈。“只是因为她看见这台机器写的东西比她自己写的要好多了。”

自那以后,奈普明智起来,将目光集中在二流作家身上。二流之上的作家数量少之又少,没有什么大不了的。很显然,引诱其上钩是很容易做到的。

最终,经过几个月的工作之后,清单上约有百分之七十的作家被他说服,签订了合同。他发现,上了年纪的作家最容易对付,因为他们的思路近于枯竭,整日与酒为伴。年轻一些的作家更麻烦些,他们趋于侮辱加谩骂。有时候,他接近他们时,他们还会有暴力倾向。这样,奈普一轮轮跑下来,受伤还不止一次呢。

但是,总体来看,开端良好,令人满意。这样算来,整个去年的时间——也就是这台机器投入运行的第一年时间,用英语出版发行的小说和故事中,估计至少有一半是阿道夫·奈普的这部伟大的自动写作机器生产出来的。

这一点令你吃惊吗?

对此,我无法肯定。

更糟糕的还在后头呢。现今,随着这一秘密传播开来,更多的人匆忙赶来，要与奈普搭上关系。自始至终，对那些签名优柔寡断的人来说，压力变得越来越大。

就在这一刻，我坐在这儿，听着另一个房间里，我那九个挨饿的孩子正在那儿号叫，我感觉自己的手越来越靠近、越来越靠近那份黄金一般的合同了——那份合同就放在书桌的另一头。

赐予我们力量吧，噢，上帝，哪怕是让我们的孩子挨饿。

第三章　功成名就

现代汉语中,“功成名就”这一成语应演变自“功成名遂”。《墨子·修身》有语云:“名不徒生,而誉不自长,功成名遂,名誉不可虚假①。”功绩建立起来,名声也就随之而来,可谓水到渠成。看来,功与名是相辅相成的,“功成”则“名”自来,“名遂”或“名就”则在于“功成”。

功名的取得不是一蹴而就的,也不是一朝一夕的事情,而是要经过一番艰苦的拼搏。其间,酸甜苦辣咸,五味杂陈,而功成名就者,当属最终尝到甜蜜滋味的人,正所谓“宝剑锋从磨砺出,梅花香自苦寒来”(古代无名氏《警世贤文·勤奋篇》)。这期间也不乏各种感慨:“三十功名尘与土,八千里路云和月”(宋代岳飞②《满江红·怒发冲冠》)、“功名富贵若长在,汉水亦应西北流”③(唐代李白《江上吟》)、“功名富贵须待命,命若不来知奈何”④(唐代白居易《浩歌行》)、“回首功名一梦中”⑤(宋代陆游《渔父·灯下读玄真子渔歌因怀山阴故

---

① 转引自“商务印书馆辞书研究中心. 新华成语词典. 北京:商务印书馆,2002:246”。

② 关于这首词是否系岳飞所作,存在争议。本书视之为岳飞所作。

③ 转引自《全唐诗》第166卷第003首。

④ 转引自《全唐诗》第435卷第003首。

⑤ 转引自“中华诗库”网站,网址:http://www.shiku.org/。

隐追拟》)、"鬓底青春留不住。功名薄似风前絮。何似瓮头春没数"①(宋代毛滂《渔家傲·鬓底青春留不住》)等。

英国作家罗尔德·达尔最终功成名就,也是经历了类似的过程,所不同的是,他有了一番"苦练"。在中国人常说的"万事开头难"的情况下,可以说,达尔开了个好头,可谓"Well- begun is half done",但是功成名就之前,他也走过一段艰辛之路。他笔下的人物也是如此。

达尔笔下的"非凡亨利"是一个功成名就的典范。亨利这个人物类似中国武侠小说中的主人公,经过一番艰苦的"修炼",最终身怀"绝技"。但是,跟中国武侠小说中的套路有所不同的是,身怀"绝技"后的亨利,走的却是中国现代"雷锋"式的路线——做好事不留名。亨利跟雷锋的差别,就在于亨利身上还保留着"武侠"的风范——劫富济贫,只不过亨利采取的手段跟"大侠"采取的手段不同罢了。

那么,就让我们走进罗尔德·达尔的世界,去探寻功成名就的秘密吧。

第一节　《非凡亨利》(上部)
The Wonderful Story of Henry Sugar (Part A)

罗尔德·达尔的《非凡亨利》(*The Wonderful Story of Henry Sugar*)收录在《〈非凡亨利〉及另外六篇故事集》(*The Wonderful Story of Henry Sugar and Six More*)一书中。这个故事类似于中国金庸等作家笔下的武侠小说,其主人公经过一番艰苦的修炼,最后练成神功,具有非凡的能力。有所不同的是,本篇小说中的主人公亨利·休格将神功用在世界各地的大赌场上,将赢来的钱用于孤儿院的建设,让孤儿感受到家的温暖。

---

① 转引自"古诗文网",网址:http://so.gushiwen.org/。

通读这部小说,再加上作家达尔在小说中的"旁白",让人感觉到其中的人物和事件都是真实的,而事实上,这篇小说里的故事,就像中国的武侠小说一样,应该都是编造出来的。这充分说明罗尔德·达尔非凡的想象能力和创作功力。

一、原作导读

这篇故事情节复杂,角度转换较多,是"故事中嵌套故事"类型的小说,一个主线故事中一共嵌套了三个分支故事。

亨利·休格是个典型的"富二代",是个浪荡的花花公子。他喜欢赌博,但不能说他赢得都很"光彩"——赌博过程中不乏使用欺诈手段。

夏日的一个周末,亨利驱车前往吉尔福德,到威廉·温德姆爵士的宅邸做客。不巧的是,那天雨下个不停,什么室外游戏也进行不了,只能待在房间里,这令亨利十分沮丧。百无聊赖之际,他溜溜达达地走进了主人家的书房,无意中在书架上瞥见了一本十分单薄的书,"发现它实际上不过是一个硬皮练习本,也就是学校里小学生使用的那种练习本"(... saw that it was actually nothing more than a cardboard- covered exercise- book of the kind children use at school)。里面的内容是一个叫约翰 . F. 卡特赖特的外科医生写的,扉页写下了这样的字样:1934 年 12 月在印度孟买市对伊姆拉汗这位不用眼睛能够看得见的人的采访报告(A REPORT ON AN INTERVIEW WITH IMHRAT KHAN, THE MAN WHO COULD SEE WITHOUT HIS EYES by Dr John F. Cartwright, BOMBAY, INDIA, DECEMBER, 1934)。于是,亨利开始阅读起来,进入第一个嵌套的故事:

有一天,卡特赖特医生跟同事坐在孟买的办公室休息。这时,一个名叫伊姆拉汗的印度男子走了进来,请求帮助。这名男子声称自己不用眼睛能够看到东西,要在一个流动剧团做开场表演,请求卡特赖特医生及同事帮忙宣传一下——用绷带将他的双眼密密实实缠住,以证明他的确具备这样的能力。缠完绷带之后,卡特赖特医生跟同事亲眼看到这名印度男子骑着自行车轻松穿过拥挤的车流。那天晚上,卡特赖特医生请伊姆拉汗吃饭,要他讲述他的神功是如何练成的。于是,他讲了起来,展开了第二个嵌套的故事:

年轻的伊姆拉汗被魔术深深地吸引,于是,他追随一名魔术师,做他的助手,以便学习魔术。一段时间过后,他发现所谓的魔术不过是靠手疾眼快来完成的,极度失望,决定去修炼一种奇特的本领——瑜伽。问题是,真正的瑜伽大师踪迹难寻,况且,伊姆拉汗修炼瑜伽的动机不是那么纯正:出名和发财。要知道,瑜伽大师要是抛头露面、公开表演的话,就会有生命危险。经过多方打探,伊姆拉汗最终找到了一位名叫班纳吉的瑜伽大师,并暗中观看大师修炼"悬空"神功。班纳吉大师发现后,愤怒之至,将他驱赶出去,但他照例每天都来。万般无奈,班纳吉只好将他推荐给自己的一个朋友,要他从自己的朋友那儿修炼瑜伽。找到班纳吉的那位朋友后,伊姆拉汗最终开始了修炼之路,练成了不用眼睛也能看见东西的神功,甚至能看透纸牌。

卡特赖特医生听了伊姆拉汗的故事,十分震惊,认为他的超能力能够创造医学奇迹:帮助失明的人看见东西,帮助失聪的人听见声音。但是第二天,还没等他看到伊姆拉汗,就听说他在睡梦中死去了。

"据说,他死在床上,"守门人说。"他睡着了,再也没有醒过来,这样的事儿时有发生。"

"They say he died in his bed," the gatekeeper said. "He went to sleep and never woke up. These things happen."

故事至此,卡特赖特医生的采访报告结束了。

二、原作释读

这篇小说篇幅较长,叙事角度切换较多,阅读中需要仔细辨别。同时,还要注意领会某些专业领域的词汇和表达,如文学、音乐、生理学等领域里的词汇和表达,但大部分还是容易理解的,障碍不是很多,可以流畅地阅读和理解。

The Wonderful Story of Henry Sugar①

Henry Sugar was forty-one years old and unmarried. He was also wealthy. He was wealthy because he had had a rich father who was now dead. He was unmarried because he was too selfish to share any of his money with a wife.

He was six feet two inches tall, but he wasn't really as good-looking as he thought he was.

He paid a great deal of attention to his clothes. He went to an expensive tailor for his suits, to a shirtmaker for his shirts, and to a bootmaker for his shoes.

He used a costly aftershave lotion② on his face, and he kept his hands soft with a cream that contained turtle oil.

His hairdresser trimmed his hair once every ten days, and he always took a manicure③ at the same time.

His upper front teeth had been capped at incredible expense because the originals had had a rather nasty yellowish tinge. A small mole④ had been removed from his left cheek by a plastic surgeon.

---

① 本部小说原文出自"DAHL R. *The Wonderful Story of Henry Sugar and Six More*. London: Penguin Books Ltd., 2002"。

② lotion: *Noun* [mass noun] a thick, smooth liquid preparation designed to be applied to the skin for medicinal or cosmetic purposes(治疗用的)洗液;洗剂;(化妆用的)搽液;涂剂

③ manicure: *Noun* a cosmetic treatment of the hands involving cutting, shaping, and often painting of the nails, removal of the cuticles, and softening of the skin 修指甲

④ mole: *Noun* a small, often slightly raised blemish on the skin made dark by a high concentration of melanin 痣;瘤

He drove a Ferrari① car which must have cost him about the same as a country cottage.

He lived in London in the summer, but as soon as the first frosts appeared in October, he was off to the West Indies② or the South of France, where he stayed with friends. All his friends were wealthy from inherited money.

Henry had never done a day's work in his life, and his personal motto, which he had invented himself, was this: It is better to incur③ a mild rebuke④ than to perform an onerous⑤ task. His friends thought this was hilarious⑥.

Men like Henry Sugar are to be found drifting like seaweed all over the world. They can be seen especially in London, New York, Paris,

① Ferrari：一个著名汽车的品牌，通常译作"法拉利"。

② West Indies: a chain of islands extending from the Florida peninsula to the coast of Venezuela, lying between the Caribbean and the Atlantic 西印度群岛(佛罗里达半岛与委内瑞拉海岸之间的一系列岛屿，位于加勒比海和大西洋之间。)

③ incur: *Verb* [with obj.] become subject to (something unwelcome or unpleasant) as a result of one's own behaviour or actions(因自身行为举止)遭受；招致；惹来(e.g. I will pay any expenses incurred. 我将支付任何由我招致的费用。)

④ rebuke: *Noun* an expression of sharp disapproval or criticism 指责；叱责；训斥(e.g. He hadn't meant it as a rebuke, but Neil flinched. 他无意训斥尼尔，但他却畏缩了。)

⑤ onerous: *Adjective* (of a task, duty, or responsibility) involving an amount of effort and difficulty which is oppressively burdensome(任务、责任等)繁重的；费力的；困难的(e.g. He found his duties increasingly onerous. 他发现自己的职责越来越繁重了。)

⑥ hilarious: *Adjective* extremely amusing 极有趣的；引人发笑的

Nassau①, Montego Bay②, Cannes③ and St Tropez④. They are not particularly bad men. But they are not good men either. They are of no real importance. They are simply a part of the decoration.

All of them, all wealthy people of this type, have one peculiarity in common: they have a terrific urge to make themselves still wealthier than they already are. The million is never enough. Nor is the two million. Always, they have this insatiable longing to get more money. And that is because they live in constant terror of waking up one morning and finding there's nothing in the bank.

These people all employ the same methods for trying to increase their fortunes. They buy stocks and shares, and watch them going up and down. They play roulette⑤ and blackjack⑥ for high stakes in casinos.

---

① Nassau: *Noun* a port on the island of New Providence, capital of the Bahamas; pop. 172,000 (1990) 拿骚(巴哈马联邦首都,新普罗维登斯岛一港口,1990年人口172,000。)

② Montego Bay: a free port and tourist resort on the north coast of Jamaica; pop. 82,000 (1991) 蒙特哥贝(牙买加北海岸自由港和旅游胜地,1991年人口82,000。)

③ Cannes: *Noun* a resort on the Mediterranean coast of France; pop. 69,360 (1990). An international film festival is held there annually 戛纳(法国地中海岸度假胜地,1990年人口69,360,每年在此举办国际电影节。)

④ St Tropez or Saint-Tropez, a Provenscal town, 104 kilometres (65 miles) to the east of Marseille, in the Var department of the Provence-Alpes-Ca te d'Azur region of southeastern France. It is also the principal town in the canton of Saint-Tropez. 圣特罗佩(位于法国东南部普罗旺斯—阿尔卑斯—蓝色海岸大区瓦尔省的一座小镇,东面离省府马赛104公里,即65英里,也是省内的主要城市。)

⑤ roulette: *Noun* [mass noun] a gambling game in which a ball is dropped on to a revolving wheel with numbered compartments, the players betting on the number at which the ball comes to rest 轮盘赌

⑥ blackjack: *Noun* [mass noun] (chiefly N. Amer.) a gambling card game in which players try to acquire cards with a face value totalling 21 and no more(主要为北美英语用法)21点(牌戏)

They bet on horses. They bet on just about everything. Henry Sugar had once staked a thousand pounds on the result of a tortoise race on Lord Liverpool's tennis lawn. And he had wagered① double that sum with a man called Esmond Hanbury on an even sillier bet, which was as follows: they let Henry's dog out into the garden and they watched it through the window. But before the dog was let out, each man had to guess beforehand what would be the first object the dog would lift its leg against. Would it be a wall, a post, a bush or a tree? Esmond chose a wall. Henry, who had been studying his dog's habits for days with a view to making this particular bet, chose a tree, and he won the money.

With ridiculous games such as these did Henry and his friends try to conquer the deadly boredom of being both idle and wealthy.

Henry himself, as you may have noticed, was not above cheating a little on these friends of his if he saw the chance. The bet with the dog was definitely not honest. Nor, if you want to know, was the bet on the tortoise race. Henry cheated on that one by secretly forcing a little sleeping-pill powder into the mouth of his opponent's tortoise an hour before the race.

And now that you've got a rough idea of the sort of person Henry Sugar was, I can begin my story.

One summer week-end, Henry drove down from London to Guildford② to stay with Sir William Wyndham. The house was magnificent, and so were the grounds, but when Henry arrived on that Saturday after-

---

① wager: *Verb* to risk or stake (an amount or a possession) on an uncertain outcome; bet 在(某物)上赌钱;打赌(e. g. I am ready to wager a package of cigarettes that he will come. 我敢打赌一盒香烟,他一定来。)

② Guildford: *Noun* a city in southern England; pop. 63,090 (1981) 吉尔福德(英格兰南部城市,1981 年人口 63,090。)

noon, it was already pelting[①] with rain. Tennis was out, croquet[②] was out. So was swimming in Sir William's outdoor pool. The host and his guests sat glumly[③] in the drawing-room, staring at the rain splashing against the windows. The very rich are enormously resentful of bad weather. It is the one discomfort that their money cannot do anything about.

Somebody in the room said, "Let's have a game of canasta[④] for lovely high stakes."

The others thought that a splendid idea, but as there were five people in all, one would have to sit out. They cut the cards. Henry drew the lowest, the unlucky card.

The other four sat down and began to play. Henry was annoyed at being out of the game. He wandered out of the drawing-room into the great hall. He stared at the pictures for a few moments, then he walked on through the house, bored to death at having nothing to do. Finally, he mooched into the library.

Sir William's father had been a famous book collector, and all the four walls to this huge room were lined with books from floor to ceiling. Henry Sugar was not impressed. He wasn't even interested. The only

---

① pelt: *Verb* [no obj.] (pelt down) (of rain, hail, or snow) fall quickly and very heavily(雨、冰雹或雪)下得很大;猛降

② croquet: *Noun* [mass noun] a game played on a Lawn, in which wooden balls are driven through a series of square-topped hoops by means of mallets 槌球游戏(一种用长柄木槌击打木球使之穿过一系列球门的户外游戏)

③ glum: *Adjective* looking or feeling dejected; morose 沮丧的;郁闷的(e.g. The princess looked glum but later cheered up. 公主看起来闷闷不乐,但后来又振作起来。)

④ canasta: *Noun* [mass noun] a card game resembling rummy, using two packs. It is usually played by two pairs of partners, and the aim is to collect sets (or melds) of cards 凯纳斯特纸牌戏

books he read were detective novels and thrillers. He ambled① aimlessly round the room, looking to see if he could find any of the sort of books he liked. But the ones in Sir William's library were all leather-bound volumes with names on them like Balzac②, Ibsen③, Voltaire④,

---

① amble: *Verb* [no obj., with adverbial of direction] walk or move at a slow, relaxed pace 漫步;悠闲散步(e. g. They ambled along the riverbank. 他们沿着河岸散步。)

② Honoré de Balzac (1799—1850), French novelist. He is chiefly remembered for his series of ninety-one interconnected novels and stories known collectively as La Comédie humaine, which includes Eugénie Grandet (1833) and Le Père Goriot (1835) 奥诺雷·德巴尔扎克(1799—1850):法国小说家,以包括91部系列小说的巨著《人间喜剧》闻名,包括《欧也妮·葛朗台》(1833)和《高老头》(1835)等。

③ Henrik Ibsen (1828—1906), Norwegian dramatist. He is credited with being the first major dramatist to write tragedy about ordinary people in prose. Ibsen's later works, such as The Master Builder (1892), deal increasingly with the forces of the unconscious and were admired by Sigmund Freud. Other notable works: Peer Gynt (1867), A Doll's House (1879), Ghosts (1881) 亨利克·易卜生(1828—1906):挪威戏剧家;被认为是首位以散文体描写普通人悲剧的主要戏剧家;其晚期作品,如《建筑师索尔尼斯》(1892),越来越多涉及无意识的力量,为西格蒙德·弗洛伊德所欣赏;其他代表作品:《彼尔·英特》(1867)、《玩偶之家》(1879)以及《群鬼》(1881)。

④ Voltaire (1694—1778), French writer, dramatist, and poet; pseudonym of Frans ois-Marie Arouet. He was a leading figure of the Enlightenment, and frequently came into conflict with the Establishment as a result of his radical views and satirical writings. Notable works: Lettres philosophiques (1734) and the satire Candide (1759) 伏尔泰(1694—1778),法国作家、剧作家、诗人,弗朗索亚马利·阿卢埃的笔名;启蒙运动的代表人物,其激进的观点和讽刺作品经常与统治集团发生冲突;代表作品:《哲学书简》(1734)和讽刺作品《老实人》(1759)。

Johnson[①] and Pepys[②]. Boring rubbish, the whole lot of it, Henry told himself. And he was just about to leave when his eye was caught and held by a book that was quite different from all the others. It was so slim he would never have noticed it if it hadn't been sticking out a little from the ones on either side. And when he pulled it from the shelf, he saw that it was actually nothing more than a cardboard-covered exercise-book of the kind children use at school. The cover was dark blue, but there was nothing written on it. Henry opened the exercise-book. On the first page, hand-printed in ink, it said:

A REPORT ON AN INTERVIEW
WITH IMHRAT KHAN, THE MAN WHO
COULD SEE WITHOUT HIS EYES
by
Dr John F. Cartwright

---

① Samuel Johnson (1709—1784), English lexicographer, writer, critic, and conversationalist; known as Dr Johnson. A leading figure in the literary London of his day, he is noted particularly for his Dictionary of the English Language (1755), edition of Shakespeare (1765), and The Lives of the English Poets (1777). James Boswell's biography of Johnson records details of his life and conversation. 塞缪尔·约翰逊(1709—1784):英国辞典编纂家、作家、批评家、雄辩家;通称约翰逊博士;作为当时伦敦文学界的重要人物,他所编纂的《英语辞典》(1755),编辑的莎士比亚作品(1765)以及《英国诗人传》(1777)使他闻名遐迩;詹姆斯·博斯韦尔的《塞缪尔·约翰逊传》详细记录了他的生平和谈话。

② Samuel Pepys (1633—1703), English diarist and naval administrator. He is particularly remembered for his Diary (1660—1669), which describes events such as the Great Plague and the Fire of London. 塞缪尔·佩皮斯(1633—1703):英国日记作者和海军行政长官,尤以其记载了诸如伦敦大瘟疫、大火灾等事件的《日记》(1660—1669)而出名。

BOMBAY[1], INDIA

DECEMBER, 1934

That sounds mildly interesting, Henry told himself. He turned over a page. What followed was all hand-written in black ink. The writing was clear and neat. Henry read the first two pages standing up. Suddenly, he found himself wanting to read on. This was good stuff. It was fascinating. He carried the little book over to a leather armchair by the window and settled himself comfortably. Then he started reading again from the beginning.

This is what Henry read in the little blue exercise-book:

I, John Cartwright, am a surgeon at Bombay General Hospital. On the morning of the second of December, 1934, I was in the Doctors' Rest Room having a cup of tea. There were three other doctors there with me, all having a well-earned tea-break. They were Dr Marshall, Dr Phillips and Dr Macfarlane. There was a knock on the door. "Come in," I said.

The door opened and an Indian came in who smiled at us and said, "Excuse me, please. Could I ask you gentlemen a favour?"

The Doctors' Rest Room was a most private place. Nobody other than a doctor was allowed to enter it except in an emergency.

"This is a private room," Dr Macfarlane said sharply.

"Yes, yes," the Indian answered. "I know that and I am very sorry

---

① Bombay: *Noun* a city and port on the west coast of India, capital of the state of Maharashtra; pop. 9,990,000 (1991). Official name (from 1995) Mumbai 孟买(印度西部的港口城市,马哈拉施特拉邦首府; 1991 年人口为 9,990,000。官方名 Mumbai (1995 年后))。

to be bursting in like this, sirs, but I have a most interesting thing to show you."

All four of us were pretty annoyed and we didn't say anything.

"Gentlemen," he said. "I am a man who can see without using his eyes."

We still didn't invite him to go on. But we didn't kick him out either.

"You can cover my eyes in any way you wish," he said, "You can bandage my head with fifty bandages and I will still be able to read you a book."

He seemed perfectly serious. I felt my curiosity beginning to stir. "Come here," I said. He came over to me. "Turn round." He turned round. I placed my hands firmly over his eyes, holding the lids① closed. "Now," I said. "One of the other doctors in the room is going to hold up some fingers. Tell me how many he's holding up."

Dr Marshall held up seven fingers.

"Seven," the Indian said.

"Once more," I said.

Dr Marshall clenched both fists and hid all his fingers.

"No fingers," the Indian said.

"Once more," I said.

Dr Marshall clenched both fists and hid all his fingers.

"No fingers," the Indian said.

I removed my hands from his eyes. "Not bad," I said.

"Hold on," Dr Marshall said. "Let's try this." There was a white

---

① lid: *Noun* (often as "lids") an eyelid 眼皮(e. g. eyes now hooded beneath heavy lids 此刻被沉沉下垂的眼皮遮住了的双眼)

doctor's coat hanging from a peg① on the door. Dr Marshall took it down and rolled it into a sort of long scarf. He then wound it round the Indian's head and held the ends tight at the back. "Try him now," Dr Marshall said.

I took a key from my pocket. "What is this?" I asked.

"A key," he answered.

I put the key back and held up an empty hand. "What is this object?" I asked him.

"There isn't any object," the Indian said. "Your hand is empty."

Dr Marshall removed the covering from the man's eyes. "How do you do it?" he asked. "What's the trick?" "There is no trick," the Indian said. "It is a genuine thing that I have managed after years of training."

"What sort of training?" I asked.

"Forgive me, sir," he said. "But that is a private matter."

"Then why did you come here?" I asked.

"I came to request a favour of you," he said.

The Indian was a tall man of about thirty with light brown skin, the colour of a coconut. He had a small black moustache. Also, there was a curious matting of black hair growing all over the outsides of his ears. He wore a white cotton robe, and he had sandals② on his bare feet.

"You see, gentlemen," he went on, "I am at present earning my living by working in a travelling theatre, and we have just arrived here in Bombay. Tonight we give our opening performance."

"Where do you give it?" I asked.

---

① peg: *Noun* such an object attached to a wall on which to hang garments 挂衣钉;挂衣钩

② sandal: *Noun* a light shoe with either an openwork upper or straps attaching the sole to the foot 拖鞋;凉鞋

"In the Royal Palace Hall," he answered. "In Acacia Street. I am the star performer. I am billed on the programme as[①] 'Imhrat Khan, the man who sees without his eyes'. And it is my duty to advertise the show in a big way. If we don't sell tickets, we don't eat."

"What does this have to do with us?" I asked him.

"Very interesting for you," he said. "Lots of fun. Let me explain. You see, whenever our theatre arrives in a new town, I myself go straight to the largest hospital and I ask the doctors there to bandage my eyes. I ask them to do it in the most expert fashion. They must make sure my eyes are completely covered many times over. It is important that this job is done by doctors, otherwise people will think I am cheating. Then, when I am fully bandaged, I go out into the streets and I do a dangerous thing."

"What do you mean by that?" I asked.

"What I mean is that I do something that is extremely dangerous for someone who cannot see."

"What do you do?" I asked.

"It is very interesting," he said. "And you will see me do it if you will be so kind as to bandage me up first. It would be a great favour to me if you will do this little thing, sirs."

I looked at the other three doctors. Dr Phillips said he had to go back to his patients. Dr Macfarlane said the same. Dr Marshall said, "Well, why not? It might be amusing. It won't take a minute."

"I'm with you," I said. "But let's do the job properly. Let's make absolutely sure he can't peep."

---

① bill sb./sth. as sth.: to describe sb./sth. in a particular way; to advertise sb./sth. as sth(把人或事物)说成是……;宣传为……(e.g. Some patients are receiving what has been billed as a revolutionary treatment. 有些病人正在接受所谓的革命性治疗。)

"You are extremely kind," the Indian said. "Please do whatever you wish."

Dr Phillips and Dr Macfarlane left the room.

"Before we bandage him," I said to Dr Marshall, "let's first of all seal down his eyelids①. When we've done that we'll fill his eye-sockets with something soft and solid and sticky."

"Such as what?" Dr Marshall asked.

"What about dough?"

"Dough would be perfect," Dr Marshall said.

"Right," I said. "If you will nip② down to the hospital bakery and get some dough, I'll take him into the surgery and seal his lids."

I led the Indian out of the Rest Room and down the long hospital corridor to the surgery. "Lie down there," I said, indicating the high bed. He lay down. I took a small bottle from the cupboard. It had an eyedropper in the top. "This is something called collodion③," I told him. "It will harden over your closed eyelids so that it is impossible for you to open them."

"How do I get it off afterwards?" he asked me.

"Alcohol will dissolve it quite easily," I said. "It's perfectly harm-

---

① eyelid: *Noun* each of the upper and lower folds of skin which cover the eye when closed 眼皮;眼睑

② nip: *Verb* [no obj., with adverbial of direction] (Brit. informal) go quickly(英国英语非正式用法)跑开(e.g. I'm just nipping down to the Post Office. 我正一溜烟儿地向邮局跑去。)

③ collodion: *Noun* [mass noun] a syrupy solution of nitrocellulose in a mixture of alcohol and ether, used for coating things, chiefly in surgery and in a former photographic process 火棉胶;硝棉胶;胶棉

注:火棉胶是一种透明或半透明而极易燃的浆状液体,由二硝化纤维素、醚和乙醇混合而成,干燥后可形成透明坚韧之薄膜,用作局部皮肤保护剂以闭合小伤口,如擦伤及割伤,固定外科敷料和保持药物与皮肤的接触。

less. Close your eyes now."

The Indian closed his eyes. I applied collodion over both lids. "Keep them closed," I said. "Wait for it to harden." In a couple of minutes, the collodion had made a hard film over the eyelids, sticking them down tight. "Try to open them," I said.

He tried but couldn't.

Dr Marshall came in with a basin of dough. It was the ordinary white dough used for baking bread. It was nice and soft①. I took a lump of the dough and plastered it over one of the Indian's eyes. I filled the whole socket and let the dough overlap on to the surrounding skin. Then I pressed the edges down hard. I did the same with the other eye.

"That isn't too uncomfortable, is it?" I asked.

"No," the Indian said. "It's fine."

"You do the bandaging," I said to Dr Marshall. "My fingers are too sticky."

"A pleasure," Dr Marshall said. "Watch this." He took a thick wad of cotton-wool and laid it on top of the Indian's dough-filled eyes. The cotton-wool stuck to the dough and stayed in place. "Sit up, please," Dr Marshall said.

The Indian sat up on the bed.

Dr Marshall took a roll of three-inch bandage and proceeded to wrap it round and round the man's head. The bandage held the cotton-wool and the dough firmly in place. Dr Marshall pinned the bandage. After that, he took a second bandage and began to wrap that one not only around the man's eyes but around his entire face and head.

"Please to leave my nose free for breathing," the Indian said.

"Of course," Dr Marshall answered. He finished the job and

① nice and...: satisfactorily or adequately in terms of the quality described 令人满意地;恰到好处地(e.g. It's nice and warm in here. 这里温暖怡人。)

pinned down the end of the bandage. "How's that?" he asked.

"Splendid," I said. "There's no way he can possibly see through that."

The whole of the Indian's head was now swathed① in thick white bandage, and the only thing you could see was the end of his nose sticking out. He looked like a man who had had some terrible brain operation.

"How does that feel?" Dr Marshall asked him.

"It feels good," the Indian said. "I must compliment you gentlemen on doing such a fine job."

"Off you go, then," Mr. Marshall said, grinning at me. "Show us how clever you are at seeing things now!"

The Indian got off the bed and walked straight to the door. He opened the door and went out.

"Great Scott!" I said. "Did you see that? He put his hand right on to the doorknob!"

Dr Marshall had stopped grinning. His face had suddenly gone white. "I'm going after him," he said, rushing for the door. I rushed for the door as well.

The Indian was walking quite normally along the hospital corridor. Dr Marshall and I were about five yards behind him. And very spooky② it was to watch this man with the enormous white and totally bandaged head strolling casually along the corridor just like anyone else. It was especial-

---

① swathe: *Verb* [with obj.] (often as "be swathed in") wrap in several layers of fabric 用几层布包起来(e. g. His hands were swathed in bandages. 他的手被绷带层层裹起来。)

② spooky: *Adjective* (informal) sinister or ghostly in a way that causes fear and unease(非正式)阴森恐怖的(e. g. I bet this place is really spooky late at night. 我敢说这个地方晚上真的很阴森吓人。)

ly spooky when you knew for a certainty that his eyelids were sealed, that his eye-sockets were filled with dough, and that there was a great wad of cotton-wool and bandages on top of that.

I saw a native orderly① coming along the corridor towards the Indian. He was pushing a food-trolley. Suddenly the orderly caught sight of the man with the white head, and he froze. The bandaged Indian stepped casually to one side of the trolley and went on.

"He saw it!" I cried. "He must have seen that trolley! He walked right round it! This is absolutely unbelievable!"

Dr Marshall didn't answer me. His cheeks were white, his whole face rigid with shocked disbelief.

The Indian came to the stairs and started to go down them.

He went down with no trouble at all. He didn't even put a hand on the stair-rail. Several people were coming up the stairs. Each one of them stopped, gasped, stared and quickly got out of his way.

At the bottom of the stairs, the Indian turned right and headed for the doors that led out into the street. Dr Marshall and I kept close behind him.

The entrance to our hospital stands back a little from the street, and there is a rather grand series of steps leading down from the entrance into a small courtyard with acacia trees② around it. Dr Marshall and I came out into the blazing sunshine and stood at the top of the steps. Below us, in the courtyard, we saw a crowd of maybe a hundred people. At least half of them were barefoot children, and as our white-headed Indian

---

① orderly: *Noun* an attendant in a hospital responsible for the non-medical care of patients and the maintenance of order and cleanliness(医院)护理员;勤杂工

② acacia or acacia tree: *Noun* a tree or shrub of warm climates which bears spikes or clusters of yellow or white flowers and is typically thorny. Also called wattle, especially in Australia 金合欢属植物;刺槐

walked down the steps, they all cheered and shouted and surged towards him. He greeted them by holding both hands above his head.

Suddenly I saw the bicycle. It was over to one side at the bottom of the steps, and a small boy was holding it. The bicycle itself was quite ordinary, but on the back of it, fixed somehow to the rear wheel-frame, was a huge placard①, about five feet square. On the placard were written the following words:

IMHRAT KHAN, THE MAN WHO SEES
WITHOUT HIS EYES!
TODAY MY EYES HAVE BEEN BANDAGED BY
HOSPITAL DOCTORS!
APPEARING TONIGHT AND
ALL THIS WEEK AT
THE ROYAL PALACE HALL,
ACACIA STREET, AT 7 P.M.
DON'T MISS IT!
YOU WILL SEE MIRACLES PERFORMED.

Our Indian had reached the bottom of the steps and now he walked straight over to the bicycle. He said something to the boy and the boy smiled. The Indian mounted the bicycle. The crowd made way for him. Then, lo and behold②, this fellow with the blocked-up, bandaged eyes

---

① placard: *Noun* a printed or handwritten notice or sign for public display, either fixed to a wall or carried during a demonstration 布告;海报;告示牌;标语牌

② lo and behold: used to present a new scene, situation, or turn of events, often with the suggestion that though surprising, it could in fact have been predicted (以介绍新景象、情况或事情的转变,常表示某事看似奇特但可以预料)哎哟,看看(e.g. You took me out and, lo and behold, I got home to find my house had been ransacked. 你把我弄出来,哎哟看看,我回到家却发现家里已被洗劫一空。)

now proceeded to ride across the courtyard and straight out into the bustling honking traffic of the street beyond! The crowd cheered louder than ever. The barefoot children ran after him, squealing and laughing. For a minute or so, we were able to keep him in sight. We saw him ride superbly down the busy street with motor-cars whizzing past him and a bunch of children running in his wake. Then he turned a corner and was gone.

"I feel quite giddy①," Dr Marshall said. "I can't bring myself to believe it."

"We have to believe it," I said. "He couldn't possibly have removed the dough from under the bandages. We never let him out of our sight. And as for unsealing his eyelids, that job would take him five minutes with cotton-wool and alcohol."

"Do you know what I think," Dr Marshall said. "I think we have witnessed a miracle."

We turned and walked slowly back into the hospital.

For the rest of the day, I was kept busy with patients in the hospital. At six in the evening, I came off duty and drove back to my flat for a shower and a change of clothes. It was the hottest time of year in Bombay, and even after sundown the heat was like an open furnace. If you sat still in a chair and did nothing, the sweat would come seeping out of your skin. Your face glistened with dampness all day long and your shirt stuck to your chest. I took a long cool shower. I drank a whisky and soda sitting on the veranda, with only a towel round my waist. Then I put on some clean clothes. At ten minutes to seven, I was outside the Royal

---

① giddy: *Adjective* disorientating and alarming, but exciting 令人迷惑、吃惊又激动的;眼花缭乱的(e.g. He has risen to the giddy heights of master. 他已升到令人飘飘然的大师高度。)

Palace Hall in Acacia Street. It was not much of a place. It was one of those smallish seedy① halls that can be hired inexpensively for meetings or dances. There was a fair-sized crowd of local Indians milling② round outside the ticket office, and a large poster over the entrance proclaiming that THE INTERNATIONAL THEATRE COMPANY was performing every night that week. It said there would be jugglers③ and conjurers④ and acrobats and sword-swallowers and fire-eaters and snake-charmers and a one-act play entitled The Rajah⑤ and the Tiger Lady. But above all this and in far the largest letters, it said IMHRAT KHAN, THE MIRACLE MAN WHO SEES WITHOUT HIS EYES.

I bought a ticket and went in.

The show lasted two hours. To my surprise, I thoroughly enjoyed it. All the performers were excellent. I liked the man who juggled⑥ with cooking-utensils. He had a saucepan, a frying-pan, a baking tray, a huge plate and a casserole⑦ pot all flying through the air at the same time. The snake-charmer had a big green snake that stood almost on the

---

① seedy: *Adjective* shabby and squalid 破旧肮脏的(e. g. an increasingly seedy and dilapidated property 日益破旧不堪的房产)

② mill: *Verb* [no obj.] (mill about/around) (of people or animals) move around in a confused mass 无目的地乱转;绕圈子(e. g. People milled about the room, shaking hands. 大家在房间里转来转去互相握手。)

③ juggler: *Noun* one that juggles objects or performs other tricks of manual dexterity 玩杂耍的人

④ conjurer: *Noun* one that performs magic tricks; a magician 魔术师

⑤ rajah or raja: *Noun* (historical) an Indian king or prince(历史上的用法)拉甲(指印度王或王公)

⑥ juggle: *Verb* [with obj.] continuously toss into the air and catch (a number of objects) so as to keep at least one in the air while handling the others, typically for the entertainment of others 抛耍;(多个物品)不停抛接不使坠下

⑦ casserole: *Noun* a large covered dish, typically of earthenware or glass, used for cooking such stews(尤指陶制或玻璃制的)焙盘;砂锅;炖锅

tip of its tail and swayed to the music of his flute. The fire-eater ate fire and the sword-swallower pushed a thin pointed rapier① at least four feet down his throat and into his stomach. Last of all, to a great fanfare② of trumpets, our friend Imhrat Khan came on to do his act. The bandages we had put on him at the hospital had now been removed.

Members of the audience were called on to the stage to blindfold him with sheets and scarves and turbans③, and in the end there was so much material wrapped around his head he could hardly keep his balance. He was then given a revolver. A small boy came out and stood at the left of the stage. I recognized him as the one who had held the bicycle outside the hospital that morning. The boy placed a tin can on the top of his head and stood quite still. The audience became deathly silent as Imhrat Khan took aim. He fired. The bang made us all jump. The tin can flew off the boy's head and clattered to the floor. The boy picked it up and showed the bullet-hole to the audience. Everyone clapped and cheered. The boy smiled.

Then the boy stood against a wooden screen and Imhrat Khan threw knives all around his body, most of them going very close indeed. This was a splendid act. Not many people could have thrown knives with such accuracy even with their eyes uncovered, but here he was, this extraordinary fellow, with his head so swathed in sheets it looked like a great snowball on a stick, and he was flicking the sharp knives into the screen

---

① rapier: *Noun* a thin, light sharp-pointed sword used for thrusting(击剑用的)轻剑

② fanfare: *Noun* a short ceremonial tune or flourish played on brass instruments, typically to introduce something or someone important(欢迎仪式上的)号角齐鸣

③ turban: *Noun* a man's headdress, consisting of a long length of cotton or silk wound round a cap or the head, worn especially by Muslims and Sikhs(穆斯林和锡克人的)包头巾

within a hair's breadth of the boy's head. The boy smiled all the way through the act, and when it was over the audience stamped its feet and screamed with excitement.

Imhrat Khan's last act, though not so spectacular, was even more impressive. A metal barrel was brought on stage. The audience was invited to examine it, to make sure there were no holes. There were no holes. The barrel was then placed over Imhrat Khan's already bandaged head. It came down over his shoulders and as far as his elbows, pinning the upper part of his arms to his sides. But he could still hold out his forearms and his hands. Someone put a needle in one of his hands and a length of cotton thread in the other. With no false moves, he neatly threaded the cotton through the eye of the needle. I was flabbergasted①.

As soon as the show was over, I made my way backstage. I found Mr. Imhrat Khan in a small but clean dressing-room, sitting quietly on a wooden stool. The little Indian boy was unwinding the masses of scarves and sheets from around his head.

"Ah," he said. "It is my friend the doctor from the hospital. Come in, sir, come in."

"I saw the show," I said.

"And what did you think?"

"I liked it very much. I thought you were wonderful."

"Thank you," he said. "That is a high compliment."

"I must congratulate your assistant as well," I said, nodding to the small boy. "He is very brave."

"He cannot speak English," the Indian said. "But I will tell him

---

① flabbergast: *Verb* [with obj.] [usu. as *adj.* flabbergasted] (informal) surprise (someone) greatly; astonish(非正式)使大吃一惊;使目瞪口呆(e.g. This news has left me totally flabbergasted. 这条消息已经让我完全目瞪口呆了。)

what you said." He spoke rapidly to the boy in Hindustani[①] and the boy nodded solemnly but said nothing.

"Look," I said. "I did you a small favour this morning. Would you do me one in return? Would you consent to come out and have supper with me?"

All the wrappings were off his head now. He smiled at me and said, "I think you are feeling curious, doctor. Am I not right?"

"Very curious," I said. "I'd like to talk to you."

Once again, I was struck by the peculiarly thick matting of black hair growing on the outsides of his ears. I had not seen anything quite like it on another person. "I have never been questioned by a doctor before," he said. "But I have no objection. It would be a pleasure to have supper with you."

"Shall I wait in the car?"

"Yes, please," he said. "I must wash myself and get out of these dirty clothes."

I told him what my car looked like and said I would be waiting outside.

He emerged fifteen minutes later, wearing a clean white cotton robe and the usual sandals on his bare feet. And soon the two of us were sitting comfortably in a small restaurant that I sometimes went to because it made the best curry[②] in the city. I drank beer with my curry. Imhrat Khan drank lemonade.

---

① Hindustani: *Noun* [mass noun] a group of mutually intelligible languages and dialects spoken in NW India, principally Hindi and Urdu, widely used throughout India as a lingua franca 印度斯坦语(印度西北部一组通行的语言和方言,主要为印地语和乌尔都语,在印度作为族际通用语广泛使用。)

② curry: *Noun* a dish of meat, vegetables, etc., cooked in an Indian-style sauce of strong spices and turmeric and typically served with rice 咖喱菜肴

"I am not a writer," I said to him. "I am a doctor. But if you will tell me your story from the beginning, if you will explain to me how you developed this magical power of being able to see without your eyes, I will write it down as faithfully as I can. And then, perhaps, I can get it published in the British Medical Journal or even in some famous magazine. And because I am a doctor and not just some writer trying to sell a story for money, people will be far more inclined to take seriously what I say. It would help you, wouldn't it, to become better known?"

"It would help me very much," he said. "But why should you want to do this?"

"Because I am madly curious," I answered. "That is the only reason."

Imhrat Khan took a mouthful of curried rice and chewed it slowly. Then he said, "Very well, my friend. I will do it."

"Splendid!" I cried. "Let's go back to my flat as soon as we've finished eating and then we can talk without anyone disturbing us."

We finished our meal. I paid the bill. Then I drove Imhrat Khan back to my flat.

In the living-room, I got out paper and pencils so that I could make notes. I have a sort of private shorthand of my own that I use for taking down the medical history of patients, and with it I am able to record most of what a person says if he doesn't speak too quickly. I think I got just about everything Imhrat Khan said to me that evening, word for word, and here it is. I give it to you exactly as he spoke it:

"I am an Indian, a Hindu①," said Imhrat Khan, "and I was born

① Hindu: *Noun* a follower of Hinduism 印度教教徒

in Akhnur, in Kashmir[①] State, in 1905. My family is poor and my father worked as a ticket inspector on the railway. When I was a small boy of thirteen, an Indian conjurer comes to our school and gives a performance. His name, I remember, is Professor Moor—all conjurers in India call themselves 'professor'—and his tricks are very good. I am tremendously impressed. I think it is real magic. I feel—how shall I call it—I feel a powerful wish to learn about this magic myself, so two days later I run away from home, determined to find and to follow my new hero, Professor Moor. I take all my savings, fourteen rupees[②], and only the clothes I am wearing. I am wearing a white dhoti[③] and sandals. This is in 1918 and I am thirteen years old."

"I find out that Professor Moor has gone to Lahore, two hundred miles away, so all alone, I take a ticket, third class, and I get on the train and follow him. In Lahore, I discover the Professor. He is working at his

---

① Kashmir: *Noun* a region on the northern border of India and NE Pakistan. Formerly a state of India, it has been disputed between India and Pakistan since partition in 1947, with sporadic outbreaks of fighting. The north-western part is controlled by Pakistan, most of it forming the state of Azad Kashmir, while the remainder is incorporated into the Indian state of Jammu and Kashmir 克什米尔(印度北部和巴基斯坦东北部边境的一个地区,旧时为印度的一个邦,1947 年对该地区实行分治后,印度和巴基斯坦之间就此一直纷争不断,不定时地爆发战争;该地区的西北部归巴基斯坦管辖,其大部分组成阿扎德克什米尔,而西北部以外的其余部分则并入印度的查谟与克什米尔邦。)

② rupee: *Noun* the basic monetary unit of India, Pakistan, Sri Lanka, Nepal, Mauritius, and the Seychelles, equal to 100 paisa in India, Pakistan, and Nepal, and 100 cents in Sri Lanka, Mauritius, and the Seychelles 卢比(印度、巴基斯坦、斯里兰卡、尼泊尔、毛里求斯和塞舌尔的基本货币单位,在印度、巴基斯坦和尼泊尔 1 卢比等于 100 派沙,在斯里兰卡、毛里求斯和塞舌尔 1 卢比等于 100 分。)

③ dhoti: *Noun* (Indian) a garment, worn mainly by men, consisting of a piece of material tied around the waist and extending to cover most of the legs(印度)缠腰布

conjuring in a very cheap-type show. I tell him of my admiration and offer myself to him as assistant. He accepts me. My pay? Ah yes, my pay is eight annas① a day."

"The Professor teaches me to do the linking-rings trick and my job is to stand in the street before the theatre doing this trick and calling to the people to come in and see the show."

"For six whole weeks this is very fine. It is much better than going to school. But then what a terrible bombshell I receive when suddenly it comes to me that there is no real magic in Professor Moor, that all is trickery and quickness of the hand. Immediately the Professor is no longer my hero. I lose every bit of interest in my job, but at the same time my whole mind becomes filled with a very strong longing. I long above all things to find out about the real magic and to discover something about the strange power which is called yoga②."

"To do this, I must find a yogi③ who is willing to let me become his disciple④. This is not going to be easy. True yogis do not grow on trees. There are very few of them in the whole of India. Also, they are fanatically religious people. Therefore, if I am to have success in finding a teacher, I too will have to pretend to be a very religious man."

"No, I am actually not religious. And because of that, I am what

---

① anna: *Noun* a former monetary unit of India and Pakistan, equal to one sixteenth of a rupee 安那(印度和巴基斯坦旧时的货币单位,等于1卢比的1/16。)

② yoga: *Noun* [mass noun] a Hindu spiritual and ascetic discipline, a part of which, including breath control, simple meditation, and the adoption of specific bodily postures, is widely practised for health and relaxation 瑜伽;瑜伽术(印度的一种传统健身法,练习包括呼吸控制、简单的静坐默想和身体的特定姿势,被广泛用作健身和休憩手段。)

③ yogi: *Noun* a person who is proficient in yoga 瑜伽修行者

④ disciple: *Noun* a follower or pupil of a teacher, leader, or philosophy 追随者;学生;门徒(e. g. a disciple of Rousseau 卢梭的门徒)

you would call a bit of a cheat. I wanted to acquire yoga powers purely for selfish reasons. I wanted to use these powers to get fame and fortune."

"Now this was something the true yogi would despise more than anything in the world. In fact, the true yogi believes that any yogi who misuses his powers will die an early and sudden death. A yogi must never perform in public. He must practise his art only in absolute privacy and as a religious service, otherwise he will be smitten to death. This I did not believe and I still don't."

"So now my search for a yogi instructor begins. I leave Professor Moor and go to a town called Amritsar in the Punjab①, where I join a travelling theatre company. I have to make a living while I am searching for the secret, and already I have had success in amateur acting at my school. So for three years I travel with this theatre group all over the Punjab and by the end of it, when I am sixteen and a half years old, I am playing top of the bill. All the time I am saving money and now I have altogether a very great sum, two thousand rupees."

"It is at this moment that I hear news of a man called Banerjee. This Banerjee, it is said, is one of the truly great yogis of India, and he possesses extraordinary powers. Above all, people are telling of how he has acquired the rare power of levitation, so that when he prays his whole body leaves the ground and becomes suspended in the air eighteen inches from the soil."

"Ah-ha, I think. This surely is the man for me. This Banerjee is the one that I must seek. So at once, I take my savings and leave the

---

① Punjab: *Noun* a region of NW India and Pakistan, a wide, fertile plain traversed by the Indus and the five tributaries which gave the region its name. 旁遮普地区(印度西北部和巴基斯坦一个地区,是印度河与旁遮普河的五条支流流经的广阔而肥沃的草原,该地区正因旁遮普河而得名。)

theatre company and make my way to Rishikesh, on the banks of the Ganges①, where rumour says that Banerjee is living."

"For six months I search for Banerjee. Where is he? Where? Where is Banerjee? Ah yes, they say in Rishikesh, Banerjee has certainly been in the town, but that is a while ago, and even then no one saw him. And now? Now Banerjee has gone to another place. What other place? Ah well, they say, how can one know that. How indeed? How can one know about the movements of such a one as Banerjee. Does he not live a life of absolute seclusion②? Does he not? And I say yes. Yes, yes, yes. Of course. That is obvious. Even to me."

"I spend all my savings trying to find this Banerjee, all except thirty-five rupees. But it is no good. However, I stay in Rishikesh and make a living by doing ordinary conjuring tricks for small groups and for suchlike③. These are the tricks I have learned from Professor Moor and by nature my sleight of hand④ is very good."

"Then one day, there I am sitting in the small hotel in Rishikesh and again I hear talk of the yogi Banerjee. A traveller is saying how he

---

① Ganges: *Noun* a river of northern India and Bangladesh, which rises in the Himalayas and flows some 2,700 km (1,678 miles) south-east to the Bay of Bengal, where it forms the world's largest delta. The river is regarded by Hindus as sacred. Hindi name Ganga 恒河(位于印度和孟加拉国北部,发源于喜马拉雅山脉,向东南流约 2,700 公里,即 1,678 英里流入孟加拉湾,并在那里形成世界上最大的三角洲;该河被印度人视为神河。印地语名"Ganga"。)

② seclusion: *Noun* [mass noun] the state of being private and away from other people 隔绝;隐居(e. g. They enjoyed ten days of peace and seclusion. 他们享受了十天与世隔绝的宁静生活。)

③ suchlike: *Pronoun* things of the type mentioned 这一类事物(e. g. carpets, old chairs, tables, and suchlike 地毯、旧椅子、桌子,以及诸如此类的东西)

④ sleight of hand: manual dexterity, typically in performing conjuring tricks (尤指变戏法时的)敏捷手法(e. g. A nifty bit of sleight of hand got the ashtray into the correct position. 一记漂亮的手法把烟灰缸放到了正确的位置。)

has heard that Banerjee is now living in the jungle, not so very far away, but in the dense jungle and all alone."

"But where?"

"The traveller is not sure where. 'Possibly,' he says, 'it is over there, in that direction, north of the town,' and he points with his finger."

"Well, that is enough for me. I go to the market and begin to bargain for hiring a tonga①, which is a horse and cart, and the transaction is just being completed with the driver when up comes a man who has been standing listening nearby and he says that he too is going in that direction. He says can he come part of the way with me and share the cost. Of course I am delighted, and off we go, the man and me sitting in the cart, and the driver driving the horse. Off we go along a very small path which leads right through the jungle."

"And then what truly fantastic luck should happen! I am talking to my companion and I find that he is a disciple of none other than the great Banerjee himself and that he is going now on a visit to his master. So straight out I tell him that I too would like to become a disciple of the yogi."

"He turns and looks at me long and slow, and for perhaps three minutes he does not speak. Then he says, quietly, 'No, that is impossible.'"

"All right, I say to myself, we shall see. Then I ask if it is really true that Banerjee levitates when he prays."

"'Yes,' he says. 'That is true. But no one is allowed to observe the thing happening. No one is ever allowed to come near Banerjee when he is praying.'"

---

① tonga: *Noun* a light horse-drawn two-wheeled vehicle used in India 印度轻便双轮马车

"So we go on a little further in the tonga, talking all the time about Banerjee, and I manage by very careful casual questioning, to find out a number of small things about him, such as what time of day he commences with his praying. Then soon the man says, 'I will leave you here. This is where I dismount.'"

"I drop him off and I pretend to drive on along my journey, but around a corner I tell the driver to stop and wait. Quickly I jump down and I sneak back along the road, looking for this man, the disciple of Banerjee. He is not on the road. Already he has disappeared into the jungle. But which way? Which side of the road? I stand very still and listen."

"I hear a sort of rustling in the undergrowth. That must be him, I tell myself. If it is not him, then it is a tiger. But it is him. I see him ahead. He is going forward through thick jungle. There is not even a little path where he is walking, and he is having to push his way between tall bamboos and every kind of heavy vegetation. I creep after him. I keep about one hundred yards behind him because I am frightened he may hear me. I can certainly hear him. It is impossible to proceed in silence through very thick jungle, and when I lose sight of him, which is most of the time, I am able to follow his sound."

"For about half an hour this tense game of follow-the-leader goes on. Then suddenly, I can no longer hear the man in front of me. I stop and listen. The jungle is silent. I am terrified that I may have lost him. I creep on a little way, and all at once, through the thick undergrowth, I see before me a little clearing, and in the middle of the clearing are two huts. They are small huts built entirely of jungle leaves and branches. My heart jumps and I feel a great surging of excitement inside me because this, I know for certain, is the place of Banerjee, the yogi."

"The disciple has already disappeared. He must have gone into one of the huts. All is quiet. So now I proceed to make a most careful inspection of the trees and bushes and other things all around. There is a small water-hole beside the nearest hut, and I see a prayer-mat beside it, and that, I say to myself, is where Banerjee meditates and prays. Close to this water-hole, not thirty yards away, there is a large tree, a great spreading baobab① tree with beautiful thick branches which spread in such a way you can put a bed on them and lie on the bed and still not be seen from underneath. That will be my tree, I say to myself. I shall hide in that tree, and wait until Banerjee comes out to pray. Then I will be able to see everything."

"But the disciple has told me that the time of prayer is not until five or six in the evening, so I have several hours to wait. Therefore I at once walk back through the jungle to the road and I speak to the tonga driver. I tell him he too must wait. For this, I have to pay him extra money, but it doesn't matter because now I am so excited I don't care about anything for the moment, not even money."

"And all through the great noontime heat of the jungle I wait beside the tonga, and on through the heavy wet heat of the afternoon, and then, as five o'clock approaches, I make my way quietly back through the jungle to the hut, my heart beating so fast I can feel it shaking my whole body. I climb up my tree and I hide among the leaves in such a way that I can see but cannot be seen. And I wait. I wait for forty-five minutes."

"A watch? Yes, I have on a wristwatch. I remember it clearly. It was a watch I won in a raffle② and I was proud to own it. On the face of

① baobab: *Noun* a short tree with a very thick trunk and large edible fruit, living to a great age 猴面包树

② raffle: *Noun* a lottery in which the prizes are goods rather than money 抽彩售物(e. g. He won a car in the raffle. 他在兑奖售物活动中赢得了一辆汽车。)

my watch it said the maker's name, The Islamia Watch Co., Ludhiana①. And so with my watch I am careful to be timing everything that goes on because I want to remember every single detail of this experience."

"I sit up in the tree, waiting."

"Then, all at once, a man is coming out of the hut. The man is tall and thin. He is dressed in an orange-coloured dhoti and he carries before him a tray with brass pots and incense-burners. He goes over and sits down cross-legged on the mat by the water-hole, putting the tray on the ground before him, and all the movements that he makes seem somehow very calm and gentle. He leans forward and scoops a handful of water from the pool and throws it over his shoulder. He takes the incense-burner and passes it back and forth across his chest, slowly, in a gentle, flowing manner. He puts his hands palm downward on his knees. He pauses. He takes a long breath through his nostrils. I can see him take a long breath and suddenly I can see his face is changing, there is a sort of brightness coming over all his face, a sort of... well, a sort of brightness on his skin and I can see his face is changing."

"For fourteen minutes he remains quite still in that position, and then, as I look at him, I see, quite positively I see his body lifting slowly ... slowly... slowly off the ground. He is still sitting cross-legged, the hands palm downward on the knees, and his whole body is lifting slowly off the ground, up into the air. Now I can see daylight underneath him. Twelve inches above the ground he is sitting... fifteen inches... eighteen... twenty... and soon he is at least two feet above the prayer-mat."

---

① Ludhiana: *Noun* a city in NW India, in Punjab south-east of Amritsar; pop. 1,012,000 (1991) 卢迪亚纳(印度西北部城市,位于旁遮普邦阿姆利则市东南,1991 年人口 1,012,000。)

"I stay quite still up there in the tree, watching, and I keep saying to myself, now look carefully. There before you, thirty yards away, is a man sitting in great serenity① upon the air. Are you seeing him? Yes, I am seeing him. But are you sure there is no illusion? Are you sure there is no deception? Are you sure you are not imagining? Are you sure? Yes, I am sure, I say. I am sure. I stare at him, marvelling. For a long while I keep staring, and then the body is coming slowly down again towards the earth. I see it coming. I see it moving gently downward, slowly downward, lowering to the earth until again his buttocks rest upon the mat."

"Forty-six minutes by my watch the body has been suspended! I timed it."

"And then, for a long long while, for over two hours, the man remains sitting absolutely still, like a stone person, with not the slightest movement. To me, it does not seem that he is breathing. His eyes are closed, and still there is this brightness on his face and also this slightly smiling look, a thing I have not seen on any other face in all my life since then."

"At last he stirs. He moves his hands. He stands up. He bends down again. He picks up the tray and goes slowly back into the hut. I am wonderstruck②. I feel exalted. I forget all caution and I climb down quickly from the tree and run straight over to the hut and rush in through the door. Banerjee is bending over, washing his feet and hands in a basin. His back is towards me, but he hears me and he turns quickly and

---

① serenity: *Noun* [mass noun] the state of being calm, peaceful, and untroubled 平静;宁静(e.g. an oasis of serenity amidst the bustling city 繁忙的城市中宁静的绿洲)

② wonderstruck: *Adjective* (of a person) experiencing a sudden feeling of awed delight or wonder(人)惊奇不已的;惊诧万分的

straightens up. There is great surprise on his face and the first thing he says is, 'How long have you been here?' He says it sharply, as if he is not pleased."

"At once I tell the whole truth, the whole story about being up in the tree and watching him, and at the end I tell him there is nothing I want in life except to become his disciple. Please will he let me become his disciple?"

"Suddenly he seems to explode. He becomes furious and he begins shouting at me: 'Get out!' he shouts. 'Get out of here! Get out! Get out! Get out!' and in his fury he picks up a small brick and flings it at me and it strikes my right leg just below the knee and tears the flesh. I have the scar still. I will show it to you. There, you see, just below the knee."

"Banerjee's anger is terrible and I am very frightened. I turn and run away. I run back through the jungle to where the tonga-driver is waiting, and we drive home to Rishikesh. But that night I regain my courage. I make for myself a decision and it is this: that I will return every day to the hut of Banerjee, and I will keep on and on at him until at last he has to take me on as a disciple, just to get himself some peace."

"This I do. Each day I go to see him and each day his anger pours out upon me like a volcano, him shouting and yelling and me standing there frightened but also obstinate and repeating always to him my wish to become a disciple. For five days it is like this. Then, all at once, on my sixth visit, Banerjee seems to become quite calm, quite polite. He explains he cannot himself take me on as a disciple. But he will give me a note, he says, to another man, a friend, a great yogi, who lives in Hardwar[1]. I am to go there and I will receive help and instruction."

Imhrat Khan paused and asked me if he might have a glass of water. I fetched it for him. He took a long slow drink, then he went on with his story:

"This is in 1922 and I am nearly seventeen years old. So I go to Hardwar. And there I find the yogi, and because I have a letter from the great Banerjee, he consents to give me instruction."

"Now what is this instruction?"

"It is, of course, the critical part of the whole thing. It is what I have been yearning for and searching for, so you can be sure I am an eager pupil."

"The first instruction, the most elementary part, consists of having to practise the most difficult physical exercises, all of them concerned with muscle control and breathing. But after some weeks of this, even the eager pupil becomes impatient. I tell the yogi it is my mental powers I wish to develop, not my physical ones."

"He replies, 'If you will develop control of your body, then the control of your mind will be an automatic thing.' But I want both at once, and I keep asking him, and in the end he says, 'Very well, I will give you some exercises to help you to concentrate the conscious mind.'"

"'Conscious mind?' I ask. 'Why do you say conscious mind?'"

"'Because each man has two minds, the conscious and the sub-conscious. The sub-conscious mind is highly concentrated, but the conscious mind, the one everyone uses, is a scattered, unconcentrated

① Hardwar: *Noun* a city in Uttar Pradesh, northern India, on the River Ganges; pop. 188,960 (1991). It is a place of Hindu pilgrimage 赫尔德瓦尔(印度北部北方邦的一个城市,位于恒河畔,1991年人口188,960,为印度教朝圣地。)

thing. It is concerning itself with thousands of different items, the things you are seeing around you and the things you are thinking about. So you must learn to concentrate it in such a way that you can visualize at will one item, one item only, and absolutely nothing else. If you work hard at this, you should be able to concentrate your mind, your conscious mind, upon any one object you select for at least three and a half minutes. But that will take about fifteen years.'"

"'Fifteen years!' I cry."

"'It may take longer,' he says. 'Fifteen years is the usual time.'"

"'But I will be an old man by then!'"

"'Do not despair,' the yogi says. 'The time varies with different people. Some take ten years, a few can take less, and on extremely rare occasions a special person comes along who is able to develop the power in only one or two years. But that is one in a million.'"

"'Who are these special people?' I ask. 'Do they look different from other people?'"

"'They look the same,' he says. 'A special person might be a humble roadsweeper or a factory worker. Or he might be a rajah. There is no way of telling until the training begins.'"

"'Is it really so difficult,' I ask, 'to concentrate the mind upon a single object for three and a half minutes?'"

"'It is almost impossible,' he answers. 'Try it and see. Shut your eyes and think of something. Think of just one object. Visualize it. See it before you. And in a few seconds your mind will start wandering. Other little thoughts will creep in. Other visions will come to you. It is a very difficult thing.'"

"Thus spoke the yogi of Hardwar."

"And so my real exercises begin. Each evening, I sit down and close my eyes and visualize the face of the person I love best, which is my brother. I concentrate upon visualizing his face. But the instant my mind begins to wander, I stop the exercise and rest for some minutes. Then I try again."

"After three years of daily practice, I am able to concentrate absolutely upon my brother's face for one and a half minutes. I am making progress. But an interesting thing happens. In doing these exercises, I lose my sense of smell absolutely. And never to this day does it come back to me."

"Then the necessity for earning my living to buy food forces me to leave Hardwar. I go to Calcutta① where there are greater opportunities, and there I soon begin to make quite good money by giving conjuring performances. But always I continue with the exercises. Every evening, wherever I am, I settle myself down in a quiet corner and practise the concentrating of the mind upon my brother's face. Occasionally, I choose something not so personal, like for example an orange or a pair of spectacles, and that makes it even more difficult."

"One day, I travel from Calcutta to Dacca② in East Bengal③ to give

---

① Calcutta: *Noun* a port and industrial centre in eastern India, capital of the state of West Bengal and the second-largest city in India; pop. 10,916,000 (1991). It is situated on the Hooghly River near the Bay of Bengal. 加尔各答(印度东部港市和工业中心,西孟加拉邦首府,印度第二大城市,1991年人口10,916,000,位于靠近孟加拉湾的胡格利河畔。)

② Dacca or Dhaka: *Noun* the capital of Bangladesh, on the Ganges delta; pop. 3,637,890 (1991) 达卡(孟加拉国首都,位于恒河三角洲,1991年人口3,637,890。)

③ Bengal: *Noun* a region in the north-east of the Indian subcontinent, containing the Ganges and Brahmaputra River deltas. In 1947 the province was divided into West Bengal, which has remained a state of India, and East Bengal, now Bangladesh. 孟加拉(印度次大陆东北部地区,包括恒河和布拉马普特拉河三角洲;1947年分为东西两部分,西孟加拉现仍为印度的一个邦,东孟加拉现为孟加拉国。)

a conjuring show at a college there, and while in Dacca, I happen to be present at a demonstration of walking on fire. There are many people watching. There is a big trench dug at the bottom of a sloping lawn. The spectators are sitting in their hundreds upon the slopes of the lawn looking down upon the trench."

"The trench is about twenty-five feet long. It has been filled with logs and firewood and charcoal, and a lot of paraffin① has been poured on it. The paraffin has been lit, and after a while the whole trench has become a smouldering red-hot furnace. It is so hot that the men who are stoking it are obliged to wear goggles. There is a high wind and the wind fans the charcoal almost to white heat."

"The Indian fire-walker then comes forward. He is naked except for a small loincloth②, and his feet are bare. The crowd becomes silent. The fire-walker enters the trench and walks the whole length of it, over the white-hot charcoal. He doesn't stop. Nor does he hurry. He simply walks over the white-hot coals and comes out at the other end, and his feet are not even singed③. He shows the soles of his feet to the crowd. The crowd stares in amazement."

"Then the fire-walker walks the trench once more. This time he goes even slower, and as he does it, I can see on his face a look of pure and absolute concentration. This man, I tell myself, has practised yoga.

---

① paraffin: *Noun* (also as "paraffin oil" or "liquid paraffin") (Brit.) a colourless, flammable, oily liquid similarly obtained and used as fuel, especially kerosene(英国英语)煤油

② loincloth: *Noun* a single piece of cloth wrapped round the hips, typically worn by men in some hot countries as their only garment(热带地区男子唯一用以遮体的)腰布

③ singe: *Verb* [with obj.] burn (something) superficially or lightly 把……浅表(或轻微)烧焦(e.g. The fire had singed his eyebrows. 火把他的眉毛烧焦了。)

He is a yogi."

"After the performance, the fire-walker calls out to the crowd, asking if there is anyone brave enough to come down and walk on the fire. There is a hush in the crowd. I feel a sudden surge of excitement in my chest. This is my chance. I must take it. I must have faith and courage. I must have a go. I have been doing my concentration exercises for over three years now and the time has come to give myself a severe test."

"While I am standing there thinking these thoughts, a volunteer comes forward from the crowd. It is a young Indian man. He announces that he would like to try the fire-walk. This decides me, and I also step forward and make my announcement. The crowd gives us both a cheer."

"Now the real fire-walker becomes the supervisor. He tells the other man he will go first. He makes him remove his dhoti, otherwise, he says, the hem① will catch fire from the heat. And the sandals must be taken off."

"The young Indian does what he is told. But now that he is close to the trench and can feel the terrible heat coming from it, he begins to look frightened. He steps back a few paces, shielding his eyes from the heat with his hands."

"'You don't have to do it if you don't want to,' the real fire-walker says."

"The crowd waits and watches, sensing a drama."

"The young man, though scared out of his wits, wishes to prove how brave he is, and he says, 'Of course I'll do it.'"

"With that, he runs towards the trench. He steps into it with one foot, then the other. He gives a fearful scream and leaps out again and

---

① hem: *Noun* the edge of a piece of cloth or clothing which has been turned under and sewn(布或衣服已缝好的)褶边(e. g. The hem on her skirt needs sewing. 她裙子上的褶边需要缝一缝。)

falls to the ground. The poor man lies there screaming in pain. The soles of his feet are badly burned and some of the skin has come right away. Two friends of his run forward and carry him off."

"'Now it is your turn,' says the fire-walker. 'Are you ready?'"

"'I am ready,' I say. 'But please be silent while I prepare myself.'"

"A great hush has come over the crowd. They have seen one man get badly burned. Is the second one going to be mad enough to do the same thing?"

"Someone in the crowd shouts, 'Don't do it! You must be mad!' Others take up the shout, all telling me to give up. I turn and face them and raise my hands for silence. They stop shouting and stare at me. Every eye in that place is upon me now."

"I feel extraordinarily calm."

"I pull my dhoti off over my head. I take off my sandals. I stand there naked except for my underpants. I stand very still and close my eyes. I begin to concentrate my mind. I concentrate on the fire. I see nothing but white-hot coals and I concentrate on them being not hot but cold. The coals are cold, I tell myself. They cannot burn me. It is impossible for them to burn me because there is no heat in them. I allow half a minute to go by. I know that I must not wait too long because I am only able to concentrate absolutely upon any one thing for a minute and a half."

"I keep concentrating. I concentrate so hard that I go into a sort of trance. I step out on to the coals. I walk fairly fast the whole length of the trench. And behold, I am not burned!"

"The crowd goes mad. They yell and cheer. The original fire-walker rushes up to me and examines the soles of my feet. He can't believe what he sees. There is not a burn mark on them."

"'Ayee!' he cries. 'What is this? Are you a yogi?'"

"'I am on the way, sir,' I answer proudly. 'I am well on the way.'"

"After that, I dress and leave quickly, avoiding the crowd."

"Of course I am excited. 'It is coming to me,' I say. 'Now at last the power is beginning to come.' And all the time I am remembering something else. I am remembering a thing that the old yogi of Hardwar said to me. He said, 'Certain holy people have been known to develop so great a concentration that they could see without using their eyes.' I keep remembering that saying and I keep longing for the power to do likewise myself. And after my success with the fire-walking, I decided that I will concentrate everything upon this single aim—to see without the eyes."

For only the second time so far, Imhrat Khan broke off his story. He took another sip of water, then he leaned back in his chair and closed his eyes.

"I am trying to get everything in the correct order," he said. "I don't want to miss anything out."

"You're doing fine," I told him. "Carry on."

"Very well," he said. "So I am still in Calcutta and I have just had success with fire-walking. And now I have decided to concentrate all my energy on this one thing, which is to see without the eyes."

"The time has come, therefore, to make a slight change in the exercises. Each night now I light a candle and I begin by staring at the flame. A candle-flame, you know, has three separate parts, the yellow at the top, the mauve① lower down, and the black right inside. I place the candle sixteen inches away from my face. The flame is absolutely lev-

---

① mauve: *Adjective* of a pale purple colour 淡紫色的

el with my eyes. It must not be above or below. It must be dead level because then I do not have to make even the tiniest little adjustment of the eye muscles by looking up or down. I settle myself comfortably and I begin to stare at the black part of the flame, right in the centre. All this is merely to concentrate my conscious mind, to empty it of everything around me. So I stare at the black spot in the flame until everything around me has disappeared and I can see nothing else. Then slowly I shut my eyes and begin to concentrate as usual upon one single object of my choice, which as you know is usually my brother's face."

"I do this every night before bed and by 1929, when I am twenty-four years old, I can concentrate upon an object for three minutes without any wandering of my mind. So it is now, at this time, when I am twenty-four, that I begin to become aware of a slight ability to see an object with my eyes closed. It is a very slight ability, just a queer little feeling that when I close my eyes and look at something hard, with fierce concentration, then I can see the outline of the object I am looking at."

"Slowly I am beginning to develop my inner sense of sight."

"You ask me what I mean by that. I will explain it to you exactly as the yogi of Hardwar explained it to me."

"All of us, you see, have two senses of sight, just as we have two senses of smell and taste and hearing. There is the outer sense, the highly developed one which we all use, and there is the inner one also. If only we could develop these inner senses of ours, then we could smell without our noses, taste without our tongues, hear without our ears and see without our eyes. Do you not understand? Do you not see that our noses and tongues and ears and eyes are only... how shall I say it? ... are only instruments which assist in conveying the sensation itself to the brain."

"And so it is that I am all the time striving to develop my inner senses of sight. Each night now I perform my usual exercises with the candle-flame and my brother's face. After that I rest a little while. I drink a cup of coffee. Then I blindfold myself and sit in my chair trying to visualize, trying to see, not just to imagine, but actually to see without my eyes every object in the room."

"And gradually success begins to come."

"Soon I am working with a pack of cards. I take a card from the top of the pack and hold it before me, back to front, trying to see through it. Then, with a pencil in my hand, I write down what I think it is. I take another card and do the same again. I go through the whole of the pack like that and when it is over I check what I have written down against the pile of cards beside me. Almost at once I have a sixty to seventy per cent success."

"I do other things. I buy maps and complicated navigating charts and pin them up all around my room. I spend hours looking at them blindfold, trying to see them, trying to read the small lettering of the place-names and the rivers. Every evening for the next four years, I proceed with this kind of practice."

"By the year 1933—that is only last year—when I am twenty-eight years old, I can read a book. I can cover my eyes completely and I can read a book right through."

"So now at last I have it, this power. For certain I have it now, and at once, because I cannot wait with impatience, I include the blindfold act in my ordinary conjuring performance."

"The audience loves it. They applaud long and loud. But not one single person believes it to be genuine. Everyone thinks it is just another clever trick. And the fact that I am a conjurer makes them think more than ever that I am faking. Conjurers are men who trick you. They trick you with cleverness. And so no one believes me. Even the doctors who blindfold me in the most expert way refuse to believe that anyone can see without his eyes. They forget there may be other ways of sending the image to the brain."

"What other ways?" I asked him.

"Quite honestly, I don't know exactly how it is I can see without my eyes. But what I do know is this: when my eyes are bandaged, I am not using the eyes at all. The seeing is done by another part of my body."

"Which part?" I asked him.

"Any part at all so long as the skin is bare. For example, if you put a sheet of metal in front of me and put a book behind the metal, I cannot read the book. But if you allow me to put my hand around the sheet of metal so that the hand is seeing the book, then I can read it."

"Would you mind if I tested you on that?" I asked.

"Not at all," he answered.

"I don't have a sheet of metal," I said. "But the door will do just as well."

I stood up and went to the bookshelf. I took down the first book that came to hand. It was Alice in Wonderland. I opened the door and asked my visitor to stand behind it, out of sight. I opened the book at random and propped it on a chair the other side of the door to him. Then I stationed myself in a position where I could see both him and the book.

"Can you read that book?" I asked him.

"No," he answered. "Of course not."

"All right. You may now put your hand around the door, but only the hand."

He slid his hand around the edge of the door until it was within sight of the book. Then I saw the fingers on the hand parting from one another, spreading wide, beginning to quiver slightly, feeling the air like the antennae of an insect. And the hand turned so that the back of it was facing the book.

"Try to read the left page from the top," I said.

There was silence for perhaps ten seconds, then smoothly, without pause, he began to read: 'Have you guessed the riddle yet?' the Hatter said, turning to Alice again. 'No, I give it up,' Alice replied. 'What'sthe answer?' 'I haven't the slightest idea,' said the Hatter. 'Nor I,' said the Hare. Alice sighed wearily. 'I think you might do something better with the time,' she said, 'than waste it asking riddles with no answers...'

"It's perfect!" I cried. "Now I believe you! You are a miracle!" I was enormously excited.

"Thank you, doctor," he said gravely. "What you say gives me great pleasure."

"One question," I said. "It's about the playing-cards. When you held up the reverse side of one of them, did you put your hand around the other side to help you to read it?"

"You are very perceptive①," he said. "No, I did not. In the case of the cards, I was actually able to see through them in some way."

"How do you explain that?" I asked.

"I don't explain it," he said. "Except perhaps that a card is such a flimsy② thing, it is so thin, and not solid like metal or thick like a door. That is all the explanation I can give. There are many things in this world, doctor, that we cannot explain."

"Yes," I said. "There certainly are."

"Would you be kind enough to take me home now," he said. "I feel very tired."

---

① perceptive: *Adjective* having or showing sensitive insight 有感知能力的;有洞察力的(e.g. an extraordinarily perceptive account of their relationship 一篇有关他们关系的入木三分的报道)

② flimsy: *Adjective* comparatively light and insubstantial; easily damaged 轻而不牢固的;脆弱的;易损坏的(e.g. a flimsy barrier 脆弱的屏障)

I drove him home in my car.

That night I didn't go to bed. I was far too worked up to sleep. I had just witnessed a miracle. This man would have doctors all over the world turning somersaults in the air! He could change the whole course of medicine! From a doctor's point of view, he must be the most valuable man alive! We doctors must get hold of him and keep him safe. We must look after him. We mustn't let him go. We must find out exactly how it is that an image can be sent to the brain without using the eyes. And if we do that, then blind people might be able to see and deaf people might be able to hear. Above all, this incredible man must not be ignored and left to wander around India, living in cheap rooms and playing in second-rate theatres.

I got so steamed up thinking about this that after a while I grabbed a notebook and a pen and started writing down with great care everything that Imhrat Khan had told me that evening. I used the notes I had made while he was talking. I wrote for five hours without stopping. And at eight o'clock the next morning, when it was time to go to the hospital, I had finished the most important part, the pages you have just read.

At the hospital that morning, I didn't see Dr Marshall until we met in the Doctors' Rest Room in our tea-break.

I told him as much as I could in the ten minutes we had to spare. "I'm going back to the theatre tonight," I said. "I must talk to him again. I must persuade him to stay here. We mustn't lose him now."

"I'll come with you," Dr Marshall said.

"Right," I said. "We'll watch the show first and then we'll take him out to supper."

At a quarter to seven that evening, I drove Dr Marshall in my car to Acacia Road. I parked the car, and the two of us walked over to the Royal Palace Hall.

"There's something wrong," I said. "Where is everybody?"

There was no crowd outside the hall and the doors were closed. The poster advertising the show was still in place, but I now saw that someone had written across it in large printed letters, using black paint, the words TONIGHT'S PERFORMANCE CANCELLED. There was an old gatekeeper standing by the locked doors.

"What happened?" I asked him.

"Someone died," he said.

"Who?" I asked, knowing already who it was.

"The man who sees without his eyes," the gatekeeper answered.

"How did he die?" I cried. "When? Where?"

"They say he died in his bed," the gatekeeper said. "He went to sleep and never woke up. These things happen."

We walked slowly back to the car. I felt an overwhelming sense of grief and anger. I should never have allowed this precious man to go home last night. I should have kept him. I should have given him my bed and taken care of him. I shouldn't have let him out of my sight. Imhrat Khan was a maker of miracles. He had communicated with mysterious and dangerous forces that are beyond the reach of ordinary people. He had also broken all the rules. He had performed miracles in public. He had taken money for doing so. And, worst of all, he had told some of those secrets to an outsider—me. Now he was dead.

"So that's that," Dr Marshall said.

"Yes," I said. "It's all over. Nobody will ever know how he did it."

This is a true and accurate report of everything that took place concerning my two meetings with Imhrat Khan.

signed John F. Cartwright, M. D.

....

Bombay, 4th December, 1934

(To be continued . . .)

三、翻译探索

本篇小说的翻译中,有些数字的书写是用阿拉伯数字还是用汉字的数字,这个问题值得考虑。具体来说,原文用英语单词表示的数字,是对应地译成汉字中的数字(如"一""二""三"等),还是转换成阿拉伯数字呢?这恐怕要具体问题具体分析,同时还要考虑到汉语的出版规范。下面的探索性译文,在这方面恐怕会存在一些问题,有待进一步探索。

非凡亨利

亨利·休格四十一岁,仍未结婚。他这个人很富有,富有的原因是,他有一个有钱的父亲,但他父亲现在已经去世。他至今未婚,未婚的原因是,他这个人太自私,哪怕是自己的一分钱也不愿意跟对方分享。

他身高一米八八,但模样并没有他自我感觉的那样帅气。

他极其讲究衣着穿戴。他去裁缝那儿量身定做套装,价格不菲;去衬衫制造商那儿定做衬衫,还去鞋匠那儿定做自己穿的鞋。

剃完胡须后,他经常再往脸上擦昂贵的护脸霜,往手上涂抹龟油膏,以使手部皮肤柔软。

每隔九天的时间,他的美发师就为他修剪一次头发,同时也习惯性地修剪一下指甲。

他的上门牙做了一层覆盖膜,价格贵得超乎想象,因为上门牙原先呈微黄色,相当难看。他的左脸颊长了一颗小痣,就让整形医生将其摘除。

他开的是一辆法拉利跑车,其价格几乎相当于一座乡间别墅。

夏季,他住在伦敦,但是,只要十月份第一场霜降下来,他就立刻出发到西印度群岛,或者去法国南部跟朋友一起共度时光,他所有的朋友都是继承了遗产的有钱人。

亨利的一生中从来没有做过一天正经的工作,还自己发明创造了一条个人的人生信条:与其辛辛苦苦忙活一阵,不如不痛不痒让人指责一番。他的朋友认为这个信条滑稽可笑。

像亨利这样的人到处看得到,他们像海草一样在全世界飘荡。特别是在伦敦、纽约、巴黎、拿骚、蒙特哥贝、戛纳以及圣特罗佩这样的地方,这样的人到处可见。虽然他们不是坏得出奇,但也不是什么好人。他们的存在也没有什么真正重要的意义,只是起到装饰的作用。

所有这一类的人,也就是所有这一类富有的人,都有一个共同的癖性:极其渴望让自己变得更为富有,尽管他们已经是腰缠万贯了。对一百万,他们从来没有感到过满足,两百万也不会满足。他们总是欲壑难填,唯一的愿望就是弄到更多的钱,其原因就是,他们总是生活在这样一个恐惧当中:某天早晨醒来,发现银行里一分钱存款都没有了。

这样的人都使用一些相同的方法来竭力增加财富的积累。他们买股票、购股份,然后看着股票、股份起起落落;在赌场,他们押高额赌注、玩轮盘赌和二十一点游戏;他们也赌马,简直是无所不赌。有那么一次,亨利·休格用一千英镑下注,赌一场乌龟比赛的结果,地点是在利物浦子爵的网球场草坪上。还有一次,他下的注比乌龟比赛时下的注翻了一倍,跟一个名叫埃斯蒙德·汉伯里的一个人打赌,赌的内容更加愚蠢可笑,具体如下:他们将亨利的狗放进花园,然后,他们透过窗户观察。但是,把狗放进去之前,大家必须先猜猜:狗将腿抬起首先碰到的是什么物体,是墙壁、柱子、灌木丛,还是树?埃斯蒙德猜的是墙壁,亨利猜的是树。结果,亨利赢了,因为之前好几天他一直在研究自己那条狗的习性,就是冲着这次奇特的赌局来的。

亨利跟他的这些朋友就是借助如此荒诞不经的游戏活动,竭力消磨由于无所事事和钱多富有而带来的无聊乏味、枯燥厌倦的感觉。

你或许已经注意到了，要是逮着机会的话，亨利本人也好不到哪里去，也会对他的这些朋友采取点作弊的伎俩。毫无疑问，用狗打赌这件事儿根本就没有诚信可言。要是你还想知道的话，乌龟比赛那场赌局也没有什么诚信可言，那场比赛他也作弊了。比赛开始前一个小时，他神不知鬼不觉地强行往对手的乌龟嘴里塞了点安眠药的粉末。

到现在为止，对亨利·休格是何许人也，你已经有了一个大致的了解，那么，我就可以开始讲述下面的故事了。

有一年夏天的一个周末，亨利驱车从伦敦赶往吉尔福德，要跟威廉·温德姆爵士一起消磨时光。爵士家的房子美轮美奂，庭园壮丽无比，可不凑巧的是，亨利星期六那天下午赶到的时候，天空已经是大雨滂沱了。这样的话，网球打不了啦，槌球游戏玩不了啦，在威廉爵士家室外游泳池游泳的打算也泡汤啦。男主人和诸位客人坐在会客室里，个个愁眉不展，盯着大雨噼里啪啦击打着窗户。有钱人是最憎恨坏天气的，坏天气令他们的钱派不上用场。

屋子里有人提议："我们大家来一局四人玩的凯纳斯特纸牌游戏吧，再押上高额赌金，肯定会很棒的。"

听的人认为这个建议很棒，但是，由于在座的总共有五个人，其中一个人必须得退出。于是，大家摸牌决定谁退出。亨利摸到了点数最小的一张，很遗憾地退出了。

其余四个人就座，开始玩牌。亨利出局，感到有些恼火，就溜达着走出会客室，来到了大厅，盯着大厅里的图片看了好一会儿。由于无事可做，他郁闷、厌倦得要死，随即穿过房间，无聊闲荡之中走进了图书室。

威廉爵士的父亲是位出名的书籍收藏家。偌大的图书室四壁，从地面到天花板都摆满了各类图书，但这对亨利·休格来说，没有什么稀奇的，甚至也提不起任何兴趣儿。他只喜欢读侦探小说，以及惊险、刺激的书籍。他漫无目的地在屋子里转悠着，想看看能否找到一本自己喜欢的书。可问题是，威廉爵士图书室里的藏书都是一些皮革面的书，上面写着名字，如：巴尔扎克、易卜生、伏尔泰、约翰逊、佩皮斯等。亨利对自己说,这全都是些枯燥的垃圾书。就在他要走开的当儿,其中的一本书吸引住他的眼球,这本书相当与众不同,是一本十分单薄的书,要是它没有从两边的书中探出一点来,他永远也注意不到它的存在。他将这本书从书架上抽了出来,发现它实际上不过是一个硬皮练习本,也就是学校里小学生使用的那种练习本。封皮是深蓝色的,上面什么都没有写。亨利打开练习本,本子的第一页有手写的墨水字体,内容如下:

1934 年 12 月
在印度孟买市
对伊姆拉汗
这位不用眼睛能够看得见的人
的采访报告
采访人:
约翰.F. 卡特赖特

亨利对自己说,这听起来还有点儿意思啊。于是,他翻过一页,结果发现余下的部分都是手写的黑色墨水字迹,字写得清晰而工整。亨利站在那儿,读完了开始的两页。读着读着,突然之间,他感觉自己有了读完这本小册子的渴望。这可是本好东西,很引人入胜。他拿着这本小册子走到靠窗的一把皮革扶手椅子那儿,舒舒服服地坐了下来,然后就又从头开始阅读起来。

下面文字就是亨利从那个小小的蓝色练习本上读到的:

我叫约翰·卡特赖特,是孟买总医院的一名外科医生。1934 年 12 月 2 日上午,我在医生休息室喝咖啡。休息室里除了我,还有三名医生,分别是马歇尔医生、菲利普斯医生和麦克法兰医生。我们大家都在享受着这来之不易的短暂休息。这时,有人敲门。“进来。”我说。

门开了,一个印度人推门进来,微笑着对我们说:“请原谅,我可以请你们几位绅士帮一个忙吗?”

医生休息室是一个私人的地方,除了医生,别人是不允许进入的,除非有紧急情况发生。

“这是私人场所。”麦克法兰医生尖声说道。

“是,是,”印度人回答。“我知道。先生们,我这样突然闯进来,很抱歉,可是,有一件极其有趣儿的事儿,我想展示给你们看看。”

我们四个人都很恼火,谁都没有开口说话。

“各位先生,”他说。“我这个人,不用眼睛能够看见东西。”

我们仍然没有邀请他进来的意思,但也没有要将他踢出门外的打算。

“你们可以蒙上我的双眼,随你们怎么蒙都可以,”他继续说,“可以将我的头部缠上五十层绷带,但我仍然能够将一本书的内容读给你们听。”

他看起来非常认真,不像是在开玩笑。我感觉,我的好奇心被他搅动起来了。“到这儿来。”我说。他向我走来。“转过身去。”于是,他转过身去。我用双手合拢上他的眼皮,紧紧捂住他的双眼。“听着,”我说。“这个屋子里有一名医生要伸出手指头来,告诉我他伸出了几根手指头。”

马歇尔医生伸出七只手指。

“七。”印度人回答。

“再来一次。”我说。

马歇尔医生两手握紧,攥成拳头,所有手指都藏了起来。

“一根手指也没有,”印度人说。

“再来一次。”我说。

马歇尔医生又两手握紧,攥成拳头,所有手指都藏了起来。

“一根手指也没有。”印度人说。

我把双手从他眼睛上移开。“不错。”我说。

“等一等,”马歇尔医生说。“我们试试这个。”门上有一个挂衣钩,上面挂了一件医生穿的白大褂。马歇尔医生将它取下,卷成一个长条毛巾形状,然后缠到了印度人的头部,并用手在他的脑后紧紧攥住它的两端。“现在试试他吧。”马歇尔医生说。

我从衣兜里掏出一把钥匙。“这是什么?”我问。

“一把钥匙。”他回答。

我将钥匙放回去,举起一只空空的手。“这个是什么东西?”我问他。

“什么东西都没有,”印度人说。“你的手是空的。”

马歇尔医生将缠绕他眼睛的白大褂移开。“你是怎么做到的?”他问。“有什么把戏呢?”

“什么把戏都没有,”印度人说。“这是真本事,训练了好多年,才好不容易得来的。”

“什么样的训练?”我问。

“请原谅,先生,”他说。“可问题是,这是隐私,是要保密的。”

“那么,为什么要来这儿展示?”我问。

“我来是请求你们帮一个忙的。”他说。

这名印度男子个子高高的,约有三十岁,留了一撮黑黑的小胡子,皮肤呈淡棕色,就是椰子果的颜色。很奇特的是,他的两只耳朵外面分别长满一团黑毛。他身穿一件白色的棉长袍,光脚穿着一双凉鞋。

“先生们,要知道,”他继续说,“我目前在一个流动剧团做事,挣口饭吃。我们刚刚到达孟买这个地方,今晚要做开场表演。”

“在哪儿表演?”我问。

“在皇宫礼堂,”他回答。“就在阿卡西亚大街上的那个。我是表演的主角,节目里我被冠以‘不用眼睛能够看得见的人——伊姆拉汗’,我有义务为这场表演大张旗鼓地进行宣传。票要是卖不出去,我们就没有饭吃。”

“这与我们有什么关系?”我问他。

“对你们来说,这很有意思,”他说。“乐趣多多,让我解释一下吧。你们知道,无论何时我们剧团到达一个新的城镇,我就亲自直接去当地最大的那家医院,请求那里的医生给我的双眼缠上绷带,以最为专业的手法缠上绷带，并且一定要确保我的眼睛一层又一层地被完完全全遮盖地严严实实。这项工作由医生来完成是很重要的，否则的话，就会有人认为我是在作弊。我被绷带彻底缠好，就走到大街上，去做一件很危险的事情。”

“你那样说是什么意思呢？”我问。

“我的意思是说，对于某个眼睛看不见的人来说，上街去做某件十分危险的事情。”

“什么事情呢？”我问。

“是一件很有意思的事情，”他说。“如果你们帮帮忙先给我缠好绷带，你们就会看着我做这件事情了。先生们，如果你们愿意为我做这件小事，你们就帮了我的大忙啦。”

我看了看其他三位医生。菲利普斯医生说，他必须到病人那里去，麦克法兰医生也是这么说的。马歇尔医生说：“好吧，何乐而不为呢？或许很有趣的，况且，一分钟不到就能缠完。”

“我跟你一起干，”我说。“但是，我们要尽职尽责将这工作完成，一定要绝对确保他无法向外偷看。”

“感激不尽啊，”印度人说。“你们愿意怎么做，就请你们尽管去做好了。”

菲利普斯医生和麦克法兰医生离开了房间。

“开始给他缠绷带之前，”我对马歇尔医生说，“我们首先将他的眼睑封起来。封完后，再用某种柔软的、可靠的、发粘的材料将他的眼窝填满。”

“说说看，什么材料呢？”马歇尔医生问。

“生面团怎么样？”

“生面团是再好不过了。”马歇尔医生回应。

“好的，”我说。“你赶快去医院面包房拿些生面团回来，我带他去手术室，先封他的眼睑。”

我带着印度人离开休息室，沿着医院长长的过道向手术室走去。“在那上面躺下，”我指着一张高高的床说道，他随即躺下。我从柜橱里取出一个小瓶子，瓶子顶上插了一个眼药滴管。“这东西叫火棉胶,"我告诉他说。"滴到你闭合的眼睑后,它就会变硬,这样你就不可能睁开眼睛啦。"

"完事后,怎么把它去掉呢?"他问我。

"酒精会相当容易地将其溶解掉,"我说。"完全无害。现在,闭上眼睛。"

印度人随即闭上眼睛。我将火棉胶滴到他的两只眼睑上。"眼睛不要睁开,"我说。"等着它变硬。"

两三分钟的时间里,火棉胶就在眼睑上面硬化成一层膜,将眼睛紧紧粘住。"睁眼试试,"我说。

他试着睁眼,但是睁不开。

马歇尔医生端着一盆生面团走进来,就是烘烤面包用的普通白面团,柔软得恰到好处。我拿出一块面团,敷到印度人其中一只眼睛上,整只眼窝都敷满了,并使面团与周围的皮肤重叠到一起,最后将面团的边缘使劲压了压。对另一只眼睛,我也如法炮制。

"感觉不太舒服,是吗?"我问。

"不,"印度人回答。"还可以的。"

"你缠绷带吧,"我对马歇尔医生说。"我的手指太粘了。"

"乐意之至,"马歇尔医生说。"瞧着吧。"他拿出一块厚厚的脱脂棉铺到印度人敷满生面团的眼睛上,脱脂棉粘到面团上就定住了。"请你坐起来。"马歇尔医生说。

印度人在床上坐了起来。

马歇尔医生拿来一卷七厘米半宽的绷带,开始绕着这名男子的头部一圈又一圈地缠了起来。绷带将脱脂棉和生面团牢牢地固定到位。缠完后,马歇尔医生将绷带头别住,然后拿起另一卷绷带,这次缠的不仅仅是眼睛,整个脸部连头一起都缠裹起来。

"请将我的鼻子留出来呼吸。"印度人说。

"那当然,"马歇尔医生回答。缠完后,他将绷带头固定好。"怎么样?"他问。

"妙极了,"我回答。"他的眼睛根本不可能透过来看到东西的。"

现在,这名印度人的整个头部被厚厚的白色绷带包裹起来,唯一能看到的部位就是凸出的鼻子尖,他整个人看起来就像是刚刚动过可怕的脑部手术似的。

"感觉怎么样?"马歇尔医生问他。

"感觉很好,"印度人回答。"工作很出色,我必须向两位先生表示祝贺了。"

"那就走吧,"马歇尔医生说,并冲我露齿一笑。"现在,向我们展示一下你看东西的聪明度吧。"

印度人下了床,径直向门口走去,然后打开门,走了出去。

"好家伙!"我说。"你看到没有?他的手抓到了门把手,不偏不倚!"

马歇尔医生将嘴合拢,不再微笑了,脸一下子变白了。"我要跟着他走。"他说完,匆忙奔向门口,我也向门口奔去。

这名印度人沿着医院的过道走着,并无异常之处。我和马歇尔医生跟在后面,离他有四米半的距离。这名男子头部缠满了一大片白色的绷带,却像其他人一样沿着过道随意走着,看起来就很阴森恐怖了,而当你确定他的眼睑被封上、眼窝敷满了生面团、面团上铺满了脱脂棉、脱脂棉上又缠了一层层绷带的时候,看起来就特别阴森恐怖了。

我看见医院里的一名当地的勤杂工沿着过道向印度人走来。这名勤杂工推着一辆食品车,突然间看到了这位白头男,一下子僵住了。但是,头裹绷带的印度白头男却很随意地向食品车旁边跨出一步,继续向前走去。

"他看见车啦!"我叫道。"他一定是看到那辆食品车啦!还绕着走过去!这简直是绝对地不可思议!"

马歇尔医生对我的话没有回应。他的脸颊刷白,由于极度震惊和难以置信,他的整个脸部都僵住了。

印度人走到楼梯处,开始向下迈步。

他下楼梯毫不费力,甚至连手都没有碰一下楼梯扶手。同时,还有几个人上楼,都停下脚步气喘吁吁地盯着他看,然后纷纷避让开来。

到了楼梯底部,印度人右转,朝通往大街的门口走去。我和马歇尔医生紧随其后。

我们医院的大门口离大街稍微有点距离,从大门口到一个小小的院落,其间有相当高的一段台阶。那个小院落的周围生长着金合欢树。我跟马歇尔医生走出来,外面阳光照耀,我们俩就站在台阶的顶部,向下方的院落看去,看到下面有一大群人,约摸有一百人吧,其中至少有一半是光着脚的孩子。我们这位印度白头男下台阶的时候,下面那些人欢呼、喊叫起来,向他蜂拥而来,而他则双手举过头顶,向他们示意、问候。

突然之间,我看见了一辆自行车,就放在台阶底部的一侧。一个小男孩扶着那辆车,那是一辆极其普通的自行车,但是,在车的后部,后轮的框架上,绑着一个标语牌,也不知道是怎么绑上去的,牌子是方形的,约有一米五见方,上面写着:

伊姆拉汗,
是一个不用眼睛就能够看见东西的人!
今天,我请求医院的医生将我的双眼
用绷带缠得紧紧!
今天晚上以及本周所有晚上
从七点开始表演。
表演地点是位于阿卡西亚大街的
皇宫礼堂。
切莫错过!
你们即将看到奇迹上演!

现在,我们帮助的这位印度人已经到达台阶的底部,径直走到自行车那儿,只见他跟小男孩说了什么,小男孩微微一笑。印度人跨上自行车,人群为他让开了路。接下来,哎呀呀,看呐,可了不得啦,这个小伙子虽然眼睛缠着绷带,什么也看不见,却开始骑着车穿过院落,直奔下方的大街而去,而大街上则是车水马龙,喇叭声此起彼伏!人群发出更加响亮的欢呼声。那些光着脚的小孩子跟着他后面奔跑,边跑边兴奋地尖叫、欢笑。在大约一分钟左右的时间内,我们一直能够看到他,只见他娴熟地骑着车行走在繁忙的大街上,摩托车飕飕地从他身旁经过,还有一大群孩子紧随其后。紧接着,他转了一个弯,消失不见了。

"我感到迷惑不解却兴奋不已,"马歇尔医生说。"我本人对此难以置信。"

"我们必须得相信,"我说。"绷带下方的生面团,他是不可能弄掉的。再者说,我们一直在场啊。至于眼睑的密封层,他得用脱脂棉和酒精,至少花上五分钟的时间才能清除掉。"

"你知道我是怎么想的吗?"马歇尔医生问。"我想,我们刚刚见证了奇迹的发生。"

我们转身,慢慢地往回走,回到了医院。

这一天余下的时间里,我一直在医院里忙着病人的事儿。晚上六点,我下了班,开车回到我住的公寓,冲完凉,换好衣服。现在是孟买一年中最炎热的时候,即使太阳落山,仍然很热,就像开了盖的大熔炉。即便你一动不动地坐在椅子上什么也不做,汗水也会从你的皮肤上渗出。一整天的时间里,你的脸就会因为潮湿而闪闪发亮,衬衫也会粘到胸部。我冲凉冲了很长时间,然后坐在阳台上,只是在腰间围上一条毛巾,喝了一杯加苏打水的威士忌,随后我就穿上干净的衣服。

六点五十分,我到达阿卡西亚大街的皇宫礼堂,那其实不算是什么宫殿,只不过是一个稍小一些的、破破烂烂的礼堂,花不了几个钱就可以租来开个会,或者举办个舞会什么的。已经有为数不少的当地印度人在售票处外面转来转去,礼堂的入口处上方一个大大的招牌上面写了些文字,意思是:国际剧团公司那一周的每天晚上都有节目表演,有杂耍、魔术、杂技、吞剑、吞火、耍蛇,还有一出独幕剧,名字叫《王公与虎女郎》。但是,在所有这些宣传之上,用最大的字体写着:伊姆拉汗,不用眼睛能够看见东西的奇人。

我买了一张票,走了进去。

整个表演时长两个小时。令我意想不到的是,这些节目从头到尾我都喜欢,所有的表演者都十分出色。我很喜欢用厨具表演杂耍的那名男子,同一时间里,他不断抛接长柄深平底锅、煎锅、焙烤浅盘、大盘子、砂质炖锅,让它们在空中飞舞。耍蛇人耍的是一条大绿蛇,那条蛇几乎是用尾巴尖支撑着站了起来,还随着笛子音乐摇摆舞动。吞火表演者将火吞了进去,吞剑那个演员将一把薄薄的、尖尖的薄剑顺着嗓子眼儿往下至少推进去一米二的长度,吞进了胃里。最后,伴随着号角齐鸣,我们的朋友伊姆拉汗出场表演了。现在,我们在医院里给他绑的绷带已经去掉了。

观众席里有几名观众被叫上台来,并让他们用床单、围巾、包头巾之类的东西把他的眼睛一层层蒙上。蒙到最后,由于头上缠的东西过多,他几乎站立不稳。接着,有人递给他一把左轮手枪,随即一个小男孩出现,站在舞台的左边。我认出来了,这个小男孩就是当天在医院外面扶自行车的那个。小男孩把一个锡罐放到自己的头顶上,然后站在那儿一动不动。他瞄准,观众鸦雀无声。“啪”的一声枪响,我们大家都跳了起来。锡罐从小男孩的头上飞了起来,“当啷”一声落到地板上。小男孩随即捡起锡罐,向观众展示子弹打出的孔洞。大家鼓掌、欢呼,小男孩微笑着。

接下来,小男孩紧贴着一个木制隔断站立,伊姆拉汗抛掷飞刀,飞刀纷纷落在男孩身体周围,多数飞刀离小男孩的身体非常近。这个表演甚是绝妙,要知道,即使不把眼睛蒙上,也没有多少人会如此准确无误地抛掷飞刀的,但是,眼前这个人做到了,真是一个非同寻常的小伙子,更何况他的整个脑袋还用布单层层缠绕,致使他整个人看起来就像一根棍子上挑着一个大雪球。即便这样,他甩起尖尖的飞刀,一点也没有伤到小男孩的脑袋,哪怕离脑袋仅有一根头发丝宽的距离。小男孩自始至终微笑着。表演完毕,观众跺着脚,兴奋得狂叫。

伊姆拉汗的最后一个表演,尽管不是那么蔚为壮观、引人入胜,却更加令人难忘。有人将一只铁桶拿上舞台,邀请观众上来检查,确定没有任何孔洞,铁桶也的确没有孔洞。然后,铁桶套到伊姆拉汗已经缠得严严实实的头部,一直套到双肩,直至胳膊肘那儿。这样,他的上臂就被固定在身体的两侧,而小臂和手仍然可以举起来。有人往他的一只手里放了一根针,另一只手里放了一段棉线。于是,他麻利地用棉线穿过针眼,一点误差都没有,看得我目瞪口呆。

表演一结束,我就向后台走去。在一间小小的、却很干净的化妆室里,我找到了伊姆拉汗先生,他一声不响地坐在一只木凳上。那个印度小男孩正从他的头上,一圈一圈地往下解缠了一层又一层的围巾和床单。

"噢,"他说。"我在医院里交的医生朋友来了。进来,先生,进来。"

"我看了表演,"我说。

"你认为怎么样?"

"我很喜欢。我想,你很棒啊。"

"谢谢,"他回应。"有劳你夸奖啦。"

"我也必须向你的助手表示祝贺,"我向小男孩点了点头,说道。"他很勇敢。"

"他不会说英语,"印度人说。"但是,我会向他转达你的话。"他迅速用印度斯坦语向小男孩做了转达,小男孩听完,严肃地点了点头,但是什么也没说。

"听着,"我说。"今天上午我对你也算是尽了一点微薄之力,那么,你能否帮我一个小忙?你能答应我,跟我出去吃晚饭吗?"

现在,他头上缠的东西都清除干净了。他冲我一笑,说道:"医生,我想你有了求知欲,我说的对吗?"

"求知欲很强,"我回答。"我想跟你聊聊。"

他的两只耳朵外面长出的两团厚厚的黑毛再一次吸引了我,这样的黑毛我没有在第二个人身上看到过。"以前,从来没有医生问过我什么问题,"他说。"但是,我没有异议,与你共进晚餐,我很荣幸。"

“我可以在车里等你吗?”

“可以,请便,”他回答。“我必须得洗一洗,然后脱掉这些脏兮兮的衣服。”

我告诉他我的车是什么样子的,并且交代说,我要出去等。

十五分钟过后,他穿着一身白色的棉长袍走了出来,还是光着脚穿那双凉鞋。没有多久,我们已经舒适惬意地坐在一家小餐馆里了。有时候我去那家餐馆,是因为那里有全城最好吃的咖喱菜肴。我一边喝着啤酒,一边吃着咖喱菜,但伊姆拉汗只喝柠檬汁。

“我不是作家,”我对他说。“我是医生,但是,如果你愿意从头对我讲述你的故事,如果你愿意向我解释你是如何修得这种魔力——不用眼睛能够看得见,我将尽我所能,一五一十地写出来。那样的话,或许我能够将其发表到《英国医学学报》,或者发表在某个著名的杂志上。再者说,我是一名医生,而不是某位卖故事赚钱的作家,人们更有可能相信我说话的真实性,这会更加有助于提高你的知名度,难道不是吗?”

“会使我受益匪浅的,”他说。“可问题是,你为什么想要这么做呢?”

“因为我有疯狂的求知欲,”我回答。“这就是唯一的原因所在。”

伊姆拉汗吃进一小口咖喱米饭,慢慢地嚼着,随后说道:“很好,我的朋友。我这就告诉你。”

“太棒了!”我叫道。“一吃完,我们就回我的公寓吧。然后,我们就可以随意交谈,不会有人打扰的。”

吃完饭,我付了账。然后,我开车带伊姆拉汗回到我住的公寓。

在起居室里,我拿出纸和铅笔要做记录。出于记录患者病历的需要,我已经练就了一种个人独有的速记法,使用这种方法,在对方语速不是太快的情况下,我能够记录下对方述说的大部分内容。我想,那天晚上我已经记下伊姆拉汗对我说过的几乎一切内容,逐字逐句记录如下。他当时是怎么说的,我现在就精确地为你写了下来:

“我是一名印度人，也是一名印度教徒，”伊姆拉汗说，“1905 年，我出生于克什米尔邦的阿克努尔市。我家里很穷，父亲是铁路检票员。我还是一个十三岁小男孩的时候，一位印度魔术师来到了我们学校，做了一场表演，演技很好，令我印象十分深刻。我记得他称自己为穆尔教授——在印度，所有魔术师都自称为‘教授’。我想，那才是真正的魔术，我感觉——怎么才能说明白我的感觉呢？我感觉，我产生了一股强烈的愿望，要亲自学习这种魔术。因此，两天后我离家出走了，决定找到摩尔教授——我心目中的新英雄，并随他学艺。我带上了所有积攒下来的钱，一共十四卢比，带的所有衣服就是现在我身上穿的，也就是一件缠腰布式的衣服和凉鞋。时间是 1918 年，我十三岁。

“结果我发现，穆尔教授已经出发，去往拉合尔，那可是三百二十公里以外的地方啊，但我还是买了一张三等火车票，登上火车，独自一人去追赶他。到达拉合尔，我找到了教授，他正在一些场所做表演，这些场所给的报酬都很低。我告诉他，我是多么崇拜、钦佩他，并提出自愿做他的助手。他收下了我。报酬多少？哦，有报酬，一天八安那，相当于半个卢比。

“教授教我圆环链接戏法，我的工作就是站在剧院前面的大街上表演这个戏法，吸引人们进来观看演出。

“整整六周时间过去了，进展得非常顺利，比上学好多了。但是突然之间，我一下子意识到，穆尔教授身上没有什么真正的魔术可言，他只不过是耍耍手腕而已，靠的是眼疾手快。意识到这一点对我来说，不亚于引爆了一枚重磅炸弹。顷刻之间，教授已不再是我心目中的英雄，我对这份工作的信心也丧失殆尽，但与此同时，我的整个心里充满了一个极其强烈的渴望，渴望找到真正的魔术，渴望去寻找某种被称为瑜伽的奇异魔力，这种渴望压倒了一切。

“要想修炼瑜伽，我必须找到一位愿意收我为徒的瑜伽修行大师，这可不是一件容易的事情。真正的瑜伽大师可不是随随便便就能从树上冒出来的。在整个印度，这样的大师寥寥无几，更何况，他们还笃信宗教、极度虔诚。所以，我要想成功地找到这样一位老师，就要装扮成一名虔诚的教徒。

“不是的,事实上,我不是什么教徒,正是由于这一点,你可以认为我有点欺骗的味道,我意欲练就瑜伽神功,纯粹是出于我的私心——我想运用这种神功来获取名望和财富。

“而这却是真正的瑜伽大师所不齿的行为,他们对这种行为的鄙视超出了这个世界上任何的东西。事实上,真正的瑜伽修行者相信,不管是谁修炼瑜伽,只要滥用它的神力,死神就会在突然之间降临。瑜伽修行者永远都不能在大庭广众之下表演,他必须在绝对静谧之处隐居下来,把瑜伽作为一种宗教仪式来修炼。否则的话,他就会招来横祸而毙命。这一点,我倒是不信,而且至今仍然不信。

“所以现在,我就开始寻找瑜伽大师了。我辞别穆尔教授,去了旁遮普邦的一个叫作阿姆利则的城镇。在那里,我加入一个流动剧团公司。寻找的路途中,我一定要填饱肚子,况且上学时我还成功地做过业余表演呢。因此,三年的时间里,我跟随这一剧团走遍了旁遮普邦,到最后我十六岁半的时候,我成了剧团的顶梁柱。这期间,我一直攒钱,到现在,我已经攒了很大一笔钱,总共有两千卢比了。

“就在此时,我听到一名男子的消息,这名男子名叫班纳吉。据说,这个班纳吉是一位真正的印度瑜伽大师,拥有非同寻常的能力。最为重要的是,人们都在讲述他如何修炼成旷世奇功——悬浮术,也就是说,他在祷告时,整个身体离开地面,悬浮在半空中,离下方的地面有四十五厘米高。

“啊哈,我想,踏破铁鞋无觅处。这位当然就是我要找的人了,我一定要找到这位班纳吉。所以,不容片刻耽搁,我带上存款,离开了剧团公司,赶往跨越恒河两岸的小城——瑞诗凯诗。据传说,班纳吉就生活在这座小城。

“我寻找班纳吉,苦苦搜寻了六个月。他人在何方?在哪里?班纳吉在哪里?哦,是的,人们说他在瑞诗凯诗,那么,他就一定在这个小城里了,但是,那是一段时间以前的事情,即使那时在小城里,也没有人看到过他。那么,如今呢?如今,班纳吉已经去往另一个地方,另一个地方是什么地方?哦,他们说,谁知道会是什么地方,又怎么会知道是什么地方呢？一个人怎么会知道像班纳吉这样一位大师的行踪呢？难道他过的是一种绝对与世隔绝的生活吗？难道他与世隔绝吗？要我回答,是的。是的,是的,是与世隔绝的。当然是的,这很明显。即使我这样的人,也看得出来。

“我花掉了几乎所有的存款去寻找这位班纳吉,只剩下三十五卢比,但没有任何结果。于是,我待在瑞诗凯诗,为一些小剧团之类的团体表演一般性的魔术戏法,以此来维持生活。那些戏法是从穆尔教授那里学来的,加之我这方面的天赋,这些戏法我变得很漂亮,手法敏捷。

“接下来有一天,我坐在瑞诗凯诗的一家小旅馆里,又一次听到有人谈起了班纳吉瑜伽大师。一名旅行者讲述他是如何听人说起班纳吉的:班纳吉现在孤身一人生活在丛林中,路途不是很远,但是,丛林茂密得很。”

“可是,丛林在哪里?”

“这名旅行者不太确定具体的位置。‘有可能,’他说,‘在那边,就那个方向,在小城的北方,’他边说边用手指比划着。

“好吧,有了方向,对我来说,就足够了。于是,我去市场,一番讨价还价要雇一辆轻便马车,包括一匹马和一辆车。就在与车夫即将成交的当儿,冒出一名男子,他说他也往那个方向去,部分路程跟我的相同,可以跟我合租节省费用。当然,我巴不得有这样的事儿。说走就走。我跟这名男子坐在车里,车夫赶着马车,沿着一条窄窄的小路,径直穿过了丛林。

“接下来,意想不到的好运竟然降临到我的头上！与我的这位旅伴交谈中,我竟然发现,他的师傅不是别人,正是这位班纳吉大师本人,而且这名徒弟现在正赶着去看师傅呢。所以,我就直截了当地对他说,我也想做这位瑜伽师傅的徒弟。

“他慢慢转过身,看了我很长时间,大概有三分钟,一句话都没说。过了一会儿,他平静地说:‘不,那是不可能的事。’

“我心里说,好吧,可不可能就走着瞧吧。接着我问他,班纳吉祷告时悬浮在半空中是不是真事儿。

"'是真的,'他回答。'真事儿,但悬浮时,不允许任何人在场观看。班纳吉祷告时,没有任何一个人得到过允许靠近现场。'

"我们乘坐着轻便马车,往丛林深处又走了一段距离,这期间不停地谈论着班纳吉。我尽量小心谨慎又随意自然地问这问那,了解了很多有关这位大师的细枝末叶,比如什么时间大师开始祷告啦等。没过多大工夫,这位男子说:'就在此告别吧,我到地方要下车了。'

"我把他送下车,然后假装继续赶路。一到转角处,我就吩咐车夫停下,在那儿等着,我则快速跳下车,沿着小路往回溜,去寻找这名刚下车的旅伴,也就是班纳吉大师的徒弟。小路上不见他的踪影,他已经消失在丛林之中,但是,消失在哪个方位?小路的左边,还是右边?我静静地站着,听听有无动静。

"听到下层灌木丛中窸窣作响,我寻思着,那一定是他。不是他,就是老虎,但确实是他,就在前头,正穿过稠密的灌木丛前行。他走的地方连一条小径都没有,他不得不扒拉开高高的竹子以及各种茂密的植物往前行走。我蹑手蹑脚地跟在后面,与他保持九十多米的距离,太近了我怕他听到我的声音,但我肯定能听到他的声音。穿行在十分浓密的灌木丛中间,不可能不发出声音的。要是他离开了我的视线——多数时间是这样的,我就循着他的声音跟过去。

"这种令神经紧绷的、'跟着走'的游戏持续了大约半个小时,突然之间,我一下子再也听不到前面那个人的声音了。我停下来,听了听,丛林一片寂静,于是,我就害怕找不见他了。我蹑手蹑脚又走了一点距离,突然,透过厚厚的下层灌木丛,我看见前方有一小块空地,空地中间立着两间小屋,是两间小小的屋子,完全是用灌木丛的叶子和枝条搭建而成的。我的心狂跳起来,感觉有一股巨大的兴奋从内心喷涌出来,因为我肯定地知道,这就是班纳吉这位大师的居所。

"已经看不到那名徒弟,他一定进入了其中的一间小屋。四周静悄悄的,因此,我现在要开始极其谨慎地探查这儿的树木、树丛以及周围的其他的东西。最近的那座小屋旁边有一个小水坑,我看见水坑旁边放了一个祷告时用的跪垫,我就对自己说,那里就是班纳吉祷告时打坐默念的地方。靠近小水坑不到三十米远的地方,生长着一棵大树,那是一棵大大的、枝杈蔓延的猴面包树,浓密的枝条漂亮地伸展开来,上面要是放上一张床,躺在床上,树下的人也不会发现。我暗自寻思,那棵树就要为我所用了,我藏到树上,等着班纳吉出来祷告,然后,我就可以目睹一切了。

“可问题是,那个徒弟对我说过,他师傅的祷告时间是傍晚五点或六点,那么,我要等好几个小时。因此,我立即穿越丛林回到小路上,对车夫交代了几句,告诉他必须等我。要他等下去,我就得多付钱给他,但是,这已经无关紧要了,因为现在我兴奋异常,此时此刻什么都不在乎了,即便是金钱。

“整个中午的时光,忍受着丛林里极度的炎热,我在轻便马车旁等待着,一直等到极其潮湿、炎热的下午即将结束。接近五点的时候,我悄悄地穿过灌木丛,回到小屋那儿,一边走,一边能感觉到我的心怦怦直跳,跳得我整个身体都跟着震动。我爬上那棵专属我的大树,藏到叶子中间,确保我能看见别人但别人看不见我。然后,就等待着,一等就是四十五分钟。

“手表?是的,我戴了一只腕表,这一点我记得很清楚。这只表是我在一次有奖购物中赢得的奖品。拥有这样一只表我很自豪,表盘上写着制造商的名字:卢迪亚纳市伊斯拉米亚手表公司。因此,我要用这只表仔仔细细地为所发生的一切计时,要记住这次经历的每一个细节部分。

“我端坐在树上,等待着。

“接下来,突然之间,一名男子走出小屋。这名男子又高又瘦,身穿一件橘黄色的缠腰布式的衣服。他将一个托盘举到胸前,托盘上放了一只黄铜罐和一只香炉。他走了过去,盘腿坐到水坑旁的垫子上,托盘则放到身前的地面上。不知怎么的,他所有的动作都显得平静、和缓。他身体前倾从水坑里捧出一捧水洒到肩膀上,随后拾起香炉,慢慢地在胸前、身后传递着,举止和缓而流畅。他双手掌心向下放到膝盖上,暂停下来。接下来,鼻孔吸气深呼吸。我也看见了,他深深呼吸一下。突然,我看见他脸色改变,整个脸部呈现某种明亮的色调,某种……怎么说呢,皮肤呈现某种明亮色调,我看得出,他的脸色在改变。

“十四分钟的时间里,他保持那样的姿势一动不动。接着,我再看他的时候,我看见——肯定地看见了,他的身体抬了起来,慢慢地……慢慢地……离开了地面,但他仍然盘腿而坐,掌心朝下放在膝盖上,整个身体却慢慢地离开了地面,升到半空中。现在,我看见了他身底下透过来的日光,他端坐在半空中,身体离地面三十八厘米……四十六厘米……五十厘米……不大工夫,他离坐垫至少六十厘米高了。

“我在树上看着,大气不敢出,不断地提醒自己:现在,看仔细了。就在你眼前,就在不到三十米远的地方,一名男子安详、宁静地端坐在半空中。你正在看吗?是的,我正在看。可是,你肯定不是幻觉吗?你肯定不是骗局吗?你肯定不是在想象吗?你肯定吗?我说道:是的,我肯定,我敢肯定。我盯着他,惊叹不已。有很长一段时间,我目不转睛地看着,接着,他的身体慢慢地下降,我看着他下降的。我看着他和缓地向下移动,慢慢地下移,直到再一次触碰地面、屁股落到垫子上为止。

“我计时了。依照我的手表,他的身体在半空中悬浮了四十六分钟!

“接着,有很长一段时间——两个多小时吧,这位男子就坐在那儿,保持绝对静止的状态,纹丝未动,好像是一个石头人。在我看来,他似乎没有呼吸,只见他双眼紧闭,脸部仍然呈现出方才那种明亮的色调,却稍微露出一点笑容。自那以后,这种面部表情我在其他人脸上再也没有看到过。

“最后,他开始动弹了。他移动双手,站了起来,又弯下身去,端起托盘,慢慢走回小屋。我万分惊奇、兴奋异常,不顾一切飞速爬下树,径直跑向小屋,随即推门而入。班纳吉背对着我,正弯腰在一只盆子里洗手洗脚,但是,他听到我的声音,快速转头,直起腰来。他的脸上露出非常吃惊的表情,问的第一句话便是:‘你在这里待了多长时间?’他这话问得很尖刻,好像很不高兴的样子。

“我立刻实话实说,讲出我爬树、观察的整个过程。最后,我对他说,我这辈子别无所求,只想做他的徒弟,并请求他:希望能收我做他的徒弟。

"突然之间,他似乎一下子怒气冲天,恼怒不已,开始冲着我大喊:'滚出去!'他这样喊道。'从这里滚出去! 滚出去! 滚出去! 滚出去!'大怒之下,他抓起一小块砖头,朝我抛过来。砖头砸到我的右腿,正好砸到膝盖下方,里边的肉都露了出来。现在还有一道疤痕呢,我露出来给你看看,就在那儿,你看看,就在膝盖下面。

"班纳吉怒不可遏,把我吓坏了,转身就跑,穿越丛林,跑回到车夫等我的地方,然后我们赶回瑞诗凯诗。但是,那天晚上,我又恢复了勇气,我自己做出一个决定,是这样的:我每天都去班纳吉的小屋一趟,坚持不懈,直到最后他感到厌烦、为图清静收我为徒为止。

"我这样做了。每天我都去看他,每次他的愤怒都像是火山喷发,向我倾泻而来,他大喊、大叫,而我只是站在那儿,虽然害怕却也倔强,总是重复着要做他的徒弟的愿望。就这样,五天过去了。接着,第六天去的时候,突然一下子班纳吉似乎变得相当平静、相当文明了。他解释说,他本人不能收我为徒,但是他说,他可以为我写一张便条给另一个人,也就是他的朋友,是一位瑜伽大师,住在赫尔德瓦尔。于是,我要去那儿得到帮助和指导。"

伊姆拉汗暂停下来,问我是否可以给他一杯水喝。我取来一杯水,他接过去慢慢地一口喝了下去,然后接着讲他的故事:

"时间是1922年,我将近十七岁了。接下来,我去了赫尔德瓦尔,在那儿找到了这位瑜伽大师。由于我有班纳吉大师的引荐信,他同意给我指导。"

"那么,是什么样的指导呢?"

"当然是整个修炼过程中最关键的部分,正是我渴望得到、苦苦寻找的。所以,你可以肯定地认为,我这个学生是如饥似渴型的。

"第一项指导,也是最为基础的部分,包括难度最大的身体训练,必须得训练,训练涉及的都是肌肉控制和呼吸方面的。可是,这样的训练持续几周之后,即便是如饥似渴型的学生也变得焦躁起来。我对大师说,我希望修炼的是思维能力,不是身体能力。

"他回答:'如果你愿意修炼去控制你的身体,那么,控制心理就是水到渠成的事情了。'我不断地请求他,两者我要同时修炼。最后,他说道:'很好,我要教你做些训练,帮助你把精力全部集中在你的意识心理上面。'

"'意识心理?'我问。'你为什么要说意识心理?'

"'因为每个人有两个心理:意识心理和潜意识心理。潜意识心理得到了高度的集中,但是意识心理,也就是每个人都会用到的心理,却是分散的,得不到集中。在意识心理这方面,精力放在数以千计的、不同的事务上,放在你周围看到的一切事物上,放在你思考的所有事情上。所以,你必须学会将意识心理集中起来。集中起来之后,你就可以随心所欲地看到一样东西,只有一样东西,绝对没有其他别的什么东西。如果你刻苦训练,你就能够全神贯注,将意识心理集中到任何一样你所挑选出来的物体上面,而且集中的时间至少三分半钟。问题是,达到这个效果需要十五年的时间。'

"'十五年!'我大叫。

"'或许更长,'他说。'一般需要十五年时间。'

"'可是,到那时,我就老了!'

"'也不要绝望,'瑜伽大师说。'时间长短因人而异,有些人需要十年,少数人则更少。在极端稀少的情况下,会出现某位奇人,一两年的时间就能练就这种功力,但是,这样的奇人是百万里挑一,出现的几率十分渺茫。'

"'这样的奇人都是些什么样的人呢?'我问。'他们与众不同吗?'

"'一模一样,'他说。'奇人或许就是某个普通的扫大街的,或许是工厂的工人,或许是王公。要是不开始修炼,根本无法说清楚到底谁是奇人。'

"'三分半钟时间内,将意识心理集中到单个的物体上,'我问,'真的有那么难吗?'

"'那几乎是不可能的,'他回答。'不信就试试看。闭上双眼,想着某个东西，只想一样东西，将其形象化，仿佛就在你眼前。用不了几秒钟的时间，你就开始走神了，其他琐碎的思想就悄悄混进来，你就会看到其他的视觉形象啦。所以，这件事情很难做到。'

"赫尔德瓦尔的瑜伽大师就是这样对我说的。

"就这样，我真正的训练开始了。每天晚上我都坐下来，闭上眼睛，将我最爱的人的脸形象化，那个人就是我的兄弟。我将精力集中到他的脸上，但是，看到他的脸的那一刻，我就开始走神。于是，我就停下来，休息几分钟，然后再继续训练。

"每日就这样训练，训练三年之后，我能够将注意力绝对地集中到我兄弟的脸上，持续一分半钟时间。我不断地取得进步，但却发生了件有意思的事儿。训练过程中，我的味觉完全丧失，直到今日，还没有恢复过来。

"接着，为了能有钱买食物来填饱肚子，我被迫离开赫尔德瓦尔。于是，我去了加尔各答，那里有更多的机会。在那里，我表演魔术，很快就有了不错的收入，但是，我从未中断训练。不管身在何处，每天晚上，我都会到一个安静的角落坐下修炼，将精力集中到我兄弟的脸上。我偶尔也选择某些非人的形象来修炼，比如一只橘子、一副眼镜什么的，这样做更是增加了修炼的难度。

"有一天，我从加尔各答出发去孟加拉东部的达卡，到那里的一所大学做魔术表演。在达卡期间，我碰巧观看了一场火上行走表演，很多人都在观看。在一个山坡草坪的底部挖了一条大沟，成百上千的观众坐在草坪的斜坡上，向沟里面俯瞰。

"大沟足有七米半长，沟里填满了原木、柴火、木炭，上面又浇上了煤油。煤油被点燃，燃烧了一会之后，整个沟就变成了一个燃烧起来的、赤红色的熔炉，温度高得连照管燃料的人也不得不戴上护目镜。风刮得很急，几乎把木炭上正在燃烧的火苗变成了白色。

"那个要赤脚在火上行走的印度人走上前来。除了腰间一条缠腰带之外，他身体其他部位都是裸露的。人群发出'嘘'的一声，只见他走进大沟，踩在白色炽热的木炭上向前走着，不慌不忙，没有停顿。他径直从白色炽热的木炭上面走过，从沟的另一头走了出去，双脚一点烧焦的迹象都没有。他抬起脚底给观众看,看得观众目瞪口呆、惊奇不已。

"然后,他又走了一遍,这次走得更慢。他一边走,我一边观察,看到他脸上露出一种不折不扣的、绝对聚精会神的表情。我对自己说,这个人练过瑜伽,是一位瑜伽大师。

"表演完毕,他向人群喊话,问是否有人勇敢地下来,到火上行走。人群一片安静。我感到我的胸膛里突然间涌出一股抑制不住的兴奋:我的机会来了,我必须抓住,必须有信心和勇气去一试身手。现在,我已经进行了三年多的训练,训练自己精力集中的程度,现在严峻考验自己能力的时刻到了。

"就在我站在原地想着这些事情的时候,人群中走出一位自愿者,是一名年轻的印度男子。他宣称,他要试试踩火行走。这一举动使我打定了主意,我也站了出来,做了声明。此时,人群为我们两个人发出喝彩声。

"现在,方才那位真正的踩火者成了监督,他吩咐那名男子先走,要求他将缠腰布式的衣服脱掉,并且说,要是不脱的话,布的褶边就会因为太热而起火,凉鞋也必须脱掉。

"这位印度年轻人一一照做,可是,一旦走近大沟,感受到里面散发出的可怕的热量,他就开始害怕起来,向后退缩了几步,用双手护住眼睛,免受热量的辐射。

"'要是你不愿意,就不必勉强。'真正的踩火者说道。

"人群等待着、观察着,感觉要有戏剧性的场面出现。

"这位年轻人尽管吓得有点儿魂不附体,还是希望证明一下自己的勇敢程度,于是说道:'我当然愿意。'

"话音刚落,他就向大沟跑去,一只脚踏了进去,另一只脚也踏了进去。只听得他发出一声恐惧的尖叫,又一次跳了出来,跌倒在地。这名可怜的男子躺在地上,痛苦地尖叫。他的脚底都严重烧伤,某些部位的皮肤都脱落了。他的两个朋友跑上前来将他抬走。

"'现在,轮到你了,'踩火者说。'准备好了吗?'

"'准备好了,'我说。'但是,我做预备动作的时候,请保持安

静。'

"人群中传来一阵高高的'嘘'声。他们已经目睹一个人严重烧伤,那么,第二个人还会那么疯狂,去重蹈覆辙吗?

"人群中有人喊:'不要去!你一定疯了!'其他人也跟着喊,所有人都告诫我不要去冒险。我转身面对他们,举起双手示意安静。他们停止喊叫,目不转睛地看着我。现在,那里的每一只眼睛都盯到了我的身上。

"我感到出奇的平静。

"我将身上缠腰带式的衣服举过头顶,脱了下来,然后又脱掉凉鞋。除了一条内裤,我几乎裸体站在那儿。我静静地站着,闭上了眼睛,开始集中精力,集中到火上面。我眼前只有白色炽热的木炭,没有其他别的任何东西。我集中精力于木炭,看到它们是寒冷的,而不是炎热的。我对自己说,木炭是寒冷的,无法烧到我。它们是不可能烧到我的,因为它们没有一点热量。半分钟时间过去了,这是容许的,但我知道,我不能耽搁太久,因为我的注意力绝对集中到任何一样物体上的时间只有一分半钟。

"我不断地集中精力,致使我进入了一种恍惚的状态。我迈开脚步,踩上了木炭。我走过整条大沟,走得相当快。哇,天呐,火没有烧到我!

"人群疯狂得沸腾了,他们喊叫着、欢呼着。那位正宗的踩火者匆忙奔我而来,检查起我的脚底,简直无法相信他的眼睛:我的脚底没有一丁点儿的烧痕。

"'啊呀呀!'他叫道。'这位什么来头?你修炼过瑜伽吗?'

"'先生,我正在修炼之中,'我自豪地回答。'进步很大。'

"我怕人群围上来,说完之后,就穿好衣服,快速离开了。

"当然,我很激动。'我的功力逐渐产生,'我说。'现在,我的功力最终开始出现了。'但我一直记着另外某件事情,是赫尔德瓦尔的那位老瑜伽大师对我说过的一件事情,我一直记着呢。他当时说:'某些神圣之人已经修炼出一种极强的集中注意力的功力——不用眼睛能够看得见。'我一直记得他的这句话,一直渴望自己能修炼成这种功力。这次踩火行走获得成功之后,我做出决定,要把所有的精力集中到这一目标上——不用眼睛能够看得见。"

到现在为止,伊姆拉汗给我讲着他的故事,中间只停下过两次。这次是第二次,停下来的时候,他又喝了一小口水。然后,他坐在椅子上将身体向后一靠,闭上了双眼。

"我要尽力将一切按顺序说出来,"他说。"我不想有半点遗漏。"

"你讲得很不错,"我对他说。"继续。"

"很好,"他说。"所以,我还在加尔各答,刚刚成功地完成了火上行走。现在,我决定将所有的精力都集中到一件事情上,那就是,不用眼睛能够看见东西。

"所以,想在训练中做点稍微的改变,现在是时候了,于是,每天晚上我都点燃一支蜡烛,然后开始盯着火焰看。你要知道,蜡烛的火焰分为三个不同的区域:最顶部的是黄色区域,稍微往下一点的是浅紫色区域,最内层的是黑色区域。我将蜡烛放在我眼前四十厘米远的地方,火焰与眼睛完全齐平——不能高于眼睛,也不能低于眼睛。之所以必须绝对地齐平,是因为那时眼睛要是上、下看的话,我就不必去调整眼肌,哪怕最微小的调整也不用。我舒舒服服地坐下来,开始盯着火焰的黑色区域看,也就是正中心的那部分。所有这一切的目的就是要集中我的意识心理,将我周围的一切从意识中排除。所以,我就盯着火焰的黑色部分看,一直看到周围的一切都消失、其他任何东西都看不见为止。接着,我慢慢闭上眼睛,将注意力集中到我选出的单个物体上,你也知道,那就是我兄弟的脸,就像我通常所做的那样。

"每天晚上入睡前,我都这样做。到了1929年,也就是我二十四岁的时候,我能够将注意力集中到单个物体上的时间维持在三分钟,而且一点儿都不走神儿。所以,二十四岁时,我开始意识到我有了一种微弱的能力——眼睛蒙上,也能看到东西。这只是一种很微弱的能力,也就是一种奇怪而轻微的感觉:闭上眼睛,使劲儿盯着某个东西,聚精会神,就能看出那个东西的轮廓。

“慢慢地,我开始修炼自己的内部视觉。

“你问我内部视觉是什么意思啊,我就跟你解释一下吧,就像当初赫尔德瓦尔的那位瑜伽大师向我解释的那样,跟你解释一下。

“你要知道,我们所有人都有两种类型的视觉,就跟两种类型的嗅觉、味觉、听觉一样。有外部类型,是高度发达的感觉类型,也就是人人都使用的感觉类型。还有一种是内部类型。要是我们大家都能开发出这种内部感觉类型,就好了:不用鼻子能够嗅到,不用舌头能够尝到,不用耳朵能够听到,不用眼睛能够看到。你明白不?我们的鼻子、舌头、耳朵和眼睛仅仅是……怎么说好呢?……仅仅是一些仪器,这些仪器能将感受传递给大脑,你难道不明白吗?

“所以,正是因为这一点,我始终努力要修炼我的内部视觉。现在每天晚上,我先用蜡烛的火焰和我兄弟的脸做常规性的练习,然后就休息一小会儿,喝上一杯咖啡。接下来,我就蒙上眼睛,坐在椅子上开始做形象化练习,不光是去想象,还要尽量去看——实际上就是不用眼睛去看屋子里的每一样物体。

“渐渐地,成功的影子开始出现了。

“很快,我就用一副纸牌来修炼了。我从一副牌的顶部抽出一张,背面朝前举到眼前,试着要看透是一张什么牌。然后,我就手持铅笔,我认为是张什么牌,就将其写下来。再抽出一张,如法炮制。就这样,我抽完整副扑克所有的牌。抽完、写完后,我就将写下的内容与旁边的那摞牌比照、核实,刚开始就获得了百分之六十到七十的成功率。

“我也拿其他东西做练习。我买了些地图和复杂的导航图,将它们钉得满屋子都是。连续好几个小时蒙着眼睛盯着它们,尽量要看见它们,尽量要读出上面小字体写的地名和河流的名称。接下来的四年时间里,每天晚上我就这样练习着。

“到了 1933 年,就是去年,我已经二十八岁,已经能够读出一本书的内容。将眼睛完全蒙上后,我能够从头至尾读出一本书的内容。

“所以现在,我终于练就了这样的功力。毫无疑问,我现在修炼成功,就立刻将这种蒙住眼睛看东西的特技用到我一般性的魔术表演中,因为我迫不及待地要一试身手。

"观众十分喜欢观看,掌声持久、响亮,可没有任何一个人相信那是真的,都认为那不过又是一种聪明的技法。我是一名魔术师,这一点使他们坚定不移地相信我就是在做手脚。魔术师就是玩把戏的,用聪明和机敏让你上当。因此,没人相信我。即使是使用极其专业的手法为我蒙上眼睛的医生也拒绝相信:有人不用眼睛会看见东西。但是,医生们也许都不记得了,或许有其他方式可以将影像传达给大脑。"

"其他什么方式?"我问他。

"老老实实地说,我不是很清楚,为什么不用眼睛也能看见东西,但我确确实实知道,我的眼睛被缠上后,我根本就不需要使用眼睛,身体另外一个部位也能够完成看的动作。"

"哪一个部位?"我问他。

"只要皮肤是裸露的,任何的部位都能够做到。比如说,如果你将一块金属板放到我面前,再将一本书放到金属板的后面,我无法读到书。但是,如果你允许我将一只手放到金属板的周围,这样的话,手就是在看书了,那么,我也就能够读到书的内容了。"

"你介意我就你说的测试一下吗?"我问。

"一点也不介意。"他回答。

"我手头没有金属板,"我说。"可是,门完全可以代替。"

我起身走到书架那儿,随手拿下一本书,书名是《爱丽丝漫游奇境》。我打开门,让他站到门后,我看不见他。我随意将书翻开,支到一把椅子上,他则站在门的另一边。然后,我自已站到一个既能看见他又能看到书的位置上。

"你能读那本书吗?"我问。

"不,"他回答。"当然不能。"

"那好吧。现在,你将一只手放到门周围,只放手啊。"

他将手放到门边移动着,一直移动到能看到书为止。接着,我看到他将五指叉开,手指彼此分得很开,开始轻微地颤抖,就像昆虫的触角在空中触摸着,然后手掌翻转过来,手背对着书的方向。

“书左面的那一页,尽量从顶部开始,读吧。”我吩咐。

大约十秒钟的沉默过后,他开始流畅地读了起来,没有任何停顿:“‘你猜到谜底了吗?’帽匠问,又转身面对爱丽丝。‘没有,我不猜了,’爱丽丝回答,‘谜底是什么呢?’‘我一点都不知道。’帽匠回答。‘我也不知道。’三月兔说。爱丽丝厌倦地叹了口气。‘我认为,你应该珍惜时间,做点更好的事儿,’爱丽丝说,‘而不是白白浪费时间出了个谜语,却没有谜底……’”

“太棒啦!”我叫道。“现在,我相信你了! 你创造了奇迹!”我激动不已,兴奋异常。

“有一个问题,”我说。“有关纸牌的一个问题。你将每张纸牌的反面举起来时,你是否将手放到纸牌另一面的边缘来帮你读出纸牌的内容呢?”

“你这个人很善于观察啊,”他说。“不,我不那样做。就纸牌而言,我实际上能通过某种方式看穿。”

“这话怎么解释呢?”我问。

“我不想多做解释,”他说。“或许因为纸牌这种东西既脆弱又单薄吧,不像金属板那样密实,也不像门那样厚实。我只能这样解释了。医生,这个世界上有很多的东西我们无法加以解释。”

“是的,”我说道。“当然是有很多这样的东西。”

“现在,你可否送我回家? 感激不尽。”他说。“我感觉很累。”

于是,我开车送他回家。

那天晚上,我彻夜未眠,由于过度的激动和兴奋,怎么也睡不着。我刚刚见证了一个奇迹。这名男子会让全世界的医生在空中大翻筋斗、无所适从! 他会改变整个医学的进程啊! 从医生的角度来说,他是最有价值的活人! 我们这些做医生的一定要留住他、确保他的安全,一定要照顾好他,不能让他走开。不使用眼睛能够将影像传送给大脑,我们一定要准确无误地查找出其工作原理。要是找到了答案,那么,盲人或许就能够看见,聋人或许就能够听见。最为重要的是,对于这样的奇人,不能无视他的存在任其在整个印度流浪、住廉价房间、在二流剧团表演。

这件事儿我越想越激动、兴奋,随后我就抓起笔记本和铅笔,开始将当晚伊姆拉汗对我讲述的一切写了下来,写得极其用心、仔细,并参照他谈话时我所做的笔记。我一刻没停,写了五个小时。到了第二天早晨八点,也就是去医院上班的时间,我写完了最为重要的部分,也就是你刚才读到的那几页的内容。

第二天上午在医院里,我没有看见马歇尔医生,只是后来在医生休息室喝茶时遇到了他。

在好不容易挤出来的十分钟时间里,我尽可能多地向他讲述了晚上的那件事儿。"今晚我要回剧院一趟,"我说。"我必须再跟他谈谈,必须说服他留下来,现在万万不可让他走开。"

"我跟你一起回去。"马歇尔医生说。

"好吧,"我说。"我们先看表演,然后带他出去吃晚饭。"

那天晚上六点四十五分的时候,我开车带马歇尔医生来到了阿卡西亚路。停好车后,我们朝皇宫礼堂走去。

"有点不对劲儿啊,"我说。"人都哪去了?"

礼堂外看不见聚集的人群,礼堂大门也关闭了。宣传表演的广告牌还在那里,但是现在,我却看到有人用大写印刷字体,在牌子上面这样写道:今晚表演取消。紧锁的大门边站着一位年迈的看门人。

"发生什么事儿?"我问他。

"有人死了。"他回答。

"谁?"我问,已经预感到是谁了。

"是那位不用眼睛能够看得见的。"守门人回答。

"他是怎么死的?"我大声问。"什么时候?在什么地方?"

"据说,他死在床上,"守门人说。"他睡着了,再也没有醒过来,这样的事儿时有发生。"

我们慢慢地走回停车的地方。一股巨大的痛苦和愤怒涌了上来:昨晚我怎么竟然允许这个身价不菲的人回家啊。我本可以留住他,本可以把我的床给他睡,本可以照看好他,我本可以不让他离开我的视线啊。伊姆拉汗创造了奇迹,他同神秘而危险的力量交流,而一般人根本触及不到这种力量。他也打破了所有的规则,在大庭广众之下展示奇迹,展示的目的是赚钱。最为糟糕的是,他还把诸多秘密讲给一个外人——我。现在,他死了。"

"所以嘛,就是那样的。"马歇尔医生说。

"是的,"我说。"就这样子了,谁都不会知道他是如何做到的。"

两次跟伊姆拉汗会面后,我把所有发生的事情写成上述报告,报告真实准确。

签名:约翰.F. 卡特赖特(医学博士)

1934 年 12 月 4 日于孟买

(待续……)

第二节《非凡亨利》(下部)

The Wonderful Story of Henry Sugar (Part B)

罗尔德·达尔的《非凡亨利》(*The Wonderful Story of Henry Sugar*)收录在《〈非凡亨利〉及另外六篇故事集》(*The Wonderful Story of Henry Sugar and Six More*)一书中。这个故事类似于中国金庸等作家笔下的武侠小说,其主人公经过一番艰苦的修炼,最后练成神功,具有非凡的能力。有所不同的是,本篇小说中的主人公亨利·休格将神功用在世界各地的大赌场上,将赢来的钱用于孤儿院的建设,让孤儿感受到家的温暖。

通读这部小说,再加上作家达尔在小说中的"旁白",让人感觉到其中的人物和事件都是真实的,而事实上,这篇小说里的故事,就像中国的武侠小说一样,应该都是编造出来的。这充分说明罗尔德·

达尔非凡的想象能力和创作功力。

一、原作导读

亨利·休格读完卡特赖特医生的报告,决定自己要修炼瑜伽神功,目的只是要看透纸牌,好闯遍赌场无敌手。于是,他将这本薄册子悄悄放入衣兜,据为己有,回家修炼……三年后,亨利能够在四秒钟之内读出纸牌的内容,到附近赌场小试身手,大获成功。但是,他并没有像预想的那样开心,瑜伽修炼改变了他的人生观,他要把赢来的钱用到慈善事业上——修建孤儿院,让孤儿有家可归。在余下的二十年时间里,他“周游”了世界近四百家赌场,建起了二十一所孤儿院。亨利这一非凡成就的取得,与两个人的辅助不无关系,一个人是约翰·温斯顿,专门经管他的账目,另一个人是马克斯·恩格斯曼,跟他游走四方,为他乔装打扮。

亨利去世后,叙事角度切换到“我”,也就是整部小说的写作者,但“我”是“隐身”的——地位是无足轻重的,起到了“纽带”或者“桥梁”的作用,可以看成作家达尔本人的化身。“我”的介入展开了第三个嵌套的故事:

我不是马克斯·恩格斯曼,也不是约翰·温斯顿,那么所有这一切我是怎么知道的?又怎样在第一时间把这个故事写出来的呢?亨利去世后不久,约翰·温斯顿从瑞士给我打来电话。电话那头的约翰·温斯顿给我讲了讲亨利·休格的秘密生涯。那已不是什么秘密了,亨利已死,再也不会去赌博了。我一边听着这个故事,一边深深为之着迷。

But how do I, who am neither Max Engelman nor John Winston, happen to know all this? And how did I come to write the story in the first place? Soon after Henry's death, John Winston telephoned me from Switzerland. John Winston told me something about Henry Sugar's secret career. It was secret no longer. Henry was dead and would never gamble again. I listened, enthralled.

"我"同意要把这个故事写出来,于是,飞到洛桑见到了马克斯·恩格斯曼和约翰·温斯顿两个人,他们跟"我"谈了有关亨利的事情。

"最后一个问题,"我说。"你总是称呼他亨利·休格,然而,你却告诉我说,这不是他的真名。我写这个故事的时候,难道你不想让我写出他的真名吗?"

"不想,"约翰·温斯顿回答。"我和马克斯都答应过他,永远也不披露他的真名实姓。哦,或早或晚,也许会泄露出去,毕竟他出生于英国的一个显赫家族。要是你不去设法追根究底的话,我会很感激的。就普普通通地称呼他亨利·休格先生吧。"

实际上,我也是那么做的。

"One last question," I said. "You keep calling him Henry Sugar. And yet you tell me that wasn't his name. Don't you want me to say who he really was when I do the story?"

"No," John Winston said. "Max and I promised never to reveal it. Oh, it'll probably leak out sooner or later. After all, he was from a fairly well-known English family. But I'd appreciate it if you don't try to find out. Just call him plain Mr. Henry Sugar."

And that is what I have done.

二、原作释读

这篇小说篇幅较长,叙事角度切换较多,阅读中需要仔细辨别。同时,还要注意领会某些专业领域的词汇和表达,如文学、音乐、生理学等领域里的词汇和表达,但大部分还是容易理解的,障碍不是很多,可以流畅地阅读和理解。

The Wonderful Story of Henry Sugar

(Continued from the above)

"Well, well, well," said Henry Sugar. "Now that is extremely interesting."

He closed the exercise-book and sat gazing at the rain splashing against the windows of the library.

"This," Henry Sugar went on, talking aloud to himself, "is a terrific piece of information. It could change my life."

The piece of information Henry was referring to was that Imhrat Khan had trained himself to read the value of a playing-card from the reverse side. And Henry the gambler, the rather dishonest gambler, had realized at once that if only he could train himself to do the same thing, he could make a fortune.

For a few moments, Henry allowed his mind to dwell upon the marvellous things he would be able to do if he could read cards from the back. He would win every single time at canasta and bridge and poker. And better still, he would be able to go into any casino in the world and clean up at blackjack and all the other high-powered card games they played!

In gambling casinos, as Henry knew very well, nearly everything depended in the end upon the turn of a single card, and if you knew beforehand what the value of that card was, then you were home and dry①!

But could he do it? Could he actually train himself to do this thing?

He didn't see why not. That stuff with the candle-flame didn't ap-

---

① home and dry: (chiefly Brit.) having successfully achieved or being within sight of achieving one's objective(主要为英国英语的用法)大功告成;成功在望(e. g. At 3: 0 up they should have been home and dry. 以3比0领先的情况下他们本来应该取胜的。)

pear to be particularly hard work. And according to the book, that was really all there was to it—just staring into the middle of the flame and trying to concentrate upon the face of the person you loved best.

It would probably take him several years to bring it off, but then who in the world wouldn't be willing to train for a few years in order to beat the casinos every time he went in?

"By golly," he said aloud, "I'll do it! I'm going to do it!"

He sat very still in the armchair in the library, working out a plan of campaign. Above all, he would tell nobody what he was up to. He would steal the little book from the library so that none of his friends might come upon it by chance and learn the secret. He would carry the book with him wherever he went. It would be his bible. He couldn't possibly go out and find a real live yogi to instruct him, so the book would be his yogi instead. It would be his teacher.

Henry stood up and slipped the slim blue exercise-book under his jacket. He walked out of the library and went straight upstairs to the bedroom they had given him for the week-end. He got out his suitcase and hid the book underneath his clothes. He then went downstairs again and found his way to the butler's pantry①.

"John," he said, addressing the butler, "can you find me a candle? Just an ordinary white candle."

Butlers are trained never to ask reasons. They simply obey orders. "Do you wish a candle-holder as well, sir?"

"Yes. A candle and a candle-holder."

"Very good, sir. Shall I bring them to your room?"

"No. I'll hang around here till you find them."

---

① pantry: *Noun* a small room or closet, usually off a kitchen, where food, tableware, linens, and similar items are stored(食品、餐具等的)储藏室(e.g. A pantry adjoins the kitchen. 食品储藏室与厨房毗连。)

The butler soon found a candle and a candle-holder. Henry said, "And now could you find me a ruler?" The butler found him a ruler. Henry thanked him and returned to his bedroom.

When he was inside the bedroom, he locked the door. He drew all the curtains so that the place was in twilight. He put the candle-holder with the candle in it on the dressing-table and pulled up a chair. When he sat down, he noticed with satisfaction that his eyes were exactly level with the wick① of the candle. Now, using the ruler, he positioned his face sixteen inches from the candle, which was what the book said must be done.

That Indian fellow had visualized the face of the person he loved best, which in his case was a brother. Henry didn't have a brother. He decided instead to visualize his own face. This was a good choice because when you are as selfish and self-centred as Henry was, then one's own face is certainly the face one loves best of all. Moreover, it was the face he knew best of all. He spent so much time looking at it in the mirror, he knew every twist and wrinkle.

With his cigarette-lighter, he lit the wick. A yellow flame appeared and burned steadily.

Henry sat quite still and stared into the candle-flame. The book had been quite right. The flame, when you looked into it closely, did have three separate parts. There was the yellow outside. Then there was the mauve inner sheath②. And right in the middle was the tiny magic area of absolute blackness. He stared at the tiny black area. He focused his eyes upon it and kept staring at it, and as he did so, an extraordinary thing

---

① wick: *Noun* a strip of porous material up which liquid fuel is drawn by capillary action to the flame in a candle, lamp, or lighter 灯芯;烛芯;(打火机的)油绳

② sheath: *Noun* a close-fitting cover for something, especially something that is elongated in shape, in particular(尤指形状细长的)紧贴覆盖物

happened. His mind went absolutely blank, and his brain ceased fidgeting around, and all at once it felt as though he himself, his whole body, was actually encased within the flame, sitting snug and cosy within the little black area of nothingness.

With no trouble at all, Henry allowed the image of his own face to swim into sight before him. He concentrated upon the face and nothing but the face. He blocked out all other thoughts. He succeeded completely in doing this, but only for about fifteen seconds. After that, his mind began to wander and he found himself thinking about gambling casinos and how much money he was going to win. At this point, he looked away from the candle and gave himself a rest.

This was his very first effort. He was thrilled. He had done it. Admittedly he hadn't kept it up for very long. But neither had that Indian fellow on the first attempt.

After a few minutes, he tried again. It went well. He had no stop-watch[1] to time himself with, but he sensed that this was definitely a longer go than the first one.

"It's terrific!" he cried. "I'm going to succeed! I'm going to do it!" He had never been so excited by anything in his life.

From that day on, no matter where he was or what he was doing, Henry made a point of practising with the candle every morning and every evening. Often he practised at midday as well. For the first time in his life he was throwing himself into something with genuine enthusiasm. And the progress he made was remarkable. After six months, he could concentrate absolutely upon his own face for no less than three minutes without a single outside thought entering his mind.

The yogi of Hardwar had told the Indian fellow that a man would

① stop-watch or stopwatch: *Noun* a special watch with buttons that start, stop, and then zero the hands, used to time races(赛跑用的)秒表;跑表

have to practise for fifteen years to get that sort of result!

But wait! The yogi had also said something else. He had said (and here Henry eagerly consulted the little blue exercise-book for the hundredth time), he had said that on extremely rare occasions a special person comes along who is able to develop the power in only one or two years.

"That's me!" Henry cried. "It must be me! I am the one-in-a-million person who is gifted with the ability to acquire yoga powers at incredible speed! Whoopee[①] and hurray[②]! It won't be long now before I'm breaking the bank[③] in every casino in Europe and America!"

But Henry at this point showed unusual patience and good sense. He didn't rush to get out a pack of cards to see if he could read them from the reverse side. In fact, he kept well away from card games of all kinds. He had given up bridge and canasta and poker as soon as he had started working with the candle. What's more, he had given up razzing around to parties and weekends with his rich friends. He had become dedicated to this single aim of acquiring yoga powers, and everything else would have to wait until he had succeeded.

Some time during the tenth month, Henry became aware, just as Imhrat Khan had done before him, of a slight ability to see an object with his eyes closed. When he closed his eyes and stared at something hard, with fierce concentration, he could actually see the outline of the object he was looking at.

---

① whoopee: Exclamation expressing wild excitement or joy(表示激动、快乐等)哈哈

② hurray or hooray: Interjection used as an exclamation of pleasure, approval, elation, or victory(表示高兴、赞同、欣喜、胜利等)好哇;加油

③ break the bank: (in gambling) win more money than is held by the bank(赌博中)赢光庄家的钱

"It's coming to me!" he cried. "I'm doing it! It's fantastic!"

Now he worked harder than ever at his exercises with the candle, and at the end of the first year he could actually concentrate upon the image of his own face for no less than five and a half minutes!

At this point, he decided the time had come to test himself with the cards. He was in the living-room of his London flat when he made this decision and it was near midnight. He got out a pack of cards and a pencil and paper. He was shaking with excitement. He placed the pack upside down before him and concentrated on the top card.

All he could see at first was the design on the back of the card. It was a very ordinary design of thin red lines, one of the commonest playing-card designs in the world. He now shifted his concentration from the pattern itself to the other side of the card. He concentrated with great intensity upon the invisible underneath of the card, and he allowed no other single thought to creep into his mind. Thirty seconds went by.

Then one minute...

Two minutes...

Three minutes...

Henry didn't move. His concentration was intense and absolute. He was visualizing the reverse side of the playing-card. No other thought of any kind was allowed to enter his head.

During the fourth minute, something began to happen. Slowly, magically, but very clearly, the black symbols became spades① and alongside the spades appeared the figure five.

The five of spades!

Henry switched off his concentration. And now, with shaking fin-

① spade: *Noun* (spades) one of the four suits in a conventional pack of playing cards, denoted by a black inverted heart-shaped figure with a small stalk(纸牌中的)黑桃

gers, he picked up the card and turned it over.

It was the five of spades!

"I've done it!" he cried aloud, leaping up from his chair. "I've seen through it! I'm on my way!"

After resting for a while, he tried again, and this time he used a stop-watch to see how long it took him. After three minutes and fifty-eight seconds, he read the card as the king of diamonds①. He was right!

The next time he was right again and it took him three minutes and fifty-four seconds. That was four seconds less.

He was sweating with excitement and exhaustion. "That's enough for today," he told himself. He got up and poured himself an enormous drink of whisky and sat down to rest and to gloat② over his success.

His job now, he told himself, was to keep practising and practising with the cards until he could see through them instantly. He was convinced it could be done. Already, on the second go, he had knocked four seconds off his time. He would give up working with the candle and concentrate solely upon the cards. He would keep at it day and night.

And that is what he did. But now that he could smell real success in the offing③, he became more fanatical than ever. He never left his flat except to buy food and drink. All day and often far into the night, he crouched over the cards with the stop-watch beside him, trying to reduce the time it took him to read from the reverse side.

---

① diamond: *Noun* (diamonds) one of the four suits in a conventional pack of playing cards, denoted by a red figure of such a shape 方块(扑克牌的四种花色之一)

② gloat: *Verb* [no obj.] contemplate or dwell on one's own success or another's misfortune with smugness or malignant pleasure 沾沾自喜;幸灾乐祸(e.g. His enemies gloated over his death. 敌人对他的死幸灾乐祸。)

③ in the offing: likely to happen or appear soon 很可能即将发生(或出现)的(e.g. There are several initiatives in the offing. 有好几个倡议即将出台。)

Within a month, he was down to one and a half minutes.

And at the end of six months of fierce concentrated work, he could do it in twenty seconds. But even that was too long. When you are gambling in a casino and the dealer is waiting for you to say yes or no to the next card, you are not going to be allowed to stare at it for twenty seconds before making up your mind. Three or four seconds would be permissible. But no more.

Henry kept at it. But from now on, it became more and more difficult to improve his speed. To get down from twenty seconds to nineteen took him a week of very hard work. From nineteen to eighteen took him nearly two weeks. And seven more months went by before he could read through a card in ten seconds flat.

His target was four seconds. He knew that unless he could see through a card in a maximum of four seconds, he wouldn't be able to work the casinos successfully.

Yet the nearer he got towards the target, the more difficult it became to reach it. It took four weeks to get his time down from ten seconds to nine, and five more weeks to go from nine to eight. But at this stage, hard work no longer bothered him. His powers of concentration had now developed to such a degree that he was able to work for twelve hours at a stretch with no trouble at all. And he knew with absolute certainty that he would get there in the end. He would not stop until he did. Day after day, night after night, he sat crouching over the cards with his stop-watch beside him, fighting with a terrible intensity to knock those last few stubborn seconds off his time.

The last three seconds were the worst of all. To get from seven seconds to his target of four took him exactly eleven months!

The great moment came on a Saturday evening. A card lay face down on the table in front of him. He clicked the stop-watch and began to concentrate. At once, he saw a blob① of red. The blob swiftly took shape and became a diamond. And then, almost instantaneously, a figure six appeared in the top left-hand corner. He clicked the watch again. He checked the time. It was four seconds! He turned the card over. It was the six of diamonds! He had done it! He had read it in four seconds flat!

He tried again with another card. In four seconds he read it as the queen of spades. He went right through the pack, timing himself with every card. Four seconds! Four seconds! Four seconds! It was always the same. He had done it at last! It was all over. He was ready to go! And how long had it taken him? It had taken him exactly three years and three months of concentrated work.

And now for the casinos!

When should he start? Why not tonight?

Tonight was Saturday. All the casinos were crowded on Saturday nights. So much the better. There'd be less chance of becoming conspicuous. He went into his bedroom to change into his dinner-jacket and black tie. Saturday was a dressy② night at the big London casinos.

He would go, he decided, to Lord's House. There are well over one hundred legitimate casinos in London, but none of them is open to the general public. You must become a member before you are allowed to walk in. Henry was a member of no less than ten of them. Lord's House

---

① blob: *Noun* an indeterminate roundish mass or shape 形状不易确定的一团(e. g. A big pink blob of a face was at the window. 窗口出现了一张肉团团的粉红色大脸。)

② dressy: *Adjective* requiring or given to wearing such clothes 需着装考究的;需着礼服的;习惯穿考究衣服的

was his favourite. It was the finest and most exclusive① in the country.

Lord's House was a magnificent Georgian② mansion in the centre of London, and for over two hundred years it had been the private residence of a Duke. Now it was taken over by the bookmakers, and the superb high-ceilinged rooms where the aristocracy and often royalty used to gather and play a gentle game of whist③ were today filled with a new kind of people who played a very different sort of game.

Henry drove to Lord's House and pulled up outside the great entrance. He got out of the car, but left the engine running. Immediately, an attendant in green uniform came forward to park it for him.

Along the kerb④ on both sides of the street stood perhaps a dozen Rolls-Royces⑤. Only the very wealthy belonged to Lord's House.

"Why hello, Mr. Sugar!" said the man behind the desk whose job it was never to forget a face. "We haven't seen you for years!"

"I've been busy," Henry answered.

He went upstairs, up the marvellous wide staircase with its carved

---

① exclusive: *Adjective* catering for or available to only a few, select customers; high class and expensive 高级的;奢华的(e.g. one of Britain's most exclusive clubs 英国最高级的俱乐部之一)

② Georgian: *Adjective* of or characteristic of the reigns of the British Kings George I - IV (1714—1830) (与)英国乔治一世至乔治四世统治时期(1714—1830)(有关)的;乔治王朝的;乔治王朝风格的

③ whist: *Noun* [mass noun] a card game, usually for two pairs of players, in which points are scored according to the number of tricks won 惠斯特牌(两对人玩的一种纸牌游戏)

④ kerb or curb: *Noun* a stone edging to a pavement or raised path(人行道或凸起小道的)石砌路缘

⑤ Rolls-Royce:一个著名汽车的品牌,通常译作"劳斯莱斯"。

mahogany① banisters②, and entered the cashier's office. There he wrote a cheque for one thousand pounds. The cashier gave him ten large pink rectangular plaques③ made of plastic. On each it said £ 100. Henry slipped them into his pocket and spent a few minutes sauntering④ through the various gaming rooms to get the feel of things again after such a long absence. There was a big crowd here tonight. Well-fed women stood around the roulette wheel like plump hens around a feeding hopper. Jewels and gold were dripping over their bosoms and from their wrists. Many of them had blue hair. The men were in dinner-jackets and there wasn't a tall one among them. Why, Henry wondered, did this particular kind of rich man always have short legs? Their legs all seemed to stop at the knees with no thighs above. Most of them had bellies coming out a long way, and crimson faces, and cigars between their lips. Their eyes glittered with greed.

All this Henry noticed. It was the first time in his life that he had looked with distaste upon this type of wealthy gambling-casino person. Up until now, he had always regarded them as companions, as members of the same group and class as himself. Tonight they seemed vulgar. Could it be, he wondered, that the yoga powers he had acquired over the last three years had altered him just a little bit?

He stood watching the roulette. Upon the long green table people were placing their money, trying to guess which little slot the small white

---

① mahogany: *Noun* [mass noun] hard reddish-brown timber from a tropical tree, used for quality furniture 红木;桃花心木

② banister or bannister: *Noun* the structure formed by the uprights and handrail at the side of a staircase(楼梯)扶手

③ plaque: *Noun* a flat counter used in gambling(用于赌博的扁平)筹码

④ saunter: *Verb* [no obj., with adverbial of direction] walk in a slow, relaxed manner, without hurry or effort 闲逛;漫步(e.g. Adam sauntered into the room. 亚当悠闲地踱进房间。)

ball would fall into on the next spin of the wheel. Henry looked at the wheel. And suddenly, perhaps more from habit than anything else, he found himself beginning to concentrate upon it. It was not difficult. He had been practising the art of total concentration for so long that it had become something of a routine. In a fraction of a second, his mind had become completely and absolutely concentrated upon the wheel. Everything else in the room, the noise, the people, the lights, the smell of cigar smoke, all this was wiped out of his mind, and he saw only the white numbers around the rim. The numbers went from 1 to 36, with an O between 1 and 36. Very quickly, all the numbers blurred and disappeared in front of his eyes. All except one, all except the number 18. It was the only number he could see. At first it was slightly muzzy① and out of focus. Then the edges sharpened and the whiteness of it grew brighter, more brilliant, until it began to glow as though there was a bright light behind it. It grew bigger. It seemed to jump towards him. At that point, Henry switched off his concentration. The room swam back into vision.

"Have you all finished?" the croupier② was saying.

Henry took a £ 100 plaque from his pocket and placed it on the square marked 18 on the green table. Although the table was covered all over with other people's bets, his was the only one on 18.

The croupier spun the wheel. The little white ball bounced and skittered③ around the rim. The people watched. All eyes were on the little

---

① muzzy: *Adjective* (of a person's eyes or a visual image) blurred(人的眼睛或视觉形象)模糊不清的(e. g. a slightly muzzy picture 有点儿模糊的照片)

② croupier: *Noun* the person in charge of a gaming table, gathering in and paying out money or tokens 赌台管理员(主要经管收进和赔付赌注)

③ skitter or skeeter: *Verb* [no obj.] [no obj., with adverbial of direction] move lightly and quickly or hurriedly 轻捷跑动(e. g. The girls skittered up the stairs. 女孩子们轻捷地跑上楼。)

ball. The wheel slowed. It came to rest. The ball jiggled[1] a few more times, hesitated, then dropped neatly into slot 18.

"Eighteen!" called the croupier.

The crowd sighed. The croupier's assistant scooped up the piles of losing plaques with a long-handled wooden scooper. But he didn't take Henry's. They paid him thirty-six to one. Three thousand six hundred pounds for his hundred. They gave it to him in three one-thousand pound plaques and six hundreds.

Henry began to feel an extraordinary sense of power. He felt he could break this place if he wanted to. He could ruin this fancy high-powered expensive joint in a matter of hours. He could take a million off them and all the stony-faced sleek[2] gentlemen who stood around watching the money rolling in would be scurrying[3] about like panicky rats.

Should he do that?

It was a great temptation.

But it would be the end of everything. He would become famous and would never be allowed into a casino again anywhere in the world. He mustn't do it. He must be very careful not to draw attention to himself.

Henry moved casually out of the roulette room and passed into the room where they were playing blackjack. He stood in the doorway watching the action. There were four tables. They were oddly shaped, these

---

① jiggle: *Verb* [no obj.] move about lightly and quickly from side to side or up and down 颠簸;急颤;抖动(e. g. The car jiggled on its springs. 汽车在车弹簧上轻轻颠簸。)

② sleek: *Adjective* (of a person) having a wealthy and well-groomed appearance(人)富态的;衣冠楚楚的(e. g. a sleek and ambitious junior Minister 一位衣冠楚楚、具有雄心壮志的年轻部长)

③ scurry: *Verb* [no obj., with adverbial of direction] (of a person or small animal) move hurriedly with short quick steps(人或小动物)小步快跑(e. g. Pedestrians scurried for cover. 行人小跑步寻找躲避之处。)

blackjack tables, each one curved like a crescent[1] moon, with the players sitting on high stools around the outside of the half-circle and the dealers standing inside.

The packs of cards (at Lord's House they used four packs shuffled together) lay in an open-ended box known as a shoe, and the dealer pulled the cards out of the shoe one by one with his fingers... The reverse side of the card in the shoe was always visible, but no others.

Blackjack, as the casinos call it, is a very simple game. You and I know it by one of three other names, pontoon[2], twenty-one or vingt-et-un. The player tries to get his cards to add up to as near twenty-one as possible, but if he goes over twenty-one, he's bust[3] and the dealer takes the money. In nearly every hand, the player is faced with the problem of whether to draw another card and risk being bust, or whether to stick with what he's got. But Henry would not have that problem. In four seconds, he would have "seen through" the card the dealer was offering him, and he would know whether to say yes or no. Henry could turn blackjack into a farce[4].

In all casinos, they have an awkward rule about blackjack betting which we do not have at home. At home, we look at our first card before we make a bet, and if it's a good one we bet high. The casinos don't allow you to do this. They insist that everyone at the table makes his bet

---

① crescent: *Noun* the curved sickle shape of the waxing or waning moon 月牙形;新月形;弦月形;(月亮)镰刀形

② pontoon: *Noun* [mass noun] (Brit.) the card game blackjack or vingt-et-un(英国英语)二十一点扑克游戏

③ bust: *Verb* [no obj.] (in blackjack and similar card game) exceed the score of 21, so losing one's stake(玩二十一点及类似牌戏)超点输掉赌注;涨裂

④ farce: *Noun* a comic dramatic work using buffoonery and horseplay and typically including crude characterization and ludicrously improbable situations 闹剧;笑剧;滑稽戏

before the first card of the hand is dealt. What's more; you are not allowed to increase your bet later on by buying a card.

None of this would disturb Henry either. So long as he sat on the dealer's immediate left, then he would always receive the first card in the shoe at the beginning of each deal. The reverse side of the card would be clearly visible to him, and he would "read through" it before he made his bet.

Now, standing quietly just inside the doorway, Henry waited for a place to become vacant on the dealer's left at any of the four tables. He had to wait twenty minutes for this to happen, but he got what he wanted in the end.

He perched himself on the high stool and handed the dealer one of the £ 1,000 plaques he had won at roulette. "All in twenty-fives, please," he said.

The dealer was a youngish man with black eyes and grey skin. He never smiled and he spoke only when necessary. His hands were exceptionally slim and there was arithmetic in his fingers. He took Henry's plaque and dropped it in a slot in the table. Rows of different coloured circular chips lay neatly in a wooden tray in front of him, chips for £ 25, £ 10 and £ 5, maybe a hundred of each. With his thumb and forefinger, the dealer picked up a wedge of £ 25 chips and placed them in a tall pile on the table. He didn't have to count them. He knew there were exactly twenty chips in the pile. Those nimble fingers could pick up with absolute accuracy any number of chips from one to twenty and never be wrong. The dealer picked up a second lot of chips, making forty in all. He slid them over the table to Henry.

Henry stacked the chips in front of him, and as he did so, he glanced at the top card in the shoe. He switched on his concentration and in four seconds he read it as a ten. He pushed out eight of his chips, £ 200. This was the maximum stake allowed for blackjack at Lord's

House.

He was dealt the ten, and for his second card he got a nine, nineteen altogether.

Everyone sticks on nineteen. You sit tight and hope the dealer won't get twenty or twenty-one.

So when the dealer came round again to Henry, he said, "Nineteen," and passed on to the next player.

"Wait," Henry said.

The dealer paused and came back to Henry. He raised his brows and looked at him with those cool black eyes. "You wish to draw to nineteen?" he asked somewhat sarcastically. He spoke with an Italian accent and there was scorn as well as sarcasm in his voice. There were only two cards in the pack that would not bust a nineteen, the ace (counting as a one) and the two. Only an idiot would risk drawing to nineteen, especially with £ 200 on the table.

The next card to be dealt lay clearly visible in the front of the shoe. At least, the reverse side of it was clearly visible. The dealer hadn't yet touched it.

"Yes," Henry said. "I think I'll have another card."

The dealer shrugged and flipped the card out of the shoe. The two of clubs① landed neatly in front of Henry, alongside the ten and the nine.

"Thank you," Henry said. "That will do nicely."

"Twenty-one," the dealer said. His black eyes glanced up again into Henry's face, and they rested there, silent, watchful, puzzled. Henry had unbalanced him. He had never in his life seen anyone draw on nineteen. This fellow had drawn on nineteen with a calmness and a certainty that was quite staggering. And he had won.

---

① club: *Noun* (clubs) one of the four suits in a conventional pack of playing cards, denoted by a black trefoil(纸牌四花色之一的)梅花

Henry caught the look in the dealer's eyes, and he realized at once that he had made a silly mistake. He had been too clever. He had drawn attention to himself. He must never do that again. He must be very careful in future how he used his powers. He must even make himself lose occasionally, and every now and again he must do something a bit stupid.

The game went on. Henry's advantage was so enormous, he had difficulty keeping his winnings down to a reasonable sum. Every now and again, he would ask for a third card when he already knew it was going to bust him. And once, when he saw that his first card was going to be an ace, he put out his smallest stake, then made a great show of cursing himself aloud for not having made a bigger bet in the first place.

In an hour, he had won exactly three thousand pounds, and there he stopped. He pocketed his chips and made his way back to the cashier's office to turn them in for real money.

He had made £ 3,000 from blackjack and £ 3,600 from roulette, £ 6,600 in all. It could just as easily have been £ 660,000. As a matter of fact, he told himself he was now almost certainly able to make money faster than any other man in the entire world.

The cashier received Henry's pile of chips and plaques without twitching a muscle. He wore steel spectacles, and the pale eyes behind the spectacles were not interested in Henry. They looked only at the chips on the counter. This man also had arithmetic in his fingers. But he had more than that. He had arithmetic, trigonometry① and calculus② and algebra and Euclidean geometry③ in every nerve of his body. He was a human calculating-machine with a hundred thousand electric wires in his brain. It took him five seconds to count Henry's one hundred and twenty chips.

"Would you like a cheque for this, Mr. Sugar?" he asked. The cashier, like the man at the desk downstairs, knew every member by name.

"No, thank you," Henry said. "I'll take it in cash."

"As you wish," said the voice behind the spectacles, and he turned away and went to a safe at the back of the office that must have contained millions.

By Lord's House standards, Henry's win was fairly small potatoes. The Arab oil boys were in London now and they liked to gamble. So did the shady diplomats from the Far East and the Japanese businessmen and the British tax-dodging④ real-estate operators. Staggering sums of money were being won and lost, mostly lost, in the large London casinos ev-

---

① trigonometry: *Noun* [mass noun] the branch of mathematics dealing with the relations of the sides and angles of triangles and with the relevant functions of any angles 三角学

② calculus: *Noun* (also as "infinitesimal calculus") [mass noun] the branch of mathematics that deals with the finding and properties of derivatives and integrals of functions, by methods originally based on the summation of infinitesimal differences. The two main types are differential calculus and integral calculus 微积分(主要有微分和积分)

③ Euclidean geometry: geometry based upon the postulates of Euclid, esp. the postulate that only one line may be drawn through a given point parallel to a given line 欧几里得几何

④ dodge: *Verb* [with obj.] avoid (someone or something) by a sudden quick movement 躲开(e. g. Marchers had to dodge missiles thrown by loyalists. 行进的人们不得不躲开忠实者的投掷物。)

ery day.

The cashier returned with Henry's money and dropped the bundle of notes on the counter. Although there was enough here to buy a small house or a large automobile, the chief cashier at Lord's House was not impressed. He might just as well have been passing Henry a pack of chewing-gum for all the notice he took of the money he was dishing out.

You wait, my friend, Henry thought to himself as he pocketed the money. You just wait. He walked away.

"Your car, sir?" said the man at the door in the green uniform.

"Not yet," Henry told him. "I think I'll take a bit of fresh air first."

He strolled away down the street. It was nearly midnight. The evening was cool and pleasant. The great city was still wide awake. Henry could feel the bulge in the inside pocket of his jacket where the big wad of money was lying. He touched the bulge with one hand. He patted it gently. It was a lot of money for an hour's work.

And what of the future?

What was the next move going to be?

He could make a million in a month.

He could make more if he wanted to.

There was no limit to what he could make.

Walking through the streets of London in the cool of the evening, Henry began to think about the next move.

Now, had this been a made-up story instead of a true one, it would have been necessary to invent some sort of a surprising and exciting end for it. It would not be difficult to do that. Something dramatic and unusual. So before telling you what really did happen to Henry in real life, let us pause here for a moment to see what a competent fiction writer would have done to wrap this story up. His notes would read something like this:

1. Henry must die. Like Imhrat Khan before him, he had violated the code of the yogi and had used his powers for personal gain.

2. It will be best if he dies in some unusual and interesting manner that will surprise the reader.

3. For example, he could go home to his flat and start counting his money and gloating over it. While doing this, he might suddenly begin to feel unwell. He has a pain in his chest.

4. He becomes frightened. He decides to go to bed immediately and rest. He takes off his clothes. He walks naked to the cupboard to get his pyjamas. He passes the full-length mirror that stands against the wall. He stops. He stares at the reflection of his naked self in the mirror. Automatically, from force of habit he begins to concentrate. And then . . .

5. All at once, he is "seeing through" his own skin. He "sees through" it in the same way that he "saw through" those playing-cards a while back. It is like an X-ray picture, only far better. An X-ray can see only the bones and the very dense areas. Henry can see everything. He sees his arteries and veins with the blood pumping through him. He can see his liver, his kidneys, his intestines and he can see his heart beating.

6. He looks at the place in his chest where the pain is coming from... and he sees... or thinks he sees... a small dark lump inside the big vein leading into the heart on the right-hand side. What could a small dark lump be doing inside the vein? It must be a blockage of some kind. It must be a clot①. A blood-clot!

7. At first, the clot seems to be stationary. Then it moves. The movement is very slight, no more than a millimetre or two. The blood inside the vein is pumping up behind the clot and pushing past it and the

① clot: *Noun* a thick mass of coagulated liquid, especially blood, or of material stuck together(尤指血液的)凝块;黏团

clot moves again. It jerks forward about half an inch. This time, up the vein, towards the heart. Henry watches in terror. He knows, as almost everyone else in the world knows, that a blood-clot which has broken free and is travelling in a vein will ultimately reach the heart. If the clot is a large one, it will stick in the heart and you will probably die...

That wouldn't be such a bad ending for a work of fiction, but this story is not fiction. It is true. The only untrue things about it are Henry's name and the name of the gambling casino. Henry's name was not Henry Sugar. His name has to be protected. It still must be protected. And for obvious reasons, one cannot call the casino by its real name. Apart from that, it is a true story.

And because it is a true story, it must have the true ending. The true one may not be quite so dramatic or spooky as a made-up one could be, but it is nonetheless interesting. Here is what actually happened.

After walking the London streets for about an hour, Henry returned to Lord's House and collected his car. Then he drove back to his flat. He was a puzzled man. He couldn't understand why he felt so little excitement about his tremendous success. If this sort of thing had happened to him three years ago, before he'd started the yoga business, he'd have gone crazy with excitement. He'd have been dancing in the streets and rushing off to the nearest nightclub to celebrate with champagne.

The funny thing was that he didn't really feel excited at all. He felt melancholy. It had somehow all been too easy. Every time he'd made a bet, he'd been certain of winning. There was no thrill, no suspense, no danger of losing. He knew of course that from now on he could travel around the world and make millions. But was it going to be any fun doing it?

It was slowly beginning to dawn upon① Henry that nothing is any fun if you can get as much of it as you want. Especially money.

Another thing. Was it not possible that the process he had gone through in order to acquire yoga powers had completely changed his outlook on life?

Certainly it was possible.

Henry drove home and went straight to bed.

The next morning he woke up late. But he didn't feel any more cheerful now than he had the night before. And when he got out of bed and saw the enormous bundle of money still lying on his dressing-table, he felt a sudden and very acute revulsion② towards it. He didn't want it. For the life of him, he couldn't explain why this was so, but the fact remained that he simply did not want any part of it.

He picked up the bundle. It was all in twenty-pound notes, three hundred and thirty of them to be exact. He walked on to the balcony of his flat, and there he stood in his dark-red silk pyjamas looking down at the street below him.

Henry's flat was in Curzon Street, which is right in the middle of London's most fashionable and expensive district, known as Mayfair③. One end of Curzon Street runs into Berkeley Square, the other into Park Lane. Henry lived three floors above street level, and outside his bed-

---

① dawn on sb.: (also "dawn upon sb.", but more formal) If an idea, the truth or a fact dawns on you, you realize it for the first time 使开始明白;使渐渐领悟;使开始理解(e.g. It suddenly dawned on us that we were lost. 我们突然意识到我们迷路了。)

② revulsion: *Noun* [mass noun] a sense of disgust and loathing 厌恶;反感(e.g. News of the attack will be met with sorrow and revulsion. 袭击的消息将让人们悲伤和反感。)

③ Mayfair: *Noun* a fashionable and opulent district in the West End of London 梅费尔区(伦敦西区富人居住区)

room there was a small balcony with iron railings that overhung the street.

The month was June, the morning was full of sunshine, and the time was about eleven o'clock. Although it was a Sunday, there were quite a few people strolling about on the pavements.

Henry peeled off a single twenty-pound note from his wad and dropped it over the balcony. A breeze took hold of it and blew it sideways in the direction of Park Lane. Henry stood watching it. It fluttered① and twisted in the air and eventually came to rest on the opposite side of the street, directly in front of an old man. The old man was wearing a long brown shabby overcoat and a floppy② hat, and he was walking slowly, all by himself. He caught sight of the note as it fluttered past his face, and he stopped and picked it up. He held it with both hands and stared at it. He turned it over. He peered closer. Then he raised his head and looked up.

"Hey there!" Henry shouted, cupping a hand to his mouth. "That's for you! It's a present!"

The old man stood quite still, holding the note in front of him and gazing up at the figure on the balcony above.

"Put it in your pocket!" Henry shouted. "Take it home!" His voice carried far along the street, and many people stopped and looked up.

Henry peeled off another note and threw it down. The watchers be-

---

① flutter: *Verb* [no obj.] (of a bird or other winged creature) fly unsteadily or hover by flapping the wings quickly and lightly(鸟或其他有翼动物)拍翅而飞;振翼;盘旋(e.g. A couple of butterflies fluttered around the garden. 几只蝴蝶在花园里飞舞。)

② floppy: *Adjective* tending to hang or move in a limp, loose, and ungainly way 松软的;松松垮垮的;下垂的(e.g. The dog had floppy ears. 这狗的耳朵耷拉着。)

low him didn't move. They simply watched. They had no idea what was going on. A man was up there on the balcony and he had shouted something, and now he had just thrown down what looked like a piece of paper. Everyone followed the piece of paper as it went fluttering down, and this one came to rest near a young couple who were standing arm in arm on the pavement across the street. The man unlinked his arm and tried to catch the paper as it went past him. He missed it but picked it up from the ground. He examined it closely. The watchers on both sides of the street all had their eyes on the young man. To many of them, the paper had looked very much like a bank-note of some kind, and they were waiting to find out.

"It's twenty pounds!" the man yelled, jumping up and down. "It's a twenty-pound note!"

"Keep it!" Henry shouted at him. "It's yours!"

"You mean it?" the man called back, holding the note out at arm's length. "Can I really keep it?"

Suddenly there was a rustle of excitement along both sides of the street and everyone started moving at once. They ran out into the middle of the road and clustered underneath the balcony. They lifted their arms above their heads and started calling out, "Me! How about one for me! Drop us another one, guv'nor[①]! Send down a few more!"

Henry peeled off another five or six notes and threw them down.

There were screams and yells as the pieces of paper fanned out in the wind and floated downward, and there was a good old-fashioned scrimmage[②] in the streets as they reached the hands of the crowd. But it

---

① guv'nor: *Noun* (Brit. informal) a man in a position of authority such as one's employer or father (often used as a term of address)(英国英语非正式用法)老板;老爸;先生(一种对父亲、雇主等尊长的称呼)

② scrimmage: *Noun* a confused struggle or fight 混战;扭斗

was all very good-natured. People were laughing. They thought it a fantastic joke. Here was a man standing three floors up in his pyjamas, slinging① these enormously valuable notes into the air. Quite a few of those present had never seen a twenty-pound note in their lives until now.

But now something else was beginning to happen.

The speed with which news will spread along the streets of a city is phenomenal②. The news of what Henry was doing flashed like lightning up and down the length of Curzon Street and into the smaller and larger streets beyond. From all sides, people came running. Within a few minutes, about a thousand men and women and children were blocking the road underneath Henry's balcony. Car-drivers who couldn't pass got out of their vehicles and joined the crowd. And all of a sudden, there was chaos in Curzon Street.

At this point, Henry simply raised his arm and swung it out and flung the entire bundle of notes into the air. More than six thousand pounds went fluttering down towards the screaming crowd below.

The scramble that followed was really something to see. People were jumping up to catch the notes before they reached the ground, and everyone was pushing and jostling and yelling and falling over, and soon the whole place was a mass of tangled, yelling, fighting human beings.

Above the noise and behind him in his own flat, Henry suddenly heard his doorbell ringing long and loud. He left the balcony and opened

---

① sling: *Verb* [with obj. and adverbial of direction] (informal) throw; fling (often used to express the speaker's casual attitude) (非正式)抛;扔(常用来表达说话人随意的态度)(e.g. Sling a few things into your knapsack. 随便扔几件东西进你的背包。)

② phenomenal: *Adjective* very remarkable; extraordinary 显著的;杰出的;不寻常的;惊人的(e.g. The town expanded at a phenomenal rate. 该城以惊人的速度扩大。)

the front door. A large policeman with a black moustache stood outside with his hands on his hips. "You!" he bellowed① angrily. "You're the one! What the devil d'you② think you're doing?"

"Good morning, officer," Henry said. "I'm sorry about the crowd. I didn't think it would turn out like that. I was just giving away some money."

"You are causing a nuisance!" the policeman bellowed. "You are creating an obstruction③! You are inciting a riot and you are blocking the entire street!"

"I said I was sorry," Henry answered. "I won't do it again, I promise. They'll soon go away."

The policeman took one hand off his hip and from the inside of his palm he produced a twenty-pound note.

"Ah-ha!" Henry cried. "You got one yourself! I'm so glad! I'm so happy for you!"

"Now you just stop that larking about④!" the policeman said. "Because I have a few serious questions to ask you about these here twenty-pound notes." He took a notebook from his breast pocket. "In the first place," he went on, "where exactly did you get them from?"

"I won them," Henry said. "I had a lucky night." He went on to give the name of the club where he had won the money and the policeman wrote it down in his little book. "Check it up," Henry added. "They'll

---

① bellow: *Verb* [reporting verb] shout something with a deep loud roar 吼叫;大声发出;大声喝道(e. g. He bellowed out the order. 他大吼着发出命令。)

② d'you = do you

③ obstruction: *Noun* (Law) the action of impeding the movement of traffic on a highway(法律)(在公路上)妨碍交通

④ lark about/around: (old-fashioned, BrE, informal) to enjoy yourself by behaving in a silly way(古旧的英国英语非正式用法)傻玩;胡闹;嬉戏(e. g. Some kids were larking about in the shopping centre. 有些孩子在购物中心嬉戏。)

tell you it's true."

The policeman lowered the notebook, and looked Henry in the eye. "As a matter of fact," he said, "I believe your story. I think you're telling the truth. But that doesn't excuse what you did one little bit."

"I didn't do anything wrong," Henry said.

"You're a blithering① young idiot!" the policeman shouted, beginning to work himself up all over again. "You're an ass and an imbecile②! If you've been lucky enough to win yourself a tremendous big sum of money like that and you want to give it away, you don't throw it out the window!"

"Why not?" Henry asked, grinning. "It's as good a way of getting rid of it as any."

"It's a damned stupid silly way of getting rid of it!" the policeman cried. "Why didn't you give it where it would do some good? To a hospital, for instance? Or an orphanage? There's orphanages all over the country that hardly have enough money to buy the kids a present even for Christmas! And then along comes a little twit③ like you who's never even known what it's like to be hard up and you throw the stuff out into the street! It makes me mad, it really does!"

"An orphanage?" Henry said.

"Yes, an orphanage!" the policeman cried. "I was brought up in one so I ought to know what it's like!" With that, the policeman turned away and went quickly down the stairs towards the street.

Henry didn't move. The policeman's words, and more especially

---

① blithering: *Adjective* [attrib.] (informal) complete; utter (used to express annoyance or contempt) (非正式)(表示恼怒或轻蔑)完全的;十足的

② imbecile: *Noun* (informal) a stupid person(非正式)笨人

③ twit: *Noun* (informal, chiefly Brit.) a silly or foolish person(主要为英国英语非正式用法)笨蛋;傻瓜;白痴

the genuine fury with which they had been spoken, smacked our hero right between the eyes.

"An orphanage?" he said aloud. "That's quite a thought. But why only one orphanage? Why not lots of them?" And now, very quickly, there began to come to him the great and marvellous idea that was to change everything.

Henry shut the front door and went back into his flat. All at once, he felt a powerful excitement stirring in his belly. He started pacing up and down, ticking off the points that would make his marvellous idea possible.

"One," he said, "I can get hold of a very large sum of money each day of my life."

"Two. I must not go to the same casino more than once every twelve months."

"Three. I must not win too much from any one casino or somebody will get suspicious. I suggest I keep it down to twenty thousand pounds a night."

"Four. Twenty thousand pounds a night for three hundred and sixty-five days in the year comes to how much?"

Henry took a pencil and paper and worked this one out.

"It comes to seven million, three hundred thousand pounds," he said aloud.

"Very well. Point number five. I shall have to keep moving. No more than two or three nights at a stretch in any one city or the word will get around. Go from London to Monte Carlo①. Then to Cannes. To Biarritz②. To Deauville. To Las Vegas③. To Mexico City④. To Buenos Aires⑤. To Nassau. And so on."

"Six. With the money I make, I will set up an absolutely first-class orphanage in every country I visit. I will become a Robin Hood⑥. I will take money from the bookmakers and the gambling proprietors and give it

---

① Monte Carlo: a resort in Monaco, forming one of the four communes of the principality; pop. 12,000 (1985). It is famous as a gambling resort and as the terminus of the annual Monte Carlo rally 蒙特卡洛(摩纳哥旅游胜地,该公国的四大行政区之一,1985 年人口 12,000;以赌博业和一年一度的蒙特卡洛汽车拉力赛最后一站著名。)

② Biarritz: *Noun* a seaside resort in SW France, on the Bay of Biscay; pop. 28,890 (1990) 比亚里茨(法国西南部海滨风景区,位于比斯开湾,1990 年人口 28,890。)

③ Las Vegas: a city in southern Nevada; pop. 258,295 (1990). It is noted for its casinos and nightclubs 拉斯维加斯(内华达州南部城市;1990 年人口 258,295,以赌场和夜总会闻名。)

④ Mexico City: the capital of Mexico; pop. 13,636,130 (1990). Founded in about 1300 as the Aztec capital Tenochtitlán, it was destroyed in 1521 by the Spanish conquistador Cortés, who rebuilt it as the capital of New Spain 墨西哥城(墨西哥首都,1990 年人口 13,636,130;约建立于 1300 年,为阿兹特克人首府,称作特诺奇蒂特兰;1521 年被西班牙征服者科尔特斯所毁,后科尔特斯将其重建为新西班牙首都。)

⑤ Buenos Aires: the capital city and chief port of Argentina, on the River Plate; pop. 2,961,000 (1991) 布宜诺斯艾利斯(阿根廷首都及主要港口城市,位于普拉特河畔;1991 年人口 2,961,000。)

⑥ Robin Hood: a semi-legendary English medieval outlaw, reputed to have robbed the rich and helped the poor. Although he is generally associated with Sherwood Forest in Nottinghamshire, it seems likely that the real Robin Hood operated in Yorkshire in the early 13th century. 罗宾汉(中世纪英国一个半传奇式劫富济贫的英雄,虽然人们通常把他与诺丁汉郡的舍伍德森林联系在一起,但是真正的罗宾汉很可能 13 世纪初在约克郡活动。)

to the children. Does that sound corny[1] and sentimental? As a dream, it does. But as a reality, if I can really make it work, it wouldn't be corny at all, or sentimental. It would be rather tremendous."

"Seven. I will need somebody to help me, a man who will sit at home and take care of all that money and buy the houses and organize the whole thing. A money man. Someone I can trust. What about John Winston?"

John Winston was Henry's accountant. He handled his income-tax affairs, his investments and all other problems that had to do with money. Henry had known him for eighteen years and a friendship had developed between the two men. Remember, though, that up until now, John Winston had known Henry only as the wealthy idle playboy who had never done a day's work in his life.

"You must be mad," John Winston said when Henry told him his plan. "Nobody has ever devised a system for beating the casinos."

From his pocket, Henry produced a brand-new unopened pack of cards. "Come on," he said. "We'll play a little blackjack. You're the dealer. And don't tell me those cards are marked. It's a new pack."

Solemnly, for nearly an hour, sitting in Winston's office whose windows looked out over Berkeley Square, the two men played blackjack. They used matchsticks as counters, each match being worth twenty-five pounds. After fifty minutes, Henry was no less than thirty-four thousand pounds up!

John Winston couldn't believe it. "How do you do it?" he said.

---

① corny: *Adjective* (informal) trite, banal, or mawkishly sentimental(非正式)陈腐的;老套的;感伤的(e.g. It sounds corny, but as soon as I saw her I knew she was the one. 这听起来是挺俗套的。可当我第一眼看见她时,我就知道她是我的意中人了。)

"Put the pack on the table," Henry said. "Face down."

Winston obeyed.

Henry concentrated on the top card for four seconds. "That's a knave① of hearts②," he said. It was.

"The next one is... a three of hearts." It was. He went right through the entire pack, naming every card.

"Go on," John Winston said. "Tell me how you do it." This usually calm and mathematical man was leaning forward over his desk, staring at Henry with eyes as big and bright as two stars. "You do realize you are doing something completely impossible?" he said.

"It's not impossible," Henry said. "It is only very difficult. I am the one man in the world who can do it."

The telephone rang on John Winston's desk. He lifted the receiver and said to his secretary, "No more calls please, Susan, until I tell you. Not even my wife." He looked up, waiting for Henry to go on.

Henry then proceeded to explain to John Winston exactly how he had acquired the power. He told him how he had found the notebook and about Imhrat Khan and then he described how he had been working non-stop for the past three years, training his mind to concentrate.

When he had finished, John Winston said, "Have you tried walking on fire?"

"No," Henry said. "And I'm not going to."

"What makes you think you'll be able to do this thing with the cards in a casino?"

Henry then told him about his visit to Lord's House the night before.

---

① knave: *Noun* another term for jack in cards(纸牌)同"J"(jack)

② heart: *Noun* (hearts) one of the four suits in a conventional pack of playing cards, denoted by a red figure of such a shape(纸牌)红桃

"Six thousand, six hundred pounds!" John Winston cried. "Did you honestly win that much in real money?"

"Listen," Henry said. "I just won thirty-four thousand from you in less than an hour!"

"So you did."

"Six thousand was the very least I could win," Henry said. "It was a terrific effort not to win more."

"You will be the richest man on earth."

"I don't want to be the richest man on earth," Henry said. "Not any more." He then told him about his plan for orphanages.

When he had finished, he said, "Will you join me, John? Will you be my money man, my banker, my administrator and everything else? There will be millions coming in every year."

John Winston, a cautious and prudent accountant, would not agree to anything at all on the spur of the moment. "I want to see you in action first," he said.

So that night, they went together to the Ritz Club on Curzon Street. "Can't go to Lord's House again now for some time," Henry said.

On the first spin of the roulette wheel, Henry staked £ 100 on number twenty-seven. It came up. The second time he put it on number four; that came up too. A total of £ 7,500 profit.

An Arab standing next to Henry said. "I have just lost fifty-five thousand pounds. How do you do it?"

"Luck," Henry said. "Just luck."

They moved into the Blackjack Room and there, in half an hour, Henry won a further £ 10,000. Then he stopped.

Outside in the street, John Winston said, "I believe you now. I'll come in with you."

"We start tomorrow," Henry said.

"Do you really intend to do this every single night?"

"Yes," Henry said. "I shall move very fast from place to place, from country to country. And every day I shall send the profits back to you through the banks."

"Do you realize how much it will add up to in a year?"

"Millions," Henry said cheerfully. "About seven million a year."

"In that case, I can't operate in this country," John Winston said. "The taxman will have it all."

"Go anywhere you like," Henry said. "It makes no difference to me. I trust you completely."

"I shall go to Switzerland①," John Winston said. "But not tomorrow. I can't just pull up and fly away. I'm not an unattached bachelor like you with no responsibilities. I must talk to my wife and children. I must give notice to my partners in the firm. I must sell my house. I must find another house in Switzerland. I must take the kids out of school. My dear man, these things take time!"

Henry drew from his pocket the £17,500 he had just won and handed them to the other man. "Here's some petty cash to tide you over until you get settled," he said. "But do hurry up. I want to get cracking."

Within a week, John Winston was in Lausanne②, with an office high up on the lovely hillside above Lake Geneva. His family would follow him as soon as possible.

And Henry went to work in the casinos.

---

① Switzerland: *Noun* a mountainous, landlocked country in central Europe; pop. 6,673,850 (1990); official languages, French, German, Italian, and Romansh; capital, Berne. 瑞士(欧洲中部一个多山的内陆国,1990年人口6,673,850;官方语言为法语、德语、意大利语、罗曼什语;首都伯尔尼。)

② Lausanne: *Noun* a town in SW Switzerland, on the north shore of Lake Geneva; pop. 122,600 (1990) 洛桑(瑞士西南部城市,位于日内瓦湖北岸;1990年人口122,600。)

One year later, he had sent a little over eight million pounds to John Winston in Lausanne. The money was sent five days a week to a Swiss company called ORPHANAGES S. A. Nobody except John Winston and Henry knew where the money came from or what was going to happen to it. As for the Swiss authorities, they never want to know where money comes from. Henry sent the money through the banks. The Monday remittance① was always the biggest because it included Henry's take for Friday, Saturday and Sunday, when the banks were closed. He moved with astonishing speed, and often the only clue that John Winston had to his whereabouts was the address of the bank which had sent the money on a particular day. One day it would come perhaps from a bank in Manila②. The next day from Bangkok③. It came from Las Vegas, from Curacao, from Freeport, from Grand Cayman, from San Juan, from Nassau, from London, from Biarritz. It came from anywhere and everywhere so long as there was a big casino in the city.

For seven years, all went well. Nearly fifty million pounds had arrived in Lausanne, and had been safely banked away. Already John Winston had got three orphanages established, one in France, one in England, and one in the United States. Five more were on the way.

① remittance: *Noun* a sum of money sent, especially by post, in payment for goods or services or as a gift(尤指邮汇)汇款;汇款额

② Manila: *Noun* the capital and chief port of the Philippines, on the island of Luzon; pop. 1,599,000 (1990) 马尼拉(菲律宾首都和主要港口,地处吕宋岛;1990年人口1,599,000。)

③ Bangkok: *Noun* the capital and chief port of Thailand, on the Chao Phraya waterway, 40 km (25 miles) upstream from its outlet into the Gulf of Thailand; pop. 5,876,000 (est. 1990) 曼谷(泰国首都和主要港口,位于昭披耶河畔,距泰国湾40公里,即25英里,1990年估计人口5,876,000。)

Then came a bit of trouble. There is a grapevine① among casino owners, and although Henry was always extraordinarily careful not to take too much from any one place on any one night, the news was bound to spread in the end.

They got wise to him② one night in Las Vegas when Henry rather imprudently took one hundred thousand dollars from each of three separate casinos that all happened to be owned by the same mob.

What happened was this. The morning after, when Henry was in his hotel room packing to leave for the airport, there was a knock on his door. A bell-hop③ came in and whispered to Henry that two men were waiting for him in the lobby. Other men, the bell-hop said, were guarding the rear exit. These were very hard men, the bell-hop said, and he did not give much for Henry's chances of survival if he were to go downstairs at this moment.

"Why do you come and tell me?" Henry asked him. "Why are you on my side?"

"I'm not on anyone's side," the bell-hop said. "But we all know you won a lot of money last night and I figured you might give me a nice

---

① grapevine: *Noun* (informal) used to refer to the circulation of rumours and unofficial information(非正式)谣言(或非官方消息)不胫而走(e.g. I'd heard on the grapevine that the business was nearly settled. 我听到有小道消息在说,这笔业务已经差不多定下来了。)

② be/get wise to sb./sth.: (informal) be/become aware of sth. or aware of sb's (usually bad) behaviour 察觉;明白;知道(某人的恶行等)(e.g. He thought he could fool me but I'm wise to him. 他以为能耍得了我,其实我清楚他是什么样的人。)

③ bell-hop or bellhop: *Noun* (N. Amer.) another term for bellboy(北美用法)同"bellboy"(信差;做杂役的男侍者)

present for tipping you off[①]."

"Thanks," Henry said. "But how do I get away? I'll give you a thousand dollars if you can get me out of here."

"That's easy," the bell-hop said. "Take your own clothes off and put on my uniform. Then walk out through the lobby with your suitcase. But tie me up before you leave. I've gotta[②] be lying here on the floor tied up hand and foot so they won't think I helped you. I'll say you had a gun and I couldn't do nothing."

"Where's the cord to tie you up with?" Henry asked.

"Right here in my pocket," the bell-hop said, grinning.

Henry put on the bell-hop's gold and green uniform, which wasn't too bad a fit. Then he tied the man up good and proper with the cord and stuffed a handkerchief in his mouth. Finally, he pushed ten one-hundred dollar bills under the carpet for the bell-hop to collect later.

Down in the lobby, two short, thick, black-haired thugs[③] were watching the people as they came out of the elevators. But they hardly glanced at the man in the green and gold bell-hop's uniform who came out carrying a suitcase and who walked smartly across the lobby and out through the swing-doors that led to the street.

At the airport, Henry changed his flight and took the next plane to Los Angeles. Things were not going to be quite so easy from now on, he told himself. But that bell-hop had given him an idea.

In Los Angeles, and in nearby Hollywood and Beverly Hills, where

---

① tip someone off: (informal) give someone information about something, typically in discreet or confidential way(非正式)向某人透露消息;暗中通知某人(e. g. They were arrested after police were tipped off by local residents. 当地居民暗中通知警察后他们被逮捕了。)

② gotta = got to

③ thug: *Noun* a violent person, especially a criminal 恶棍;暴徒;罪犯

the film people live, Henry sought out the very best make-up man in the business. This was Max Engelman. Henry called on him. He liked him immediately.

"How much do you earn?" Henry asked him.

"Oh, about forty thousand dollars a year," Max told him.

"I'll give you a hundred thousand," Henry said, "if you will come with me and be my make-up artist."

"What's the big idea?" Max asked him.

"I'll tell you," Henry said. And he did.

Max was only the second person Henry had told. John Winston was the first. And when Henry showed Max how he could read the cards, Max was flabbergasted.

"Great heavens, man!" he cried. "You could make a fortune!"

"I already have," Henry told him. "I've made ten fortunes. But I want to make ten more." He told Max about the orphanages. With John Winston's help, he had already set up three of them, with more on the way.

Max was a small dark-skinned man who had escaped from Vienna① when the Nazis② went in. He had never married. He had no ties. He became wildly enthusiastic. "It's crazy!" he cried. "It's the craziest

① Vienna: *Noun* the capital of Austria, situated in the north-east of the country on the River Danube; pop. 1,533,180 (1991). From 1278 to 1918 it was the seat of the Habsburgs. It has long been a centre of the arts, especially music; Mozart, Beethoven, and the Strauss family were among the great composers who lived and worked there. German name Wien. 维也纳(奥地利首都,位于奥地利东北部多瑙河畔,1991年人口1,533,180,1278~1918年为哈布斯堡王朝所在地,长期以来一直是艺术,尤其是音乐中心,曾在此生活和工作的著名作曲家有莫扎特、贝多芬、施特劳斯家族。德语名"Wien"。)

② Nazi: *Noun* (historical) a member of the National Socialist German Workers' Party(历史上的用法)(德国)国社党党员;纳粹分子

thing I've ever heard in my life! I'll join you, man! Let's go!"

From then on, Max Engelman travelled everywhere with Henry and he carried with him in a trunk such an assortment① of wigs, false beards, sideburns②, moustaches and make-up materials as you have never seen. He could turn his master into any one of thirty or forty unrecognizable people, and the casino managers, who were all watching for Henry now, never once saw him again as Mr. Henry Sugar. As a matter of fact, only a year after the Las Vegas episode, Henry and Max actually went back to that dangerous city, and on a warm starry night Henry took a cool eighty thousand dollars from the first of the big casinos he had visited before. He went disguised as an elderly Brazilian diplomat, and they never knew what had hit them.

Now that Henry no longer appeared as himself in the casinos, there were, of course, a number of other details that had to be taken care of, such as false identity cards and passports. In Monte Carlo, for example, a visitor must always show his passport before being allowed to enter the casino. Henry visited Monte Carlo eleven more times with Max's assistance, every time with a different passport and in a different disguise.

Max adored the work. He loved creating new characters for Henry. "I have an entirely fresh one for you today!" he would announce. "Just

---

① assortment: *Noun* a miscellaneous collection of things or people 各种各样的人(或物)(e. g. The room was filled with an assortment of clothes. 房间里摆满了各种各样的衣服。)

② sideburn: *Noun* (often as "sideburns") a strip of hair grown by a man down each side of the face in front of his ears 连鬓胡子

wait till you see it! Today you will be an Arab sheikh[①] from Kuwait[②]!"

"Do we have an Arab passport?" Henry would ask. "And Arab papers?"

"We have everything," Max would answer. "John Winston has sent me a lovely passport in the name of His Royal Highness Sheikh Abu Bin Bey!"

And so it went on. Over the years, Max and Henry became as close as brothers. They were crusading brothers, two men who moved swiftly through the skies, milking the casinos of the world and sending the money straight back to John Winston in Switzerland, where the company known as ORPHANAGES S.A. grew richer and richer.

Henry died last year, at the age of sixty-three; his work was completed. He had been at it for just on twenty years.

His personal reference book listed three hundred and seventy-one major casinos in twenty-one different countries or islands. He had visited them all many times and he had never lost.

According to John Winston's accounts, he had made altogether one hundred and forty-four million pounds.

He left twenty-one well-established well-run orphanages scattered about the world, one in each country he visited. All these were administered and financed from Lausanne by John and his staff.

But how do I, who am neither Max Engelman nor John Winston,

---

① sheikh or shaikh or shaykh or sheik: *Noun* an Arab leader, in particular the chief or head of an Arab tribe, family, or village(阿拉伯)酋长;族长;家长;村长

② Kuwait: *Noun* a country on the NW coast of the Persian Gulf; pop. 1,200,000 (est. 1991); official language, Arabic; capital, Kuwait City 科威特(波斯湾西北海岸国家;1991 年估计人口 1,200,000,官方语言阿拉伯语;首都科威特市。)

happen to know all this? And how did I come to write the story in the first place?

I will tell you.

Soon after Henry's death, John Winston telephoned me from Switzerland. He introduced himself simply as the head of a company calling itself ORPHANAGES S. A., and asked me if I would come out to Lausanne to see him with a view to writing a brief history of the organization. I don't know how he got hold of my name. He probably had a list of writers and stuck a pin into it. He would pay me well, he said. And he added. "A remarkable man has died recently. His name was Henry Sugar. I think people ought to know a bit about what he has done."

In my ignorance, I asked whether the story was really interesting enough to merit being put on paper.

"All right," said the man who now controlled one hundred and forty-four million pounds. "Forget it. I'll ask someone else. There are plenty of writers around."

That needled[1] me. "No," I said. "Wait. Could you at least tell me who this Henry Sugar was and what he did? I've never even heard of him."

In five minutes on the phone, John Winston told me something about Henry Sugar's secret career. It was secret no longer. Henry was dead and would never gamble again. I listened, enthralled.

"I'll be on the next plane," I said.

"Thank you," John Winston said. "I would appreciate that."

In Lausanne, I met John Winston, now over seventy, and also Max

① needle: *Verb* (informal) provoke or annoy (someone), especially by continual criticism or questioning(非正式)(尤指通过不断地批评或质疑)刺激;激将;挑逗;惹……发火(e. g. I just said that to Charlie to needle him. 我对查理说那些话就是想刺激他。)

Engelman, who was about the same age. They were both still shattered by Henry's death. Max even more so than John Winston, for Max had been beside him constantly for over thirteen years. "I loved him," Max said, a shadow falling over his face. "He was a great man. He never thought about himself. He never kept a penny of the money he won, except what he needed to travel and to eat. Listen, once we were in Biarritz and he had just been to the bank and given them half a million francs to send home to John. It was lunchtime. We went to a place and had a simple lunch, an omelette① and a bottle of wine, and when the bill came, Henry hadn't got anything to pay it with. I hadn't either. He was a lovely man."

John Winston told me everything he knew. He showed me the original dark-blue notebook written by Dr John Cartwright in Bombay in 1934, and I copied it out word for word.

"Henry always carried it with him," John Winston said. "In the end, he knew the whole thing by heart."

He showed me the accounts books of ORPHANAGES S. A. with Henry's winnings recorded in them day by day over twenty years, and a truly staggering sight they were.

When he had finished, I said to him, "There's a big gap in this story, Mr. Winston. You've told me almost nothing about Henry's travels and about his adventures in the casinos of the world."

"That's Max's story," John Winston said. "Max knows all about that because he was with him. But he says he wants to have a shot at

① omelette or omelet: *Noun* a dish of beaten eggs cooked in a frying pan and served plain or with a savoury or sweet topping or filling 煎蛋饼;炒蛋

writing it[①] himself. He's already started."

"Then why not let Max write the whole thing?" I asked.

"He doesn't want to," John Winston said. "He only wants to write about Henry and Max. It should be a fantastic story if he ever gets it finished. But he is old now, like me, and I doubt he will manage it."

"One last question," I said. "You keep calling him Henry Sugar. And yet you tell me that wasn't his name. Don't you want me to say who he really was when I do the story?"

"No," John Winston said. "Max and I promised never to reveal it. Oh, it'll probably leak out sooner or later. After all, he was from a fairly well-known English family. But I'd appreciate it if you don't try to find out. Just call him plain Mr. Henry Sugar."

And that is what I have done.

(The end)

三、翻译探索

本篇小说的翻译中,有些数字的书写是用阿拉伯数字还是用汉字的数字,这个问题值得考虑。具体来说,原文用英语单词表示的数字,是对应地译成汉字中的数字(如"一""二""三"等),还是转换成阿拉伯数字呢?这恐怕要具体问题具体分析,同时还要考虑到汉语的出版规范。下面的探索性译文,在这方面恐怕会存在一些问题,有待进一步探索。

---

① have/take a shot (at sth./at doing sth.): (also "give sth. a shot") (informal) try to do sth. (非正式)试图;设法(做某事)(e.g. I don't know if I'll be any good at editing the newsletter, but I'll give it a shot. 我不知道自己有没有能力编辑这份时事通讯,不过我会试试看。)

非凡亨利

(接上)

"哇,哇,哇,"亨利·休格说。"现在看来,那真是太有意思啦。"

他合上练习本,坐了下来,眼睛盯着窗外的雨,只见雨滴"啪啦、啪啦"拍打着窗户。

"这是一条,"亨利·休格继续自言自语地大声说道,"特别棒的信息,能够改变我的人生。"

亨利所说的这条信息指的就是,伊姆拉汗经过一番修炼,能够从反面读出纸牌的内容。亨利是一个赌徒,一个不择手段的赌徒,根本没有诚信可言。他立刻意识到,如果能训练自己做到同样的事情,就发大财了。

有好一会儿,亨利任由自己的大脑思考着:要是能够从纸牌的背面读出内容来,那么,他将能做出多少美妙的事情啊。那样的话,不管是玩凯纳斯特纸牌游戏、桥牌,还是扑克牌游戏,他每一局都能稳操胜券。更美妙的是,世界上每一个赌场他都能进去玩一玩,赢遍二十一点赌局以及其他所有高额赌注的牌类游戏啊!

亨利清楚得很,在所有的赌场里,几乎所有的赌局最终都是一张牌定输赢。要是你预先知道那张是什么牌的话,那么,你就大功告成啦!

可问题是,他能做到吗?他能够自我修炼做到这一点吗?

他看不出有什么原因做不成。用蜡烛火焰训练那件事儿,看起来也不是特别难啊。况且,根据练习本上所写,真的没有什么大不了的啊——不就是盯着火焰的中心看、努力将注意力集中到你最爱的人的脸上嘛。

或许他需要花掉好几年的时间才能练成,但是,花上几年的时间练成了,就可以在赌场里打败任何对手,这个世界上有谁会不愿意呢?

"天呐,"他大声说。"我要训练!我这就去训练!"

他静静地坐在图书室的扶手椅子上,谋划着作战计划。首先,不要告诉任何人他要忙些什么。他会从图书室偷出这个小小的练习本,这样他的朋友谁都不可能偶然地看到这个本子而学到这些绝技。偷出来后,无论走到哪儿,他都随身携带,变成他的个人秘籍。他也不可能出去找一位活着的、真正的瑜伽大师来指导自己,因此,这个本子就是他的瑜伽秘籍,就是他的师傅。

亨利站起身,将那个薄薄的蓝色练习本塞到夹克衫里面,走出图书室,径直上楼走进了这个周末归他使用的那间卧室。他拿出手提衣箱,将书藏到衣服下面,然后又下楼,寻路走向男管家的储藏室。

"约翰,"他对男管家说,"你能给我找根蜡烛吗? 就是普通的白色蜡烛。"

管家受到的训练就是:从不问原因,只要一味地遵从。"先生,你还想要一个烛台吗?"

"是的。一支蜡烛和一个烛台。"

"遵命,先生。需要送到你的房间吗?"

"不,我在周围转悠一下,等着你找蜡烛和烛台。"

这位男管家很快就找到了蜡烛和烛台。亨利说:"现在,能给我找个直尺吗?"于是,管家给他找了个直尺。亨利谢过管家,返回卧室。

进入卧室后,他将门锁上,还把所有的窗帘都放了下来,使整个房间的光线不是十分的明亮。他将蜡烛插到烛台上,将烛台放到梳妆台上,随手拉来一把椅子坐下。他注意到,他的双眼正好与烛芯齐平,令他感到十分满意。现在,他用直尺量了量,将脸定位到离蜡烛四十厘米远的地方。也就是本子里说明的必须达到的距离。

那个印度小伙子已经将其最爱的人的脸形象化,那个人就是他的兄弟,但亨利没有兄弟,他打算取而代之,把自己的脸形象化。这是个不错的选择,如果一个人像亨利那样自私自利、唯我独尊的话,那么,自己的脸当然就是自己的最爱。更进一步说,亨利最了解自己的这张脸了,他每天都要花掉那么长时间瞧着镜子里自己的脸,了解脸上的每一条曲线和皱纹。

他用点烟的打火机将烛芯点燃,一股黄色的火苗随即出现,并持续稳定地燃烧起来。

亨利一动不动地坐着,眼睛盯着蜡烛的火焰。本子里说得相当正确:靠近看蜡烛的火焰,火焰确实分为三个不同的区域:外围是黄色区域,内壳是淡紫色区域,正中心是微小的、颇具魔力的纯黑区域。他就盯着这个微小的黑色区域看,将眼睛聚焦到那上面,一直盯着看。盯着、盯着,一件异乎寻常的事情发生了:他的内心一片空白,大脑也不再烦躁不安地思考了。突然间,他一下子感觉自己整个人、整个身体好像被包裹在火焰之中,感觉自己就坐在那个小小的、虚无的黑色区域,温暖舒适、惬意无比。

亨利不费吹灰之力就让自己的脸游移到自己眼前。他将注意力集中到这张脸上,其他的一切他都不加理会,将所有其他想法都封锁到外面。精力集中这件事儿他是完全做到了,但持续时间只有十五秒。十五秒过后,他的内心就开始漂移了,竟然思考起在赌场赌博的场景,以及会赢多少钱这方面的事儿。到了这一时刻,他就从蜡烛那儿移开目光,休息一下。

这是他最先的尝试,而且做成了,这令他激动不已。诚然,精力集中的时间不是很长,可话说回来,那个印度小伙子第一次尝试的时间也不是很长。

几分钟过后,他又试了一下,效果不错。尽管他没有秒表可以计时,但感觉这一次肯定比第一次要长些。

“太棒了!”他叫道。“我要成功了!我要成功了!”一生中,从来没有什么事情令他如此兴奋。

从那天起,亨利不管身在何处,或者忙些什么事情,每天早晨和晚上必定用蜡烛做练习,正午也经常练习。带着真挚的热情投身于某件事情,这是他一生中从来没有过的,而且,取得的进步也很显著。经过半年的训练之后,他能够将注意力绝对地集中到自己脸上,持续时间不低于三分钟,而且外部思想一丝一毫也不会进入他的内心。

赫尔德瓦尔的那位瑜伽大师曾经对那个印度小伙子说过,一个人要想达到那样的效果,必须得修炼十五年啊!

可是,且慢!这位瑜伽大师也说过别的事情。说过什么呢(想到这儿,亨利第一百次翻开了那个小小的蓝色练习本查找起来)?他说过,在极其特殊的条件下,世上会出现一个特别的人,只用一两年时间就能练就这种功力。

"那个人就是我啊!"亨利叫道。"一定是我!我就是一百万人当中的一个,具有这样的天赋和能力,可以用惊人的速度获得惊人的瑜伽神功!哇呀呀,好呀,加油!现在看来,用不了多久,我就会将欧洲和美洲所有赌场里庄家的钱赢光。"

但是此时此刻,亨利显示出非凡的耐性和极强的判断力。他没有急不可耐地拿出一副纸牌,看看能否从反面读出牌的内容。实际情况是,他谨慎地避开了所有的牌类游戏。刚一开始用蜡烛训练的时候,他就不玩桥牌、凯纳斯特纸牌游戏和扑克牌游戏了。更奇特的是,他也不再到处参加聚会,也不再与有钱的朋友周末相聚,而是全身心瞄准一个目标:练就瑜伽神功,其他所有的事情必须等到他达到了目标再说。

练到第十个月的某个时候,就像当初伊姆拉汗所做的那样,亨利也意识到自己具有一种轻微的能力——闭上眼睛,能够看见一个物体了。闭上眼睛使劲儿盯着某个物体、注意力高度集中的时候,实际上他已经能够看出那个物体的轮廓。

"功力开始出现了!"他叫道。"我就要接近目标了!太美妙啦!"

现在,他比以前更加刻苦地用蜡烛进行练习。第一年接近尾声的时候,他实际上能够将注意力集中到自己的脸部影像的时间至少维持在五分半钟!

此时此刻,他做了个决定:用纸牌试一下自己的功力,时机已到。做这个决定的时候,已经接近午夜,他就待在伦敦公寓的起居室里。于是,他拿出一副纸牌,还有铅笔和纸,兴奋得浑身发抖。他将纸牌正面朝下放在前面,注意力集中到最上面的那张牌上面。

刚开始的时候,他所能够看到的就是牌背面的图案,那是一种全世界纸牌中最为常见的、普普通通的图案——细细的红色线条。现在,他将精力从牌的图案转向牌的另一面,将注意力集中到牌的下面看不见的部分,聚精会神、心无旁骛,决不让任何一丝其他的想法溜进自己的内心。三十秒钟过去了。

接着,一分钟……

两分钟……

三分钟……

亨利没有动弹,聚精会神、心无旁骛。他正在将纸牌的反面形象化,其他的任何想法一概不允许进入大脑。

第四分钟的时间里,开始有情况发生了,速度很慢,却很清晰,如魔法一般——黑色的符号变成了黑桃,黑桃旁边出现了数字"5"。

黑桃5!

亨利停了下来。现在,他伸出颤抖的手指,拾起那张牌,翻了过来。

哇,真的是黑桃5!

"我成功了!"他从椅子上跳了起来,大声喊道。"我把牌看透了!我入道了!"

休息一会儿之后,他又试了一次,这次他用秒表计时,看看需要多长时间。他读出了这张牌:方块K,用时三分五十八秒。正确无误!

再试一次的时候,他又读对了,用时三分五十四秒,少用了四秒钟。

由于兴奋,他浑身冒汗,精疲力竭。"今天不能再继续了。"他自我告诫。于是,他起身倒了一大杯威士忌喝了下去,坐下来一边休息,一边想着刚才的成就,沾沾自喜。

他对自己说,现在的任务就是用纸牌练习、再练习,一直练到拿起牌就能看透为止。他相信,自己能做到这一点。毕竟在刚才的第二次的计时尝试中,他就少用了四秒钟。蜡烛练习就此放弃,只把精力放在纸牌上,他要不分昼夜坚持用纸牌练习。

于是,他就这样去做了。既然他已经嗅到了成功在即的味道,就要更加全身心地投入。除了买吃的、买喝的,他一刻也没离开过公寓。白天一整天的时间一直到大半夜,他都蹲在那里,低头看着纸牌,身旁放着秒表,尽力要缩短从反面读出纸牌内容所需的时间。

一个月的时间里,他将时间缩短到一分半钟。

经过半年的高强度修炼,在半年时间接近尾声的时候,二十秒内他就能完成任务了,但二十秒的时间也是太长了。在赌场里赌博时,发牌人等着你说"要"或"不要",然后给你发下一张牌,是不容许你盯着牌看上二十秒,然后再决定要还是不要的。三四秒钟还是允许的,但是,不能再长了。

亨利继续训练,但是从现在起,要想提高速度,难度是越来越大。从二十秒降低到十九秒,他苦苦练了整整一周的时间。从十九秒降低到十八秒,他苦苦练习将近两周时间。又过去了七个月的时间,他正好用十秒钟看透一张牌。

但是,他的目标是四秒钟。他清楚,若不是最多用四秒钟看透一张牌,就无法成功地赢遍赌场。然而,越是靠近目标,达到目标的难度就越大。他用去了四周的时间,才将时间从十秒压缩到九秒,又用了五周时间,才从九秒压缩到八秒。但是,到了这个阶段,辛苦对他来说已经没有什么大不了的啦。他集中注意力的能力已经修炼到这样一个程度:一口气练十二个小时,轻轻松松不在话下。他也绝对地肯定,最终他会练成,不练成誓不罢休。日复一日,夜复一夜,他蹲坐在那儿,俯身纸牌上方,身旁放着秒表,精力绝对高度集中地奋战着,力图将那固执、倔强的最后几秒钟抹去。

从七秒降低到四秒,减掉最后三秒是最为艰苦卓绝的。为达此目标,他整整用了十一个月啊!

伟大的时刻在一个星期六的晚上到来。一张纸牌正面朝下放在他前方的桌子上,他"咔嚓"一按秒表,就开始集中精力。转瞬间,他看到一团红色,并迅速出现了形状,变成方块,几乎与此同时,左上角出现了一个数字"6"。他又"咔嚓"一按秒表,看了看时间,正好四秒!他将牌翻过来,正是方块6!他成功了!他读出牌的内容,用时正好四秒钟!

他用另一张牌又试了一次。四秒钟之内,他读出了黑桃Q。紧接着,他计时读完整副牌。都是四秒！都是四秒！都是四秒！每张牌用时都是一样的。最终,他成功了！一切都结束了,他整装待发！

那么,他一共用去多长时间？他集中精力、马不停蹄地苦战了正好三年零三个月。

现在该转战赌场了！

什么时候开始呢？

何不今晚就开始？

现在是星期六的晚上,所有赌场这个时候都人满为患,这是再好不过的啦,不大可能引起怀疑。他走进卧室,换上无尾礼服,戴上黑领结。星期六晚去伦敦的大赌场,衣着是需要考究一些的。

他决定去劳德豪斯。伦敦有一百多家赌场,但是,没有一家的大门朝平头百姓敞开着,你得先成为会员,才允许你进门。亨利已经是十多家赌场的会员了,但他最喜欢的一家就是劳德豪斯,这家是全国最精良、最奢华的一家。

劳德豪斯位于伦敦的中心,是一栋乔治亚时期风格的大厦,美轮美奂。二百多年以来,它一直是某位公爵的私人宅邸。现如今,它已经被一些赌注经纪人接管,里面挤满了新面孔,玩着一种全新的游戏,但这里过去可不是这个样子。这里的房间质量上乘,天花板高高地悬在上方,一度是贵族,甚至是皇族聚会的场所,聚会时他们玩着高雅的惠斯特纸牌游戏。

亨利驱车来到劳德豪斯,将车停在大门口的外面。他下了车,但没有让车熄火。与此同时,一名穿绿色制服的侍者走上前来,为他停放车辆。

沿着大街两侧的镶边石停放着约十二辆劳斯莱斯车。看来,只有极其富有的人才配得上来劳德豪斯。

“嗨,休格先生,你好！”坐在执勤台后面的男子问候道,他的工作就是永远记住每一张面孔。“多年不见你来了！”

“我一直很忙。”亨利回答。

他踏上宽阔华丽的楼梯上楼,楼梯的扶手是红木制的,上面雕刻了图案。他走进出纳员办公室,开列了一张一千英镑的支票,出纳员随即递给他十枚大大的、长条形的、塑料做的粉红色筹码,每枚筹码上写着“100£ ”(“£ ”是“英镑”的符号——译者注)。亨利将筹码塞进衣兜,然后闲逛了几分钟,出了这个赌室,又进入那个赌室,目的是想找回久违的感觉,毕竟很长时间没来了嘛。今晚人很多。营养充足的女士们站在轮盘赌轮子的周围下注,如同肥圆的母鸡绕着饲料槽啄食。她们的胸前和手腕上都佩带着黄金和珠宝的饰品,她们很多人头发是蓝色的。男士则个个身穿无尾礼服,没有一位个头高挑。哇,亨利纳闷:这种有钱人都长着短腿吗?他们的腿在膝盖部位就似乎停止了生长,膝盖以上没有大腿了。多数男士肚子远远地向前凸出,脸色深红,双唇间夹着雪茄,眼睛则散发出贪婪的目光。

这一切,亨利都注意到了。这是他平生第一次用反感的目光注视着这类富有的赌徒。就在刚才,他还一直把他们看成同伴,认为自己也是他们这个群体、阶层的一员。可是今晚,他们看起来粗俗不堪。

他感到疑惑:是不是在过去的三年多时间里他练就的瑜伽神功让他整个人稍有改变?

他站在那儿,看着轮盘赌室里的场景。人们将钱放到绿色的长桌子上,尽力猜测:轮盘下一轮转动后,白色的小球会落进哪一个小槽内。亨利看了一眼轮盘,突然之间,或许是由于习惯成自然,而不是其他别的原因,他竟然开始全神贯注于轮盘之上。这不是什么难事了,因为他一直练习在这种完全集中注意力的技能,练了这么长时间之后,已经变成某种常规性的动作了。就在转瞬之间,他的内心完全彻底地集中到轮盘上了,房间里其他的一切——吵闹之声、赌博的人们、各种灯光、雪茄的味道,都从他的内心消失了。他的眼里只有轮盘边缘白色的数字,数字从“1”到“36”不等,“1”和“36”之间标的是“0”。眨眼间,所有的数字模糊起来,在他的眼前消失。但是,只有一个数字“18”除外,其他的统统消失不见,他能够看到唯一的数字就是“18”。刚开始的时候,这个数字稍微有点模糊,焦距不对,接着数字的边缘清晰起来,白色的部分越来越明亮、越来越耀眼。到了最后,这个数字本身开始闪耀起来,就好像它的后面燃起一盏明亮的灯,似乎向着他一下子跳了过来。就在那一时刻,他停了下来,屋子里的场景在他的眼中恢复如初。

“你们都下完了吗?”赌台台长问。

亨利从兜里掏出一枚100英镑的筹码,放到绿色桌子上标有数字“18”的方格内。尽管赌台上摆满了其他人下的注,但是只有他把筹码放到了“18”的方格内。

台长转动了轮盘。白色的小球绕着轮盘的边缘跳跃着、滚动着。大家看着,所有的眼睛都盯向小球。轮盘慢了下来,逐渐停止,小球随即轻轻摇晃几下、飘来荡去,然后利索地落入“18”号槽内。

“18!”赌台台长叫道。

人群发出叹息声。台长的助手用一把长柄木铲将输家的一堆堆筹码铲走,但是,他并没有铲走亨利的,亨利赢了,赔率是三十六比一,他押了一百,一共赢了三千六百英镑。赌场付给他三枚面额为一千英镑的筹码,还有六枚面额为一百英镑的筹码。

亨利开始感觉到浑身有一股异乎寻常的力量,感觉如果自己愿意,就可以摧毁这个地方。不出三个小时,他就可以毁掉这座别致的、高能的、昂贵的公共场所。他可以从这里赢走一百万,让钱“哗哗”地流进他的腰包,让周围那些表情冷酷、身体富态的绅士们一个个都看傻了眼,就像惊恐万状的老鼠,四处奔跑,乱作一团。

他应该那样做吗?

那样做的诱惑力太大了。

且慢,要是那样做了,一切都完蛋了。他会变得远近闻名,世界任何地方的赌场都永远不会允许他进入了。他一定不能那样做,一定要谨小慎微,一定要不显山不露水。

亨利随意地从轮盘赌室溜达出来,走进二十一点赌室。他站在门口处,观察着里面的一切。里面有四张桌子,每张桌子都是曲线型的,呈月牙状,赌家绕着半圆的外围坐在高凳子上,发牌的庄家则站在里面。

一只末端开口的盒子被称为“发牌盒”,里面装了好几副纸牌

(劳德豪斯的规矩是,一只发牌盒里装四副洗好的纸牌),庄家用手指一张、一张地将发牌盒里的纸牌抽出……发牌盒里,纸牌的反面总是可见的,但另一面根本看不见。

赌场称这种游戏为"二十一点",是一种十分简单的游戏活动。你我对它的了解也许是通过另外三个名字:宝通、二十一以及威特恩。玩家尽可能将手中的牌点累加起来等于二十一或者接近二十一,但如果超出二十一,玩家就因超点涨裂而输掉,庄家得钱。在几乎每一局牌戏中,玩家都面临这样的抉择:是冒着涨裂输掉的危险再要一张牌,还是不要牌、保住手里已得到牌的点数?但是,对亨利来说,这个抉择不成什么问题。四秒钟之内,他就会"穿透"庄家要发给他的牌,他就会知道是喊"要",还是"不要"。这样,他就能将二十一点赌局玩转于股掌。

在所有的赌场里,他们为二十一点赌局设立了一个棘手的规则,在家里玩就没有这样的规则。在家里,我们看到第一张牌后,才开始下注,要是第一张牌好的话,我们下的注就高些,但赌场里不允许你这样做。在赌场里,他们坚持要桌旁的每个人先下注,然后再发第一张牌。更厉害的是,赌场里也不允许你随后通过买下某张牌的方式来加注。

但是,这一切都妨碍不到亨利。只要他坐在庄家的最左边,那么,在每一局开始的时候,他就总能得到发牌盒里的第一张牌。对他来说,牌的另一面总是清晰可见的,而且下注前,他会"读透"那张牌。

现在,站在门内一声不响的亨利等待着,等着庄家左边的位置腾出来,四张桌子只要有一张腾出这样的空位就可以。为了这样的空位,他必须得等二十分钟,但最终,他还是如愿以偿了。

他稳稳地坐到高凳子上,将从轮盘赌中赢到的其中一枚"£ 1 000"的筹码递给庄家。"拜托,都给我换成面额为二十五的。"他说。

发牌的庄家是一名年纪不大的男子,两只眼睛黑黑的,皮肤灰灰的。他从未笑过,没有必要时也从不说话。他的两只手特别的纤细,手指仿佛写满了数字,随时能算出结果。他拿起亨利递过来的筹码,扔进桌子上的一个槽里。他前面放了一只木制托盘,上面整整齐齐地码放一排排颜色各异的圆形筹码。有的面额是"£ 25",有的是"£ 10",还有的是"£ 5",每一种筹码的数量或许有一百枚之多。这位发牌手大拇指跟食指并用,拿起一摞面额为"£ 25"的筹码,往桌子上一放,将筹码堆得高高的。他准确无误地知道,那一堆共有二十枚筹码,连数都不用数。他那灵敏的手指能够拿起数量不等的筹码——从一枚到二十枚,而且绝对准确,从未出错。发牌的庄家又拿起一摞筹码,凑够四十枚,滑到亨利身前的桌面上。

亨利将筹码在身前摞起来,同时瞥了眼发牌盒顶部那张牌。他集中起注意力,四秒之内读出上面有个数字"10",于是,他将其中的八枚筹码向前推出,总共二百英镑,这个数目是劳德豪斯二十一点赌局允许下的最大的注。

十点那张牌发给了他,第二张牌是九点,这样,总共是十九点了。

大家都跟到了十九点。这样,只需直挺挺地坐着,希望庄家的牌不是二十点,或者二十一点。

基于这点考虑,庄家再一次走到亨利跟前说:"十九点。"然后,他就径直向下一位玩家走去。

"等等。"亨利发话了。

庄家暂停下来,回到亨利那儿。他皱起额头,用那双冷漠的黑眼睛看了看亨利。"都十九点了,你还想要牌?"他带有某种挖苦、讽刺的腔调问道。他说起话来带有意大利口音,声音里既有嘲弄又有挖苦的意思。手中的牌加到了十九点,再要的话,发牌盒里只有两张牌不会让你的点数涨裂:纸牌A(算作一点)和纸牌2。到了这个时候,蠢蛋才冒险再要牌,特别是在桌面的赌注是二百英镑的情况下。

发牌盒前面那张还没有发下去的牌是清晰可见的,至少,那张牌的反面是清晰可见的。那张牌,庄家连碰也没有碰一下呢。

"是的,"亨利回答。"我想,我还要一张。"

庄家耸了耸肩,猛地将那张牌抽了出来,一张梅花2随即利索地甩到亨利的眼前,跟"10"和"9"并排放着。

"谢谢,"亨利说。"太漂亮了。"

“二十一点。”庄家说道。他黑黑的眼睛随即抬起,紧盯着亨利的脸,打量着,没有移开,也没有说话,显得疑惑不解。亨利让他思维失衡,他一生中从没看到有什么人达到了十九点还要牌的,而眼前这个伙计到了十九点竟然还要牌,而且镇定自若、信心十足,离谱得让人震惊,最后还赢了。

亨利捕捉到庄家眼中的神情,立刻意识到,自己犯下了愚蠢的错误。有点锋芒外露了,一定不能再这样做了。在如何使用神功方面,他以后一定要特别小心谨慎,甚至一定要做到偶尔让自己输一输,一定要时不时做点愚蠢的事情。

赌局继续进行。亨利的优势过于强大,很难将赢钱的数额下降到合理的水平。偶尔有些时候,在明明知道要涨裂的情况下,他也会要第三张牌。竟有那么一次,他看到要发的第一张牌是A,但却投出最小的筹码,然后又叫苦不迭,大声骂自己:刚开始的时候怎么没有下大注呀。

一个小时的时间里,他正好赢了三千英镑。于是,他当即收手,把筹码揣好,回到出纳员办公室,准备将筹码换成了现金。

玩二十一点,他赢了三千英镑,玩轮盘赌,赢了三千六百英镑,算下来总共赢了六千六百英镑,赢到六十六万英镑也是轻而易举的事情。他自己琢磨起来,现在显而易见、几乎可以肯定的是,整个世界上没有谁的赚钱速度能比他快。

出纳员接过亨利那堆大小不一的筹码,面不改色心不跳。他戴着一副钢质架眼镜,眼镜后面那双灰白的眼睛对亨利没有产生丝毫的兴趣,只是盯着柜台上的筹码。这名男子的手指也仿佛写满了数字,随时能算出结果,但是,他却略胜一筹。他不但能算数,还会三角学、微积分、代数、欧几里得几何学,而且身体每一根神经都熟谙此道。他简直就是一台具有人类生命的计算机,大脑中通上了千万条的电线,只需五秒钟的时间,他就数出亨利的筹码有一百二十枚。

“休格先生,给你开张支票好吗?”他问。就像楼下执勤台处的那名男子一样,这位出纳员也记住了每位会员的名字。

“不,谢谢,”亨利回答。“我要现金。”

"遵命。"眼镜后面发出了声音。随后,他转过身体,走到办公室后面一个保险柜那儿,柜里的钱一定有数百万英镑之多。

按照劳德豪斯的标准,亨利赢的钱算是小巫见大巫啦。现在,那些阿拉伯的石油王子就在伦敦,他们喜欢赌博,那些中东来的可疑的外交官、日本来的商人、英国本土逃税的房地产经营商都喜欢赌博。每天在伦敦的大型赌场里,他们输赢的数目十分惊人,但多数情况下输的居多。

出纳员返回,将亨利换的那捆钞票往柜台上一甩。尽管这捆钱足以买下一所小房子,或者一辆大汽车,但劳德豪斯这位出纳主管却没有看上眼。对于刚才他甩给亨利的那捆钱,没准儿他只是认为那是一包口香糖呢。

亨利一边往衣兜里揣着钱,一边想:你等着瞧,我的朋友,你就等着瞧吧。他随即走开。

"先生,你要开车走吗?"门口穿绿色制服的男侍者问道。

"先不开,"亨利回答。"我想,我先呼吸一点新鲜空气。"

他沿着大街溜达开了。将近半夜了,但这座大城市仍然毫无睡意。晚上空气凉爽,令人愉快,亨利能够感觉到夹克衫的内兜鼓鼓囊囊的,他用一只手摸了摸,还轻轻地拍了拍,那里放的是刚才赢的那一大摞钞票。对于一个小时的付出而言,这些钱可是相当大的一笔数目。

那么,以后呢?

下一步要干什么?

照这样,他可以月赚百万之多。

要是他愿意,还可以赚得更多。

至于到底能赚多少,那就是无边无际的啦。

凉爽的夜晚行走在伦敦的大街上,亨利开始想下一步该怎么办。

现在,这个故事要是虚构编造的,而不是真实发生的话,就很有必要为之增添一个出人意料、令人激动的结尾。再者,编出这样一个富于戏剧色彩的、异乎寻常的结尾也不是什么难事。那么,实际生活中的亨利到底怎么样了,在告诉你真相之前,让我们在这儿暂停一会

儿,看看一位合格胜任的小说家会写些什么来为这个故事收口。这样一位小说家的写作笔记会是这样的:

1. 亨利必须得死。就像在亨利之前的伊姆拉汗一样,亨利触犯了瑜伽修炼者的法则,出于个人盈利的目的使用神功。

2. 如果亨利的死法非同寻常、引起读者的兴趣、令读者意想不到的话,那将达到最佳效果。

3. 比如说,他可以回到自己的公寓,然后开始数钱,并沾沾自喜起来。此时,他或许突然之间感到身体不适、胸口疼痛。

4. 他开始害怕起来,决定立马上床休息。他脱光衣服,赤身裸体地走向衣橱去换睡衣。经过靠墙放置的落地镜时,他停了下来,看着镜子里裸露的自己。很自然地,他就开始不由自主地地集中精力,于是……

5. 突然之间,他一下子“看穿”自己的皮肤,就像回来之前曾经“看穿”那些纸牌一样。那情景如同X光透视一样,但效果要好得多。X光透视图中只能看到骨骼和身体密度大的区域,而亨利能够看到一切。他看到了自己的动脉血管、静脉血管,看到血液通过这些血管输送,还看到了肝、肾、肠子,以及自己的心跳。

6. 他看着胸部发出疼痛的部位……看到了……或者说,他认为自己看到了……大静脉血管内有一个小小的黑色肿块,这条大静脉在右手一侧跟心脏相连。小小的肿块在静脉内能干些什么呢?一定是某种阻塞物,一定是一个凝块,也就是血栓啊!

7. 刚开始的时候,血栓似乎是静止不动的,但是接着,它开始移动了。移动的距离很不明显,也就是一两毫米的距离。血栓后面静脉内的血液被泵起来,挤着血栓流过,血栓又移动了。只见它猛地动了一下,动了约有一点三厘米的距离。这次是沿着静脉向心脏方向移动。亨利看着,恐惧万分。他知道——这个世界上几乎人人都知道,静脉里的血栓要是挣脱束缚、移动起来的话,最终会达到心脏。要是血栓很大的话,就会粘在心脏里,人或许就会因此死去……

对于一部小说作品来说,那将是一个相当糟糕的结尾,但是,本篇故事不是虚构的小说,而是真实发生的。这个故事不真实的地方是亨利的名字以及赌场的名字。亨利的真名不叫亨利·休格,他的真名出于保护的目的而不得不被隐去,而且至今依然不能公之于世。出于某些显而易见的缘由,赌场的真名也不能写出来。除此之外,这个故事都是真实的。

正是由于这是一篇真实的故事,它必须有一个真实的结尾。真实的结尾或许不像虚构的结尾那样富于戏剧性,或者阴森恐怖,可不管怎么说,其结尾还是蛮有意思的。下面就是实际发生的事情。

在伦敦的大街上溜达了大约一个小时,亨利返回了劳德豪斯,取了汽车,开回自己的公寓。他感到迷惘,无法理解为什么自己取得了巨大的成功,却感觉不出有多大的兴奋。三年前,也就是开始练习瑜伽之前,他身上要是发生这类事情的话,他会兴奋得发狂,他会到大街上一番手舞足蹈之后,冲进最近的一家夜总会喝香槟庆祝的。

有意思的是,他根本没有真正地兴奋起来,反而闷闷不乐。不知为什么,这一切都过于轻松:每次下注,他都成竹在胸,没有波澜,没有悬念,更没有输钱的危险。当然,他也知道,从现在起他可以周游世界,赚取百万。可是,那样做会有一点点的乐趣吗?

慢慢地,亨利开始明白,某个东西要是能随心所欲地想拿多少就拿多少——特别是金钱,那将毫无乐趣可言。

还有一件事。在修炼瑜伽神功的过程中,他的人生观就此完全改变,有没有这个可能呢?

当然,这是可能的。

亨利开车回到家,直接上床睡觉。

第二天早晨,他起得很晚,但并不比前一天的晚上欢快、兴奋多少。从床上爬起来、看到那一大捆钱还放在梳妆台上的时候,他突然觉得,自己对钱产生了一种强烈的反感。在他的人生里,再也不想要钱了。他也无法解释为什么会这样,但事实胜于雄辩:他就是不想再要一分钱了。

他拿起那捆钱,都是面额二十英镑的纸币,正好三百三十张。他走到公寓的阳台上,穿着一身暗红色的丝绸睡衣站在那儿,俯瞰下方的大街。

亨利的公寓位于柯曾大街——伦敦正中心最为时尚和昂贵的一个区域,人们称之为梅费尔区,也就是伦敦的上流社会区。柯曾大街的一头通向贝克莱广场,另一头通向帕克莱恩。亨利住的地方从街面算起是四楼,卧室外侧是一个小阳台,安装了铁栏杆,站在阳台上,整条街道尽收眼底。

当时是七月的一个上午约十一点钟,阳光明媚。尽管是星期天,但是下方的人行道上还是有相当多的人溜达来、溜达去。

亨利从这一大摞钞票中抽出一张二十英镑的,从阳台上丢了下去。一阵微风吹了过来,将纸币吹向一边,朝帕克莱恩方向飞去。亨利站在那儿看着,只见它在空中飘动着、旋转着,最终落到大街的对面,径直落到一位老人的面前。这位老人穿着一件长长的、破旧的棕色外衣,戴着一顶松松垮垮的帽子。当时,他正独自一人慢慢地行走,一下子看见钞票从面前飘过。于是,他停下脚步,将其拾起。他双手举起钞票,眼睛盯着它,然后将它翻过来,凑近了细瞧,随即抬起头,向上方看去。

“嗨,说你呢!”亨利一只手在嘴边收拢成杯状喊道。“那是给你的!是件礼物!”

老人一动不动地站着,将钞票举到身前,看着上方阳台上的身影。

“揣到兜里吧!”亨利喊道。“拿回家!”他的声音沿着大街传得很远,很多人停下脚步,抬头观瞧。

亨利又抽出一张钞票,扔了下去。下方那些观瞧者没有离开,只是观瞧着。他们根本不清楚发生了什么事儿,感到纳闷:上方阳台上有一名男子喊着什么,接着扔下一个像纸片一样的东西。大家跟随着飘落的纸片,纸片最后落到一对年轻夫妇近旁,他俩正挽着手臂穿过大街。丈夫松开手臂,意欲抓住飞过的纸片,但没抓住,随后从地面上将其拾起,仔细查看起来。大街两边的观瞧者都看向这个年轻的男子,对于他们中很多人而言,这个纸片看起来极其类似纸币那样的东西,都等着要看个究竟。

“是二十英镑啊!”男子叫道,激动得手舞足蹈。“是一张二十英镑的钞票!”

“留着吧!”亨利冲他喊道。“属于你啦!”

“你当真?”男子将钞票高高举起,回喊道。“真的给我了吗?”

突然间,大街两侧发出一阵“唰唰”的响动,大家立即开始行动,纷纷涌向道路的中间,簇拥在阳台的下方。他们将手臂举过头顶,开始呼喊:“我呢!给我一张呀!老板,再给我们扔一张吧!再多扔几张啊!”

亨利随即又抽出五六张纸币,扔了下去。

纸币在风中“哗啦啦”散开、下落之时,人们不停地尖叫、呼喊。纸币即将落入手中的时候,大街上出现了那种古老的、混乱的哄抢场面。但是,大家都很友好,而且兴高采烈,认为这是一场离奇的玩笑:一名男子穿着睡衣,高高地站在四楼的阳台上,随手将这些面额巨大的纸币向空中抛洒。在场的那些人中,有相当一部分人还是平生第一次看到面额为二十英镑的钞票。

可是现在,另外一件事情即将发生。

在一座城市的大街上,消息的传播速度之快是惊人的,而且非同凡响。亨利的所作所为就如同上空的闪电,瞬间传遍柯曾大街,也传入了柯曾大街以外的大街小巷。于是,人们从四面八方奔涌而来。才几分钟的工夫,男女老少约有一千人堵塞了亨利阳台下面的街道。车开不过去,司机就纷纷下车,加入到人群之中。突然之间,柯曾大街就陷入了喧嚣和混乱。

就在此刻,亨利干脆抬起胳膊,向外一甩,将整捆的钞票扬到空中。六千多英镑就这样纷纷扬扬,飘向下方涌动的人群。

随之而来的哄抢场面颇为壮观。趁着纸币还没有落地,人们争相跳起,捕捉纸币。大家你推我搡、你争我夺、你呼我喊、你起我跌。很快,整个街道乱成了一锅粥:有打斗的、也有喊叫的,大家互不相让。

亨利站在上面,看着喧嚣混乱的场面,突然听到自己身后公寓内的门铃响了起来,而且一个劲儿地响个不停。于是,他离开阳台,打开了公寓的正门。一名大块头警察站在门外,他留着黑胡子,双手放在屁股上。“你!”他气愤地大喝一声。“那个人就是你!你知道你到底在做些什么吗?”

“长官,上午好,”亨利问候。“招来那么多人,我很抱歉。我没想到结果会是这个样子。我只是赠送一些钱,随手扔了出去。”

“你这是在扰乱地方治安!”警察咆哮着。“你这是在妨碍交通!你煽动人们聚众闹事,整条大街到处是人,堵了个水泄不通!”

“我说过,我很抱歉,”亨利回应。“我许诺,我不会再这么做了。他们很快就会散开。”

这名警察将一只手从屁股上拿开,摊开手掌,里面露出一张二十英镑的钞票。

“啊哈!”亨利叫了起来。“你自己也弄到了一张!我很高兴!我十分为你高兴!”

“现在,赶紧停止这种胡闹行为!”警察说。“关于这事,这么多二十英镑的钞票,我要严肃问你几个问题。”他随即从胸兜里掏出一个记录本。“首先,”他继续说,“你是从哪儿弄到这些钱的?”

“我赢的,”亨利说。“那天晚上,我手气很好。”接着,他告诉警察他赢钱那家场所的名字,警察记到了小本子上。“去核实一下吧,”亨利补充道。“这事儿是真是假,他们会告诉你。”

警察放低记录本,直视着亨利。“实际上,”他说,“我相信你的故事。我认为,你讲的是实话,可是,那也不能为你的所作所为开脱。”

“我没有做错任何事情。”亨利说。

“你就是一个幼稚的大蠢蛋!”警察喊道,情绪又开始激动起来。“你就像一头蠢驴,绝对是个白痴!要是你真那么幸运,赢了那么大一笔钱,还想送给别人,干吗非要从窗户扔出去?”

“为什么不呢?”亨利露齿一笑,说道。“扔出去也是给出去的一个好方法。”

“这简直是个该死的、愚蠢的、笨拙的方法!”警察大叫。“为什么不把钱送到需要钱的地方,去做点好事?比如说,一所医院,或者一座孤儿院？全国上上下下,有多少孤儿院,连给孩子买礼物的钱都没有,更别提圣诞礼物了！偏偏这个时候,竟出了你这么个傻瓜,从来不知道缺钱是什么滋味,竟然把钱扔出窗外,丢到大街上！简直把人气疯了,我真的快疯了!"

"孤儿院?"亨利说。

"是啊,就是孤儿院!"警察叫道。"我就是在孤儿院里长大的,我知道那里是什么样子!"说完,警察就迅速转身离开,下了楼梯向大街走去。

亨利没有动地方。警察的那番话,特别是话中真情流露出的那种冲天的怒气,如同一记响亮的耳光,在我们男主人公的脸上拍了下去。

"孤儿院?"他大声说。"这个想法相当不错。可是,为什么仅仅是一座孤儿院呢？为什么不是很多、很多座孤儿院呢?"现在,他很快想到了一个崇高、绝妙的主意,这个主意会改变一切。

亨利关上正门,走回公寓。就在转瞬之间,一种强烈的兴奋在他的内心翻腾。他开始在屋子里来回踱步,把那些能将他的绝妙主意变成现实的那些点一一打上了勾。

"第一点,"他说,"活着的每一天,我都要赚取一大笔钱。"

"第二点,每年对于同一家赌场,我去的次数一定不能超过一次。"

"第三点,不管是在哪家赌场,或者从哪个人身上,我一定不要赢得太多而引起怀疑。我给自己的建议是,将每晚赢钱的数量控制在两万英镑以下。"

"第四点,每晚两万英镑,那么一年三百六十五天,总数加起来是多少?"

亨利拿出纸和铅笔,将总数计算了一下。

"总数是七百三十万英镑。"他大声说。

"很不错。第五点,我要不断地换地方。在任何一个城市,我一口气待的时间决不能超过两三个晚上,否则,消息就会传开。路线是这样的:从伦敦开始,到蒙特卡洛,再接下来分别到戛纳、比亚里茨、多维尔、拉斯维加斯、墨西哥城、布宜诺斯艾利斯以及拿骚等地方。大致就是这样类似的路线。

"第六点,我将用我赚的钱在去过的每一个国家建立一个绝对一流的孤儿院。我要做一位罗宾汉式的绿林好汉,从赌注经纪人或者赌场经营者那里赢钱,再把赢的钱送给儿童。这听起来有点落入俗套,或者是心血来潮?作为一个梦境,的确如此,但作为一个现实,要是我能把这个现实付诸行动,那么,就一点也不会落入俗套,或者心血来潮。这将成为一项巨大的工程。

"第七点,我需要一个人来帮我,这个人就坐在家中,看管好所有的钱,然后购买房舍,并组织、安排好所有事情,也就是一个金融家的角色。这个人应该是一个我能够信得过的人。约翰·温斯顿这个人怎么样呢?"

约翰·温斯顿是亨利的会计,处理他的所得税方面的事务,还解决投资等所有与钱相关方面的问题。亨利认识他已经有十八个年头了,两人之间已经建立起一种深厚的友情。尽管如此,但要记住的是,时至今日约翰·温斯顿只知道亨利是一个富有的、懒散的花花公子,一生中从来都没有做过一天像样的工作。

"你一定是疯了,"亨利讲述完他的计划时,约翰·温斯顿这样说道。"还没有什么人能设计出一套体系来击垮赌场的。"

亨利从兜里掏出一副扑克,那是一副崭新的扑克,还没有开封呢。"来吧,"他说。"我们就简单玩一玩二十一点游戏。你坐庄发牌,但不要对我说这些纸牌被做上了标记,这可是一副新牌啊。"

这两个人坐在温斯顿的办公室里——从办公室的窗户可以俯瞰贝克莱广场,正儿八经地玩起了二十一点,玩了将近一个小时。他们用火柴杆计数,每根火柴当二十五英镑用。五十分钟过后,亨利赢了不下三万四千英镑!

约翰·温斯顿简直无法相信。"你是怎么做到的?"他问。

"把这副牌放到桌子上,"亨利说。"正面朝下。"

温斯顿照做了。

于是,亨利就聚精会神地盯着最上面的那张牌,持续了四秒钟。“最上面的是张红桃J。”他说。的确如此。

“下一张是……红桃3。”一点没错。他继续将整副牌看了个遍,说出了每张牌的内容。

“接着讲,”约翰·温斯顿说。“给我讲讲你是怎么做到的。”一般情况下,这位擅长数学计算的会计总是镇定自若,但这次却将身体伏在书桌上方,一双眼睛瞪得大大的、闪闪发亮,就像两只星星。“你知道不知道,你正在做的事情根本就是不可能的?你真的意识到了?”他说。

“这事儿不是不可能,”亨利说。“只是,这事儿做起来难度很大,我是这个世界上唯一能做成这件事儿的人。”

约翰·温斯顿书桌上的电话铃响了。他拿起听筒,对秘书说道:“苏珊,没有得到我的通知,请不要再将电话接进来,即便是我妻子打来的也不行。”他抬起头,等着亨利继续讲。

接着,亨利一五一十地向他解释自己是如何练成这种神功的,告诉他自己是如何发现那个练习本,还告诉他有关伊姆拉汗的事情,最后向他描述自己在过去的三年里如何不间歇地修炼自己的注意力。

讲完后,约翰·温斯顿说:“你练过火上行走吗?”

“没有,”亨利回答。“我也不打算那样做。”

“是什么东西使你认为,你能够在赌场里做成辨认纸牌这件事情的?”

亨利接着告诉他自己前一天晚上去劳德豪斯赌场那件事儿。

“六千六百英镑啊!”约翰·温斯顿大叫。“说实话,你真的赢了那么多真钱吗?”

“听着,”亨利说。“刚才一个小时还不到,我就赢了你三万四千英镑啊!”

“的确不假。”

“我把赢钱的上限控制在六千英镑,”亨利说。“要想控制好,别超过那个数目,你需要付出极大的努力才能做到。”

“你将成为地球上最富有的人。”

“我不想做地球上最富有的人,”亨利说。“再也不想了。”接着,他告诉约翰关于设立孤儿院的计划。

讲完后,他说:“约翰,你愿意跟我一起干吗？你愿意做我的金融家、银行家、管理家等角色吗？愿意来帮我处理事务吗？每年会有数百万进账的。”

约翰·温斯顿,这位向来行事谨慎、考虑周全的会计,是绝不会一时冲动、大脑发热就对什么事儿持赞同态度的。“我得先看看真刀真枪地干一次。”他说。

因此,那天晚上他俩一起来到了位于柯曾大街的里茨夜总会。“这阵子,劳德豪斯是不能再去啦。”亨利说。

轮盘赌的第一轮中,亨利将“£ 100”押到“27”这个号码上,结果出人意料地赢了。第二轮的时候,他将“£ 100”押到“4”这个号码上,结果又出人意料地赢了。总共净赢七千五百英镑。

紧挨着亨利站着的一名阿拉伯人说道:“我刚刚输掉五万五千英镑。你是怎么赢的?”

“靠运气,”亨利说。“运气好而已。”

他们又来到二十一点赌室。在那儿半个小时工夫,亨利又赢了一万英镑,然后,他就罢手不赌了。

来到外面,走在大街上,约翰·温斯顿说:“现在,我相信你了,我跟你一起干。”

“我们明天开始。”亨利说。

“你真的打算每一天晚上都做这件事情吗?”

“是的,”亨利说。“从一个地方到另一个地方,从一个国家到另一个国家,我会迅速转移的。每一天,我都将通过银行将赢的钱寄给你。”

“你知道,一年赢的总数会是多少吗?”

“数百万吧,”亨利兴高采烈地说。“一年大约七百万。”

“那样的话,可不能在这个国家做这个事,”约翰·温斯顿说。“这个国家的税收检查员会把钱都收走的。”

“去哪个国家,随你挑,”亨利说。“我完全信任你,对我来说,到哪个国家都没有任何区别。”

“我看还是去瑞士,”约翰·温斯顿说。“可问题是,明天不行,我不能一抬屁股就走人。我和你不一样,我是一个有家室的人,我有牵挂、有负担。走前,我必须得跟老婆和孩子谈谈,必须得给孩子转学,必须得通知一下公司里的合伙人,必须得把现在的房子卖掉,然后在瑞士再买一处房子。我亲爱的老兄,这些事情做起来需要时间啊!”

亨利从兜里掏出刚刚赢来的一万七千五百英镑,递给了身边的这位男子。“这点钱微不足道,希望能帮你渡过难关、安顿下来,”他说。“但是,一定要抓紧,我想立马开始。”

不到一周的时间里,约翰·温斯顿就到了洛桑,他的办公室坐落在一个漂亮的山坡上,高高地俯瞰着日内瓦湖,他的家人很快也来到了这里。

亨利也开始到各大赌场展开行动。

一年后,亨利已经先后将八百多万英镑的钱寄到了身在洛桑的温斯顿手中。一周有五天的时间,钱源源不断地寄给瑞士的一家公司,名叫“S. A. 孤儿院联盟”。除了约翰·温斯顿和亨利之外,谁都不知道这些钱来自哪里、用在什么地方。至于瑞士的当权者,他们永远都别想知道这些钱来自哪里,亨利是通过银行寄出这些钱的。周一的那笔汇款数额总是最大的,因为这其中包括了他周五、周六和周日赢到的所有的钱,这三天银行不营业。他转移的速度很快,让人吃惊,约翰·温斯顿只能从他寄钱的银行的地址,了解到他的行踪。前一天的地址或许是马尼拉一家银行的,而后一天或许就是曼谷的。有的地址是拉斯维加斯的,有的是库拉索岛的,有的是弗里波特的,有的是大开曼岛的,有的是圣胡安的,有的是拿骚的,有的是伦敦的,还有的是比亚里茨的。什么地方的地址都有,不管是什么地方,只要那儿的城市里有大的赌场,就会留下那儿的地址。

七年以来,一切进展顺利。有将近五千五百万英镑的钱汇到了洛桑,然后又安全地转走。约翰·温斯顿已经建起三个孤儿院:一个在法国,一个在英国,还有一个在美国。另外,还有五个孤儿院正在建设之中。

接下来,有了点儿麻烦。有关亨利的消息在赌场老板之间不胫而走,尽管他总是谨慎再谨慎:不管是哪一天晚上,不管在什么地方,不能赢太多的钱。可最后,消息还是传播开来。

有一天晚上在拉斯维加斯,他们察觉到他的行为。当时,亨利有点欠考虑,在当地的三家不同的赌场里分别赢了十万美元,但不凑巧的是,那三家赌场是由同一伙人经营的。

当时的情况是这样的。第二天早晨,亨利在宾馆打点行装准备去机场,这时有人敲门。敲门的是宾馆里的男侍者,他低声对亨利说,有两名男子在前厅里等他,还有其他几名男子在后面的出口那儿把守。男侍者还说,他们都是些冷酷无情的家伙,但是,此时此刻亨利要是下楼会有多大的机会脱身,他并没有多说什么。

"你为什么上来告诉我?"亨利问他。"你为什么要站在我这一边?"

"我不站在任何人的一边,"男侍者说。"但是,我们都知道,你昨晚赢了一大笔钱。于是,我寻思着,我要是暗中向你通风报信,你会送我一件不错的礼物。"

"多谢,"亨利说。"但是,我如何脱身?如果你能帮我从这儿出去,我就给你一千美元。"

"那很容易,"男侍者回答。"脱下你的衣服,穿上我的制服,然后提起你的手提箱,通过前厅径直走出去。但是,走前要把我捆起来。我被捆绑着手脚躺在这儿的地板上,他们就不会认为是我帮的你。我会说,你有枪在手,我无计可施。"

"我上哪儿弄绳子捆绑你?"亨利问。

"就在我的衣兜里。"男侍者说完,张开嘴笑了。

亨利穿上男侍者的金绿色制服,这身装束看起来还不赖。然后,他用绳子将这名侍者结结实实地捆绑好,还在嘴里塞上一条手绢。最后,他将十张一百美元的钞票塞到地毯下面,好让这名侍者以后来取。

楼下的前厅里,两个矮粗的黑发恶棍盯着从电梯里走出来的每一个人,但是,他们几乎不会注意身着金绿色制服的男侍者。一名男侍者拎着一只手提箱从电梯里出来,麻利地走过前厅,穿过双开式弹簧门,向大街走去。

一到机场,亨利就更换了航班,换成下一次航班飞往洛杉矶。他对自己说,从现在起,事情办起来不会如此轻松了,可是那个男侍者却给了他一点启示。

到达好莱坞后,在好莱坞附近以及电影明星居住的贝弗利希尔斯市,亨利探访到电影业中最好的化妆师,那人就是马克斯·恩格斯曼。亨利前去拜访,对他立刻就有了好感。

"你挣多少钱?"亨利问他。

"噢,一年大约四万美元吧。"马克斯回答。

"要是你愿意跟随我,专门为我化妆的话,"亨利说,"我给你年薪十万。"

"你有什么伟大的想法?"马克斯问。

"我说给你听。"亨利说。随后,亨利对他讲了事情的原委。

马克斯是第二个知道亨利身怀绝技的人,第一个知道的是约翰·温斯顿。亨利展示自己的读牌神功,马克斯看得目瞪口呆。

"老天啊,伙计!"他大叫。"你能发大财啊!"

"早就发了,"亨利对他说。"我已经发了十次财,可我还想再发十次。"随后,他告诉马克斯有关孤儿院的事情:在约翰·温斯顿的帮助下,他已经建起三所孤儿院,还有更多的孤儿院正在建设之中。

马克斯是一位小个子、黑皮肤的男子,纳粹进入维也纳的时候,他从那里逃了出来。他从未结婚,没有什么束缚和羁绊。听完亨利的话后,他兴奋得不得了。"真了不得啊!"他叫道。"这是我一生中听到的最了不得的一件事!我跟你一起干,伙计!我们这就出发!"

从那时候起,马克斯·恩格斯曼开始跟随亨利周游四方。他随身携带一只箱子,箱子里装着各式各样的、你从未见过的东西,有假发、假胡须、连鬓胡子、小胡子,以及许多化妆用品。他能够将自己跟随的大师变成三十种或者四十种不同身份的人,让人辨认不出,就连现在一直提防亨利的那些赌场老板,没有一次能够辨认出化妆后的亨利·休格。事实上,拉斯维加斯那个插曲发生后仅仅一年的时间里,亨利和马克斯竟然还回到过那个危险的城市。当时是一个温暖的、满天星星的夜晚,亨利赢了整整八万美元,赢钱的地点就是他以前去过、还出过事的那三家大赌场中的第一家。他化妆成了一位年迈的巴西外交官进了赌场,赌场里那帮家伙永远也不知道他们是怎么再次倒霉的。

现在,既然亨利不是以自己的本来面目出现在赌场里,当然就有很多其他方面的细节需要照顾周全,例如假身份证和假护照等。举例来说吧。在蒙特卡洛,赌客在被允许进入赌场前,总是要出示护照。在马克斯的协助下,亨利又到蒙特卡洛去了十一次,每次去的时候,用的护照都不一样,化的妆也不一样。

马克斯非常喜爱这份差事,非常喜欢为亨利创造出新的形象。"今天,我要为你化出个全新的形象来!"他总是会这样宣布。"你就等着看效果吧!今天,你将变成一名来自科威特的阿拉伯酋长!"

"我们有阿拉伯护照吗?"亨利总是会这么问。"在这儿,我们有阿拉伯证件吗?"

"我们什么都有,"马克斯总是会这样回答。"约翰·温斯顿已经以皇家殿下阿布本贝酋长的名义给我发来一本漂亮的护照!"

就这样,事情继续开展下去。多年以来,马克斯和亨利亲如兄弟,兄弟俩配合作战,在天空飞来飞去,迅速辗转于世界各地,挤干世界上的赌场,将挤出来的钱直接发回给身在瑞士的约翰·温斯顿,瑞士的那个名为"S. A. 孤儿院联盟"的公司也变得越来越富有。

亨利去年去世,也就是他六十三岁的那年。他的工作已经完成,为此他整整忙碌了二十三年的时间。

他的私人参考手册上列出了三百七十一家大型的赌场,这些赌场分布在二十一个不同的国家或者岛屿上。他多次拜访过这些赌场,一次也没有失过手。

根据约翰·温斯顿的账目,亨利一共赢了一亿四千四百万英镑。

他死后留下二十一所设施完善、运行良好的孤儿院,这些孤儿院分散在世界各地,每拜访一个国家,他都要在那里建一所这样的孤儿院。约翰和他的手下在洛桑管理、资助这些孤儿院。

我不是马克斯·恩格斯曼,也不是约翰·温斯顿,那么所有这一切我是怎么知道的?又怎样在第一时间把这个故事写出来的呢?

听我跟你说说吧。

亨利去世后不久,约翰·温斯顿从瑞士给我打来电话。电话里,他只是简单地自我介绍,说他是一家名为"S. A. 孤儿院联盟"的公司的主管,问我是否愿意来洛桑见见他,目的是要我为他的组织写一部简史。我不清楚他从什么地方搞到我的名字,他手头或许有一个清单,上面列出一些作家的名字,并用大头针别上。他说,他会给我优厚的报酬,接着补充道:"一个非凡之人最近去世了,他的名字叫亨利·休格。我想,人们应该对他的所作所为有所了解。"

由于对情况一无所知,我就问他,这个故事是否真正有意思到值得发表的程度。

"那么,好吧,"这位男子说,他现在手头控制着一亿四千四百万英镑。"算了吧,我问别人去,作家到处都是。"

他的话刺激了我。"别这样,"我说。"等等。你可不可以至少告诉我这位亨利·休格是谁,他做了什么事情?我从未听说过这个人啊。"

五分钟过后,电话那头的约翰·温斯顿给我讲了讲亨利·休格的秘密生涯。那已不是什么秘密了,亨利已死,再也不会去赌博了。我一边听着这个故事,一边深深为之着迷。

"我这就坐下一班飞机过去。"我说。

"谢谢你,"约翰·温斯顿说。"我很感激。"

在洛桑,我见到了当时已年过七旬的约翰·温斯顿,也遇见了跟他年龄相仿的马克斯·恩格斯曼。他们仍然沉浸在亨利去世的悲痛中,马克斯甚至比约翰·温斯顿更加悲痛,因为至少十三年以来,他一直跟亨利形影不离。"我很爱他,"马克斯说着,脸上浮现出一丝茫然的表情。"他很伟大,从来不为自己着想,赢的钱自己从来没留过一分,用在旅行和吃饭方面的花销除外。听着,有一次我俩在比亚里茨的时候,他刚在一家银行将五十万法郎汇给了约翰。当时正是吃午饭的时间,我俩去了一个地方,简单吃了点,点了个煎蛋饼和一瓶葡萄酒。结账的时候,亨利身上一分钱都没有了,我身上也没有。他真是一个可爱的人。"

约翰·温斯顿跟我讲了他所知道的一切,还给我看了看约翰·卡特赖特医生1934年写于孟买的那个原始的、深蓝色的练习本,我将里面的内容一字不差地抄写下来。

"亨利总是将它随身携带,"约翰·温斯顿说。"到了最后,他背下了整本的内容。"

他给我看了"S. A. 孤儿院联盟"的账本,每本都一天、一天地记载着亨利赢钱的数目,记了二十多年,真是令人难以置信。

他讲完后,我说:"温斯顿先生,你的故事有很多空白的地方,有关亨利的旅行和在世界各地赌场的冒险经历,你几乎只字未提。"

"那个故事属于马克斯,"约翰·温斯顿说。"马克斯了解那方面的一切,因为他那时跟亨利在一起。可问题是,他说,他要尝试着自己去写,而且已经开始写了。"

"那样的话,为什么不让马克斯将整个故事都写出来?"我问。

"他不想都写,"约翰·温斯顿回答。"他只想写关于自己和亨利的故事。要是写完的话,这将是一个美妙、奇异的故事。可是,他现在年纪大了,跟我一样大了。他能否完成,我持怀疑态度。"

"最后一个问题,"我说。"你总是称呼他亨利·休格,然而,你却告诉我说,这不是他的真名。我写这个故事的时候,难道你不想让我写出他的真名吗?"

"不想,"约翰·温斯顿回答。"我和马克斯都答应过他,永远也不披露他的真名实姓。哦,或早或晚,也许会泄露出去,毕竟他出生于英国的一个显赫家族。要是你不去设法追根究底的话,我会很感激的。就普普通通地称呼他亨利·休格先生吧。"

实际上,我也是那么做的。

(终结)

参考文献

［1］DAHL R. The Wonderful Story of Henry Sugar and Six More ［M］. London: Penguin Books Ltd., 2002

［2］DAHL R. The Best of Roald Dahl ［M］. London: Penguin Books Ltd., 2006

［3］DAHL R. The Collected Short Stories of Roald Dahl ［M］. London: Penguin Books Ltd., 1992

［4］陈钰. 畸形精神世界的工笔画家——谈罗尔德·达尔的小说创作特色［J］. 武汉：外国文学研究，1985(4)：66-69.

［5］商务印书馆辞书研究中心. 新华成语词典［M］. 北京：商务印书馆，2002.

［6］新华社译名室. 世界人名翻译大辞典［M］. 北京：中国对外翻译出版公司，2007.

［7］周定国. 世界地名翻译大辞典［M］. 北京：中国出版集团，中国对外翻译出版公司，2008.

后　记

我们对罗尔德·达尔“非儿童类”短篇故事(小说)进行研究和翻译已经持续了四个年头了。其间,因教学和其他科研的缘由,有所间断,但多数时间是在研读和翻译达尔的这部分短篇小说中度过的。所研读、翻译的达尔这部分短篇作品共计六十篇。

在研究和翻译罗尔德·达尔这部分作品的过程中,历尽了艰辛,特别是在翻译过程中,不时会遇到这样或那样的“坎坷”。达尔在写作过程中,时常会“卖弄”自己所掌握的某些专业方面的知识,如葡萄酒、收藏、音乐、医学等,这就逼着译者硬着头皮去熟悉相应的知识。另外,达尔还偶尔会“显摆”一下自己英语之外的词汇,如法语、拉丁语等,这对于译者来说,未免有些“捉襟见肘”了——有的词,任凭怎么查也不得结果。达尔原文中的某一段有时会罗列出若干的专有名词,本着一丝不苟的研究态度,翻译过程中译者对它们均一一查证——哪怕对其中某些表达已经相当熟悉了。对于这样的“坎坷”,下笔前会来回踱步、反复思量、仔细斟酌,正如鲁迅先生在译完《死魂灵》谈到翻译时所言:“我向来总以为翻译比创作容易,因为至少是无须构想。但到真的一译,就会遇着难关,譬如一个名词或动词,写不出,创作时候可以回避,翻译上却不成,也还得想,一直弄到头昏眼花,好像在脑子里面摸一个急于要开箱子的钥匙,却没有。”(鲁迅《“题未定”草·且介亭杂文二集》)

在研究和翻译罗尔德·达尔的这部分作品过程中,还会遇到语言及文化差异方面的“绊脚石”,处理起来颇费脑筋,正如严复在谈

《天演论》翻译的《译例言》中所言:“新理踵出,名目纷繁,索之中文,渺不可得,即有牵合,终嫌参差,译者遇此,独有自具衡量,即义定名。”另外,对于查询无果的地方,也得认真加以思考,甚至经过了很长时间才“创造性”地下笔定论,可谓“一名之立,旬月踟蹰。我罪我知,是存明哲”(严复《译例言》)。由此可见,译事之难,不亚于李太白笔下的“蜀道之难,难于上青天”了!

幸运的是,在对罗尔德·达尔这些“非儿童类”短篇小说进行研究和翻译过程中,我们得到了许多朋友和同事热情的帮助和有力的支持,感激之情无以言表。

对罗尔德·达尔短篇小说的研究和翻译源于英国朋友马礼(他的英文原名叫“*Jonathan Rackham*”,时任渤海大学外籍英语教师)2009年赠送给著者之一的一本书,书名叫《罗尔德·达尔小说精品集》(*The Best of Roald Dahl*)。在阅读这本书的过程中,得到了启发,萌生了要研究并翻译作家罗尔德·达尔“非儿童类”短篇小说的念头。我们2010年9月开始动笔,从此一发而不可收。在对原文理解过程中所遇到的难题,得到了马礼耐心而细致的解答,甚至在他回到英国后,还继续通过电子邮件、越洋电话等方式给予我们热情的解答。在此,衷心感谢好友兼同行的马礼,感谢他热情帮助!

译文从初稿到成稿,虽经数次校正和修改,仍然存在不少问题。此时,我们的学长兼兄长刘恩东先生及时伸出了援助之手,对最终的成稿在“忠实”的基础上进行了“通顺”方面的梳理。刘恩东先生虽身为大学英语教师,但是,其汉语功力不可小觑,令吾等外语研究者难以望其项背,特别是他古汉语的功力,甚至超出很多古汉语的专业研究者。有了我们兄长的梳理和理顺,毛坯一样的成稿方焕发出光彩。兄长的修改,虽然有时只是增填一个字,或者是删除一个词,但却救译文于“水火”之中。可以说,没有兄长的理顺,名为“成稿”的译文只能如同一个咿呀学语、走路不稳的婴儿。在此,衷心感谢兄长刘恩东先生,感谢他的辛苦付出!

研究伊始,一个偶然的机会,我们搜索到克里斯廷·霍华德(Kristine Howard)创建并维护的网站“罗尔德·达尔粉丝网”(Roald

Dahl Fans. com),并就罗尔德·达尔有关问题联系过霍华德女士,收到了她及时的回复。整个研究也因霍华德女士的网站而受益匪浅。在此,衷心感谢克里斯廷·霍华德女士,感谢她在网站里所提供的全面而翔实的资料!

同时,我们十分感谢大连交通大学外国语学院及渤海大学外国语学院的领导和同事给予我们热情的帮助和有力的支持!十分感谢哈尔滨工业大学出版社田新华主任在出版方面提供的有力支持!十分感谢为本书的出版而忙碌的所有编辑人员和工作人员!同时,我们十分感谢为本研究提供帮助的所有朋友和同仁!

当然,由于时间和能力所限,疏漏在所难免,还望读者赐教、斧正,并多提宝贵意见。

对罗尔德·达尔"非儿童类"短篇故事(小说)研究、翻译所成之书,难免泛泛而论,甚至是流于平庸,但是,我们本着扎实做学问、做学问如做人的思想,从起点出发,稳扎稳打,力戒浮躁之风,勿求好高骛远。

记得《礼记·中庸》里有言:"君子之道,譬如行远,必自迩,譬如登高,必自卑。"愿以此语共勉。

王　昕　王永胜

2015 年初冬